Alpha Male

Jared Conway

British Library Cataloguing In Publication Data
A Record of this Publication is available
from the British Library

ISBN 1846850657
978-1-84685-065-3

First Published February 2006 by

Exposure Publishing, an imprint of Diggory Press,
Three Rivers, Minions, Liskeard, Cornwall, PL14 5LE, UK
WWW.DIGGORYPRESS.COM

'Where do we come from? What are we? Where are we going?' –
Paul Gauguin painting. 1897.

PROLOGUE

18 MEN, 22 women, 14 children, 62 dogs, 39 cats and hundreds of other even
lesser creatures; he'd killed them all and could remember every one. A few had
been necessary, but most had been purely for enjoyment. The greatest
pleasure had been his parents and his baby sister; in their final moments, he'd
loved them most of all.

Marcus was awake. He opened his eyes and rose instantly from the bed,
flinging aside the single sheet that had been his only covering and walking
swiftly to the window looked out across a flat expanse of water. In the stark
blackness of early morning the absolute silence was overwhelming. Anything
that moved was hugely exaggerated while the slightest sound echoed into the
profound stillness of the pitch-black sea. Almost imperceptibly to the naked
eye, dawn crept over the horizon. So achingly slow was its progress that it
was unclear whether the darkness diminished or the light increased. Either
way, the effect was the same. Each time he looked up, the light was more
pronounced, until even the winking pinpricks on the distant headland faded
and disappeared. The arrival of the sun was almost an anti-climax; creeping
timidly over the rim of the world like an uncertain suitor peeking from the
shadows, before gaining confidence and spearing its brilliant fingers across the
reflective surface of the sea. From his vantage point, an open balcony looking
out over the picturesque harbour of Collioure, the watcher looked out at a
scene which had captivated successive generations of artists and remained
completely unmoved. He had slept well and was refreshed. Anything else was
an irrelevance.

Marcus turned away and strode naked to the washstand where he
scrubbed his hands and face, brushed his teeth and shaved, then collected his
clothes from the wardrobe. Frowning, he examined a brown speck on the cuff
of his shirt. It was faint enough to escape attention but he scrubbed it under
the cold tap until all traces of the stain had been removed. The shirt would
have to be replaced later, but would suffice for the moment. He dressed and
collected his single bag from beneath the antique pine table on which he'd
placed his wallet, watch and small change. He stepped over the body on the
floor, carefully checking the soles of his shoes for blood traces. Disposal of the
remains, while desirable, had become inconvenient. Having decided to leave
France, such trivial matters were no longer important. The girl was a nobody
without any possible link to himself and would be soon forgotten. Just another
dead junky, albeit one whose miserable life was remarkable only for the
luxurious trappings of the room where she'd spent her last night on earth. The
razor lay by her side, its gleaming blade and pearl handle standing out against
the dark oak floorboards. Although the razor had never made contact with his
own skin, it had been part of him for many years and had served him well. All
other aspects of his life, he would leave behind, but this old friend was too

3

precious to abandon. Marcus used the girl's discarded underwear to wipe the blade before slipping it into a battered velvet-lined case. He had no doubt that he would have need of it again.

Little more than an hour later he was in the mountains, still shrouded in gloom while the sun struggled to break above the towering peaks. *Mantet* in the French Pyrenees is remote by any standards. Razed to the ground by the Germans during the Second World War due to its status as a centre of *Maquis* resistance, the village had lain abandoned and forgotten for twenty years, its former residents either massacred at the site or sent to work camps from which they never returned. Hippies wandering the mountain drug trails between France and Spain re-discovered the village in the Sixties, repairing some of the buildings and restoring the village to life.

In more recent times, most of the houses had been renovated and the majority of the twenty or so residents involve themselves in trekking or raising horses. The area surrounding the village is a true wilderness. From the top of the *Col de Mantet*, looking back towards the towering peak of Mount *Canigou* and the spectacular *Alemany* Valley, the village lies hidden below the crest of the hill. The road ends here; beyond the village the dense forests and tortured obsidian rock formations stretch all the way to Spain.

The lure of walking through one of Europe's last remaining true wild places still draws a small number of summer visitors, but step off the marked trails for only a few hundred metres and all aspects of civilisation vanish. The house is invisible from any pathway. Even close up, it is difficult to find. A former shepherd's croft or *bergerie* long since abandoned to the elements, the rough stone walls overgrown and crumbling. In the unlikely event that a stray rambler came across the house, its derelict appearance rendered it unlikely to be worthy of closer inspection.

Beneath the broken-tiled roof was a smaller structure, hand built by its single occupant, almost square with no obvious point of entrance. Contained within the simple stone walls and well-insulated roof, it was the modern equivalent of a hermit's cave. A nearby stream had been adapted to power a small alternator, silently charging a series of batteries and providing sufficient electricity for a single light. A large double mattress, a chipped and battered oak table and a solitary chair were the only furniture. The true owner had died many years previously leaving the house to be re-claimed by the wilderness. The present occupant had found it by accident and immediately saw it's potential. His chosen occupation, the clandestine movement of narcotics and human migrants from the African Continent, required that he be based on the shores of the Mediterranean. He was not averse to spending time in 5-star hotels, but he also needed a place of absolute privacy.

Four wheel drive vehicles are as common a sight in nearby *Prades* or *Vernet Les Bains* as on the mountain roads and he attracted no more attention than any other tourist buying supplies. The sun-kissed beaches of southern France, or across the border in Spain, are only an hour away, as are the chic ski resorts of Andorra and Mont Louis. Inhabitants of remote areas keep themselves to themselves in the main and a handsome man driving through an isolated country village with a pretty girl in the passenger seat aroused no particular interest. Certainly not enough attention for anyone to note that the man was always alone on the return journey.

He was alone now, packing his few items of clothing into a single rucksack and tightening the laces on his boots ready for the arduous walk across country to the place where he had parked his vehicle. 'Time to go back,' he said aloud, speaking for the apparent benefit of the stone walls whilst detaching the connection from the batteries. The dawn he'd witnessed at sea level came much later to these high mountains and as he walked away the first faint glimmer of sunlight was just touching the surrounding hills and the distant village was stirring.

Marcus threw his bag onto the back seat of the car and stood for a moment. The decision had been made and he was ready to go back. He allowed himself a moment's reflection. Old memories flitted through his mind, some of them pleasant, but most were a constant reminder of unfinished business. The time had come to redress the balance. The boredom he'd been experiencing recently was a spur for the action that he knew he had to take. He'd taken the first step already and it was time to move on. Faces flashed through his mind. Faces of people to whom he'd never spoken; yet he knew everything about them and not a single day passed that he did not think of them.

Sunlight had cleaved its erratic way through the early morning cloud cover, the distant hills a shimmering dusky pink while the vast expanse of sky was a vivid lazuline blue. Faint traces of dew lingered on the sparse scrub nestling beneath soft rounded boulders, the freshness of the preceding night soon to be overwhelmed by the impending day. In the heat of summer every day was the same. With each brilliant shaft of light that invaded the landscape, fresh colours burst into life. By mid-day the heat had bleached the scene to a white glare, painful to the eye, and the whole valley would be baking under a remorseless sun. Tiny creatures scurried and darted, frantically seeking out shade in meagre patches of sage and bracken. Later still, the encircling hills turned to gold as the sun dipped lower in the sky until each successive peak was tipped with vivid pink and the lower slopes slipped through ever-deepening shades of indigo. Flocks of birds plunged and soared in a riot of activity until even they became still at last and settle down to roost as the last vestige of discernible colour leeched away marking the final passage of another day.

The arrival of each succeeding sunrise pushed the barriers of light and shade to the limit, yet the man standing as still as one of the ancient encircling stones experienced nature's wonders at first hand on a daily basis and it meant nothing to him. His priorities lay elsewhere. Marcus opened the car door, climbed inside and moments later the engine roared into life. He never looked back as he drove away from his remote dwelling for the last time.

'From a certain point onward there is no longer any turning back. That is the point that must be reached.' - Franz Kafka.

CHAPTER 1

MARCUS stood perfectly still, blending into the background as the busy shopping crowds streamed past. Saturday morning and the Pyramids Centre in Birkenhead was packed with bustling shoppers. His target had been in River Island for half an hour but the level of his concentration remained unbroken.

This was research. Planning ahead. The person he was waiting for was safe for now. Their time had not yet come but knowledge was everything. The more he knew about his target, the safer and more enjoyable the outcome. He had been away from England for not much more than two years and noted the increased number of tattoos on show, more commonly on young women than on men, with a wry amusement. He had survived an attack in prison from a fellow inmate that had left a jagged scar on his shoulder blade. Not much of a scar. Certainly less than the injuries suffered by his assailant. Marcus had gouged out one of the man's eyes and chewed through his testicles. Compared to that, a minor flesh wound was nothing. Marcus had persuaded a prison artist to tattoo a quotation from Friedrich Nietzsche over the scar. 'What doesn't kill me makes me stronger.' Following his release he'd discovered the quotation may have been incorrectly recorded, although his source volume of quotations in the prison library had been reputable. The quotation had been recorded elsewhere as 'What doesn't destroy us makes us stronger.' The possibility of inaccuracy was unacceptable and he'd had the entire area treated with a laser until no trace of the words remained.

A pretty teenage girl swished through the doorway, hips swinging under a short denim skirt. The tanned legs, high breasts and pert features were one hell of a package and Marcus observed that his were not the only eyes following her progress. Most of the men and a fair number of women had taken more than a passing note of the girl. Marcus smiled inwardly at the thought that many of the watchers would like to fuck the girl; but only he would want to kill her afterwards.

Donna looked at the entrance gates, the wide sweep of lawn visible beyond the gravelled drive and thought of her own humble abode. 'The rich are different,' she mused, hardly aware that she had spoken aloud. Dexter looked sharply at Donna as she demonstrated for the umpteenth time her priceless capacity for stating the bleeding obvious.

'In any particular way?'

Donna shrugged. 'The pavements,' she said feebly, gesturing at the broad expanse of slabs separating the boundary walls from the road. At least three times wider than in any other road in town as if in acknowledgement of the residents' need to distance themselves from the mere mortals driving down the Queen's Highway. Wide enough to be a bus lane although there were no bus stops on this route. Nobody ever walked here either. A token jogger perhaps but no pedestrians. Even the cleaning woman or gardener arrived by car. Dexter nodded but said nothing. Donna recognised the expression on his face. She'd seen it often enough.

Irritation.

Whether she was the cause or merely a small part of a larger problem Donna had no way of knowing. If it were anything to do with her, he'd tell her soon enough. 'This is where I'd live if I won the lottery.'

Dexter snorted. After a few moments, striding along with Donna almost running alongside to keep pace, he glanced at her. 'Or married a millionaire?'

Donna stared back at him until Dexter looked away. She allowed herself a tiny smile. The idea of marriage to a rich man had never crossed her mind. Why should it? Given her track record with men, rich or otherwise, the lottery odds were better.

'Do you even do the lottery?' Dexter growled.

'No.'

Dexter shrugged and came to a sudden halt causing Donna to over-run him. 'Waste of bloody time all this crap,' Dexter growled, 'I feel like a door to door salesman. No, sod it; I am a bloody door to door salesman. That's all this amounts to.'

Donna nodded. So, that was it. Nothing to do with her at all. Just Dexter getting his knickers in a twist over Roper's latest bright idea; tapping up the existing client list in an attempt to drum up trade in a slack period by suggesting an upgrade to their security systems. Donna knew Dexter's opinions on having descended to what amounted to little more than a peddler of burglar alarms well enough by now. As a career copper, a legend in his own field, he was somewhat less than thrilled at this aspect of the daily grind that was forced upon R and D Security by increasing overheads and a diminishing caseload.

'Back to Roper Towers then for Happy Hour?' Donna asked, trying to bring a small measure of light relief within range of the dark cloud that enveloped her senior colleague. Not that she ever thought of Dexter as a colleague. He was her boss, a benevolent despot in the main, but still commanding respect and absolute obedience from his underlings.

Dexter frowned. 'Watch yourself,' he cautioned, 'Happy Hour is no way to refer to the weekly Associates meeting at R and D Security which is of immense value and importance, as well you know.'

Donna smirked, knowing that Dexter was the only person in the world who detested the weekly meetings more than herself.

An hour and a half later, the boredom that was Wednesday mornings was in full spate. As the most junior member, all that was required of Donna was to sit and marvel as her elders and betters reported on the progress, or lack of progress, of each case with which the firm was presently dealing. Today was worse than usual as Andy, Donna's best mate and fellow lackey, was on some skive or other in Liverpool. Dexter, the only other person on the staff for whom she had the faintest liking, had been blathering away for twenty minutes now and showed no signs of coming to the end of his monologue. To Roper, joint Senior Partner alongside Dexter, staff briefings were the most important part of the job, while his equally awful sibling, Martha, was responsible for routine clerical matters. In Donna's opinion, what this amounted to in practise was finding excuses to vent her spleen on the firm's most junior member. Donna craved coffee and a Hobnob, needed a pee desperately and an itch in that unreachable spot between her shoulder blades was driving her mad.

Dexter stopped talking for a moment to glare in Donna's direction and she realised that her rendition of 'Chirpy Chirpy, Cheep Cheep' which had been in her head since she'd heard it on the car radio two hours ago was not *Sotto-Voce* after all. She gave an effulgent smile in a vain attempt to restore harmony but her efforts were doomed to failure. Dexter shook his head, visibly expressing the frequency with which Donna's behaviour continued to fall below acceptable levels. A point of view with which Roper and his sister were in complete agreement to judge by their expressions. Donna shrank down in her seat, somehow repressing the urge to parade around the room farting loudly and singing at the top of her voice. Never a good career move.

'Nothing more to report on the Borthwick case,' Dexter continued, giving every sign of going on for another half-hour at least. 'I've had Andy there for two weeks checking out all likely areas and it's definitely an inside job. As far as the other case goes, no sign of the missing punter either but I've got the address of a woman he used to live with. I'm off to see her tonight. I'll get back to Borthwick later today and give him a progress report.'

Roper nodded. Edgar Borthwick ran a casino and gaming club in Chester that had seen a rapid downturn in profits over the past few weeks. During his long career, former Detective Inspector Dexter had crossed swords with Borthwick on more than one occasion, but the respect the casino owner had for Dexter's ability had prompted him to approach R and D Security to sort out a couple of small problems. Sammy Yates, widely known by the ironic sobriquet Rowdy despite his taciturn nature, was a regular customer who'd run up a line of credit and then absconded when his luck started to turn. The situation was not unusual in the casino business. Gambling debts were not recoverable in law. All that meant was that the creditors couldn't go to court to recover the debt. A moot point as a man like Edgar Borthwick would never have considered going to court anyway. The law was long-winded and only the lawyers made a profit. Better to hire a firm like R and D Security and let them recover the debt in return for ten-per-cent commission. If they failed there were other options. Edgar Borthwick wouldn't get his money back using these other methods but the defaulter wouldn't be in any hurry to run up any more debts. He wouldn't be in a hurry to do anything for a while. Not until he came out of hospital. Dexter knew the likely fate of anyone who owed money to Edgar Borthwick and would do his best to persuade the man to pay up. He was sanguine about the retribution that would follow if the debtor failed to deliver. It wasn't his problem. Shouldn't have scarpered owing the money.

First he had to locate him. There was a finder's fee on offer. Any subsequent action was a separate matter.

The other problem was potentially more serious. Gaming Club profits don't go down for any reason other than someone being on the fiddle. Andy had been there every night, discreetly poking around as Dexter put it, and had turned up a light-fingered croupier with a debt problem. Debt would be the least of the croupier's worries when his employer received Dexter's report. Dexter continued to summarise the progress of existing cases and Donna listened with some chagrin to the areas of his monologue that concerned her own workload. Last Friday had seen the end of a two-week spell as an office cleaner at a Birkenhead solicitors' practice. She'd had to do her normal work during the day, then put an overall on and start her other duties. It may have been Friday afternoon, but the acronym, POETS' Day - Piss Off Early, Tomorrow's Saturday -did not apply at R and D Security.

In addition to cleaning the offices, Donna's duties entailed foraging through the waste-paper baskets and any unlocked cupboards attempting to find any trace of more than a hundred lost files. The Senior Partner had briefed her carefully, stressing how much he trusted his office staff but certain that the missing files were somewhere on the premises. 'One of these bastards has hidden them,' he'd added, seemingly forgetting his previous avowals of trust. The delights of a nightly rummage through mounds of empty yoghurt-pots, cigarette ends and reams of discarded paper or mauling filing cabinets away from the wall only to reveal nothing more than vast amounts of dust and fluff had been the low point of her career to date. Naturally, she'd also had to carry out the normal duties of an office cleaner and had concluded after the first night that cleaning other peoples' toilets was a pleasure she could do without. Donna spent most of the night rummaging through desk drawers and filing cabinets. Not the most fascinating work. The job would have been easier if the Senior Partner had remembered to leave a set of keys before swanning off on his holidays. Not that it made much difference. Any fool can open a filing cabinet. Most of them have a single lock at the top that secures all the drawers in each cabinet. Tilt the whole thing backwards and prop it up, fiddle underneath for the lock release and away you go.

That's the theory anyway. In practise, terrified that the whole thing would come crashing down on her dainty little fingers while she fiddled around under the cabinet, Donna was never happy until it was safely propped up, ideally with half a dozen house bricks. Unfortunately, house bricks tend to be in fairly short supply in the average office. After all this aggravation she'd not found a single missing file, although she'd located seven cheques behind one of the cupboards. On her last night at the practice she'd woken from a brief doze in the only comfortable chair to a thunderous pounding on the main door. The Regional Crime Squad had sent two uniformed officers and another man, obviously a civilian as he was wearing a Hugo Boss suit, to secure the premises following the arrest of the Senior Partner on fraud charges. Unwilling to be classed as a mere cleaner Donna identified herself as a member of R and D Security, aware that this snobbish attitude was beneath her but the Boss-suited fraud expert was rather handsome. Donna knew her own failings but invariably gave in to them.

'I should get off home, love, if I were you,' one of them had said. Not the good-looking one of course who'd never even looked her way. Probably thinking Donna's lime green overall was a bit of a turn-off. 'The bloke who set your little job up won't be around for your report. He's banged up in a cell and likely to be staying there for a while.

Office cleaning wasn't what she'd envisaged when she'd started at R and D Security and conning householders into signing up for extra burglar alarms wouldn't form part of her job description either in a perfect world.

Donna's only other case consisted of a taxi-driver who had seemingly vanished from the face of the earth. Their client, the man's girlfriend, was still waiting for him to bring back her jewellery from the repairers, insisting that he loved her and that his sudden disappearance must be a result of some accident. The police would only act if the client suspected that her boyfriend had stolen the items and as this thought was impossible for her to even contemplate she'd had no alternative but to ask an enquiry agent to find him. Donna could empathise with her trusting faith. Dexter had told her when she first started this work that she was too naive and trusting for the job. She'd told him how she hoped never to become a cynical old bastard like him but deep down Donna knew he was right. It was just not in her nature to think the worst of people. That explained a lot. Mind you, she was learning fast. Enquiries at the jewellery shop where the repairs had been carried out had established that they had valued the items at £22,000. Perhaps the missing boyfriend hadn't loved the client quite so much after he found out their value. Donna had done her best on the client's behalf, but only one result looked likely.

'And that's about it,' concluded Dexter, 'Not exactly riveting. I never thought I'd be saying this, but I'd far rather have too much on my desk than too little.'

'Indeed!' Roper interjected, uncrossing his legs and almost blinding Donna with the glare from his highly polished shoes. 'Point taken. But even in slack periods the firm continues apace. We've increased our take-up rate on security systems by thirteen percent in the past quarter.'

Dexter frowned. 'A few proper cases wouldn't go amiss,' he grumbled.

Roper smiled, dentures flashing. 'Quite so, indeed. Quite so.'

Donna winced. The Senior Partner rarely smiled, but by its very rarity, each occasion was even scarier than the last. Roper was inordinately proud of his team, his tiny insignificant fiefdom. Most of all, he liked to feel important. *Mein Fuhrer*, Dexter called him, not entirely affectionately. He's not a bad old bugger, he'd told Donna, just likes to think he's top dog now and again. No harm in it. Just play along, that's the best way. Donna was trying hard, but it was bloody difficult.

Roper turned to Donna and favoured her with an expression that could have been mistaken for benevolence in anyone else. 'Just this morning, for instance, I've taken instructions from a client. Not a major case, but perhaps within the compass of Miss O'Prey. Hmm?'

Donna strapped an expression of competence onto her face and prepared herself for the latest of a long series of menial tasks which Roper deemed appropriate to her limited talents. Her features must have passed muster as Roper glanced away, referring to a pad resting on the knees of his immaculately pressed trousers.

'As I said, nothing too difficult, but who knows where even a trivial matter may end, Miss O'Prey? Naturally, I will only expect you to deal with the immediate enquiry and anything subsequent to the strict terms of reference will be handled by one of the Senior Partners.'

Donna was outraged, but the complaints that sprung to her lips were stillborn. Dexter got there first.

'Hang on a minute,' he rumbled, 'Either Donna takes on the case or she doesn't. If she takes it, then she follows it through, wherever it leads. That's only right. Unless you're suggesting that she's likely to cock it up and have to be bailed out.'

'Not at all,' Roper blustered, his every fibre demonstrating that Dexter's guess was bang on the money. 'Although, I hardly imagine anyone wishes to see a repetition of that missing girl business again.'

Donna could no longer contain herself. 'That was well over two years ago and if rape, murder and kidnapping, can be reduced to that missing girl business, you....' She subsided into spluttering indignation, too angry to formulate any sensible argument and glanced at Dexter for help. Dexter didn't disappoint her.

'That missing girl case was as big as anything that came my way in thirty years. Murder Squad, Serious Crimes, you name it.'

Roper looked flustered. 'Well, yes. Quite so. But my point is that with hindsight, it would have been preferable for Miss O'Prey to have had rather less exposure to such a serious case at such an early stage in her career Not to mention the considerable risk to her health and well-being.' He looked to Dexter in anticipation of his partner's support.

'Bollocks!' Dexter stood and paced the room, a typical response when endeavouring to keep his famous temper in check. 'Donna not only survived serious risk to life and limb, she was directly responsible for saving the lives of others. On her own. As far as I'm concerned, she's as capable as anyone in this room of dealing with any case that comes her way. Make that more capable than most.'

Donna looked at Roper and his sister who were the only other people present apart from herself and Dexter and saw the effect of Dexter's pointed remarks. Roper's complexion was brick red while Martha looked as if Dexter had accused her of pissing in the sink. 'No-one is saying Miss O'Prey does not have our full confidence,' Roper spluttered. 'Not the case at all. I was merely attempting to assure that a relatively inexperienced associate would not be expected to carry out an investigation without a degree of support from above. In a purely advisory capacity, of course.'

'Rest assured that Donna won't need her hand held,' Dexter rumbled, still pacing as Donna pondered the wisdom of pointing out that she was in fact present and need not be referred to in the abstract. 'But, any help she needs, I'll be there to give it. If you're expecting problems with a serious case I'll be glad to take it on. Anything must be better than selling bloody burglar alarms.'

Roper was immediately contrite. Dexter's presence on a doorstep almost guaranteed success and security systems were a profitable sideline. 'Oh no. Not at all. Only a trivial matter. Ideal for Miss O'Prey.'

'What is it?' Donna enquired, trying desperately to sound both keen and professional. She'd take the case on, regardless of its importance, determined to regain the ground she'd lost in the last two years. In her early days at R and D Security she had been no more than the office junior, but the rapid escalation of her first real solo investigation into such dangerous territory had thrust her into the forefront of high profile casework. All that progress had counted for nothing when she'd suffered a minor breakdown following her narrow escape from a violent psychopath and since her return to work had been offered only trivial and unimportant cases. This latest job offer would undoubtedly be more of the same, but Donna knew she had to demonstrate her ability to take on any case and resolve it quickly and efficiently if she ever hoped to be rewarded with the demanding cases for which she longed. The problem was partly of her own making; bitterly aware that she came across as weak and feeble, seemingly unable to transfer the action woman lurking deep inside her onto the real stage. She had to credit Dexter for recognising these hidden characteristics and encouraging her at every turn, but Donna, to her own chagrin, was proving a difficult student. If that near brush with violent death had been the zenith of her career, revealing hitherto unsuspected talents, it was equally evident that she'd plumbed the depths once more following a severe battering to mind and body. Donna knew the general opinion of her peers was somewhat unflattering but had finally started to believe in herself again. Even if no one else shared that belief. Now, as three pairs of eyes swivelled in Donna's direction, Roper grunted, as if reluctantly accepting that his most junior Associate had the right to speak out.

'A sudden death. Young man. Eighteen or nineteen. Parents want answers.'

Donna blinked. Roper had switched effortlessly into military-speak, as befitted his former working life. Short snappy sentences. Information passed down; junior ranks for the briefing of.

'What sort of answers?'

'Usual background stuff. Friends. Problems of a personal nature. What made him do it? That sort of thing.'

'Do what?'

Roper looked angrily at her as if suspecting she was being deliberately obtuse. 'Kill himself of course.'

'Oh!'

13

'Suicide. No doubt about it. Parents can't seem to accept the fact. Want answers.'

'I'm sure they do,' Donna said, her voice barely audible. 'How did he...'

'Kill himself? Hanging.'

'What?' Donna felt the room sway, barely aware of Dexter's outraged bellow. 'For God's sake, man. Have you no sense at all? You know Donna's history as well as I do, yet you consider it appropriate to put a case like this her way?'

Donna's memories of finding her father's body, hanging from a stout beam over the stairwell, were ingrained on her soul, but something made her speak out. 'It's ok. I want the case.'

Dexter strode to her side, his face a concerned mask. 'Just take a minute to think about this. No one here will think any less of you if you decide to pass on this particular case.' He looked pointedly at Roper.

'No, I want it.'

Dexter's face softened. 'You don't need to do this. Why torture yourself?'

'I want it. I can do it. Who knows, maybe I need to confront a few demons head-on. That good enough reason for you?' Donna knew she was being harsh; Dexter was only thinking of her own best interests, but her response couldn't be helped. The minute Roper offered the case she'd known she would take it on. Even if only for an entirely selfish reason: the need to prove something to herself. Dexter sighed and walked away, resuming his seat without further comment.

'Splendid,' Roper announced, rubbing his hands together. 'Perhaps Miss O'Prey could liase with me later? Arrange to meet the clients?'

Donna nodded, eyes downcast, feeling Dexter's gaze on her but unable to look at him. Martha sniffed. Whether at the prospect of her brother, the Supreme Being, liasing with the miscreant O'Prey or as a reminder that important filing duties were being neglected Donna couldn't say, but it served as a spur to Roper to bring the meeting to a close. Dexter shook his head as he passed by but refrained from anything further. Donna knew he'd accept her decision, even if he was violently opposed to it. Dexter was always on at her to accept more responsibility, to take the difficult decisions even when offered an easy way out, so he could hardly complain when she did exactly that. She still had no idea why she'd put her hand up for this case, the subject of which was so painful to her, but the deed was done and she'd make sure she pursued it with as much dedication as she could muster. She'd half expected that reference would be made to the case that had part-fascinated, part-terrified her. It had been more than two years ago but the memories were as vivid as ever. Marcus Green had been imprisoned while still technically a child for the murder of two young children in a house fire. Released after thirteen years he'd returned to wreak havoc in the area and managed to turn Donna's first solo case, a supposedly routine missing person enquiry, into an investigation involving rape, kidnap and murder. She'd gone out on a limb, even defying Dexter at times, and due to her perseverance the kidnap victims had been rescued. After a final violent struggle, in which Donna and the captive women had faced imminent death, the searing heat of a blazing log cabin had consumed Marcus Green. When a subsequent search of the remains had failed to locate the body of Marcus, Donna had succumbed to a repetition of the panic attacks that had been her constant companion since her father's suicide. Beset by fears that her erstwhile captor may still be at large, Donna's rehabilitation had been prolonged, but she was back on track now, eager to resume her duties at R and D Security. It may not have been the best job in the world but it provided the stimulus she needed and ensured she had no free time to brood on past events.

The sky was that shade of blue which great painters yearn to immortalise on canvas, like a great bale of cloth stretched tight over the roof of the world, appearing close enough to reach out and touch. Marcus turned his face towards the warmth for a few moments, before resuming his vigil. He sucked his teeth as a figure shuffled into sight, then relaxed as the subject of his interest was revealed as an elderly woman.

He felt calm, indolent as a Sunday afternoon in high summer. That 'can't be bothered' feeling that he knew he had to guard against. Being back in his own country, especially here on the Liverpool dockside where he had once been well known was dangerous. The reminder was necessary. He'd been away for over two years and had become accustomed to moving freely in areas where he was treated as just another tourist among a multitude. Now all his senses were on full alert. This was the only way he could achieve his desires. For the same reason, he kept his temper firmly under control, ever fearful of the consequences. Like a dangerous beast kept caged the consequences of unchecked rage were too terrible to contemplate. Loss of temper was loss of control and without control he would be no better than the scum who stood on street corners with palms outstretched begging for small change.

He'd left England in a hurry. Being officially pronounced dead was an advantage he couldn't afford to waste. The current politically-motivated obsession with asylum seekers meant that traffic entering the port of Dover from the Continent was very closely scrutinised, but vehicles travelling in the opposite direction were rarely subject to the random searches that had become the norm on entry. It had been very easy to clamber unseen into the back of a lorry and spend the short sea crossing in the depths of the vehicle bay. On arrival in France he'd stolen a car, driven to the outskirts of Dreux and found an empty apartment in a tower block where he could recover from his injuries. With its vast illegal immigrant population conditioned to a distrust of authority, Dreux was perfect and for a man with money all things were possible. It bought him time to get himself patched up and a new identity established. By the time he moved on to the next stage of his plan he was fit and well again. A new man. Literally. He had a new passport and other documents in his suitcase and nothing to connect him to the person he used to be. The passport was not a forgery but the genuine article, well able to satisfy the most demanding official. Its previous owner would have no further need of the document; not at the bottom of a deep lake with a heavy chunk of masonry tied to his chest to ensure he stayed there. The man had been greedy; attempting to extract a greater price than what had already been agreed for the papers he'd contracted to supply. Faced with the anticipated refusal to pay the extra charges, the Frenchman drew a handgun from his belt and pointed it at the face of Marcus. Marcus barely glanced at the weapon, a Heckler and Koch USP 40 containing 13 rounds. His expression never wavered, staring into the eyes of the drug dealer whose distended pupils revealed an excessive familiarity with his stock in trade. Satisfied that the man's reactions were no match for his own, Marcus reached out and calmly deflected the barrel of the gun away from himself as an expression of intense agony contorted the face of his assailant. Marcus glanced at the slim blade buried to the hilt in the other man's groin and smiled. Reliance on the power of his weapon had made his opponent vulnerable. A handgun was only ever effective at a distance greater than arm's length. Overconfidence had persuaded the dealer to remain within killing range of his opponent. Up close and personal was home territory for Marcus, negating the apparent advantage of the opponent's weapon. Marcus had taken the documents he'd ordered, together with the dead man's passport and brokered a deal with the crack-dealing occupants of a neighbouring flat whereby the dead man's remaining drug stocks would be exchanged for permanent disposal of the body.

Marcus stirred, instantly raising his defences to the maximum, as a slight figure appeared in his field of vision. A young man dressed entirely in black, jogged between two parked cars. Marcus smiled.

'About bloody time Chris,' he called out, a smile taking away the harshness of the rebuke.

'Sorry, mate,' the youth answered, 'couldn't get away. Did you see her?' The eagerness in his voice was palpable and Marcus allowed himself a further smile.

'Yeah. Would I let you down? It's not as bad as you thought. She's still keen on you, don't worry about that. That other lad was a mistake. She knows that now.'

The youth stopped in front of Marcus. 'Great. When did you speak to her?'

'Last night. Gave her a bell like you said and she said to come round. We had a coffee and she told me straight how she'd met this other lad, but it amounted to nothing. I told her how you thought she'd stood you up and she was well gutted. I reckon if you ring her tonight she'll tell you the same. Look, I've got the motor round the corner. Fancy getting away from this dump for a while?'

Chris grimaced. 'Can't, mate. Sorry. Got the Social Services coming round later to see about getting a bath lift in and some other gear the old girl needs. I want to be there when they arrive or they'll just fob her off with some crap about budget shortages and she'll end up with fuck all.'

Marcus grinned. 'No problem. Just come for half an hour. I'll tell you everything Angela said. Once I've put your mind to rest, we can get wasted with what I've got in the glove box. Put yourself first for a change, instead of running round like a blue-arsed fly every time your old lady wants something doing.'

The youth frowned ruefully. 'Yeah, I know. I'm she's all got, aren't I? It's not her fault the old man's never there. Useless twat.'

Marcus shook his head. 'I know. It's a bitch. But this is top stuff, Chris. I can't guarantee getting anything as good as this every time. Are you in or out?'

By way of answer, the youth set off, looking over his shoulder at Marcus. 'I'm in. Move your arse, why don't you?' Marcus grinned, jogging to catch up his companion. They walked side by side along the deserted pavement and out of sight. A woman cleaning the inside of her bedroom windows caught a quick glance of Chris turning the corner. She had no idea she would be the last person to see him alive.

Donna shuffled through the papers on her desk, turning over everything one more time. Her quest was in vain as the report she'd promised faithfully would be in Dexter's hands first thing in the morning had vanished. She turned up Roper's notes containing the client's address along with numerous strict instructions concerning the manner in which he wanted the investigation to be carried out and frowned. So many instructions! Donna could reduce Roper's strictures to a few salient words and did so when Dexter had asked her for details of the case.

'Have a quick chat to the clients, but don't get them upset by asking for too many details. Ring up a couple of friends of the dead boy. See if they knew of any reasons he was depressed enough to kill himself. Write up a report, show it to Roper, then forget about it and get on with my other work.'

Dexter frowned. 'Sounds easy enough. Only one thing missing as far as I can see.'

Donna looked up and saw Dexter was waiting for her to speak.

'Do the job properly?' she said.

Dexter looked pleased. 'Spot on.'

'Why don't I go to see the clients and find out the details, then actually go and see the lad's mates in person and not just ring round like Roper suggested? Doing things that way I'd know from talking to the clients what their concerns were and could ask his mates the right questions.'

'Good. What then?'

Donna thought deeply. 'Follow my nose?'

Dexter beamed, patted her on the shoulder and walked away before Donna could even begin to think up a decent excuse about the missing report.

Chapter 2

DONNA looked at the obstacle barring her way and wondered which of them would be first to crack. She had telephoned the clients to arrange a meeting, but on arrival at the house, a mock-Tudor affair on the leafy outskirts of Little Sutton, she'd failed to find much sign of a welcome. The man standing in the doorway was a pretty forbidding sight. Above the ring of fat overflowing his shirt collar, a blotchy red face featured unusual puffed-out cheeks, like a hamster with an addiction to anabolic steroids, and thick rubbery lips. The man's nose looked as if it belonged to an even larger person and had been parked in the centre of his face on a purely temporary basis until claimed by its rightful owner. The face was framed by thick clumps of hair sprouting defiantly from his large fleshy ears. He was wearing scuffed trainers, faded jeans, a Comic-relief T-shirt and an angry expression on his face. The expression looked as if it was changed about as often as he changed his T-shirt. Not very often. The shirt, like its owner, had seen better days. But not recently. In either case.

'I've telephoned and arranged to....'

'I don't care what you say you've done,' the man interjected, 'I'm telling you you're not coming in. End of story. So, do us both a favour and sling your fucking hook.' He took a deep drag on his cigarette, watching the drifting smoke with rapt attention. Almost as if he'd never seen such a thing before.

As Donna drew a deep breath a woman appeared in the narrow gap between the man barring Donna's way and the doorframe. 'What's happening, Terry?' she said, peering out at Donna.

'Just another nosy bloody reporter,' Terry replied, half turning to reply, 'She's just leaving.'

'I'm not a journalist,' Donna shouted, 'I'm here to talk to Mister and Mrs Carter. About their son.' As she spoke, Donna took a step back as Terry's face contorted in a fresh paroxysm of rage.

'Are you Miss O'Prey?' The woman brushed past her minder with ease and stepped down from the step to confront Donna directly.

Donna smiled. 'Donna O'Prey,' she affirmed, extending her hand. The woman smiled broadly, taking Donna's hand in her own before turning to face the man behind her. 'Thanks, Terry,' she said, 'I'm expecting the young lady.'

Terry narrowed his eyes, glaring at Donna as if she'd tricked him in some way and then turned on his heels and strode back into the hall and out of sight. The woman smiled at his departing back. 'Terry's a treasure but he is inclined to take an extreme line sometimes. We have had a few problems with reporters and Neil, that's my husband, asked Terry to keep a look out. Sorry you got lumped in with the Fourth Estate rat pack.'

'That's fine,' Donna reassured her, 'You've had problems with journalists then?'

The other woman looked quizzically at Donna. 'Didn't your Mister Roper tell you? We've had no end of trouble with reporters camping outside the door. Although just why they bother, I really don't know. Its not as if Neil is

18

going to come out for a chat, is it? Public figure he may be, but there are limits.'

Donna said nothing. Roper had given her scarcely more than a name and address, no personal details at all and now it seemed the client was some form of VIP. Neil Carter? The name meant nothing to her. Donna decided to wait it out and see if meeting the man of the house would provide any clues.

'Shall we go inside? Oh, what must you think of me? Sorry, I'm Jenny Carter.'

Donna smiled back. 'Donna,' she said again, 'Donna O'Prey.'

'Come in, Donna. I'll take you through to meet Neil.' The woman stalked off into a wood-panelled hall, high heels clacking on the tiled floor and Donna trailed after her wondering how a woman who looked as good as Jenny Carter could have had a nineteen-year-old son. As if she'd read Donna's mind Jenny stopped at the far end of the hall.

'Just before we go in,' Jenny said, 'I'd better clear something up. I'm not Julian's mum. I'm the trophy wife. I'd been Neil's bit on the side for three years and then his wife, the precious Alison who he supposedly couldn't possibly give up just to marry me, fell off her horse and broke her stupid neck. We got married six weeks after the funeral. So much for him missing her.'

'Oh!' Donna didn't know what to say.

'Yeah. I reckon he didn't want to pay her off in a divorce settlement. Since we got married I realise what a tight sod he really is. If he's got any fancy ideas about replacing me he'd better start cashing in some of his investments 'cause I won't go cheaply.'

'What was Julian like?' Donna asked, trying to get the subject round to the reason she was here.

'Oh, a good laugh. Full of life. That's what made it such a shock when the silly little sod topped himself. We got on dead well, Jules and me.'

'Did you never think he was depressed or anything like that?'

'Nah! He was just a young lad. Bloody good looking as well. Everything to live for. Neil blames himself, of course, but I can't see why. Not his fault. Let me take you in to see Neil. He can tell you all this stuff much better than me. He's Julian's Dad; I'm only the floozy who married Neil for his money.'

'Did you?' Donna could have bitten her tongue off as the question came out but Jenny didn't appear fazed at all.

'I suppose I did really but he was the one doing all the chasing. He asked me. Not the other way around. Mind you, his so-called friends didn't see it like that. A right miserable crowd they are. Always going on about how wonderful Alison was and how he must miss her. Tell you the truth, I wish he'd tell the whole lot of them to bugger off and mind their own business. Neil's not the big man any more and as for his mates, loyalty to Alison doesn't stop them touching me up every chance they get. My arse is black and blue by the time our pissed-up dinner guests have gone off home with their frosty-faced old bitches.'

Donna smiled, playing the all girls together role to the max. Jenny pushed back her blonde mane, revealing a rose tattoo on an uncovered sleek shoulder and pushed open a heavy oak door. Donna followed her into a huge room, dark and sombre with acres of panelling. Heavy velvet drapes, blanking off tall sash windows, excluded any external sounds as effectively as top of the range double-glazing. The burnished hues of an immense table flanked by eight matching chairs dominated the room but there seemed no sign of human presence.

'Neil! Get your head out of that drinks cabinet. You've got a visitor.'

At the far end of the room a section of panelling swung ajar revealing itself as a concealed room and a large man stepped forward from the dark interior. He had the ruddy complexion that can indicate either a healthy outdoor life or high blood pressure. Donna would have laid odds on the latter. He was a study in sartorial elegance. The sort of thing which townies imagined a country squire would wear. Donna didn't know any country squires but if she did it was a certainty they wouldn't look like this. White open-necked shirt and a paisley cravat with the shirt collar turned back over the neck of a Harris Tweed jacket, moleskin trousers seemingly a little too snug for comfort and shiny black boots. Deep-set brown eyes under heavy brows imparted an air of menace at variance with the rest of his facial features.

'This is Donna. Donna O'Prey. Come from that Private Detective place.' Jenny said as she shoved Donna forward.

'How do?' The man said in a deep gravely voice, thrusting out a hand for Donna to shake.

Donna took the proffered hand and then realised her mouth was wide open. She quickly shut it. 'You're Neil Travis.'

The man smiled a trifle ruefully. 'Used to be. Long time ago so please don't tell me your Mum used to be a fan. It's a sensitive subject.'

Donna bit back her next remark which would have been exactly that, apart from the fan having been her Dad. Among the few tangible possessions to survive his death were half a dozen Neil Travis albums.

'Neil still writes songs, don't you darling? Jenny cooed, taking his arm and draping it around her shoulders. 'And, just a few weeks ago there was talk of the band reforming for a charity concert.'

Neil frowned. 'Not ever really likely, that,' he said gently. 'All of us far too old to rock, far too fat to strut a stage like we once did.'

Donna picked up on some hidden agenda between the two of them, but was still too surprised to pursue the thought. When Neil Travis was front man for the Furies, Mick Jagger had been his only serious rival for the title of sexiest man in Rock. Now, he was thickset, balding slightly and dressed like one of the old farts he once mocked in the lyrics of his songs but Donna had still recognised him instantly.

'Would you like a drink, Donna? *Cappuccino* or anything?' Jenny enquired, her perfectly capped teeth gleaming.

'Oh, no thanks. Perhaps I could…'

'Have something a bit stronger? Of course you can'

Donna blinked. She'd been about to suggest that she could make a start on finding out about the death of Neil's son and her hesitation had been no more than uncertainty as to the correct way of going about this. Neil removed his arm from his wife's shoulder and motioned towards one of the sofas. 'I think Donna wants to get down to business,' he said, 'Please take a seat over there, Donna and ask your questions in comfort.' He turned to Jenny. 'Why don't you go for a swim, darling? I'm sure you'll find all this a bit of a bore?' It was a clear brush-off and Jenny froze for a moment before tossing her hair back and striding away.

'Fine,' she called, over her shoulder. 'You two have your chat or whatever. I'll go and do something about the state of my nails.'

As the sound of clacking heels faded, Neil sighed heavily. 'Did you see her sodding nails?'

'Not really,' Donna said, tactfully. Actually, the nails had been the first things she'd noticed. Great long blood-red talons and obviously false.

Neil sighed. 'I don't blame you for what you're thinking. Silly old fool, old enough to know better than to get hitched to such an obvious gold-digger.' Donna said nothing and by the time she realised it would have been polite to have made some token protestation the moment had passed. Neil gave a faint smile. 'There's my answer, then,' he said. 'You're in good company, Donna. All my friends tell me exactly the same thing. And they're right. All I can say in my defence is that I married Jenny on the rebound when my wife died suddenly, thinking that sex and a bit of ego-stroking could be a substitute for what I'd lost.'

Donna sat, flicking at the edge of her notebook as Neil continued in the same vein for another couple of minutes.

'Bugger! Just listen to me airing my dirty linen and inflicting all this on you. You must think I'm a tedious old bastard rambling on and on like this?'

Donna looked directly at him. 'I don't,' she said firmly. 'What I think is that you just need to talk. Any subject would do.'

Neil looked at her closely and then abruptly sat down on the sofa opposite. 'You're a sharp one, aren't you?'

Donna shrugged. 'I know all about losing someone. You've had a double blow. First your wife and then your son. It's not easy.'

'No. It's not easy and it doesn't get any easier.' A single tear escaped from the corner of his eye and crept slowly down his cheek. 'Just when I start to think I'm beginning to cope with it all, along comes another bloody reporter looking for a fading rock star in family tragedy story and I'm back to square one. Hence the lovely Terry who's my self-appointed minder. He's a smashing bloke, used to be a roadie in the band so maybe he takes my welfare a bit too seriously. I'm surprised you got past him without being head-butted.'

Donna laughed. 'It was touch and go for a while,' she admitted. 'Do you feel up to doing this now? I can always come back another time.'

'No!' The interjection was so unexpectedly vehement that Donna jumped. 'You're here now. Let's get on with it. I told your boss, Roper isn't it?' Donna nodded. 'Told him I didn't want a quick in and out job. I want someone to look into all the circumstances of my boy's death. I've had it up to here with the police, the coroner, all that crap about Julian killing himself. Now I want the truth.'

Donna looked at him sharply. 'You don't think it was suicide?'

'Never in this world. Julian was happy, without any money worries or girlfriend hassles. Nothing.'

'What about drugs? I'm sorry to ask that, but...'

'What? Because I spent ten years out of my skull while living the sex drugs and rock 'n roll stereotype? That's the very reason I can say with such certainty that Julian didn't do drugs. Not with his old man as a constant reminder of how drugs fuck you up. Not to mention, the difficulty of hiding the signs from me. I've been there, remember, done all that. I'd be the first to know. Not to mention having gone through his room, all his stuff, with a fine-tooth comb. *Nada.*'

'Fair enough. What can you tell me? All I know so far are just the bare details.'

Neil sighed. 'I've looked into this suicide business. Read all the statistics. Just like being back at Oxford.' He laughed harshly. 'By the look on your face you didn't know that. Yes, I went to Oxford, did a law degree, but found the music business was a lot more fun and paid pretty well too.'

Donna looked at the tortured expression on his face and thought once again that her job had its shitty moments. She should be arrested for emotional breaking and entering. Peering into the sorrow and misery which had become the norm for the man opposite her who'd been hiding behind a veil of false courage and self-delusion while trying to hang on to his sanity.

'Tell me about Julian. What was he like?'

Neil shrugged his shoulders. 'Intelligent. Good head on his shoulders. Easy to get on with. I may be biased but he was the son I'd always dreamed of. Talented musician, much better than I ever was, but sensible enough to steer clear of the band scene. He was all set to get a bloody good degree behind him and make his own way in the world. All that talk of suicide is from people who didn't know him. I'd say he was the last person on earth to do away with himself.' He was crying freely now, not even bothering to wipe the tears from his face. Donna had learnt from Dexter that there was a time to interrupt and there was a time to shut up and listen. This was definitely the latter.

'I can't explain any of it. I had to sit in that courtroom and listen to a complete stranger tell me that my boy had taken the decision to end his own life. I felt so bloody useless. I just can't accept it. Part of me doesn't want to find out what happened. If Julian really did kill himself and I had no inkling of it where does that leave me? With a shit-load of guilt on my shoulders, that's where.' He stopped talking, but Donna sat very still, saying nothing and waiting for him to continue. Neil stood and walked across the room, gazing out of the window, then returned to his seat and started talking again. 'I found him. In the stable block. We don't keep horses now. My wife, sorry, I mean my late wife, was a keen rider, but after she died I sold both the horses. Too many memories. I don't suppose you know but Alison died after falling from her horse.' Donna had known that, thanks to Jenny, but said nothing. She still had her pad on her knee but had yet to open it.

'Julian had been dead for several hours according to the police. It was awful seeing him there. You can't imagine.' Donna could imagine the scene only too well but kept a tight grip on herself, willing the weakness she was feeling to pass. The night she'd found the body of her Dad hanging in the stairwell had been the worst night of her life and she'd never be free of the pain she'd felt at that time.

'I managed to get him down, but knew straight away that he was gone. Somehow I got back to the house to call the emergency services and then went back and sat with him. Jenny was in a right state. Wailing and carrying on. She was very close to Julian; they used to watch TV together. The Office, things like that. I'll say that much for her; there was never a moment's awkwardness when she turned up from nowhere as my wife. Julian was fine with her from the very beginning, as she was with him. After it was over, when the police and ambulance crew had all gone, we sat in this room, just Jenny and myself, staring into space. We couldn't speak, couldn't even begin to understand what had happened.' Neil stopped talking and attempted a smile. 'As you can see I'm not a lot further forward even now.'

'Can you suggest anyone I should talk to? Friends? Girlfriend perhaps?'

'Forget the girlfriend,' Neil snorted, 'She's no use at all. I asked her straight away if she had any idea what had really happened.' He stopped talking, staring into space.

'And?' Donna prompted.

'And nothing. She told me she thought Julian might have killed himself because he was my son. Pressure was on him because I was well known, had been well known at one time anyway, and Julian had always tried to live up to that. Make his own way in the world without my help to prove something or other to me.' He snorted again. 'Load of bollocks.'

'How serious was it? Their relationship, I mean.'

'Not as serious as she makes out. They'd been together for about a year. Julian told me months ago that she wouldn't survive his move to university. He'd got it all worked out. Typical of him to sort everything out in advance. He said he was ready for a new start. Even if that meant ditching the girlfriend. They were never going to last anyway. She was a nice enough girl and certainly looked the part but on a long-term basis? Not a chance. Julian had told me about his plans for the future. He was really up for it all. Going up to Oxford, getting his degree, everything was exciting and challenging. Does that sound like someone who couldn't cope with life or was so depressed that his only option was to kill himself?'

'No. It doesn't. What about friends? Can you suggest anyone I should talk to?'

Neil nodded. 'I've been in touch with a couple of what I'd have said were his close friends. They're as baffled as we are.' He hesitated. 'I'm not sure how relevant this is, but...'

'Go on.'

'Well, there's some mate or other, someone I don't know, who used to ring up to speak to Julian. Only in the last week or so before Julian died. I don't know his name so I couldn't get in touch. For the funeral, you know?'

Donna nodded. 'Perhaps one of his other mates will know. Leave it with me; I'll do my very best.'

'That's it, then. Can't help you at all, can I? I wish I could give you some idea of anything that would help but there's nothing. Oh, apart from this.' He almost ran across the room and rummaged in a walnut bureau, eventually retrieving a buff envelope with a cry of triumph. Neil walked across to Donna and handed the envelope to her. It wasn't sealed and when Donna shook it a king-size cigarette dropped into her lap. She looked at it blankly.

'I found this in Julian's room,' Neil explained 'Its not just any old fag. Hand-rolled. Special order I reckon.'

'Not Julian's then?'

Neil laughed. 'Not bloody likely. Silk Cut was more the mark for Julian. B and H if he fancied a change. Smoked too much really but what can you do? All his mates smoke. Better that than some of the stuff I've put away in my time, I suppose.'

'I don't understand. The cigarette?'

'Oh, may be nothing. I expect Julian was given it and kept it to smoke later. Funny though; I'd have thought he'd have at least smoked the bloody thing if he was intending to do away with himself.'

Donna nodded. 'Oh, I see.'

'He wouldn't have got a fancy ciggie like that off any of the mates I knew about. It'll probably be nothing but keep it anyway. You never know.'

'Did you show it to the police?'

Neil snorted. 'No chance. They've made their mind up it was suicide and are hardly likely to change their minds by me waving a cigarette around. They'd just assume a drugs involvement or something. Look; forget I even mentioned it. Take it away or leave it here. Please yourself.'

'I'll take it,' Donna said, decisively, slipping the cigarette back into the envelope and into her pocket. 'I need to keep an open mind. Look into everything.'

Neil reached down and took her hand in his own. 'Find out for me, Donna. Find out what happened to my boy.'

Donna looked back at him solemnly. 'I will. Believe me, I will.'

Marcus knelt down, leaning over the prone figure until he was close enough to whisper.

'Chris. Can you hear me?'

Chris opened his eyes and smiled. 'Oh yeah, loud and clear. Where the hell did you get this stuff?'

Marcus smiled back. 'The best is yet to come. Wait 'till you try the new gear. Makes weed seem tame. Even good stuff like this.'

'Bring it on. Just…'

'What?'

'You know. No hard stuff, right? I'm not into smack or anything heavy.'

Marcus looked offended. 'What do you take me for? Am I your mate or what?'

'You know you are. What's the new gear then?'

'Just a popper. Works like fucking magic. One whiff of it and you're flying. I've only got a couple for now, but I can get more at the weekend. Go for it, yeah?' He took a clear gelatine bulb out of a metal case and handed it to Chris.

'You not having one?'

'Yeah. In a minute. You first. Just snap it under your nose and breathe in. Take a good deep breath; it's too good to waste.'

'Look, I need to get back, mate. Can't leave the old girl much longer. Reckon I'll save it for later, ok?'

Marcus frowned. 'Be all right. Only lasts a few minutes, but you'll be flying. Plenty of time. You can spare a few more minutes can't you?'

Chris propped himself up on an elbow. In the clearing, surrounded by trees the light was fading fast, but the sky was still clear and bright. 'Better not. I'm half way off my head on dope as it is. Need to have a clear head if I'm to sort the Social Services crowd out.'

'See what you mean. Save it for later then. Tell you what; I can help you clear your head if you want.'

'Yeah?'

'Yeah. Easy.' Marcus rummaged in his back pocket and produced a twist of aluminium foil.

'What you got there?'

'New stuff. Clear your head in no time plus it'll keep you sharp for hours. Just what you need.' He removed two capsules from the foil and passed them across to Chris. 'Here you go. Have these on me. I don't want you going home in this state.'

Chris took the capsules and regarded them doubtfully. 'What are they?'

Marcus shrugged. 'Don't know the technical name but they're bloody magic, mate. You'll need a piss in about half an hour and all the dope in your system will be flushed out. After that you'd pass an Olympic drug test. That's what all the top athletes use. I've only got those but you need a clear head, right? Help yourself. My treat.'

'Brilliant. Thanks mate.' Chris tipped his head back and swallowed both capsules. As he settled back on the grass Marcus looked on impassively when Chris clutched his chest at a sharp stab of pain.

'Fuck!'

Marcus leant over him. 'What's up, Chris?'

Chris shook his head, motioning to his chest. 'Really hurts. Shouldn't hurt like this, should it?'

'Oh, I think that's the idea.'

Chris moaned, clutching his chest. 'What's happening?'

Marcus smiled without warmth. 'You're having a heart attack. That's a pretty heavy cocktail you've just taken in.'

'Get help.'

'Oh, I don't think so.'

'Why have you done this? I'm a mate.'

Marcus shook his head. 'No mate of mine, Chris.' He rose to his feet.

'You can't leave me,' Chris wailed, sweat standing out on his brow. His face was chalky white, lips already turning blue. Marcus kicked at his supporting arm and Chris fell back heavily, moaning at a fresh stab of pain.

'I'm not going anywhere. Not yet.' Marcus carefully scanned the area, kicking fallen leaves over the grass on which he'd been sitting.

Chris moaned, his teeth snapping together. 'Jesus!'

'Don't go yet, Chris,' Marcus said calmly, 'I need to tell you something. You listening?' The other youth did not reply. 'I come from round here. Only a few miles away actually. I had to go away because of something that happened when I was a kid. I was in the wrong place at the wrong time. Two kids died in a fire and they blamed me for it. Locked me up. I was only thirteen. Think what that did to my mother to lose a son like that. Now your folks will know what it feels like to lose a child.' His voice was calm and his expression impassive. If he ever considered the irony of his words, given that he'd killed his own father and his baby sister while he was still a child and then later his mother too when her death provided the means of faking his own death, he gave no visible sign.

'You can't do this.'

Marcus laughed. 'I already have. You're dying. Unless you get urgent attention in the next couple of minutes you're dead meat. And that's not going to happen. Nobody knows you're here. It could be days before they find you.'

Chris opened his eyes very wide. 'You bastard,' he said.

'One other thing. First night we met you were sulking like a spoilt kid over a girl that'd stood you up. I turned up and out of the kindness of my heart offered you enough weed to make you forget all about that Angela tart. Remember her now? Left you for someone better didn't she? That was me as well. I took her off you and you never even dreamt of it. All that whinging about losing her. You didn't lose her; she fucking dumped you when I came along. I picked her up and was fucking the little slag an hour later. We pissed ourselves laughing about you waiting at the bus station for her like the fucking loser you are when all the time she was with me. You couldn't even fuck her properly, could you? She told me about what a useless twat you were. No wonder she dumped you. She won't even come to your funeral.'

Chris tried to rise, then sank back on the grass.

'Won't be long now, Chris,' Marcus whispered. 'Can you feel it? You're dying now.'

Chris closed his eyes and Marcus reached out and slapped him across the face. 'Open your eyes, loser. Look at me.' Chris tried to spit at him, but the effort was too much for him. He gave a low moan, drew a deep rasping breath and then was silent. Marcus watched him for another minute, then touched his face gently with the tips of his fingers and rose to his feet. This had not been a death to treasure. Of the many people he'd killed several had died slowly. Those were the ones he'd enjoyed the best. There were others whom he'd deliberately left alive but they had begged for death and were still wishing for a release from constant pain. Marcus walked away, dismissing the body lying on the grass behind him.

'So long, Chris,' he said over his shoulder.

CHAPTER 3

Donna sighed. Her grandmother, Peg was being difficult. As usual. Following the sudden death of her father, Donna had suffered a major breakdown and Peg had taken it on herself to provide after-care when Donna had finally been discharged from hospital. She'd always called the old woman by her given name, even as a small child. Donna owed Peg a debt of gratitude she could never repay for dragging her back to the land of the living. Although there was an inevitable price to pay, as Peg could be difficult at times and at eighty-three managed to rule over great chunks of her granddaughter's life.

Dexter had called at the house on his way into work to ask why Donna's mobile was switched off. The reason couldn't have been simpler; she'd forgotten to put it on charge and now had to suffer the consequences. A major bollocking from Dexter. As if that weren't a bad enough start to the day, Peg had started on Dexter, accusing him of bullying poor little Donna.

'I was wrong, Peg. My fault. Not anyone else.' Donna said.

'I dare say. But, that's no reason for him to give you the Three Degrees.' Peg snapped.

Dexter almost smiled. Donna knew he kept a mental note of Peg's frequent liberties with the English language and this Peg-speak version of the Third Degree would no doubt be produced by Dexter at some suitable occasion in the future. He held up both hands defensively. 'Right. I shouldn't expect Donna to remember to keep her mobile charged up. I realise now that's an unreasonable expectation. I'll say no more about it.' The gleam in his eye left Donna in no doubt as to the consequences if she failed to answer her phone in the future, but his words were sufficient to pacify Peg.

'I should just think so and all. Now, if you pair clear off out of the road, I can perhaps get on. I've got to get some spuds peeled and cash poor Mister Day's pension for him.'

Donna nodded, throwing her notebook, pen and other stuff into a carrier bag. Mister Day was a neighbour and one of the unfortunates whom Peg had decided was in need of help. In his seventies and crippled with arthritis, Mister Day was in no position to reject help. Even when the self-appointed carer was ten years older than himself.

'Poor old devil,' Peg mused, 'I reckon most of his troubles are down to that wife of his. Dying on him like that. Typical. Mind you, what can you expect with her being vegetarian.' Peg uttered the word vegetarian as another person would say child molester. 'I can't be doing with all that nonsense. I've been eating meat all my life and never suffered by it.' Donna said nothing. Peg's diet would horrify any modern nutritionist, but her continued good health certainly proved something. Living on a staple diet of belly pork, beef dripping and fatty bacon, her arteries should have been as choked as the M25 on a wet Friday evening. 'I don't know why,' Peg went on, 'He doesn't try one of those homosexual doctors.'

'What?' Donna struggled to produce even this solitary word.

'One of them that Prince Charles goes to.'

'Oh,' Donna said, faintly, 'A homeopathic doctor.'

'That's what I said. Elsie Carter. you know; her with the husband?' Peg said, revelling in having news to pass on.

'What husband?'

'You know. The one who's a bit funny in the head. Anyway, not him. Elsie Carter. She reckons these new doctors can cure anything. I told her straight. Just get some decent grub inside you and you'll be right as nine-pence. Mind you, waste of time giving advice to Elsie Carter. She used to cut the fat off her bacon. Throw it in the bin. Best bit of nourishment that is, the rind.' Again Donna said nothing, unwilling to argue the merits of healthy eating with Peg. 'There you are then,' Peg went on, triumphantly, 'Goes to show.' This expression vied with 'Stands to reason' as Peg's favourite remark.

'What's Elsie Carter got to do with getting Mister Day's pension for him?'

Peg looked askance at Donna. 'Never said it did. You pair always rabbiting on would confuse a saint.'

Dexter blinked but somehow kept quiet. Donna kissed Peg on the cheek. 'See you later, you mad old bat,' she said affectionately. 'Don't know what time I'll be back. If I'm likely to be late, I'll ring you.'

Dexter coughed and Donna returned from the doorway to collect her partially charged mobile from its stand. 'I hadn't forgotten,' she said, bitterly aware that Dexter knew otherwise.

In the road, Donna brought Dexter up to date with her progress, such as it was. 'I'll see the girlfriend this morning, then try and track down a couple of his mates. Neil gave me some addresses so I'll see what turns up.'

'Neil?'

'The client. Oh, I should have said before. You'll never guess who he is?'

Dexter looked bemused.

'Neil Travis.'

'Get away?'

'Yeah. His real name's Neil Carter, but I knew him straight away.'

'Neil Travis,' Dexter mused. Donna could almost swear she detected a note of respect in his tone. 'So, what's the great man got to say about his lad's suicide?'

'Pretty much what I'd have expected. He's in denial. That's for sure. Said Julian, that's the lad's name, wasn't the sort to kill himself. Too much to live for. It sounds an odd one to me, but early days yet. I've only got one point of view.' Donna watched Dexter's face and saw a flicker of amusement. She was deliberately repeating a Dexter mantra: never reach any conclusion until all the evidence was in. It was her way of clawing back a bit of his respect after the mobile 'phone debacle.

'Fair enough. I've had a quick glance at the coroner's report. Seems pretty much cut and dried, but have a look yourself and see what you think. I've left it in your desk drawer. Keep it out of sight. I shouldn't have it by rights, but managed to call in a favour or two. I've also booked you in at the morgue. I imagine you remember how to find your way there?'

Donna grimaced. Her one and only previous visit to the morgue had been in Dexter's company where she'd distinguished herself by throwing a wobbler. A full-scale panic attack triggered off by one of the white-coated assistants tottering past carrying an overloaded tray of unrecognisable giblets.

Dexter grinned wolfishly, enjoying her discomfort. 'Yes. Thought so. Well, rest easy, you won't have to see any actual corpses. Just ask for Tommy, tell him I sent you and ask him what he remembers about your case. He's a good lad, a bit of an oddball but they all are in that job. Tommy was assisting when they did the post-mortem so he'll perhaps give you a bit more usable info than you'll get from the report. OK?'

Donna nodded. Dexter's list of useful contacts was legendary and invariably saved a great deal of time. So far, it seemed as if Dexter had been doing most of the work.

'Neil Travis,' Dexter mused. 'Fancy him being the lad's father. If I remember right, he got himself in the papers recently. Got picked up for speeding and took a swing at the traffic lads who pulled him in. Never the wisest course.'

'I didn't see that.'

'Stumped up for a decent brief and got off the assault charge, but picked up a fair old ban. Failed the breathalyser in good style. If I remember right, it showed up as 190 milligrams per 100 millilitres.'

'What's that mean? In English?'

Dexter grinned. 'Pissed out of his skull. His wife had died and he'd just come from the funeral.'

'Oh. He's got himself a new wife now.'

Dexter sniffed. 'Anything else I need to know?' he enquired, glancing at his watch.

Donna slipped her hand into her pocket and handed him the envelope. 'This was found in the lad's room. Perhaps he'd been saving it for a special occasion.'

Dexter looked at the cigarette carefully. 'Fancy,' he said, 'Hand-made. Cost a fair old bit a packet of these. You'd think he'd have smoked the bloody thing before topping himself.'

Donna nodded. 'That's what the client said.'

Dexter slipped the cigarette into his pocket. 'Leave this with me. I'll ask around. Can't be too many places around where they still do hand-rolled fags. Anything else?'

Donna shook her head. 'Any suggestions?'

Dexter shook his head. 'Your case.'

Donna nodded. That wouldn't stop him interfering if he thought she was out of her depth, but she knew he'd let her run with it until the time came that she had to ask for advice. As Dexter drove away, Donna glanced at the scrap of paper she'd torn from her notebook. It was the address of Julian's girlfriend and as yet she didn't have the remotest idea of how to go about interviewing the girl. Follow your nose, she told herself and clambered behind the wheel.

The black puppy began barking almost immediately the two boys entered the woods. A young Labrador is a lively creature and he made short work of slipping his lead and darting off into the bushes. Nick, his owner, rolled his eyes in mock fury but the sheer naughtiness of the puppy was one of the best things about him. Nick's best friend, Tom, shrieked with excitement. 'After him,' he called and the two boys took off at a run in hot pursuit. As they ran, panting with exertion but laughing out loud, the sound of barking became even more pronounced.

'He's found a rabbit,' Nick ventured hopefully, but as they burst into the clearing, both boys came to a skidding halt. The puppy stood over the figure on the ground, front legs wide apart, barking furiously. Tom took a single step forward and then stopped.

'Is he dead?' Nick asked; his voice shrill.

Tom shook his head. 'Don't know.' The boys stood still, eyes fixed on the prone body. The puppy gambolled across and Nick grabbed his collar and managed to re-attach the lead without taking his eyes off the body. Both boys turned simultaneously and then bounded away along the track on which they'd arrived.

Donna tapped her foot and waited. She'd been waiting for a good ten minutes in a windowless room and was getting more and more irritable. On arrival at the morgue she'd asked for Tommy and had been told to stay in this tiny room and wait. A loud crash in the corridor outside suggested some calamity or other and Donna wasn't surprised when the next sound to reach her ears was loud swearing. The complainant was male and the possessor of a formidably varied vocabulary. Donna poked her head outside and saw a tall thin youth, no older than herself, standing over a pile of something unmentionable on the floor. He was wearing a bloodstained green smock from which he was scraping dollops of flesh. Donna gulped and whipped back inside the room. The youth wandered off, feet scuffling on the tiled floor and the next sound Donna heard was the clip-clop of steel-tipped shoes approaching from the opposite direction.

A chubby middle-aged man with a nose that could have been the design blueprint for Concorde dominating his features scurried into the room. 'Miss O'Prey?' He enquired.

'That's right,' confirmed Donna, taking his fleshy hand and trying to ignore the fact that he was staring at her chest in a rather obvious manner.

'Just excuse me for one moment,' the man said, wrenching his gaze away from Donna's sweater for a moment, 'I'll be right back.' He went out into the corridor and she heard him berating the unfortunate youth who was now mopping the floor. 'Take that lot back, get it weighed and bag it up properly. Anyone slips over in that and you're in big trouble, lad. Got that? Now get it sorted.'

As the man returned, Donna could clearly hear the youth say 'wanker,' but apparently the object of this epithet was hard of hearing as he didn't break stride. 'Hello again. Sorry about that.'

'No problem,' Donna assured him. 'I assume you're Tommy.'

'I am indeed. Very much at your service.' Typical of an acquaintance of Dexter, Tommy had a rich Scouse accent you couldn't cut with an axe, let alone a knife. Dingle, Donna guessed. Adenoids working overtime and soft palate taking a major pounding. It's the classic Scouse, a Dingle accent. Liverpool isn't the biggest city around, but South-Enders, Scottie-Roaders, Tockie, the Dingle; every accent is different. Maybe you had to be born and bred in Liverpool to tell the difference instantly, but once tuned in to the local dialect it was as good as a home address.

Tommy was still looking at Donna's chest. She gave a troubled sigh. 'Did Dexter…'

'Indeed he did. I understand you're interested in a case of suicide.'

'That's right. Julian Carter. Do you remember it?'

Tommy smiled, revealing yellow teeth. 'Of course. I remember it very well. I assisted; was there the entire time. What exactly did you want to know? I told Mister Dexter I could let him borrow the report, but he said he'd like a verbal briefing as well and that he'd be sending his investigator down. Has there been a change of plan? Couldn't the investigator make it?'

Donna took a deep breath. 'That's me. I'm doing the investigation. It's my case.'

Tommy looked doubtful. 'Oh. I see. Well, if Mister Dexter says so. It was a clear suicide, you know?'

'Oh! You've no doubts about that?'

'None at all. I suppose the family can't come to terms with the verdict. Very common that. But, I've seen a good many suicides and this was as clear-cut as they come.'

Donna frowned. 'Oh. In what way?'

'Well now. For a start, there's the method. Hanging. Could it have been murder or was it really a suicide? The key is the bruising around the neck. Bruising is critical. With a suicide you get a bruise like this.' Tommy drew an upside-down V shape on a sheet of paper and pushed it towards Donna. 'If it's murder by strangulation, the bruising is in a ring around the neck, together with pressure marks at the back of the neck.'

'No doubt then? It had to be suicide. Because of the bruising.'

Tommy grinned. 'Unless…'

'Unless what?'

'Unless the victim was unconscious at the time and the hanging could be staged by putting his neck in a noose and shoving him off a raised platform. It would look like a suicide then. The bruising would be consistent with a suicide and there would be no way of proving otherwise.'

'So, what are you saying? It could have been murder?'

Tommy shrugged. 'Not according to my boss, so that's that. End of story. Silly bastard.'

'Who? Your boss?'

Tommy cackled. 'Well, yeah, but I didn't mean him. I meant the lad who topped himself. Bad choice.'

'In what way?'

'Hanging, for a start. If you want to do away with yourself, hanging is a pretty shite method. Most hanging suicides jump off a chair with a slip-knotted rope around their neck. If they only realised how inefficient, not to mention how agonising a method they've chosen, they'd quickly find another way of doing away with themselves. You need one hell of a drop to actually break the neck and even then there's no such thing as instantaneous death. The victim asphyxiates; all that actually means in practise is that the poor sod chokes to death. The heart carries on pumping, forcing blood through the compressed area of the neck and bursting tiny red veins in soft tissue areas such as the eyelids. Those haemorrhages are called *petechiae*. The result is not nice at all. Hanging is never a good way to die and even worse for the poor bastard who finds the body.'

Donna felt the room swaying and sat down, fortunately on the edge of a sturdy metal table.

'What's up? You look awful. Sorry, I shouldn't be going on about things like this. It's enough to make anyone feel a bit squeamish.'

'It's not that,' Donna said, her voice faint, 'My Dad hanged himself a few years back. I found him.'

'Oh, shit! I'm so sorry. I had no idea.'

Donna raised a feeble hand. 'No way you could have known. Sorry I....'

'Not your fault, love. Mine. You just sit where you are for a bit and I'll make you a cup of tea. Would that help?'

Donna nodded gratefully and swivelled round to sit in the chair properly. She felt close to tears, but she'd never revealed her inadequacies by giving in to the urge to cry. Even when she found her father's body, she'd held back the tears. She'd taken a long shower after the police had finally departed. The good thing about crying in the shower is that no one can see your weakness. Despite her best efforts to deal with her turbulent history, she'd failed dismally every time these particular memories came back to haunt her.

Seated in front of her computer screen, Sarah groaned, panting through her open mouth, as her chest tightened. It felt as if a giant ratchet was clicking inexorably round, pulling encircling steel bands closer and closer together with each turn. Her ribcage heaved silently, the virtual absence of wheezing even more dramatic than the first telltale sound. As breathing became progressively more difficult she was overcome by convulsions of coughing and spluttering. Arms waving feebly, she fell to the floor, throwing her head backwards, gasping for air as a hoarse rasping wheeze erupted in her chest. Reaching in desperation for the trailing plastic tubes leading to the nebulizer, she dislodged a pile of books, sending them crashing to the floor.

Pulling up outside the address Neil had given for Julian's girlfriend, Donna was still feeling wretched. Seemingly, everyone at the morgue had become aware of her panic attack and had rallied around. They'd all been very pleasant. Not to mention polite, helpful and friendly. After ten minutes, Donna hated them all. She missed the banter, the constant ribbing that was part and parcel of sharing an office with her equally messy and disorganised colleague, Andy. Compared to R and D Security this lot were just too *nice*. She'd collected her car from the patch of waste land that called itself a car park having paid the equivalent of a ransom demand for a kidnapped socialite in return for the dubious privilege of parking her car in a muddy puddle.

Not for the first time, Donna wondered whether Dexter's concerns about immersing herself in a case where she had such a history and high levels of personal involvement with the manner of death might just have been right. By now Dexter would surely have learned what had happened to her at the morgue and only her reluctance to appear feeble and gutless stopped her ringing Dexter and requesting he take her off the assignment.

The house was one of a block of three: red brickwork, tall Georgian windows and very classy indeed. The great sweep of Warren Drive overlooked the Mersey. High up on the hill on the approach to New Brighton, it had been a desirable address since Victoria was Queen and rich ship-owners, flush with the spoils of Empire, built houses with a view of the sea which was their gateway to prosperity

Donna tugged on the bell-pull; nothing so vulgar as a buzzer here, and was rewarded with a satisfactory clanging from the dark interior. She waited a few moments, but nobody came to the door. As she stood debating the point of ringing again, she heard a loud crash from inside the house followed by the sound of breaking glass. Donna took a step backwards, then returned and pulled on the handle once more sending loud peals echoing through the house. Another crash rang out, evidently some heavy object striking something equally solid and accompanied by a feeble cry was enough to make up her mind. Donna ran to the window to her left and heaved upwards. Nothing. She tried the one to the right with similar results. The door was impressively solid and she gave it no more than a regretful glance before running to the gate at the side. Slipping the latch first time, Donna ran around to the rear and saw a small window with frosted glass was slightly open. Reaching her hand through the gap, she managed to flick the metal hook upwards and swing the window fully open. At this stage, she stopped for a moment, considering for the first time what her instincts had suggested. Her mind was made up by a second cry, very faint but undoubtedly a sound of pain or distress. That was enough to galvanise her into action and she swung one leg over the windowsill and clambered through. As Donna dropped to the floor, she saw at once that she was in a small cloakroom and that her entrance had dislodged a terrifyingly large array of jars and bottles to the tiled floor where most of them had broken. 'Shit!' she whispered, then kicked the debris to one side and bolted for the doorway.

Heaving the door open, Donna found herself in a hallway, doors on each side and came to a skidding halt. 'Hello? Anyone there?' *Bloody stupid question.*

From behind the door on the right came a faint mewing sound followed by another dull thump. Donna flung the door open and stopped dead in the entrance. A square table, crammed with tangled tubes, medicine bottles and inhalers together with a single book, 'A Confederacy of Dunces,' and an open green plastic case directly in front of her. A computer screen flickered on a pine table; the keyboard dangling down still connected by its cable.

The girl was about eighteen or nineteen. She was lying on the floor with terrified eyes begging for help. Donna stood stock-still for a moment, looking at the girl's feeble arm movements and feeling helpless in the face of such obvious distress. The girl's lips were tinged with violet; her face deathly pale. Donna's neighbour was asthmatic and she had recognised the open case as containing a nebulizer. She reached down into the case and disentangled the tubes, unravelling the flexible plastic pipe, clamping the attached mask to the girl's face with one hand, reaching across to the machine with the other and throwing the switch. The liquid in the opaque plastic bowl vaporised and passed down the tubes emerging as steaming tendrils from the sides of the facemask. Donna held the mask tightly in position, rubbing the pale girl's narrow shoulders with her other hand. Her breathing was shallow; chest barely moving, but the dry heaving sobs had lessened. She coughed into the mask and Donna raised it for a moment. The girl looked up with streaming eyes and motioned silent thanks. Donna replaced the mask and remained seated on the floor until her patient had completely consumed the 10-ml dose.

'I don't know who you are,' the girl said, removing the mask from her face, 'Probably a burglar. But even if you are, thanks for being here. I was getting a bit desperate.'

'That's putting it mildly. I'm Donna. Donna O'Prey. Are you Sarah?'

'Yeah.'

'Well, it's you I came to see. I'm asking around, trying to find out what happened to Julian. Why he wanted to kill himself.'

'Oh shit! I might have known. His dad sent you, right? Can't get his head round the idea his son could have been so selfish as to kill himself? Am I right?'

Donna frowned. 'Sort of. I think he just wants to know why. Know what I mean?'

Sarah propped herself up on one elbow. 'Don't we all? He's not the only one who can't understand why Jules did it.'

'Does this happen often?' Donna asked, gesturing at the trailing tubes and wires, 'You getting in a state like this?'

'The asthma? I've always had it, well since the age of about two, I think. It's very common and getting more so every year.'

'Must be one hell of a restriction.'

'No, not really. Not until the last few weeks. My asthma, to start with anyway, was of the allergic type. I never had any eczema, not to speak of, so I should feel grateful for that, as they often go hand in hand. If I avoid the things that trigger an attack I would have no problems. Trouble is; I'm allergic to an awful lot of stuff. All the usual things, feathers, perfume, smoke, fresh paint, dust, mites and every animal with fur on its back. Plus a good few others, including seafood, most preservatives and strawberries. Oh, and don't forget peanuts as well. It's quite difficult to avoid everything on that list. The old bronchial tubes go merrily along, doing the job they're suppose to do until they come into contact with one of these triggers. Next thing, I'm gasping and wheezing like an old woman.

'How do you cope?'

'I take these puffer things every couple of hours. More often than I should, really, but what the hell? Some of them are relievers and some are preventative. My throat gets all raw and inflamed, because I take so many. I've got oxygen and the nebulizer for when I haven't got enough breath to use an inhaler. Then, there are the magic steroids. Not the type that makes you into an Olympic shot-putter, but bloody effective. Prednisolone is what they call an oral steroid; I'm up to 100mg every day. That's a lot, too much for the long-term effect on my health, but what can I do? I just can't function on a lower dosage. It'll sort itself out, it usually does.'

'How long have you been as bad as this?'

Sarah shrugged. 'Up to a couple of weeks ago, asthma was something I'd learned to live with. Actual attacks, bad ones like this anyway, were pretty infrequent as long as I minimised my contact with things that caused me a problem. I think of those times now as the good old days. Any restrictions that I had were pretty minor, like I was never allowed pets as a kid and had to take my own anti-allergy foam pillow around with me if I slept away from home. Then all this happened and I had a really bad attack. Just about my worst ever and I've not settled down again yet. I'll get over this. Nobody ever accused me of being a quitter.'

'Was it the news about Julian that tipped you over the edge?'

'Oh yes. I'd been fine before that. We'd been planning on going to Paris the weekend after, bought the tickets and everything. Sort of a going-away treat before he went up to Oxford.'

'Oh!'

Sarah climbed unsteadily to her feet, righted the typist's chair and sat down. Donna sat on a low chair next to her. Sarah smiled. 'See. I'm fine now. Fit as a fiddle.'

Donna thought she looked awful, face pale and drawn with big dark shadows under her eyes, but smiled re-assuredly. 'Much better,' she said. 'Would you like me to make us a cup of tea?'

'Oh, would you? The kitchen's just through that door. Would you mind if I had coffee? I'm sorry, I've only got instant.'

'No problem,' Donna assured her. 'Coffee would be great. How do you like it?'

'One sugar and just a dash of milk please.'

The kitchen was straight out of the IKEA catalogue. Quite small with pine units, but everything was included. Donna checked the water level in the kettle, flicked the switch and looked out the coffee, milk and sugar. She found some sliced ham in the 'fridge and made a plate of sandwiches. The bread was some sort of healthy-eating organic cereal mixture, dark and crunchy. Peg would most definitely not have approved, but Donna reckoned the quick snack would do the trick. Steam from the boiling kettle had misted a section of glass in the kitchen window. Donna drew a smiling face in the moisture, then realised with a start that the cartoon could scarcely have been less appropriate and hurriedly wiped it away with the heel of her hand. Clutching two china beakers and the plate of sandwiches, she walked back to where Sarah was waiting. They sipped and munched in silence for a while until Donna saw an improvement in the other girl's appearance and judged the moment was right to resume her questioning.

'Are you in touch with any of Julian's mates?'

Sarah nodded. 'A couple, yeah.' She picked moodily at a sandwich, raising one corner to check the contents before taking a neat precise bite, hardly enough to be noticed. Replacing the sandwich on her plate she picked up another, holding it in mid-air, her expression vacant.

Donna produced a sheet of paper and showed it to the other girl. 'Anyone else you can think of, apart from this list I got from Julian's dad?'

Sarah took the sheet of paper and studied it carefully. 'No. That's who I'd have suggested. Not that they'll be able to come up with any reasons for all this.'

'Neil mentioned another lad; he didn't know his name, who'd been a mate of Julian's. Do you know who that would be?'

Sarah looked blank. Glancing down at the sandwich she carefully replaced it on the plate and smoothed out a thin crease in the linen tablecloth, her fingers lingering over an embroidered flower.

'Some mate he'd only met recently, perhaps?'

Sarah frowned and then her face brightened. 'Oh, right. Not so much a mate, just someone Jules found on the Internet. Chat rooms. Someone else who was going up to Oxford. They were reading the same subjects, even going to be at the same college. Jules was dead pleased, said how much he was looking forward to meeting him. I never met him myself and I don't suppose Jules ever got the chance to meet up with him as things turned out'

'Neil said this other lad was always on the 'phone, talking to Julian.'

'I told you, they had a lot in common.'

'But he doesn't call any more. Neil would have liked to have told him what had happened, given him details of the funeral and stuff. But he's not been in touch again.'

Sarah shrugged. 'Can't help you. I never met him. Like I said.'

'Can you remember his name?'

'Don't think I ever knew his name. They had a lot in common, but that was all to do with going up to Oxford. It wasn't my favourite subject. Jules never talked to me about Oxford.'

'Why not?'

'Because he was leaving me, putting us to one side. I hoped we'd survive him going away, but it made me very insecure. Julian understood that. The subject almost never came up.'

Donna waved a hand in dismissal of the topic. 'Don't worry. It's probably not important. I'll go back to Julian's dad; see if he can remember any more details.'

'I suppose the great rock and roll star has been telling you how I was a bad influence on Julian, making him want to abandon all that talk about Oxford and run away to live in a camper van in Wales and have loads of kids?'

Donna was surprised. 'No Not at all.'

Sarah looked doubtful. 'Really?'

'No. Nothing like that. Is that true, then?'

Sarah burst out laughing. 'Oh, sure. I'd have loved it and so would Jules. But, he wanted to go to Oxford more. A lot more. Not to please his family. Not to upset me either. You didn't know him. He was dead set on going, really looking forward to it. That's why all this talk of Julian being depressed or not being able to cope is such rubbish. Julian was the most positive person ever. We were due to go to Paris. Booked the hotel and everything. Our last trip away before he left for Oxford. All his idea. He'd never have let me down about something like that. Never.'

'What then? Why did he do it?'

Sarah shrugged. 'Kill himself? He'd never do that. No chance. Something happened.'

'Like what?'

Sarah shrugged again. A tremulous smile battled for survival on the thin lips. Her features were strained, worry lines carving deep grooves into the taught skin and fanning out from the sunken eyes. Her face was flushed and blotchy. The eyes were dark shiny buttons, like smooth glossy olives in the pale pizza dough of her complexion. Her cheeks were distended orbs either side of a surprisingly pert nose. When she smiled, the slabs of her features moved and shifted dramatically before settling down again to reveal the true person hiding beneath the surface.

'I don't know. I told his mum, sorry his step-mum, that I thought he'd been killed and she went mad with me. Told me I was a silly little girl with a big mouth and that I should never say such a thing again. That's when I had my first bad asthma attack.'

'Why did she say that?'

'She said Neil would go off his head if he ever thought anyone had killed Julian. It would be even worse than believing Jules had killed himself, but I don't see that.'

'You don't?'

'No. Thinking he killed himself leaves everyone thinking they could have done something to stop him. That it must have been their fault, you know? That Jules was unhappy and we never even noticed.'

'Is that what you think?'

Sarah gave a thin smile. In fact, as smiles go, this was positively anorexic. Her voice was barely audible by now 'No. I know, *knew*, Julian. He wasn't unhappy. Just the opposite. That's how I know someone did something to him. Julian would never, ever, leave the people he loved like that. It was murder. I can't prove it and everyone else will think I'm talking rubbish, but I know. I don't know how or why, but I just know. Julian was murdered.'

38

Marcus was waiting. This was the best time of all. The anticipation. All the planning was behind him. The next one had been chosen. This could be the best yet. Young, pretty, female, she ticked all the right boxes. Plenty of time to enjoy himself before the time came to move on to the next. Over a period of time, he'd refined the methods, which afforded him optimum pleasure during the process of demonstrating control over his subjects. Rape had been the choice of conquerors throughout the ages and with good reason; enforced sexual domination stripped every last vestige of dignity from a victim. Attractive young girls were accustomed to being objects of desire and thrived on the adoration of their admirers. The next target would soon learn the transient nature of her beauty. The act of rape transcended mere sexual gratification; that was a mere by-product of the process. Marcus was concerned only with demonstrating his complete power and control over his victim. Transforming the act of love into an ordeal of pain and degradation had become the only way Marcus could attain ecstasy. Killing the girl would be a bonus.

Over the last two years Marcus had made a number of changes. The most dramatic had been in his appearance. The High Atlas region of Morocco is remote and inhospitable; the tiny fortified villages perched amongst the crags were Berber strongholds a thousand years ago and in some cases have remained untouched by the relentless march of progress and where ancient rites and traditions have survived the passing centuries. Using aromatic herbs, potions and holistic treatments that were in common usage at the time the Pyramids rose from the desert sands, it was possible to attain a state of euphoria which would be the envy of any cocaine-snorting Greenwich Village loft dweller. Of even greater importance to Marcus were the specialist services available to any person of means who was prepared to make the difficult journey through this remote area. After six months in the mountains all evidence of facial scarring had been removed, together with any indication that his hands had been severely burnt in the fire which had almost claimed his life. The treatment, all of it without the benefits of Western anaesthetic techniques had been both painful and prolonged, but had been spectacularly successful. Anyone who had known him in his former life would certainly fail to recognise him now. His skin had been darkened by repeated immersion in vats containing animal and plant dyes still in regular use locally through countless generations. His hair was thick yet cut close to the scalp and tinted lenses had turned his former blue eyes deep brown. Even his body shape had changed. Previously slender, Marcus had worked tirelessly to tone his body until he was satisfied with the results. His shoulders were broader, his waist now even slimmer, while his legs had the power to run the sheerest mountain trails without raising his heart-beat from a steady forty-five beats a minute. For six demanding months Marcus had hidden himself away, working fifteen hours a day with the healer who had taken on the task of his renewal in return for a huge sum of money. The payment was made in the traditional way: directly to the village with the healer taking only an equal share for himself.

When Marcus eventually bade farewell to the old man, whose inscrutable features gave no clue to his age, even he felt a momentary twinge of regret at the decision he was obliged to take. His new appearance and identity known only to a solitary person, the old man had to die, but even in death his clear eyes displayed not a shred of censure, merely fatalistic acceptance of this final betrayal.

The ancient trade routes of Africa are well documented throughout history, yet remain as relevant now as ever. Where once the trade was in spices and exotic fabrics, in more recent times two valuable commodities held sway: drugs and people. The re-classification by the British Government of cannabis from a Class B to a Class C narcotic in January 2004 gave Marcus his opportunity. Although large-scale dealing remained an offence, in effect the emphasis had changed and the slender resources of the Customs and Excise officials would henceforth be concentrated on Class A drugs such as heroin. Most of the cannabis entering the UK, Europe's leading consumer with an annual trade worth in excess of a billion pounds, prior to 2004 was from Pakistan or Holland. Both countries had problems in supplying the demand from over two million regular users in Britain, mainly because their delivery methods and couriers were well known to the British authorities. Marcus made contact with the drug barons who controlled hashish production from their mountain base of Ketama, high in the Rif Mountains and agreed to buy as much of the product as they were capable of supplying. In a country of immense poverty, this guarantee of regular purchase by a single customer was a great coup. With a cash value amounting to more than two billion pounds a year, the cultivation and supply of cannabis, or Kif as it is known locally, gave employment to over a million workers. A workforce fiercely loyal to their benefactors as even the humblest picker could earn double the average weekly wage in a single day.

Marcus worked quickly, organising his workforce into teams and varying his methods of transport to ensure a steady supply. Small boats sped across the narrow stretch of water between Morocco and Spain; lorries ostensibly containing perishable cargo such as fruit or cut flowers were loaded with drugs and TIR seals attached to ensure they travelled freely across Europe with a minimum of official interference Profit margins were huge. For less than a hundred pounds couriers would carry drugs taped to their bodies while crossing frontiers, each kilo of hashish having a street value well in excess of two thousand pounds on arrival in England.

After arranging the lines of supply whereby hashish from the Rif Mountains of Morocco found a ready market throughout Europe, another lucrative business opportunity took the eye of Marcus. A steady stream of economic migrants flooded northwards from the starving interior of the African continent towards Britain or other countries, which were perceived as wealthy beyond the wildest dreams of the prospective immigrants. For a man with ambition and a willingness to break inconvenient laws where necessary, opportunities were always available and Marcus quickly made use of the contacts he found on the fringes of this prosperous trade in commodities and human expectation. Within a matter of months he'd put together a team which, through sheer ruthlessness had forced the existing traders into enforced retirement. Even the arrival of the Sheehan brothers, irked at the constant disruption to their shipments and angry enough to return to active duty in the face of shortages on the streets of Liverpool, Manchester and the rest of their vast empire, proved to be no more than a brief diversion. Fat Stan as the elder Sheehan was universally known, although never within his earshot, blustered and bullied for a while, incensed that so little was known locally concerning the identity of whoever had so swiftly exercised dominance over shipments crossing the narrow strip of ocean separating the Moroccan coastline from Europe. Fat Stan and his younger brother, Dermot, made a serious error of judgement in under-estimating the ruthlessness of Marcus and his team. The Sheehan brothers fully expected their little local difficulty to be resolved by seizing the odd shipment and cracking a few heads together. When this strategy had no effect, Fat Stan put the word out that he wanted a sit-down. Marcus had agreed to the meeting, but it was to be the only concession he was prepared to make. He'd stated his terms which were unequivocal; give up your business interests and walk away. The Sheehan brothers had gone soft after many years of rich living. Their weaknesses were firmly pointed out by Marcus. Large extended families, too diverse and numerous to guard with any hope of success. 'You're out of your depth, son,' Fat Stan had blustered. 'Oldest rule in the book. We don't involve each other's families.'

'Your rules, not mine,' Marcus had assured him and had responded to their interference in his business affairs by rounding up members of the Sheehan gang and administering old-style Berber justice. Limbs were amputated, testicles removed and fed to goats, eyes gouged out. As a business strategy it was brutal, brief and effective. Fat Stan Sheehan became far more amenable after a visit from a dozen men wielding baseball bats while his younger brother, more hot-headed and less likely to listen to reason, eventually got the message in an even more painful manner. Marcus pinned him to a row of wooden railway sleepers with six-inch nails before reversing a JCB over his lower limbs. Aware of their legitimate business interests he'd taken the trouble to import the JCB from Sheehan Brothers Plant Hire and attached a thick wad of notes to the windscreen as full payment for a week's hire, even though the machine had only been used for a single day. The Sheehan brothers elected for retirement to their native Sligo where Fat Stan's nickname would soon be rendered inaccurate. A liquid diet, the legacy of a shattered jaw and ruptured spleen would see the pounds melt from his gigantic frame as he pushed Dermot's wheelchair around the grounds of their estate.

Now, that area of his life had been put on hold. It was time to resolve a matter, which had festered in his mind for many years. A desire for revenge which had grown stronger over the many years of anticipation and planning.

The girl would be part of that plan; a small part but important. Marcus waited with the patience of the hunter, savouring every moment and relentlessly eager to press on with the next stage of his plan.

Donna drove down Dee road and turned left along the long stretch of the promenade, lowering her sun visor against the glare of the sun sinking ever lower in the sky. It was that time of day when the light grew briefly sharper. The old stand-by about it always being darkest before the dawn, only in reverse. As she reached the end of the prom, the sun completed its daily passage across the sky and dipped from view, leaving behind its legacy of flame and bringing splendour to the evening sky. A few dark brooding clouds lay in parallel lines above the flaming glare of the sea which was ablaze with light, although a menacing cloud layer hinted at the impending darkness.

Donna parked up, feeling like a wet rag. The last hour or so had been stressful. She'd sat for half an hour in the Mersey Tunnel, almost at the mid-point, while the emergency crews removed a broken down van. Traffic fumes persisted on her clothes and in her sinuses. She heaved her coat off the back seat. *Chez Donna* was flanked by two similar houses on either side. Probably glad of their support. Donna suddenly realised she was starving and hurried across the road, door key at the ready. Peg wasn't around, so Donna walked through the house and checked the back garden. More yard than garden but pleasant enough in good weather. Still no sign of Peg. Donna took her washing off the line. Bone dry despite being left out throughout the last rain. Soaked through and then dried off again. Kind of an extra rinse. Donna stuffed her underwear into a plastic bag, shook the creases out of everything else and hung the clothes over her arm ready to go straight into her wardrobe. Life was too short for ironing. Closing the back door, Donna dropped the clothes on the table and walked back along the hall.

'Donna? That you?' Peg's disembodied voice assailed her ears from the floor above Donna's head.

'Who were you expecting, Bruce Willis?' Donna called up the stairs. Peg's scowling face appeared over the banisters. She'd once confessed that the sight of a man wearing a vest always reminded her of her late husband and Donna had tacked a photograph of Bruce Willis in full macho pose above Peg's bed.

'Get up here this minute. I want your advice on something.'

Donna almost ran up the stairs. If living with Peg had taught her anything, it was that the old woman never sought the advice of anyone. On arrival in the front bedroom, Donna came to a skidding halt. Peg was pirouetting in front of the full-length mirror, wearing a pair of skin-tight leggings and a satin top with fluorescent stripes. The entire outfit was a virulent shade of pink.

'Well? What do you reckon?'

Donna was speechless.

'Is this the right get-up for aerobics? You do a bit of keep fit, don't you? What do you reckon?'

Donna nodded, still incapable of speech. The contrast with her own gym clothing, a battered sweatshirt and tatty tracksuit trousers could not have been more pronounced.

'They're getting up a class for the old folk at the Concourse. Just a bit of easy stretching. I thought I'd sign up for it. I'm as stiff as a board some days by the time I've done the house through and run a few errands.'

Donna nodded once more. Peg's usual regime amounted to a full spring clean on a daily basis followed by a tour of every shop in the area carrying bags of provisions on behalf of elderly neighbours, most of whom were several years younger than herself. At eighty-plus was it any wonder she felt a few twinges now and again?

'I got this from the Oxfam. Good fit isn't it?'

'Yeah.' Donna finally found the power of speech. 'What's for tea?'

Peg shrugged. 'You'll have to fend for yourself tonight. I told Ethel I'd go with her to the hospital. She's booked a taxi. The very idea. There's a perfectly good bus if you walk up to the stop outside the library. Riding round in taxis like Lady Muck, I ask you, but there's no talking to Ethel. Her Albert's had another one of his turns. He'll not be coming out again. I've tried many a time to break it to Ethel, but she's never been one to face facts that one.'

Donna winced. Peg's idea of hospital visiting was to scrutinise the ward's state of cleanliness and interrogate the patient as to whether or not his or her affairs were in order in readiness for their inevitable and imminent death.

'I'll do myself a fry-up,' Donna announced. Peg beamed with approval. A huge grease-laden meal was her idea of sustenance.

While Peg struggled out of her aerobics outfit and got ready to visit the stricken neighbour, Donna took herself off to the kitchen. She fried two eggs and three rashers of bacon in Peg's trusty old frying pan, added half a tin of baked beans and a few scraps of cold mashed potato. When the mixture was bubbling nicely, she added brown sauce and black pepper and then ate the lot, straight out of the pan with huge chunks of bread.

Peg was wearing her best coat and sensible shoes, ready to traipse hospital corridors until she found evidence of sloppy hygiene. She looked over Donna's shoulder and gave a grunt of approval at the empty frying pan. 'Make sure you wrap up warm when you set off tomorrow. It's given out rain later.'

'I know, I know. Don't get yourself worked up. You'll do yourself a mischief, you soft old bat,' Donna mock scolded.

'I might be old, but I'm not addled,' Peg grumbled, practising for her hospital visit by brushing her fingers over every exposed surface seeking out the faintest trace of dust. Normal behaviour for a cleanliness fanatic. Donna knew her grandmother was dead right. Peg had left school at fourteen, after a pretty rudimentary education. A girl who could read and write was classed as almost over-qualified in those days and Peg went out to earn money for the family. She may not have had any fancy pieces of paper to prove how clever she was but Peg had something far more valuable. Common sense. Great dollops of it, making her, in real terms, the wisest person Donna had ever known. The rattle of the doorknocker announced the taxi's arrival and within seconds Peg had departed. Donna washed and put away her knife, fork and frying pan, swept a few stray breadcrumbs into the bin and headed for the sofa. She'd already rung Andy and made arrangements for him to join her tomorrow and was now savouring the prospect of putting her feet up and watching whatever mindless trash was served up on the television. Andy had asked if she fancied a night on the town and she'd turned him down for some reason. Just not in the mood. He may have been her best mate, but she'd little appetite for a pub-crawl at the moment. She knew only too well that Andy would try and fix her up with one of his mates, hopefully one of his straight friends, and she'd rather not get involved. Andy had often told her she was doomed to have problems with men as her relationship genes were fucked up. He was probably right. She'd never learnt how to get along with the opposite sex. Going right back to the time she was mad about a lad called Rupert when she was about seventeen. Yeah, Rupert, for fuck's sake, but he'd been absolutely bloody gorgeous. Tall, dark and wildly handsome. Skip-loads of money, a sports car and, best of all, he'd been mad about her. Donna was not so shallow these days as to be swayed by cars and good looks, well not as much as when she was seventeen anyway, but Rupert was crazy about her and that was much better than any sports car. Donna was a bit of a culture vulture back then and had thought to impress Rupert by suggesting they went to the theatre. She didn't remember what they saw, nothing too heavy anyway. Rupert had sat next to her like a statue. Donna remembered being so pleased with herself as the cast gave a really good performance and she'd loved it. She'd turned to Rupert during the interval, expecting a meaningful discussion and all he'd said was, 'Do you know how many lights there are above that stage? A hundred and seventy-three!' They never went back after the interval, but drove instead to a wine bar and met up with some of Rupert's friends. Donna finished with him that night and never saw him again. She may have been besotted, but even someone half-blind would have realised that Rupert was a moron. Today had turned out not so bad after all. The job was like her life, she reckoned, tedious and repetitive in the main, but spiced with rare moments of frantic excitement. That was what made it bearable, the job anyway. She wasn't so sure about her life; the jury was still out on that one.

CHAPTER 4

'I BET you never thought you'd be doing this for a living, did you? Funny sort of career choice.'

Donna looked at Andy and frowned. They'd been waiting for the traffic to move for at least ten minutes now and there seemed no sign of any activity in the queue in front of them.

'It's not a career, it's a job.'

Andy gave her one of his looks.

'A career is something you set out to do,' Donna persisted. 'Maybe always wanted to do. It fulfils a need and there's a distinct purpose to it.'

'Oh yeah? Like being a presenter on Blue Peter?'

Donna cringed, regretting the unguarded moment when she'd unwisely confided her earliest childhood ambition to an arch-sceptic like Andy.

'What I do is a job, not a career.'

'What's the difference?'

'A job is less than a career. Easier to go home and forget about work until the next day.' Donna was floundering a bit now; her off the cuff definition seeming weak and inaccurate in the face of Andy's obvious scorn, but she pressed on regardless. 'With a career, you actually achieve something, get somewhere.'

'Get an ulcer? Goes with the territory.'

Donna ignored him. 'Look, I just like this job, right? Most of the time anyway.'

'Seems to me, working from your definition, that you have all the negative aspects of a career, but none of the rewards. Perhaps it's a vocation.'

Donna shook her head vigorously. 'No.'

'What's the difference?'

'The difference is, if you know you won't get paid for going in and you still go in; that's a vocation. I don't do that. It's a job.'

'So let me get this straight. You and me, we have a job that consumes most of our time, can put us in hospital and they pay us fuck-all, but that's okay with you because its something to do while you're waiting for a proper career to come along? Blue Peter perhaps.'

Donna opened her mouth to reply and then shut it again and punched him on the shoulder instead. Impossible to argue with Andy; He was far too devious and she always seemed to end up on the losing side. Donna had asked him to come with her today to provide another point of view. She'd decided to go back to see Julian's father again. Sarah's allegations of foul play had left her rattled and Andy was the ideal choice to make sense of the position. Apart from being indecently good-looking, he had a sharp mind and charm to spare. If he hadn't been gay she knew their friendship would have been very different. Certainly that would have been the case if she'd had any say in the matter. She'd settled for Andy being a mate, but the bargain was still a good one. He had a fund of salacious stories, especially concerning the gay life-styles of stars of stage and screen. Donna sometimes wondered whether he made most of it up for her amusement, but remained fascinated. He'd recently told her that a favourite Hollywood actor, a man she'd admired and fantasised about since her early teens, was not only homosexual but wore sanitary pads beneath his designer underpants to counter the effects of weakened sphincter muscles, brought about by over-indulgence in gay orgies.

Andy nudged her and Donna saw that the car in front was moving at last. 'Come on, Donna. Never mind lusting after motorbike couriers.' Donna followed the direction of his eyes and saw a fat youth in leathers leering at her from alongside the car. She shuddered and moved off smoothly. The bike revved up furiously and roared past leaving a trail of blue smoke and testosterone in its wake.

'That's what you need. A real man in your life,' offered Andy. Donna ignored him. There was a hint of truth in his mocking words but fat bikers were not what Donna had in mind.

Donna sighed and half-turned towards Andy. 'Are you getting ready to play your Mister Smooth act for me?'

Andy shrugged. 'What exactly did you have in mind?'

'Oh, you know? Ask the awkward questions, but make it look like you're just being a nice guy? Can you do that?'

'No problem. Mind you, it'd be a whole lot easier if I had some idea what we are trying to prove here.' Andy's confusion was a mirror image of Donna's own uncertainty. She'd still no real idea which way to go about investigating the reasons for the death of Julian, but the most logical step, asking Dexter for advice, was being kept in reserve for now. Best to try and work it out for herself. Andy wouldn't push his opinions on her, but she knew she could rely on him to have some useful input. That was the idea, anyway.

Donna spotted a filling station and took a late decision to swing onto the forecourt, grinning broadly as Andy clawed at the passenger door handle and mimed a desperate desire for escape. She'd just remembered that on her way home one night last week she'd been stopped and warned about a failed taillight. A very polite and helpful policeman asked how far she had to travel. Donna told him the truth, about half a mile and he'd followed her home, his rear lights acting for both vehicles. No mention of a breathalyser or any necessity to produce her documents. Either the local scuffers were getting the Community Policing message at last or Donna had finally mastered the art of batting her eyes at the male sex.

After roaming the aisles of the service station for five minutes, Donna gave up and joined the queue of three waiting with varying degrees of patience while a spotty youth wearing a red overall and a back to front baseball cap changed the till roll. Donna moved further away and bumped into the man who'd joined the queue behind her. She'd been about to apologise, but he turned his head away. *Rude bastard.* Donna moved to one side, forcing him to look at her, but he looked right through her. Her attempts to make eye contact failed dismally as he kept his eyes focussed in the middle distance. Even when Donna shifted over and stood directly in front of him, it made no difference. It was as if he was blind, but Donna realised that he suffered from an even worse disability; that of being painfully shy. She was no exhibitionist herself, but couldn't deal with people like this.

When service was eventually resumed and Donna reached the head of the queue, she smiled brightly and asked the retard behind the counter where she'd find a taillight bulb.

He shook his head. 'We don't stock stuff like that.'

'You're a bloody garage. You must have a taillight bulb somewhere.'

'Nope.'

Donna gazed around in frustration. 'You've got ice-cream, Tampax, bread, sugar, baked beans, wine gums and bloody Coco-pops, but no bloody car parts?'

'We've got engine oil,' the youth protested defensively.

'Oh right. A couple of cans of engine oil, a few key rings and that's it. I just hope corner shops start selling cut-price petrol.' Donna stomped out, almost bumping into Andy in the doorway.

'What's up?'

'Nothing,' Donna grunted, 'Come on, let's get moving.' She heaved on the glass door, only to reel back as a new customer barged his way past her. Tight blue jeans and a white tee shirt. Capped sleeves to show off his sculptured biceps and Sonny Corleone shoulders. A thick neck, shaved head and a big smile. The smile was the really scary part. He favoured Donna with a nod of recognition and stalked past. Donna let out a sigh of relief as the door closed behind his massive back.

'Friend of yours?' Andy enquired, eyeing the man curiously.

'One of the local nutters. Danny Rourke. Not really the friendly type. I know him well enough to keep my distance. Used to be a bouncer at some club over the water; went down for GBH a few years ago. He's pumped himself up since I last saw him. Steroids probably and plenty of them. Mood swings and aggression. That level of dosage would turn the local vicar into a psycho and Danny boy was a dangerous bastard back when he was still in his pram. Hope he gets put away before he tops some poor bastard, that's all.'

Andy looked back through the glass doors. 'So that's what they mean by rough trade,' he said, rolling his eyes and adopting a salacious leer.

Donna shook her head and took Andy by the arm. 'Come on; let's go before you make the biggest mistake of your life by propositioning Danny Rourke.'

Samantha was sixteen and that was old enough to stay out all night if she wanted to. Her stupid parents wouldn't agree, but all they ever wanted was for her to stay home like a little kid while everyone else was going out and enjoying themselves. Everyone she'd spoken to in the chat room had told her the same thing; her parents still wanted to keep her as a baby who liked dressing up and playing with dolls. That was how they still saw her and it just wasn't fair. Miles said she owed it to herself to get a life and Miles knew everything. She'd been spending two or three hours a night on-line, supposedly doing a school project, over the last three weeks and when Miles said he'd take her to an all-nighter at the weekend, she'd said ok straight off. Mum and Dad were so pathetic; she'd told them she was spending the weekend with her friend Melanie in North Wales and all they'd said was don't forget to take plenty of warm clothes.

Miles was eighteen. He had his own car and was just so good-looking. She'd wanted to tell Melanie about him but Miles had said it would be best not to tell anyone in case they accidentally mentioned it to someone else and her folks got to hear what she was really going to be doing. Samantha tensed as a rakish sports car drew alongside. The side window hissed down. 'Are you Samantha?'

'Yes,' she said, a little uncertain.

'Miles asked me to collect you. I'm his brother, Marcus. Do you want to sling that bag in the back?' He pressed a button on the dashboard and the hood slid back and disappeared into the boot.

Samantha hopped awkwardly from one foot to the other. 'Where's Miles?'

Marcus grinned. 'Back at the house. The lazy bugger's running late as usual, so he asked me to take his motor and pick you up.'

'Is this his car?'

Marcus looked surprised. 'Yes. Why?'

'It's gorgeous.'

'It's ok, I suppose. He's had good cars since he was old enough to drive. We both have. Look, are you getting in or not? Miles will think I've upset you if I don't get you back soon and I know he's desperate to meet you at last.'

'Really?'

'Sure. Oh, I know, you're probably thinking who's this guy asking me to get in a car with him? Is that right? Well, how if I tell you your favourite band is Coldplay and you like to eat Salsa wraps and burgers? Would anyone who'd not been sent by Miles know that?'

Samantha grinned and reached out to slide her bag onto the back seat. She stepped carefully over the sill, revealing rather a lot of thigh in the process, but Marcus was the perfect gentleman and pretended not to notice.

'Buckle up and we'll be on our way. You've got lovely hair, Samantha. Or is it Sam?'

'I prefer Samantha.'

'Samantha it is, then. I must say, I never expected you to be so pretty. What are you, nineteen? Twenty?'

Samantha thought about nodding, but settled for, 'Eighteen.'

'Really? You look so confident I thought you must be older. Is that too tight?' Marcus reached over and clipped the belt into its slot. It was tight. Very tight.

'It hurts a bit. Can you slacken it off?' Samantha struggled, but couldn't seem to slacken the belt at all. Marcus ignored her, pressed the button that raised the hood and prepared to drive away.

'Keep your trap shut, you little scrubber, or you'll wish you'd never been born.' He showed her the gleam of a razor, its pearl handle winking in the sunlight. 'Behave yourself. If not, I'll cut you. Fancy a nice new face, do you? Just one scream, one move and I'll slice you up and drop you in the gutter where you belong. Got it?'

Andy had gone down a treat with Julian's family, but Donna was still far from impressed with the progress she'd made. It all seemed so unlikely, the suicide, so out of character, but if Donna had learnt one thing from Dexter it was never to rely on one point of view. Get the whole picture. Maybe, she'd been asking her questions in the wrong places. She'd never met Julian, but everything so far had suggested he wasn't the type to let down the people who loved him. The trouble with that point of view was that it was what these people wanted to believe. Her own father's death had brought home to her the clear fact that close family ties were no guarantee of knowing what anyone had running around inside their head. Her Dad was the perfect example. He'd been a heavy drinker in his youth, but after cancer took the life of Donna's mother, he'd given all that up to look after her. Donna still had no idea what had caused his sudden relapse and even less idea why he'd hung himself.

They were sitting in a big comfortable room at the back of the house. Julian's father, Jenny, Andy and herself. Jenny was flirting outrageously with Andy who diligently pretended not to notice.

'What a treat, working with a gorgeous hunk like Andy,' Jenny whispered. Donna nodded, feeling that she should be taking charge, but she'd been distracted by the bizarre mix of ancient and modern in the living room. While Donna had sunk, almost without trace, into the depths of an overstuffed chintz sofa, Andy perched with unforced elegance on a solid square of black leather mounted on a chromium-plated frame. Billowing white cotton curtains hung from what appeared to be polished scaffolding poles and on a side table, a carved naked male figure hinted at an interest in ethnic art. Donna nodded at the figure, daring Andy to respond. He pursed his lips in a gesture of admiration, rolling his eyes and pretending to wipe drools of saliva from his chin, composing himself as Jenny returned with a tea-pot modelled on a thatched cottage, china cups and a veritable mountain of biscuits. Andy lifted a saucer and glanced at the maker's name. One of his peculiarities. He originated from Stoke-on-Trent and, like any true son of the Potteries, needed to check the antecedents of any stray piece of crockery that crossed his path. Donna swore he didn't know he was doing it half of the time. What he saw must have impressed him as he lowered the saucer almost reverently to the table.

'I said, what's your next step?' Neil's voice permeated Donna's subconscious at last as she belatedly realised that the question had been directed at herself.

'Asking around,' she said, rather too quickly, aware that her attempt to look as if she'd been giving the question a degree of thought had been a complete failure. 'Looking up Julian's mates, that sort of thing.'

'I see,' Neil said, looking less than impressed.

'You're in good hands, 'Andy interjected, 'When it comes to finding out the truth, they don't come any better than Donna.'

Neil looked doubtful. At some unspoken mutual acceptance that the meeting was at an end, they all stood and walked to the doorway, Jenny clinging to Andy for support as if she were crossing a fast-flowing river rather than deep-pile Axminster. Hands were shaken; cheeks pecked and promises made to keep everyone advised of progress. In no time at all, Donna and Andy were driving back through the heavy iron gates.

'Nice bloke,' Andy offered. Donna nodded, noting without surprise that the hyper-attentive Jenny did not rate a mention. Donna drove another half mile before either spoke again. 'So, what's the plan?' Andy asked.

'No idea.'

Andy nodded. He didn't look surprised. 'I assume you won't be involving Dexter at this stage?'

'You assume correctly. My case. That's what he said.'

'Right. Would you be averse to a suggestion?'

'No.'

'Obviously, ask around. Find out from his mates what made Julian tick. But, assuming that turns up nothing helpful…' He paused.

'Yes?'

'Well, you could look into this suicide stuff. I know you've seen it from the other side, as it were, but just how common is it that a young bloke with everything to live for ends up topping himself? I don't know the answer, but perhaps it's more common than we think. There may be patterns out there that you should be aware of. Not that I'm presuming to advise you, of course. Like Dexter said, it's your case.'

Donna pondered for a couple of minutes, concentrating on her driving. As they came to a halt at a red light she broke her silence. 'I think I might go and see Kate Davies. She'll get me the facts and figures in no time.'

Andy looked surprised. 'That weirdo computer woman? I thought you'd decided she was a bit too scary for a delicate flower like you?'

Donna nodded. It was true that her previous exposure to the murky twilight zone in which Kate Davies spent her time had left her traumatised and unwilling to repeat the experience, but this would only be a simple request for information and should not lead anywhere she did not want to go. The last time she'd seen Kate, Donna had been on the track of Marcus Green. Kate had helped to narrow the search, but Donna had still been closer to violent death than she'd ever wanted to be. Marcus Green's body had never been found and in the small hours of the morning, it was his face she saw in her dreams.

Looking for her.

Waiting for his chance.

Donna knew she should have contacted Kate before now, even if only to thank her for her help, but she'd never managed to pick up the 'phone. Too many bad memories. Kate was a researcher, trawling databases and Internet sites for information on her specialised fields of enquiry. She'd shown Donna some of her files from a research project on child pornography commissioned by the Home Office; even the statistics pages made Donna feel sick. Kate chose to live in the dark world peopled by multiple murderers, violent criminals and perverts. Donna had barely peeked into that life, but didn't know how she'd cope with a repetition of the experience.

Marcus smiled. He liked it when they screamed. The girl's face was contorted, terror etching deep furrows into her brow. At this precise moment she could pass for thirty, not sixteen.

'Nobody to hear you, Samantha. We're all alone here. I bet your mum always told you never to get into a car with strange men? She was dead right, wasn't she?'

Samantha stopped screaming and looked at him, her face ashen. 'What do you want? Where's Miles?'

Marcus leaned forward and slapped her face. 'There is no Miles, you stupid little tart. Just me. You were getting yourself all excited about this lad you'd met in a chat room, good looking, plenty of money and, best of all, desperate to meet you. Well, sorry to break bad news, but all that was me. That photo I sent as an attachment was me as well, but as I used to look. I look different now. Better, don't you think?'

Samantha said nothing, but she'd stopped screaming.

Marcus smiled. 'I can untie you now, if you like. Its not like you're going anywhere, is it?'

'Can I have my clothes back?'

'Oh, I don't think so,' Marcus replied. He pulled his shirt over his head and placed it carefully on a low rail, then unzipped his trousers and stepped out of them. When Marcus was naked he reached over and untied the cords that held the girl's ankles to the end of the solid iron frame supporting the double mattress. Her arms were still tied to the top rail of the frame above her head and he checked these bindings, but left them intact. When he climbed on to the mattress, Samantha started screaming again.

'What exactly do you want me to do?'

Donna frowned. She'd forgotten how awkward Kate Davies could be. 'Just look into something for me. I'm investigating a suicide, acting for the family and I don't know where to start.'

'And?'

Donna frowned again, holding the 'phone awkwardly as she struggled to open the battered briefcase which Dexter had insisted in passing on to her. 'I don't know.' *Pathetic.*

Kate's sigh was audible even in the midst of Donna's briefcase-induced contortions. 'Start with the name.'

'Oh, right. Julian Carter. He's the son of....'

'Neil Travis,' Kate interjected, 'Yeah, I know.'

'How?'

'Bloody Nora, it was in all the papers. Old rockers are always newsworthy. I'll ring you back.'

Donna blinked as the 'phone went dead. Kate's abrupt manner was no surprise. She was a recluse, choosing to spend her life behind a security fence and any amount of high-tech gadgetry. Dexter had instigated previous contact with Kate and Donna was uncertain of her ground. Would she have to invoice Kate for the benefit of her expertise and, if that proved necessary, how did she do that? She was beginning to wish she'd never instigated contact with Kate at all when the 'phone rang out. Donna picked it up straight away.

'Hello?'

'Right then, Julian Travis, or Carter. Whatever. I've got the details here. Death by hanging. Clear suicide, according to the coroner. Open and shut. What's the problem?' Kate, straight down to business.

'Well, the family, his girlfriend and all his mates say he wouldn't have done it. Too much to live for.'

Kate sighed. 'What would they know? Only what he'd allowed them to know. You should know that better than most.'

Donna flinched as the truth of Kate's remark hit home. Her father's suicide had been a complete shock to her and remained so even now.

'I can tell you something,' Kate continued. 'It's a growth industry, suicide, mostly among young males. Stress, they reckon. Hang on a minute and I'll just….' Her voice tailed away. Donna could picture her wheeling her chair across the room in which she spent every waking hour.

'Back again, 'Kate announced a few minutes later, 'might be able to do something for you. How about next month?'

Donna swallowed. 'Oh, I thought…'

'What? You thought that I'd drop what I'm doing just to help you?'

'Well, no. But…'

'Donna, what are you like? Internet junkies don't sleep, remember? I can always find you some time from somewhere. What does Dexter say about you calling me in?'

'He doesn't actually know.'

Kate's laughter was so unexpected and so infectious that Donna found herself joining in. 'You little devil. This makes a difference. Consider me on board.'

'That's brilliant, Kate. I don't expect, you know, miracles, but anything you could suggest.'

'Leave it with me. From what I've seen so far, which isn't very much, I shouldn't get your hopes up. The only thing that concerns me more than a little is why you've put your hand up for this particular case. Surprised Dexter didn't veto it straight away.'

'I know what you're saying, but I need to start dealing with what happened to my dad and move on. I didn't want to wimp out of taking the case just because it was a suicide and my dad just happened to have killed himself.'

There was a silence on the line and when Kate spoke again her husky voice revealed some strain. 'I didn't mean your dad. You don't know, do you?'

'Know what?'

'I don't suppose many people know. I only found out because I'm always on the lookout for this sort of thing. Any connection with old cases.'

'What are you on about?'

'Neil Carter. He was on a jury, a few years back.'

Donna took a deep breath. 'Not Marcus? Marcus Green?'

'The very same. He was one of the jurors who brought in a guilty verdict and sent him down.'

CHAPTER 5

'THE Willows' was a solitary and rather austere house with missing roof slates, damp patches behind a broken metal downspout and peeling woodwork. As Donna approached the main entrance it looked even worse. Above the doorframe was a large crack, deep enough to swallow a hand, running across the whole width of the stone lintel. The doorway was in deep shade which softened the ravaged effects of time and neglect, but the paint-work was pitted like a bad case of teenage acne. A very bad case. Rusty wires poked out from the socket where a substantial bell push had once proudly stood. Donna was reminded of the mother of a school-friend she'd met recently and been shocked by the woman's appearance. In the same way, this house stood almost apologetically on its patch of land as if shamed by the ravages brought about by the failings of others.

Keeping well clear of a drip from the broken downspout, Donna banged on the solid door and waited. This was her third house visit today, contacting Julian's known mates and she fully expected it to be as useless as the other two had been. She'd spent a difficult hour with Dexter last night. His surprise at being advised by Donna that there was a connection, albeit a tenuous one, with Marcus Green, had been genuine. She had no doubt of that. The difficulty had been when he took it on himself to arbitrarily remove her from the enquiry. She'd lost her rag, shrieking that he was no better than Roper. As insults went, it was tame enough, but Dexter had at least allowed her to justify her continued involvement in the case. It had been a close call; not helped by her failure to demonstrate any progress at all, but she still had the case. In her rage, Donna had even let it slip that she'd asked Kate for help, but Dexter's response had surprised her. The gist of it had been that talking to Kate was a positive step at least. Dexter had also turned up a likely supplier of the cigarette found in Julian's room. Some back-alley place off Bold Street. Donna had listened to Dexter's complex directions and still hadn't the faintest idea where to go. She'd have to blunder around like a lost soul, but that was nothing new. Talking it all over with Andy later had also helped. He was also pretty dismissive of the Marcus Green connection. Donna couldn't remember his exact words, but the sentence he'd used had contained the words twat, stupid and paranoid. So what if Julian's father had been on the Marcus Green jury? Andy was always so straight, in everything but his sexual inclinations, that Donna felt a great swirl of relief wash over her.

Despite all that positive support, the fact remained that this morning had been a complete waste of time. The two lads she'd interviewed had been Julian's best mates and she'd learnt nothing from them. Both were equally baffled, completely unable to come up with any reasons for his decision to take his own life.

'Help you?' The teenaged girl in the doorway looked anything but helpful.

'Is Tom in?'

'Yeah. Come in.' The girl didn't ask who was calling or why. Couldn't be arsed, Donna supposed watching her shuffling down the hall in slippers which were only held together by an elastic band across each instep.

'In there,' Donna's helpful guide muttered, jerking a thumb at a partly open door and moving on down the hall. Donna pushed open the door and stopped in the entrance as she saw the size of the boy seated at a scarred table. He was massive. Not fat particularly, just enormous. His head would have been grotesque on anyone else, but on him it was just right. In proportion. He was wearing a denim shirt; presumably extra-extra-extra-large, but still tight across his shoulders, with the sleeves rolled up to reveal forearms like Popeye.

'Tom?'

He looked up and smiled. 'Yes.'

'My name's Donna. Sorry to just turn up, but your friend let me in.'

He grinned. 'That's my sister. Not my friend. Not anyone's friend actually, as I'm sure you noticed. Hormones, you know?'

He stood and offered a ham-like hand and they shook hands. Just about the right level of pressure, that fine line between a bone-crushing macho statement and a wet fish. A proper handshake. *Promising.*

'So, what can I do for you?'

Donna smiled. He may be a giant, but he was a gentle one. His voice was a soft baritone and his manners impeccable.

'I'm trying to help Julian's family. See if I can find a reason for what happened.'

'Oh, I see. Rather you than me.' Tom noted Donna's expression and was quick to explain his remark. 'What I mean is, Julian was a mate. A good mate. And, I knew him as well as I've known anyone. But, as for wanting to kill himself, I don't have a glimmer of an idea where all that came from. It's a cliché, I know, but he really did have everything to live for. The prospect of going to Oxford was very exciting for Julian, meeting new people, all that. He got on well with people, even an awkward lummox like me, and was positive about just about every aspect of his life. No way he killed himself. Absolutely no way.'

Donna sat very still. Tom had only told her the same as everyone else, but this seemed different. Perhaps it was his sheer size that was so compelling. If Tom said it was Thursday, it was Thursday. But, Donna knew it was more than that. Tom was no fool; that was certain. Both Julian's other mates had been likeable enough as people, but all they'd given her had been shock and disbelief; everything she'd expected from them, but no more. Tom gave an impression of having really known Julian. A close friend. A confidant, perhaps?

'How can you be certain? I mean, we think we know people really well and then....' Donna deliberately allowed her voice to tail away, waiting for a reaction.

'You never met Julian.' Tom spoke very calmly. It was a statement, not a question.

'No.'

'If you had met him, known him, you'd know he'd never have killed himself. That would have been weak, not to mention cruel. Julian didn't have the capacity for cruelty and he was the strongest person I ever met. Mental strength, you know?'

Donna looked at him. She'd run out of questions in the face of such certainty. Tom smiled at her. 'I don't know what you're trying to find out, but do yourself a favour. Forget any idea that Julian killed himself. I can't tell you what really happened, but that should be the area you look at. Find out who killed him.'

Donna started. Julian's girlfriend making wild accusations of foul play was one thing, but to hear the very same suggestion from Tom carried considerably more weight. It began to dawn on Donna that this case was turning out to be anything but the quick in-and-out enquiry that she'd anticipated.

'What about his other friends? Can you suggest anyone else I could talk to?'

Tom scribbled a couple of names on a sheet of paper and passed it over. Donna glanced at it and saw exactly what she expected: the same people she'd already approached. 'There's his girlfriend, of course,' Tom said, 'I assume you've been there already?'

Donna nodded.

'Not much help, am I? There's someone else, but I don't know his name. Someone he met recently.'

Donna looked up. 'Julian's dad mentioned a new mate. Said he'd not been able to get in touch, not even to tell him about the funeral.'

'Well, he wasn't at the funeral.'

Donna started. 'Do you know him then? This new friend?'

Tom shook his head like a great grizzly bear. 'No. But, I knew everyone at the funeral. It was deliberately kept pretty low-key because of the press.'

Donna nodded.

'Julian told me he'd met some bloke or other in a chat room who had a head full of ideas. His exact words.'

Donna frowned. 'Funny sort of phrase.'

'Not for Julian. He was a great enthusiast. Always on the lookout for new information, anything different. He spent hours surfing the net, looking up the weirdest things just to understand them. Information was his big thing. He thrived on it.'

'So, you don't know anything about this mysterious new mate.'

Tom poked his tongue into the side of his cheek. 'I don't know whether I'd go so far as to say mysterious,' he mused, 'From what I gathered, this lad was going up to Oxford, same college as well, so that explained them getting on so well. Julian didn't believe in mixing the species when it came to friendships. Those names I gave you? I don't actually know them, but I know who they are. They were friends of Julian's. Not friends of mine.' He shook his head. 'When someone you know, someone you like, dies suddenly like that, it's a shock. I had to go through the same thing all over again a week later. Funerals, eh?'

'A relative or another friend?'

'A good mate, Chris Wright. We went to school together and were in the same chess club. Chris was an art student, bloody talented as well. I'd actually mentioned Julian's death to him the last time I saw him. He was shocked and sympathetic. I don't suppose he thought it would be his turn next.'

Donna's mouth dropped open. 'You mean?'

Tom nodded. 'Yeah. Within the week. Not suicide though. Drug overdose. Some kids found him in the park. Funny really.' Donna was shocked and it must have shown on her face as Tom gave a gruff bark of laughter. 'I didn't mean humorous. I meant it was odd. I never took him for a drug addict. Bit of dope perhaps, but far too straight to be a heavy user.' He looked at Donna, his facial expression deadly serious. 'If I were you,' He hesitated.

'Go on,' prompted Donna.

'If I were you, I'd look into his death while you're at it. When it comes to funerals, two is overkill.'

Marcus was angry. His anger was directed at himself, but to a casual observer there would have been no outward manifestation of the rage that consumed him. The girl had fought tigerishly, forcing him to use a greater degree of force than he'd intended. Her death was inconvenient, nothing more, but the loss of control was the reason for his anger. The circumstances of the girl's death meant a change of plan and it was this that had provoked his anger. Any disruption to his plan, even when self-inflicted, was cause for concern. He looked at the body on the bed. Samantha didn't look pretty any more. She didn't look sixteen any more either. Marcus turned away, already planning the next step. His intention had been for the girl to be discovered in an alley with a needle in her arm. Plain straightforward drug overdose. With her broken nose and bruised flesh that method of disposable was no longer credible and some form of damage limitation would now be necessary if the girl's death was to appear accidental. The situation was already resolved; a back-up plan in place. He walked to the door, the decision having been made. All traces of anger had evaporated. He was ready.

The Caravan Park was deserted, closed down for 'essential maintenance' according to the sign outside the warden's caravan. His breath plumed in the still cold air as he unlocked the chain barring the entrance road and reversed his car out. The warden's van was locked, curtains drawn as a deterrent to casual visitors, but Marcus had no fear of being disturbed. The warden's body was buried in deep undergrowth at the base of the cliff and the man would not be missed until the site re-opened in six weeks time. The car had served its purpose and would now be abandoned. Granby Street, with the keys on show in the ignition, was the best way to guarantee its permanent removal. A prestige motor like this would be in a lock-up garage within the hour, ready to be re-sprayed, fitted with new plates and documents and shipped out to a new home in Eastern Europe. The new under the counter money was all coming from Russia, Romania and the former Soviet Union satellite states these days. The new consumers wanted only the best and were happy to pay top prices for it. It had been necessary to use a flashy car, as the girl would not have been so easy to impress if he'd arrived in a family saloon, but his replacement vehicle would be very different. He invariably chose a nothing car, such as a Ford Focus. Decent engine, reliable, but best of all, it would never attract attention. Even the colour would be nothing special. Safety in numbers would have suggested red, but Marcus remembered casual talk among the policemen who'd once held him captive. Talk of a snooker game where traffic police tried for a maximum break by stopping a red car, then a black one, then another red and so on. In these circumstances a red car would be more liable to be stopped than any other. Marcus had no way of knowing whether that overheard conversation was relevant now, or whether it had ever been a reliable story. The chances were very low; no more than one in a hundred, but he didn't believe in taking chances. Ever. He'd bought the Porsche from a drug dealer in London. Cash, no paperwork, no names or addresses required, purely for this one purpose. He'd been to the capital to sort out a few loose ends. Business affairs. Marcus had stayed at the Dorchester for two weeks, making contacts and shopping for essentials. Such as the three suits designed by Mark Powell and ordered from the studio at 12, Brewer Street. His various tasks completed, he'd headed north to finish the job he'd postponed for so long. Only half a dozen or so more deaths and his work would be over. He'd not be tempted to rush anything. The method he'd chosen would allow him to complete the task with a minimum of risk. This was vital; his planning had always placed avoidance of danger at the very top of the list. This excessive caution was not rooted in fear. Self-interest demanded that he be free. Marcus had been confined like an animal, for many years and knew he would take any measure necessary to avoid a repetition.

A minor concern was that, despite him having been officially pronounced dead, someone was actively seeking him out. He had planted a sophisticated device that alerted him if anyone tried to access old files or records concerning himself. The search would be useless as he'd deleted most references to himself since leaving England, but anyone still looking for traces of him would leave a signal in a file he checked regularly. The programme told him that whoever had started to seek him out was a hacker. A very good one. Not in his class, but still able to search using a specially written programme which would be undetectable to most people. He was not overly concerned at this stage, but action would have to be taken eventually. He resolved to lay down stocks of materials he would be likely to need. He would soon know the identity of the unknown snooper and discouragement would then be necessary. Marcus had not yet decided on the method this discouragement would take, but one decision had already been made: the means would be permanent and very painful indeed.

He drove away from the site, now chained and locked once more, savouring the many pleasures of a cool crisp morning. A shy, breathy wind ruffled the treetops as the sun rose in the eastern sky, pink and violet streaks tipping the distant hills. Marcus swerved slightly as a small rodent scuttled from the hedgerow and smiled broadly at the sound of tiny bones crunching beneath the fat tyres of the Porsche. Sometimes life was just perfect.

Donna had taken the Underground and, rather than go direct to Central station, had fancied a bit of a walk and got off at James Street. She'd enjoyed a stroll down Matthew Street past the old Cavern Club; the whole area crammed with tourists doing the Beatles Trail, squeezed past the crowds outside Flanagan's Apple and sneered at the cheap commemorative crap crammed into every shop window. City of Culture? Not much sign of that round here. Donna passed Wade Smith on the corner, crammed with trainers costing a week's wages, without a sidelong glance, then walked up the main drag to Bold Street. Which was where the day had turned sour.

Donna had walked up and down Bold Street for an hour, investigating every crummy warehouse and corner shop in search of the tobacconist Dexter had suggested, all to no avail. The whole area was full of barriers. What with steel shutters covering plate-glass windows, screens up at the Post Office counter, all Government offices, off licences, late-night filling stations, was it any wonder nobody trusted anyone else? With good reason. All this was part of the don't look at me and don't even think about striking up a conversation culture. Just get what you need and fuck off out again. Where speech was unavoidable, conversations had to be conducted through a plastic barrier or by means of a two-way intercom. A lifer in Walton gets treated better.

Just as she was about to give up, Donna found what she was seeking. She'd passed it at least twice, a tiny shop, blank windows, dark and dingy. Not exactly Toys R Us. The door creaked and a tiny figure materialised from the gloom as she entered. 'Can I help you?'

Donna brought out the cigarette that she'd reclaimed from Dexter and handed it over. 'I don't suppose...'

'One of mine? Yes indeed. What about it?' The man was tiny, stooped almost double which accentuated even further his lack of stature, but Donna would not have ventured a guess at his age. Old was the best she could do.

'You make them? Here?'

'Yes. And yes again. Is there some point to your visit, love, or are you here to waste my valuable time?'

Donna belatedly realised that the waspish tone was an act. The old man was smiling broadly. 'Glad to see anyone these days. Even a time-waster. What can I do for you?'

'This cigarette? Its special, is it?'

The old man looked affronted. 'Special? I'll give you special. Yes it is. Fifteen minutes to make up a single cigarette. Does that sound special to you?'

Donna nodded. 'So, this would be made to order?'

'One of the few. Let me have a good look.' He split the end of the cigarette and sniffed delicately at the exposed tobacco leaves. After a moment, he stiffened and handed back the cigarette. 'Sorry. Can't help you.'

Donna stood there, mystified. 'Can't help or won't help?'

'Same thing when it comes down to it. I remember that particular blend. Unusual. A mix of Turkish and Virginia. You needn't think I can let you have any either. Been caught out once. Never again.'

'I don't understand.'

The old man leaned forward, craning his head upward to stare at Donna. 'You're not here to collect any of these, then?'

'No. I just wanted to know if you'd made them.'

'Oh. Sorry, love. I'm a miserable old bastard these days. It's just that I made up a batch of these, oh it must be well over two years ago and the customer never came back for them. I kept them for a while, but tobacco is a right pain. It dries out and preventing that costs money. I had to chuck the whole batch away. Then, a couple of weeks ago, I get this 'phone call. Can I make up another batch? I explain about the last lot, how I had to get rid of it and he says fair enough. No problem, he says. Add it to the bill, he says.' His face contorted in rage.

'What happened?' Donna asked.

The old man shook his head in disgust. 'What happened? He sent some little toe-rag in here to collect the new batch. Picked them up, then told me he'd not be paying for the last lot, just for the batch I'd just made up.'

'It wasn't your regular customer, then?'

'No. He'd not have done that. He was a real gent. He sent in this young lad, homeless by the looks of him. Had all the details with him, so of course I gave him the package. He gave me the money, but when I asked about the other amount owing he just laughed at me and walked off. I tell you, if I'd been a few years younger...' His voice tailed away.

'I'm sorry,' Donna said. It always amazed her that people gave out information to perfect strangers without a hint of curiosity as to why she wanted to know this information. 'Can you describe him, the lad who picked up the cigarettes?'

'Scruffy little sod. Needed a shave. Got a right gob on him. Swore at me, terrible. Little bastard.'

Donna sighed. A dead end. 'What about your old customer? Can you describe him?'

'Only a youngster, but a real gentleman. Not usual these days, I can tell you. He was a good customer for about a year and always paid in full. In cash. Then he just stopped coming in. Never heard any more from him for a couple of years or so. Not until the other week anyway when I got a call out of the blue. Like he'd never been away.'

'Your old customer. What did he look like?' Donna's question seemed innocuous enough, but she felt a chill run down her spine as the old man proceeded to describe her nemesis, Marcus Green, in graphic detail.

CHAPTER 6

DONNA climbed out of the car and looked around. The house stood well back from the road, perched on a small mound. Donna walked up the drive, gravel crunching beneath her feet and climbed the steps towards the main entrance. This was a double-income housing area. Still one step below the mansions on the hill where the lady of the house would organise charity lunches and shopping expeditions to fill in her time, but down here they were still doing pretty well. Well enough to farm the kids out to child minders and employ a cleaner three mornings a week.

The mock-gothic entrance should have been the setting for a Dracula film and the views over the water were superb, although the house had a dreary and neglected feel about it. To get to the front door, it was necessary to open a vast metal gate over which was a steeply pitched tiled canopy. Donna imagined the gates to hell must have been modelled on the same pattern.

The heavy front door yawned open. Behind it was a black void.

'Hello,' Donna called out. A disembodied voice came out of the darkness.

'Whatever it is you're selling, we don't want it. Now fuck off.'

Donna sighed. Whatever happened to old-world courtesy? 'I'm not selling,' she called.

'Good. I'm not buying. So, fuck off.'

'I'd like to talk to you. It's about your son.'

After a long silence, a man stepped forward from the shadows. The scuffed and battered leather jacket was well past its prime. Like the man wearing it. But, Donna could see from its cut that the jacket had started off as a really tasty piece of kit. Top of the range. Once again, very much like its owner. He clicked his tongue and Donna felt a momentary spasm of alarm, concerned that she'd somehow caused offence, until she realised the clicking was a mere affectation and had no censorious overtones. She wished, for the umpteenth time, that her chronic insecurity would die a natural death.

'What about my son?' He looked utterly dejected and seemingly at the end of his tether. Shoulders slumping, the pain of his loss permeated every fibre of his being. Donna felt for him. This was a broken man.

Donna held out her hand. The man ignored the gesture, staring at her with such aggression that she felt a pang of alarm. 'I'm Donna O'Prey. I'm looking into a suspicious death on behalf of a client.'

The man barely glanced at her. 'So?'

'I came across the name of your son. Chris, wasn't it?'

The man nodded.

'I just thought it might help to talk to someone about Chris. Not that there's any connection or anything, but...'

'Help?' The interruption was fierce. 'Help who? Not me. Not his mother. What help can it be to us to keep dredging up old stuff? We lost a son. I've never been the father to him I should have been. I'm the first to say that. Not the best husband either, but that's something I've got to live with. It's too late for Chris. Too late now to be the father I should have been.'

'I'm sorry.'

'Sorry? What use is sorry now? I never even knew the silly little sod was on drugs. That's the sort of parent I was. Sorry doesn't work, does it? Too bloody late now for sorry.'

Donna stood on the step, uneasy at the sheer misery facing her and uncertain whether it would be best to leave at this stage rather than risk inflicting any more pain on this family. She looked directly towards the man, wondering how best to deal with an awkward situation and found him staring wistfully back at her. The man taking her arm made up Donna's mind. 'Not your fault, love,' he muttered, 'Caught me at a bad time, that's all. Not your fault. Come in and have a chat to the wife.'

He led the way into the dark interior and, after a moment's hesitation, Donna followed him. The house was a riotous mixture of eccentric styles. Heavy Victorian furniture mingled with delicate oriental pieces, while every spare surface was home to a vast collection of china ornaments. What made it all the more bizarre was the revelation that the woman who sat in the bay window gazing out at the garden was in a wheelchair. Donna couldn't imagine having to negotiate the maze of ornaments on a regular basis while confined to a wheelchair.

'Here you are, Alice. A visitor for you.' Donna's companion said brightly. Trying too hard, Donna thought.

The woman turned a stony glare in their direction and then abruptly smiled. The change was staggering. Her harsh features were transformed and the beam of welcome she bestowed on Donna was like the sun coming from behind a heavy cloud.

'Hello, love. Who are you?'

Donna moved forward. 'Donna O'Prey.'

'Hello, Donna.' The woman displayed no sense of curiosity at all.

'I wanted to say how sorry I am to hear of your loss,' Donna began, uncertain how to proceed.

'Thank you. Very kind.' The woman was trying hard to be pleasant, but even Donna could see it was all an act. This was a woman living on the edge.

The man lurking behind Donna broke in to disrupt the awkward silence. 'What about a nice cup of tea, love? How about you, Alice? Nice cup of tea, eh?'

The woman froze, then raised her head and looked directly past Donna at her husband. 'Piss off, George. When I want anything from you, I'll ask for it. Just don't hold your breath.'

George took the hint and drifted away. The woman waited until the door closed behind him, then smiled broadly at Donna. 'That's better,' she said, 'Can't stand him hanging around. He's spent the last twenty years in the alehouse and now he expects to walk in here and put on the good husband and concerned father act. Well, I'm not having it. He was no bloody use to me while Chris was growing up and he's no bloody use now. It's too late for all that.'

Donna smiled faintly and, when prompted, sat down on a hard-backed chair next to the wheelchair. 'Call me Alice,' the woman said, 'Might as well. It's my name after all.' She gave a cackle of laughter that was barely a fraction away from hysteria.

As I said to your husband,' Donna began, 'I'm looking into...'

'Why my Chris? What's he got to do with you? I'm not being rude, but...'

Donna thought she wouldn't like to hear her when she was trying to be rude, but could understand it in the circumstances. She hesitated, uncertain how to answer the question. If she was honest, she was beginning to wish she'd never come here in the first place.

'Come on. What brings you here asking about my son?'

'I don't know,' Donna answered, falling back on honesty in the absence of anything else. 'I'm looking into the sudden death of another boy, but the name of your son came up and I thought I should come and see you.'

'I see. No, bugger it; I don't do anything of the sort. Did Chris know this other boy who died? Are you telling me there was some connection?'

'No. Not at all.'

'Who was he?'

'Julian Carter. Does that mean anything?'

'That pop star's lad who killed himself? I read about it. That Julian boy. Was he on drugs?'

'No. I don't think so,' Donna replied.

'Neither was Chris.' The statement was so definite, so absolute, that Donna gasped. Just about all she knew about this woman's son was that he'd died of a drug overdose.

'When the police told me they'd found him dead I was devastated. He was such a lovely boy. I know you'd expect to hear that from his mother, but he really was. Life here has been no bed of roses, what with me stuck in this chair and his bloody father always down the pub, but Chris was wonderful. Never went out without telling me where he was going and what time he'd be back. Didn't want me worrying, you see. His death was bad enough, but when they said it was a drug overdose, that I could never accept. Not Chris.'

The vehemence of this statement fixed Donna in her chair. 'What evidence was there of, you know?' she asked, feebly.

'Drugs? The police said he'd taken a massive overdose, burst his heart. Absolute rubbish.'

'I don't know the circumstances,' Donna ventured, 'but from the little I know about drugs, it seems the first time is often the most dangerous. I think it's because the body hasn't had time to develop any tolerance.'

Alice nodded. 'That's what they told me. One of them Social Worker busybodies came round, asking if I wanted counselling. I told her I didn't want any counselling, I just wanted my Chris back here with me and no more talk of him being a drug addict. That Social Worker, she said that Chris had taken something with some fancy name or other. Very strong, it was. She also reckoned he'd got other stuff with him. In his pockets. I don't understand it. That sort of thing, wouldn't it be very expensive?'

'I suppose so,' replied Donna.

'Chris had no money to buy stuff like that. He was a student. Hadn't two pennies to rub together most of the time. Where would he have got the money from to buy drugs? That's why I thought of that Julian boy when you asked me about him. I could have understood it if he'd been the one to die from an overdose, but not Chris.' She started to cry and Donna patted her hand, feeling useless.

'I'll have to go now,' she said, 'I'm really sorry about your son.'

The last vestiges of flesh tones slipped away from Alice's features, leaving her face chalky white. 'He didn't die from what they said,' she whispered, barely loud enough for Donna to hear. 'Not drugs. You look into it. You'll see I'm right. Chris would never do that. Somebody killed him. That's what really happened.'

Donna froze, halfway out of the chair. This was the second time she'd been told that foul play was behind the sudden deaths of two different young men.

Alice released Donna's hand and sank back, looking exhausted. 'Take no notice of me,' she said, turning her face away to gaze out of the window once more, 'I'm just a silly woman who doesn't know what she's on about most of the time.' A tremulous smile battled for survival on the thin lips. Her gaunt features were strained, worry lines carving deep grooves into the taut skin and fanning out from the sunken eyes.

Donna almost tiptoed her way out of the room and ran into the hulking figure of George in the hall. Literally. Given his guilty expression he must have been listening at the door.

'Finished, have you?' His voice was hushed and as he turned to face Donna she was hit by a blast of stale booze fumes. The steady daily top-up kind of drinker rather than the occasional bender, by the looks of his complexion.

'Yes, thanks. I think so.'

'She'll not have it, you know? Drugs, I mean. Not our Chris. Mind you, I reckon she's got it right for once. He wasn't a lad for skipping over the traces. Never was. Didn't smoke, hardly ever took a drink even.' He made it sound more of a fault than a virtue. 'As for drugs, I reckon he's the last one you'd ever suspect of being on them things. Beats me where he'd got the money from.'

'That's what your wife said.'

'Did she?' The innocence of his expression was confirmation that he'd overheard every word his wife had uttered.

'She also said someone had killed him,' Donna said, impulsively.

'Maybe they did. I don't know about that. I'll tell you something though. Chris would never have taken himself off into that park for hours on end without telling his mother where he was.'

Donna nodded. They were singing from the same hymn sheet, not surprisingly in the circumstances and she would learn nothing more here. To add to the nothing she'd heard already. On an impulse she turned back and spoke directly to the man who was shuffling along behind her. 'Were either of you by any chance ever members of a jury?'

The man looked at her as if she were demented. Not surprisingly, Donna thought. Why had she asked that? Just because Julian's father had some vague connection with the man who'd nearly killed her? Was it some bizarre wish to confirm the involvement of Marcus Green? She didn't know the answer, but the description of the man who'd ordered the hand-made cigarettes had been uncannily close to Marcus. Was she justified in seeing the spectre of his presence at every turn or was it yet another case of over-reaction? She knew what Dexter would think.

Donna cleared her head of random thoughts to listen to the man's reply. His expression pre-judged the answer.

'A jury? No, not me. Not Alice, neither. Not unless she slipped out without telling me.' He chuckled. 'Even when I was pissed, which was most of the time, I reckon I'd remember that. I've hardly taken a drink since Chris died, you know? She doesn't think I'm capable of stopping, but I'll get there. I miss him, just as much as she does, you know that?'

Donna nodded. 'I can see that,' she said, truthfully. They arrived at the door and he solemnly shook her hand and wished her a safe journey home.

Marcus was on a buying spree. A set of bone-handled carving knives, together with a sharpening steel, from a kitchen supply shop in Chester, then a trip to B and Q. where he deliberated the respective merits of two rival brands of nail guns before deciding the more expensive was the better choice. A cordless power drill with an assortment of drill bits, two pairs of cotton gloves and a large electric griddle from the barbecue section completed his purchases.

Leaving the car park, he drove to the outskirts of the town and turned off the main road past a railway bridge and entered a narrow dirt track. Driving carefully on the rutted surface, he checked carefully for the presence of security cameras but saw none. Pulling up beneath the overhanging branches of a large tree, he climbed out of the car and looked carefully in each direction. Satisfied that he was alone, Marcus popped the lock on the boot and pulled out the girl's body which he propped against the car for a moment while he withdrew a white handbag from the boot, which he slammed shut behind him. Heaving the body over his shoulder without apparent effort, Marcus climbed the steep grassy bank facing him. At the top of the slope, he looked carefully around once more before arranging the body carefully in place, propping the inert figure upright with a broken fence-post. He placed a couple of items from his pocket inside the handbag and tossed the bag to one side. Examining his handiwork carefully, he nodded with satisfaction.

As Marcus reached his car, he glanced at his watch and smiled. When he reached the main road, he paused for a moment and opened the car window. His acute hearing could just about discern a faint rumbling sound in the far distance. Marcus smiled broadly, closed the car window and slipped a mint into his mouth as he drove away.

Donna luxuriated in the shower. Baths were great for wallowing in, but as a means of getting clean, they were rubbish. You lie there as dirty water is absorbed into your wide-open pores and then you get out dirtier then when you got in. No, Donna decided; give me a shower any time. The sound of the telephone intruded only briefly. The answer-phone would pick up any messages. When Peg's strident voice rang out, confirming not only that she'd returned from the shops, but also that she'd answered the telephone, Donna groaned and switched off the water. Peg wouldn't go away until Donna made an appearance and answered the call. Peg was no more likely to ask the caller to ring again later than she was capable of letting the answer-phone take a message.

Arriving in the kitchen swathed in a huge towel and dripping water everywhere Donna found Peg holding the 'phone at arm's length. 'Some woman,' she hissed, 'Wants you. Said it was urgent.'

Donna took the 'phone, trying to ignore Peg's unashamed eavesdropping and heard the voice of Alice, the woman she'd spoken to earlier.

'Miss O'Prey, please.' She sounded harassed.

'Alice? Hello, it's Donna O'Prey here.'

'Oh! At last. Your secretary is very protective. I couldn't make her accept that it was you I needed to speak to. Personally.'

Donna glared at the lurking Peg who took no notice at all. If anything she edged even closer.

'You asked George a question before you left. He's just told me.'

'Oh yes?' Donna said, politely, racking her brains as to which question Alice meant.

'About being on a jury?'

'Oh! He said not. Not you either.'

'No. He was right for once. I wanted to know why you were asking, that was all.'

'No particular reason,' Donna explained, 'I only asked because of the other boy who died. Julian Carter. One of his parents had been on a jury.'

Alice sounded puzzled. 'I don't see what....'

'Forget about it. It was a stupid question. I just had a silly idea that because Julian's father had been on a jury, it might have meant something, but as it turned out, it wasn't relevant at all. Neither of you ever served on a jury.'

There was a long silence. When Alice spoke again, her voice was very faint. 'I didn't, but Chris's dad, he was on a jury a long time ago.'

'Oh! He said he wasn't.'

Alice sighed. 'George wasn't. But George isn't Chris's father. He just thinks he is.'

'I'm sorry. I don't understand.'

Alice sighed again. 'I wasn't always stuck in a wheelchair you know. Long ago now I had an affair. Oh, it all ended years back. He was married as well. It was my decision to end it. Things were just too complicated. Especially after Chris was born.'

'Oh, I see.'

'Yes. Chris was never George's son. It was easier that way. I never let on. To either of them. George or Chris. What would be gained?'

'Are you still in touch with…?'

'Robert? Oh, yes. I had to tell him when Chris died, you know?' He's been very good all these years. Sent money regularly. Our little secret. Nobody else knew about Robert. No one else at all. He cried when I told him the news about Chris.'

'I see.'

'The thing is. Robert was on a jury once. He told me all about it. Even though he wasn't supposed to tell anyone. A big case. Some boy who killed two little girls.'

'Marcus Green,' Donna whispered.

'What did you say, dear?'

'Marcus Green,' Donna repeated, her chest tightening. She was just about conscious of the voice on the other end of the 'phone, but stood rigidly, teeth clenched, until Peg took the handset from her and replaced it on the cradle.

The locomotive eased over a slight incline and gathered speed on the long run along the straight three miles of track, which lay dead ahead. All systems green and the recently completed track renewal ensuring a smooth passage. Behind the locomotive, a long line of carriages ran straight and true, full of commuters and shoppers bound for London Euston. A slight delay on departure from Lime Street had already been clawed back and with good weather ahead the driver was confident that the current rate of progress would be maintained. Reaching top speed at the far end of the straight section, he eased back on the throttle just a shade as the long graduated curve came into sight. He'd glanced at his instruments for a second, all systems still green, which made him a fraction late in seeing the figure on the line, but the momentary delay was immaterial. He'd no chance of stopping and it would be almost another minute and a half before the train came to a final juddering halt. A mile back, the girl's broken body was spread over a hundred yards of track. The driver had barely glimpsed the white face of a young girl and the squealing brakes which had locked the great iron wheels had drowned out any screams, but he'd be seeing that same face every night for the rest of his life.

CHAPTER 7

THE next morning, Donna had spent over an hour with Dexter. It had been a traumatic meeting, entirely dominated by her boss. He'd listened to her ramblings - his word not Donna's - about the possible involvement of Marcus Green, then told her to forget it and get on with the case. Donna had ranted, argued and finally begged, but the end result was unchanged. She was to continue investigating the sudden death of Julian Carter, as the client had requested and forget about trying to prove some spurious connection with a man who had been officially pronounced dead.

Just as Donna prepared to storm out, Dexter had called her back. 'When were you planning to see Kate?'

Donna hesitated. She'd intended to see Kate in her own time, the previous hour having led her to the conclusion that Dexter wouldn't any longer be prepared to sanction any official contact.

Dexter smiled. 'I'll ok it. Just do yourself a favour and concentrate on the case as it stands. Don't waste time looking for anything else. I'll go with you if you like.'

Donna recognised the offer for what it was: Dexter wanting to keep an element of control, but was unable to justify an outright refusal. 'How about tomorrow morning?'

'Fix it up for this afternoon,' Dexter said, waving her away. 'Let me know the details and I'll see you there.'

Back in her own office, Donna glanced at the scrawled notes she'd made after talking to Alice and looked up the address of Robert Hudson, whom Alice had revealed to be the true father of her son, Chris. Dexter's high-handed attitude had irritated her, not for the first time, and she decided on the spur of the moment to go and see the man, deliberately contradicting Dexter's order to concentrate solely on matters directly relating to Julian Carter. She snatched her mobile off the charger, reached over the desk and slipped her ID card into the pocket of her jeans and then telephoned Kate Davies and arranged for her and Dexter to call that afternoon. He was only down the corridor, but she'd had enough of Dexter's company for the time being so left a message on Dexter's mobile advising him of the appointment. One act of mutiny was enough to be going on with.

Robert Hudson's address turned out to be a rambling three-storey house on the edge of a tiny village near Birkdale golf course, rather neglected on the outside, but with stunning views along the shore. The blustery winds were partly deflected by the rows of sand dunes and Donna gave a sigh of relief as she parked the car on a wide grassy verge.

Outside the front gate a trio of young mothers had gathered, pushchairs forming a barrier to anyone wishing to pass by. The three women talked at each other constantly. How well their own child was doing at school, their special talents, and all that proud parent crap. The other two didn't even make pretence of listening to the one that was speaking at any time; just waited for an opportunity to burst in and talk about their own kid. Donna thought there could be no more boring subject than other peoples' children. The topic may well have been fascinating to the parent, but remained a total turn-off to everyone else. Donna stood uncertainly for a moment, before deciding affirmative action was necessary. 'Excuse me,' she said, trying for authority. Three pairs of eyes swivelled in Donna's direction. Her sad childless status was noted and a perceptible smugness wafted through the air. Three pushchairs moved as one, just far enough to allow a non-member of the infant rearing club to squeeze past and all without a moment's break in their conversation. Donna opened the gate and walked up a wide crazy-paved path towards the house.

The front door was a solid oak affair, studded with impressive iron bolts and would have withstood a battering ram, but the deep windows on either side were wide open.

'Hello?' Donna called, deeming the effort required to lift the massive iron knocker to be beyond her capabilities, 'Anyone there?'

A face appeared at the left-hand window, looked Donna up and down and vanished again. A middle-aged woman wearing an alarmingly vibrant yellow shirt. Donna waited. After a few moments, the huge door creaked open and the same woman appeared on the step. She'd combed her hair, reducing the tangles slightly, but the shirt was even more dazzling at close quarters.

'Hello,' the woman said, smiling broadly. 'Can I help you?' Donna liked her immediately and liked her even more when she brushed aside Donna's proffered identity card and babbled introduction. 'Is this the right address for Mister Hudson? Mister Robert Hudson?'

'Right address? Oh yes. Come inside out of the wind.'

Donna stepped inside and followed the woman through a long narrow hallway, more like a hospital corridor than part of a private house, towards an open door at the end. The sound that Donna had taken to be of somebody strangling a cat turned out to be a tall thin man scraping away at a highly polished cello. He looked up as Donna entered the room and frowned. 'Hello. You're not a musician, are you?'

'Sorry,' Donna replied. 'Tone deaf, I'm afraid.'

The man clambered awkwardly to his feet, stepping around the cello as he did so. 'Just as well,' he exclaimed brightly, 'I can't get the hang of this thing. I reckon there's something wrong with it. Won't play tunes at all.'

Donna hesitated, then realised his remarks were intentionally ironic.

'The young lady wants to talk to you, Robert.' The woman who'd followed Donna into the room said, her high-pitched voice carrying clearly over the sound of a chain saw which kicked into life somewhere outside the French windows. Donna was well aware that she'd not given any reasons for calling at the house, other than asking whether Robert Hudson lived there and was already regretting the way she'd just dashed over here without any planned itinerary in place. The main problem was her uncertainty as to how to broach the subject of the boy whom she'd been told was the man's son, while in the presence of the man's wife. Her awkwardness was spared when the woman excused herself, telling her husband she was popping next door to collect a library book which the neighbour had asked her to return leaving Donna and Robert Hudson alone.

'I stopped smoking three months ago and needed something to take my mind off the cravings,' Robert said. 'This thing,' He indicated the cello with a look of disgust, 'was supposed to inspire me. I used to be pretty good on the violin years ago and thought the cello would be a natural progression. No such luck.'

Donna realised that the temporary absence of the man's wife meant she was missing an opportunity and jumped straight in. 'I need to talk to you about a rather delicate subject,' she interjected, 'I got your name from Alice. Alice Wright.'

The man's face stiffened and he gave a quick glance at the partly open door. 'Come with me,' he said, leaving the cello propped precariously against his chair and walked swiftly across the room to a second door behind him. Donna followed him through the door and up a wide staircase to a room crammed with piled-up books and magazines. Like the photograph of himself as a much younger man posing self-consciously with an enormous sporting trophy, the enormous brass ashtray was a link with his past. Donna imagined he'd hung on to the desk for the same reason. His working files, loosely stacked in chaotic piles, covered the entire surface of a side table and extended along both free sides of the room. All the paraphernalia of a well-ordered office, but without any of the order.

'Now then. What's all this about?' He was more concerned than angry, but Donna hastened to give a quick précis of her conversation with Alice Wright.

'Am I right to assume you were the father?'

'Of Chris? Yes, I was. I was very much in love with Alice, but things were complicated. To say the least. We broke up. Her idea not mine. But I had to respect her wishes. It was all very civilised. She's a strong person. Didn't need me in her life. The boy had a father. Her husband. It was for the best. We were both married to other people. Still are. I would have taken that step, but she wouldn't. Not even when she became pregnant. She ended it. Just like that. Never asked me for anything.'

Donna stood in silence as his words spilled out in short snappy sentences. When he stopped talking and stood gazing out of the window, she decided to give him a gentle push.

'But, you did send her money?'

'Yes. For the boy. Little extras. Christmas, his birthday. Never enough to embarrass Alice or cause her problems at home. Just a hundred pounds here and there. She kept the money. I know she never asked for it, she would never do that, but she never sent my cheques back. Perhaps she reckoned I could afford it.'

'Did you never ask to see the boy?'

'No. I kept in touch for a while. As a friend. Until she told me she'd prefer I didn't. I've never spoken to her since. Not until she rang me a few weeks ago.'

'What was that like? Hearing from her again after all this time?'

He turned his face towards her and Donna saw the sparkle of tears on his cheek. 'What do you think it was like? My child had died. I may not have ever really known him, but I never forgot he was my son.'

Donna flinched. 'I'm sorry. It was a stupid question.'

'Forget it. You had your reasons, I suppose.'

Donna shuffled awkwardly at his obvious discomfort. Truth to tell, she wasn't at all sure what she hoped to achieve here and having caused the man such pain she just hoped her visit would shortly start to bear fruit.

'I've got a couple of photographs. That's all. Nothing else to remember him by at all. You must think I'm pathetic, carrying on like this over a child I never knew.'

'No. Not at all.' Donna stood and watched him fall apart, wishing she'd never driven to the house.

'I've thought of him so often. She made the decision, not me. I wanted the baby. I would have left my wife for her. I told her that and I meant every word of it, but she decided it wasn't what she wanted. I suppose what it came down to was that I wasn't what she wanted. It was a bad time. I had to carry on, patch up my own marriage and try and forget about the baby.'

'Did you?'

'What? Patch up my marriage? Yes, for what that's worth.'

'No. I meant, forget about him.'

'Never.' The vehemence of his reply was such that Donna froze, unwilling to prolong this ordeal any longer. When he turned away from her and started shuffling papers on hid desk, she realised she was losing control of the interview. Not that she'd ever been in control to start with.

'You said you had some photographs?'

Robert turned back to face Donna and she saw fresh rears on his face. 'Yes. Just snaps really. Alice sent me them over the years. Very discreet about it. Always delivered to my office. His first day at school, birthday parties. That sort of thing.'

'Do you have them here?'

'Of course.'

'Doesn't your wife, you know…?'

He laughed. 'I'm not entirely stupid. I have my secrets, as I'm sure she has hers. Elaine is not one to pry, but I keep the photographs hidden away amongst my work files. All very boring stuff. No chance of Elaine ever finding them.'

'Can I see them?' Donna knew she was being pushy and that her persistence may be unwelcome, but the damage had already been done and she reasoned she may as well get as much as she could from her visit. Sympathy had very swiftly taken second place to opportunism. The familiar selfish, not so mature side of her nature. Which was the real Donna? Buggered if she knew.

Robert hesitated for a moment, clearly wanting to refuse her request, but hampered by good manners and chivalry. Unlike Donna. He frowned. 'I suppose so. Just hang on for a minute.' He left the room and Donna heard a filing cabinet slide open in the next room. She waited patiently, admiring the many small touches that brought the room to life. A delicate figurine in a niche high up on the facing wall, a faded strip of fabric running along the back of a tapestry nursing chair, bunches of herbs suspended from the immense oak beams that stretched the full length of the room. The passing years had burnished the pale floorboards in a manner impossible to duplicate by polishing. This room personified that effortless mixture of style and practicality that was almost impossible to replicate in a modern house.

Robert appeared in the doorway, looking perplexed and more than a little concerned. 'They're not there,' he said.

'Are you sure?'

'Of course I'm bloody sure,' he snapped. 'They've been in that drawer for donkey's years, ever since we moved out here. I never move them. One of the few things I'm certain about the way my memories going lately. Some days are one long Craft day.'

Donna looked perplexed. 'Sorry? Craft day?'

'Yeah. That's C.R.A.F.T as in Can't Remember A Fucking Thing.'

'Oh, I see. Perhaps your wife…?'

He shook his head. 'No. Elaine never goes in there. It's my office. She won't even clean in there in case she inadvertently moves something I desperately need. In any case, if Elaine had found them, don't you think she would have mentioned it? The boy is, was, the image of me. Why do you think I took such care to keep the bloody photographs hidden?'

Not enough care, obviously, thought Donna. 'What exactly is missing?'

'Everything. The whole file. About a dozen photographs, photocopies of school reports, things like that.'

'Oh!'

He looked at her sharply. 'What's that supposed to mean? Oh?'

Donna shook her head. 'Nothing. Do you think somebody could have taken them?'

'I don't see how.'

'Burglars, perhaps?' Donna asked, knowing it was a stupid question even as she formed the words.

He looked at her with an expression very close to contempt. 'Burglars? Around here? Not very likely. We don't lock our doors in this village. One of the reasons we moved out here to the wilds of Southport. No crime. No joy riders. Nothing like that here. In any case, I hardly think burglars would steal a few worthless photographs and ignore a Georgian silver desk set, do you?'

Donna shook her head, but knew in her heart that he was wrong. She knew that the house had been burgled. Hardly a difficult matter in an area where doors were left unlocked and that the intruder hadn't been looking for items of value. Just information. Which he'd found in the filing cabinet. Enough to confirm that Robert had once fathered a child and enough documentary evidence to trace that child. She shivered, suddenly aware that

Marcus Green had been in this very room, perhaps even stood on this same spot and felt a chill spread throughout her body.

Robert took a step towards her, concern etched on his face. 'I say. Are you ok? You've gone as white as a sheet.'

Donna heard the words, but was powerless to reply. An iron band had imprisoned her chest. She gasped for breath, staggered once and pitched forward into his outstretched arms.

Marcus sat back in the heavy chair, stretching the long muscles of his back, with some satisfaction. He'd spent well over three hours in front of the flickering light of the computer screen and the time had been well spent. The house was set well back from the road, but he'd backed his car into the garage to avoid any chance of his presence being detected. He'd lingered in the departure hall of John Lennon Airport long enough to note the addresses on each set of luggage and an apparently casual conversation with one of the waiting passengers had revealed that the couple would be away for three weeks. They'd mentioned putting their pet dog into a boarding kennel, thereby confirming there would be no one left in the house as they would otherwise have been able to look after the dog. Gaining entry to the house had been easy and he'd taken advantage of a well-stocked freezer and microwave oven to enjoy a satisfactory meal before settling himself down in the office and logging on to the Internet. The man's computer password had even been written down in his desk diary.

The fast Broadband connection had located the information he'd needed with commendable speed. Marcus had been mildly concerned that the search of the records pertaining to his identity, more accurately to his former identity, had taken place but the software he'd designed had done its job. He now had as much information as he needed to identify his pursuer. The name meant nothing to him, but he would need to act promptly to deter this intruder. Permanently.

He'd already decided to take the Range Rover that occupied the other half of the garage, leaving his own car behind. Marcus placed the slip of paper on which he'd copied the name and address from the computer screen face up on the passenger seat. Time for a shower and a change of clothing before he left the house. There was no need to hurry and the next stage of his plan would be easier under cover of darkness. His quarry lived less than an hour away.

'Don't try to move. Just stay where you are.' The disembodied voice floated down to her. Donna opened her eyes and saw the blurred outline of a middle-aged woman with deep frown lines creasing her brow.

'Where am I?' Donna heard her own voice, which sounded strange and far away, and had an irrational urge to giggle. She'd heard the same question in a hundred bad films and here she was saying exactly the same thing.

'You're fine. You fainted and Robert had the sense to put you on the bed and call out a doctor. I got home as he was on the telephone and got a bit of a turn myself, I can tell you. Strange women swooning in my house? Whatever next?' The woman was babbling, whether through concern or nervousness Donna didn't know. The voice was quintessentially English. Middle-class, middle-aged, middle-income bracket. More at home at a coffee morning in somewhere like Leamington Spa than buried out here among the sand dunes of the Fylde coast.

'Elaine?' Donna asked. She already knew the answer. Even glimpsed through the mists that still blurred her vision, the vibrant yellow shirt had been a bit of a give-away. Donna shuffled herself along the bed, trying to get comfortable. Her throat felt raw.

'That's right, dear. Just lie still. The doctor will be here any minute. Robert has explained why you're here.'

'*Has he now?*' Donna thought, but did as she was told and lay back on the pillow. Elaine stood up as a slamming door and heavy footsteps on the stairs announced the arrival of the anticipated doctor. The old boards creaked and groaned like the rigging of a galleon in full sail as a large untidy man, dressed in a combat jacket and camouflage trousers burst through the door drawing a squeal of alarm from Elaine.

'Morning,' he announced, slightly out of breath. Robert followed him through the doorway and went straight to his wife's side. 'Here is your patient,' he said to the other man, gesturing at the prone figure of Donna.

'Ah, yes. Recovering already, I think.' Donna smiled. He looked like no doctor she'd ever seen, but his affable manner lifted her spirits. Donna prided herself that she knew how to read faces and thought this was a man she could trust. The only item of jewellery was a plain gold ring on his wedding finger, while his air of quiet competence was immediately apparent, even to a complete stranger. The type of man you'd want to come along if your car broke down in the rain. When push came to shove, feminism was a fair-weather luxury as far as Donna was concerned. The new arrival slapped a battered old bag on the floor and smiled broadly. 'Please excuse my....' He gestured at his clothing. 'I was about to take my dogs and go for a ramble across the dunes, maybe chase a few rabbits. The dogs I mean. Not me. Rest assured that underneath these awful clothes I am Doctor Rennie. Dennis to my friends and especially to all young attractive female patients.'

Donna smiled, marvelling at how certain middle-aged men could get away with murder when it came to flirting, even in these days of political correctness. 'You look very professional to me,' she said, suddenly feeling much better. The doctor may have been dressed like a Vietnam veteran, but he had an easy familiarity about him that was very comforting. Doctor Rennie shooed both Elaine and Robert out of the room and sat on the edge of the bed.

'What happened, exactly?' He asked, opening his case. 'Fainting?'

Donna nodded. 'I've done it before,' she said. 'I feel fine now.'

'Let me see about that. I am the doctor here, not you.' Eyes twinkling, he produced a tiny glass contraption and pushed it gently into Donna's right ear for a few moments. Withdrawing it, he glanced at a gauge and put it away. 'Temperature just about normal. That is good.'

74

'I've never had that,' Donna said, gesturing towards her ear. 'Only under my tongue, you know?'

He nodded. 'The miracles of modern medicine. Be grateful I am a doctor and not a vet.' He mimed thrusting a huge thermometer up his own backside and roared with laughter. Donna joined in his merriment, wondering whether this was just his off-duty persona or whether he was always like this with his patients.

'You seem fine,' Doctor Rennie said after a few more tests. 'Fit as the proverbial fiddle. You say you've had this sort of thing before?'

'Panic attacks? Yes.'

'I see. Is there anything in your normal life that's likely to cause stress? Your job, for instance? What exactly is it you do?'

Donna outlined the bare bones of what she did for a living, being careful to keep well away from any reference to the specific case in which she was presently engaged.

'Fine. Now give me the real story.'

Donna looked at him with growing respect. He was sharper than he looked. 'What?'

'I've been given the run-around by experts in my time. There's a lot you're not telling me, isn't there?'

Donna frowned and then capitulated, telling this complete stranger all about her dad, her previous case and the terror she'd experienced when faced with a ruthless killer. Once she began, the words flowed and she felt a strange sense of relief. When Donna finally wound down, Doctor Rennie sat well back in his chair and looked at her as if she'd just confessed to being a spy for the medical ethics complaints department.

'I don't know whether to prescribe a sedative or apply to have you sectioned,' he said. 'One thing's for sure. If this is what you're engaged in on a daily basis, no bloody wonder you have panic attacks.'

'I'm sorry; I shouldn't have said all that. I shouldn't be involving you in my troubles.'

'I'm glad you did. I can relate to what you've just been telling me, far more than you realise. A good friend of mine went missing three years ago and I was heavily involved in attempting to help the family. Counselling is the way we describe it nowadays. It's a trendy way to describe what is just basic humanity. Very easy to describe but very difficult to actually achieve anything. In view of your involvement in crimes of violence, I can well understand why your own health is suffering. If you want my personal opinion, you're either a bloody fool or a quite remarkable young woman. And, I don't think you're a fool.'

Feeling really stupid, but completely unable to control herself, Donna burst into floods of tears, sobbing helplessly and wailing like a toddler who's been told there's no such thing as Father Christmas.

By the time Donna eventually recovered, she'd received a generous ration of sympathy. That was what had made her so pathetically weepy. She couldn't hack too much kindness; it made her feel so bloody inadequate.

'Are you on any medication at the moment?'

Donna shook her head. 'Used to take tablets, but not lately. Trying to cope without them.'

'Not entirely successfully, it would appear. Even without drugs, they're avoidable, these panic attacks of yours. All a matter of correct breathing and, of course, avoidance of stressful situations.'

Donna nodded. She'd been told this before. Sounded simple enough, taking a few deep breaths at times of stress would prevent an attack developing. She could even remember the technical name, Pranayamic breathing; flooding the bloodstream with oxygen. Donna's problem was trying to remember all that helpful advice at the time she needed it most. Simple rational explanations were just not on the agenda when the room began to sway and her legs felt as if they belonged to another person. Someone very old or very feeble. Donna had once tried to explain all this panic attack stuff to Peg. Big mistake. Peg's innate practicality blinded her to the failings of others, leaving Donna feeling more inadequate than ever. Can't even remember to breathe? How pathetic was that?

CHAPTER 8

KATE adopted the voice of an American news-reader, 'In the modern world of crime detection, the hiding places for today's criminals are constantly shrinking.' Donna laughed and Dexter glared at her.

'You always do this.' Dexter's voice was a low growl. 'Put me down, every time.'

'Yeah? You fucking dinosaur coppers are fit for nothing else. I'm not telling you how to do your job.'

'Oh, aren't you?' Dexter growled. Kate smiled sweetly but said nothing.

Donna looked at the two of them, realising there was a power struggle going on, but unable to predict its resolution. She'd met Dexter in the road outside the wall bristling with high-security devices that surrounded Kate's house.

Despite the best efforts of Doctor Rennie, Donna still felt under the weather and was trying desperately to disguise the true state of her health. Dexter looked tired, Donna thought. As if he'd got the cares of the world on his shoulders. *God knows what he thinks I look like.*

They'd gone through the complicated entry ritual which was part of the routine for a truly paranoid person like Kate Davies, but a pitched battle had ensued the minute they set foot in Kate's cluttered work room. Dexter had been acting stroppy ever since he'd arrived and Kate had met him full on with a few barbs of her own.

'Don't know why I'm even bothering to be here,' Dexter rumbled, crossing his legs awkwardly in the narrow typists' chair that had been offered to him. 'Every single time you want to start some battle or other. Is it too much to ask that once, just once, you could let me have my say without butting in all the bloody time?'

'Calm down, Dexter,' Kate said, her expression confirming Donna's suspicion that she was deliberately provoking Dexter for some reason best known to herself. 'Don't get your knickers in a twist. I only asked if you had any evidence to back up your latest problem or whether you're expecting me to do your job for you. As usual.'

'Oh, stuff it,' Dexter interrupted, red in the face with anger, 'I can see I'm wasting my time here.' Dexter's voice was a low growl and the lines across his forehead crinkled and deepened.

'Yeah. That obsession you have with Marcus Green should have taught you a lesson or two. I'm not telling you how to do your job... '

'Oh, aren't you?' Dexter snapped, looking angrier than Donna had ever seen him. 'Why don't you forget Donna ever rang you and we can both get on with our lives in peace? Waste of bloody time being here at all from where I'm sitting.'

'Nice one, Dexter.' Donna's voice came out louder than she'd intended and Dexter's head whipped round to stare at her. Even as she'd spoken, Donna knew she was out of order and his expression said as much. If anyone in this

77

room was obsessed with Marcus Green it was her and Dexter knew that better than anyone. Dexter turned away and ignored her.

'I'm sure Donna can tell me what you both need without getting in a state.' Kate was all sweetness and light now, but if her intention was to placate Dexter her words had the opposite effect.

'Right. Why don't I just bugger off and leave you two to get on with it? Donna, ring me when you get home. Let me know if you make any progress. I'll not be holding my breath.' Nodding curtly at Donna and ignoring Kate completely, Dexter lumbered to his feet and strode out of the room. Kate swivelled on her chair, watching the monitor fastened to the back wall until she saw Dexter slam the front door. She sighed, eyes still fixed to the screen until the shapeless bulk of Dexter opened the heavy metal door in the high stone wall and closed it behind him. Kate pressed a switch on her desk and a row of blue lights lit up on her desk. She grunted at this confirmation that the alarm system was working and turned back to face Donna.

The room was even more cluttered than Donna had remembered from her previous visits, more than two years ago. The waist-height worktop was cluttered with a seemingly random collection of machinery and trailing connections. At least a dozen beige or grey towers, no makers names, just plain boxes, all with a baffling array of wires protruding from the rear. Two laptops, the nearest with the familiar Toshiba logo and an Apple Power-book, the latest jumbo-screen model, were placed side by side on a Formica table. Two laser printers, a couple of scanners and other various bits and pieces filled the remaining worktop while a huge photocopier squatted menacingly against the back wall. The room resembled a branch of PC World, only better stocked. Kate smiled, noting Donna's gaze and gestured at the electronic beast that sat on the desk in front of her. 'What about this little beauty? My latest creation. I sat here for three hours last night, over-clocking it to hell and back. Nothing too good for my new baby. Isn't she beautiful?'

Donna's mind flashed back to the three pushchair brandishing women she'd seen earlier. She had seen enough doting parents in her time to know when to smile and look suitably impressed.

Kate rambled on for a couple of minutes about extra cooling fans, digital connections and state of the art modifications while Donna tried to stop her eyes glazing over. Kate stopped in mid-sentence. 'You know fuck-all about computers, don't you?'

Donna gave a rueful nod; half expecting to be castigated for her lack of knowledge, but Kate only laughed. 'Thought so. I've been making it up for the last thirty seconds and you never batted an eye-lid. You're polite though, I'll give you that.'

Donna grimaced. 'Sorry.'

'Don't worry about it. I shouldn't really expect anyone else to be interested. Give me a minute to run my checks and I'll be right with you.' Kate bent over her keyboard and tapped away for a few moments as the screen in front of her lit up and darkened in turn.

Donna had seen this study in concentration before. On a previous visit to the house Kate had explained the reasons behind her obsession with her personal security, especially with regard to the computer systems which were her only contact with the outside world and thus her main source of concern.

On that previous occasion, explaining the series of checks she made on her system on a daily basis, Kate had told Donna that she always felt a slight disappointment at the absence of any contamination. She enjoyed the challenge of searching out and destroying a virus, especially any new and unknown strain, pitting her wits against the perverted skills of some unknown hacker. Next, she checked that another computer had not penetrated her system, explaining her actions as she worked. The unique software Kate had installed to carry out an ongoing search for the electronic signature of any unseen intruder intrigued Donna; she didn't even begin to understand it but still found it fascinating.

Kate frowned, tapping in another instruction on her keyboard before turning back to face Donna.

'Why don't you tell me what you want from me? I got more than a hint when you rang that you think our old friend Marcus Green may have resurfaced.'

Donna frowned. 'Not really. Well, yes I think he might....' Her voice tailed away.

'Is he involved or not?'

'I don't know. To tell you the truth, there's no evidence at all, but...'

'But, you've got one of your feelings, is that it?'

Donna nodded. 'I know it's stupid. He was supposed to have died in that fire at his mother's house. The police were convinced that it was his body they found. Then, he turned up again, nearly bloody killed me, and I saw him trapped inside that cabin when it burnt down. There was no way he could have got out of there. I was there and I watched it burn to the ground.'

'So?'

'They didn't find his body, did they? Nobody seemed to take me very seriously when I said he was still alive. Even Dexter took a lot of persuading and nobody else was even prepared to listen to me. I've always had it in the back of my mind that he's....'

Kate reached over and touched Donna's arm. 'You think he's still out there?'

'Yeah.'

'You could be right. I've already had a quick look around,' Kate gestured at the banks of computers, 'but, so far, nothing. No trace of him. Mind you, I don't suppose for one minute that even if Marcus is still walking around somewhere he'll be using his own name. Far too clever for that. Was that what you wanted? To know if I could trace him for you? Surprised Dexter agreed to that. Sounds very unlike him.'

Donna grimaced. 'You're right. Dexter said it would be ok to ask you to help me with a case I'm working on, but the Marcus stuff has only just come out.'

'So, the real reason you're here is the suicide of Julian Carter?'

Donna nodded. 'Yes. I came across another lad who died recently as well. Found dead from an overdose, but his family reckoned that would have been right out of character. I know you'd expect them to say that, but...'

'You believe them.' It was a statement, not a question. Donna nodded.

'Fair enough. Anything else? Kate grinned. 'Actually, I'm more interested in why you think Marcus Green would come back from the grave, as it were, for the specific purpose of getting involved in any of this.'

Donna took a deep breath before blurting out all the random nonsense she'd been bottling up for days. How the common thread that linked both cases she'd looked into had been a mysterious and unidentified new friend. Kate looked less than impressed and her expression didn't change after Donna hurriedly told her about the hand-made cigarette found in Julian's room. It was only when Donna mentioned the fact that both young men had a parent who'd been on the jury that sent Marcus Green to prison that Kate sat forward, her attention absolutely focussed on Donna.

'Now, that I can relate to,' Kate said, 'I can look into that. Find if any other jurors have had problems like these two poor buggers. Clever.'

'What?'

'If there is a link, it would have taken a fair jump to find it. Two deaths, but neither of them suspicious. Suicide and a drug overdose. Regrettable, but not unusual for that age group. Not suspicious in the foul play sense. Nothing to connect the two deaths and not much call for the police to get involved.'

'What about the Julian Carter suicide? Have you had a chance to look at it yet?

'Just the bare bones of the case. Coroner's verdict and a pretty sketchy set of police records. All the medical stuff was pretty conclusive. End of story.'

Donna nodded. The manner in which Kate Davies roamed through confidential documents, seemingly at will, through the medium of her computer was no longer shocking to her. The only surprise had been that steady law-abiding Dexter had apparently condoned what Kate did in the course of her work. A classic case of the end justifying the means, she supposed.

'Everything points to suicide I suppose? Nothing to suggest anything else?'

Kate shrugged 'Murder or suicide? Or even an accident? Impossible to be absolutely certain. The main indications of suicide are that the body was fully clothed – suicides don't usually want to be found naked - and enough traces of alcohol and drugs to be significant. Plus a note. Well, sort of a note. Just one word. Sorry.'

'Eh?'

'That was the word.'

'Oh! I see what you mean.'

Kate shook her head. 'Pretty damn obvious for a suicide note, just the one word, but given the circumstances, what else needed to be said? It fits the bill. Add the note to all the other indications and you can rule out an accident.'

'But not murder?'

Kate chuckled. 'Not to a suspicious bastard like me. That's the thing with a one-word suicide note. Very easy to plant at the scene, but it could have been written in a completely different context. A hand-written page of A4 would be rather more conclusive. The coroner said suicide. No doubts at all.' Kate shrugged her shoulders. 'I'd expect him to, given the circumstances. Suicide has to be favourite, no matter what the family may feel about that.'

Donna pulled a face. 'Could you look up the other boy? Chris?'

Kate smiled and nodded as Donna passed her a notebook with all the information she had concerning the sudden death of Chris Wright. Donna waited patiently as Kate's fingers flew across the keyboard and within a few minutes was looking at an official-looking report on the screen.

'Large quantities of toxic substances found, consistent with a heavy drug user,' Kate said, paraphrasing the details aloud as she scrolled down the document. 'Enough to identify the specific substances, even after three or four days lying out in the open.'

'How do they know all this stuff?'

'Like what?'

Donna waved a hand in the air uncertainly. 'Oh, you know, time of death, all that sort of thing.'

'Time of death is reasonably straightforward in the majority of cases. If it's recent there's the temperature of the body. How long it's been cooling down. Usually, a rectal probe will determine the body temperature at the time of examination. The human body cools at a known rate, although you need to allow for fluctuations in external temperature and other variables such as the amount of body fat on the victim. That's known as Algor Mortis. Then again, blood pools in the lower areas of a body as the fluids settle. That lividity follows a pretty strict pattern, taking up to three or four hours in total, leaving an impression of deep bruising. After four hours at most, this lividity is fixed and we know that the body was found in the same place that death took place as there had been no displacement of the lividity pattern. That's Liver Mortis. Am I being too technical for you?'

Donna shook her head vigorously.

'Ok then. The next stage is Rigor Mortis. That's the manner in which a body stiffens after death. The degree of rigor is a pretty good indicator of time of death but there are any number of variables dependent on circumstances.'

'Such as?'

Kate looked at Donna's face, rapt with interest and gave an indulgent smile. 'Rigor starts with death. Firstly in the small muscles of the face, the neck, the jaw, yeah? Hardly noticeable at this stage. Then it progresses into the large muscle groups where the whole body becomes stiff and immovable, usually affecting the whole body within a twelve-hour period. It takes longer under very cold conditions while extreme heat will accelerate the process.'

'How long does a body stay like that? Or does it go away again?'

'Normally, after a day and a half say of full rigor, a body will start to reverse the process and after three days it has gone completely. In a case like this, a body left out in the open air; it's the animal kingdom that does all the work for us. Simple biology' She looked at Donna's expression and laughed. '*Calliphora Erythrocephalus,* that's the common bluebottle to you, lays its eggs on the body during the day. On the following day, the eggs hatch, but its not until the third day that they're recognisable as the maggot we all know and love. They'll feed on anything going they can find for the next few days, until they're almost at bursting point, then they pupate, ready to produce the next generation of bluebottles. The time-scale never varies. It's a far better guide to time of death than any other method. The medical team seem pretty certain of their facts, but so would I if all I had to go on was this document. Means nothing, unless you were actually there at the time. Who knows what really happened?'

Donna frowned. 'You think it could have been murder?'

'Of course it could. If Marcus Green is involved the chances are very high.'

Donna could scarcely contain her excitement. 'Do you really think it could be him?'

Kate shrugged her shoulders. 'I don't like this jury link. Everything else could be explained away, but not that. Let me dig a bit; see what else I can find to prove a link with Marcus Green. I'll tell you one thing: if it were anyone else but you asking, I'd be pretty dismissive. Marcus Green is dead. All the records say so. No wonder you've had so much trouble getting anyone else to take notice of what you were telling them. I'm different. I've always had a high regard for eyewitness testimony. Same with Dexter. When you told Dexter that Marcus Green was the one who tried to kill you, even though everyone else was convinced he'd died, he'll have taken it on board, believe me.'

'He isn't exactly falling over himself to say he believes me now.'

Kate shrugged. 'That's his way. Give him evidence, hard evidence, and it'll be a different story. Find a believable link between the deaths of these two and Marcus. Dexter will find that irresistible. And, from what I've seen so far, a clever manipulative killer like him could easily be involved.'

'This sort of thing is your area of expertise, isn't it? People like Marcus. What are they like?'

'Multiples? Most are loners with few close friends. Withdrawn and distant. Usually unmarried, but not always the case.'

'The Yorkshire Ripper?'

'Yeah. What else? Often they were abused as children, had a homosexual, or latent homosexual background. May collect pornography or have a morbid interest in death and dead bodies. May also collect weapons. Collecting can be an obsession.'

'Anything else?'

'Abnormally tidy, fastidious. All sorts of things like that. The only constants I've found are they are all skilled liars, deceivers. Plausible types who think on their feet and plan for every contingency. Most don't want to be caught.'

Donna shook her head. 'Animals!'

'Not at all. An animal will kill for a good reason. For food or to defend itself or it's young. Leaving out the occasional killing frenzy, the fox let loose in a hen-house syndrome, animals resort to killing only when it's necessary. Killing for amusement, revenge, greed or financial gain: these are human characteristics and are unknown in the rest of the animal kingdom. Multiple killers with a specific personal agenda are particularly unique.'

Donna scowled. 'I still think they're animals. Marcus especially. He preys on his victims. Like a wolf.'

'No. Not a wolf. Wolves are pack animals. Marcus is a solitary killer. Self-sufficient and self-contained. Clever too. A fox perhaps?'

Donna shook her head. No! He's a wolf. A lone wolf.'

Kate nodded, conceding the point. 'Wolf it is then.'

'You've met a lot of them?'

'A few years back I did a major Home Office study on multiple killers. Back in the days when I was still confident enough to go out. I interviewed most of the well-known faces, both here and in the States. Not a pleasant task. Most of them were willing to talk freely to me.'

'So, you've talked to all the monsters.'

'Not all of them, no. Only the unsuccessful ones.'

'How's that?

'They got caught. The very best are still out there. Still killing.'

'Like Marcus?'

'Yes. Like Marcus. But, Marcus is nothing like the others. Except for the planning. He's the cleverest one I ever came across. Look, these days most of the world uses these things,' Kate gestured at the serried rows of computers surrounding her, 'Especially when it comes to tracking criminal behaviour. But, computers aren't intelligent. They look for similarities and when they find them, lights flash, buzzers sound and everyone gets very excited. No similarity means no flashing lights. The real clever buggers know that if they can avoid a recognisable MO, their chances of avoiding detection will be so much better. A man like Marcus Green for example.'

'It is him, isn't it?'

Kate shrugged. 'Who knows? If, and it's a big if, there's any link at all between these recent deaths, then their very diversity would suggest a clever mind at work.'

'Like Marcus?'

Kate smiled indulgently. 'Maybe. Or someone very like him.'

"You always say him. Not her. Are they always male? The people who do this sort of thing?"

"Yeah. Almost always. That proves we're the gentler sex, doesn't it? As far as I can see at this stage, if this is the work of one man, he'll be a planner. A thinker. Someone ruthless and utterly without compassion. This is Marcus Green territory."

Donna pouted. 'Dexter doesn't think so. He won't accept there's a link.'

Kate laughed. 'Why am I not surprised? Dexter's old school. Bogged down with an obsession with hard evidence. Not surprising, given his background, but not you. You're more like me. Open minded. I value intuition above all other qualities. If this is the work of a multiple killer, we'll not catch him by any normal methods.'

'How then?'

'By focussing on the one thing that sets him apart. His cleverness. He'll be an obsessive planner, leaving nothing to chance. Taking no risks.'

Donna frowned. 'How will that help us?'

'Anyone who takes such care to avoid detection will leave a trail. He'll need to plan everything in detail. Which means he'll stalk his victims, know their routine in advance. Someone will see him. Good as he is, he can't be invisible. Someone somewhere has seen him. They won't realise the significance of what they've seen, but they will have seen him. That's where you come in.'

Donna looked at her blankly. Kate shook her head in mock disbelief. 'If we accept these sudden deaths of two young men are somehow linked to the trial of Marcus Green, which for now I'll accept, then what have we got so far?'

The thought came to Donna with blinding speed. 'The victims.'

Kate nodded. 'Good. And what else?'

Donna shook her head. Kate sighed heavily. 'Think about it. If there's a link between these two cases, then the next step is obvious. Two dead kids with no connection to each other, apart from the trivial fact of having a parent who was once a member of a very specific jury. So?'

Donna nodded her head. 'Oh! The other jurors?'

Kate beamed. 'Exactly. I'll have you a list of names to work on by this time tomorrow. If any other members of that jury have suffered a recent death in the family, no matter what the circumstances, well, I think even Dexter will be interested to hear of it.'

Kate stretched her arms behind her neck. She looked tired. 'Listen. Why don't you get off home? Tell Dexter I'm on the case. I'll find out what I can and get back to you. I can tell you one thing. If Marcus Green is still alive, I'd expect to find evidence of him somewhere. Maybe not by name, but one thing will not have changed.'

'What's that?'

'He likes killing. I've not seen any significant rise in the local stats for missing persons, so it looks likely that even if he has returned that this would have been very recently. Of course, if the two cases you looked at are his handiwork, then he's moved the goalposts. Still killing, but the bodies are being discovered. Without any reason to believe there is any villainy involved.'

Donna looked crestfallen. 'Don't worry,' Kate told her, 'If there's anything to find out, I'll find it. As you say, that sort of thing is my bread and butter, so rest assured, I'll be looking. If only…'

'What?'

'Oh, probably nothing. Just that I've noticed the sort of thing I was talking about, but not round here. The South of France, Spain as well, there've been a dozen or so cases of young girls going missing. More than the usual level of teenage runaways. All of them living away from home. Summer jobs at the beach, students on a gap year, young girls from all over the world. Not unusual in holiday areas with a large influx of young people, but in sufficiently high numbers for the local law to put the word out. Then again, it may be nothing. So much of all the crap I do turns out to have a perfectly rational explanation. For instance, there's been a great fuss lately over some mystery firm involved in a take-over in the wholesale drug trade. Most of the gear that finds its way onto the streets round here comes through the Sheehan family. They've had it tied up for years. Until now. Somebody else has taken over. Someone with enough balls to take on the Sheehan brothers. That takes some doing. If Dexter was here, I'd suggest he look into it. Not that I think for a minute it'll have anything to do with your case, but Dexter would be interested.' Kate had been scrolling through a series of documents as she spoke, not looking at Donna at all.

'I'll get off then, should I?' Donna said, tentatively, aware that her continued presence was an irrelevance as far as Kate was concerned.

'Right,' Kate said, frowning deeply. 'That's odd.'

'What?'

Kate looked up, still frowning. 'Oh, nothing. Somebody playing silly buggers I suppose. I'm getting traces of someone trying to crack my system. The firewall will get rid of them in a minute or so. You get off and I'll speak to you later if I find anything.'

Donna nodded and stood up. Kate smiled up at her. 'Can you see your way out?'

'Yeah. No problem.' Donna went through the heavy metal door and looked back at the house which was in darkness apart from the brightly-lit room where Kate spent the majority of her time. She pondered on the manner in which Kate chose to live. A virtual recluse. Marooned inside the thick walls of her house, her only contact with the world outside being the charged electrons that made up cyberspace. Donna shivered as if at a sudden chill and hurried back towards where her car was parked. A gibbous moon on the rise cast a faint glow, but the shadows under the trees were dark and forbidding and she was suddenly conscious that she was the only person on the road. She reached her car, started the engine and drove away, swerving to avoid a Range Rover that was slowly turning the corner with only sidelights showing.

Marcus parked the car under the heavy branches of a large tree and took a laptop computer from its leather case. He connected a mobile 'phone and was soon back inside his own software programme. He adjusted one of the settings and scrolled through the pages of data that flowed across the screen, pausing occasionally to read a section more carefully. Lips pursed, he whistled softly as his suspicions were confirmed. The woman had been actively seeking any information that could relate to himself and he even felt a grudging respect for her abilities. The system was well defended and proof against most security threats. His own superior skill as a programmer had not only gained admittance to the system, but also planted a tiny reversing programme which would be working away in the background, completely undetected by the host and systematically erasing the entire contents of the hard drive. He switched his attention to another file, taking careful note of a series of blueprints and wiring diagrams. Especially those pages referring to the home security system. The owner had obviously felt her computer to be impregnable and the ideal place to store all her important material. This was fine while the only security threat being contemplated was that relating to a common burglar, but its strength was also its greatest weakness. When the threat came from a superior intellect, able to disarm all the defensive barriers, the whole system was wide open.

Marcus switched off his computer and placed it carefully on the back seat. He left the car and padded silently towards a dark section of the wall that his careful study had confirmed to be outside the range of the security cameras.

Kate stiffened as her suspicions were confirmed. Since she'd logged back on she'd been conscious of a nagging worry and her firewall confirmed that repeated efforts had been made to access her system. This was not in itself unusual; she routinely noted casual hackers probing the defences of her system, but this recent activity was different. Normally, she could turn back the intruder having noted their identity, but all her efforts to back-trace had come to nothing. She logged off and sat back in her chair, then sat up very straight. The intruder was still there. The system still showed high-level activity, despite her having closed all active and background files.

Kate knew her system was impregnable and had devoted all her skill to ensuring this was the case, but the evidence of her own eyes could not be denied. Someone had not only gained access to her system but had managed to defeat the defences that she'd painstakingly installed over the years. She hugged her arms across her chest as icy tendrils of fear took hold and glanced nervously at the security control panel and the steady gleam from the row of tiny lights. She reached across to the telephone, just to hear another voice, the image of Dexter's solid frame fresh in her mind and then took her hand away, feeling suddenly foolish. The house's defences were formidable and her present nervousness was nothing more than an over-reaction to some teenage hacker who'd somehow got lucky and accidentally linked into her system in some way. She'd rather enjoy the challenge of locating the intruder and planning some form of retribution for his actions. She was still smiling at the prospect when the lights went out and the room was plunged into darkness.

CHAPTER 9

DONNA sighed. Dexter could be such a prat sometimes. She'd rung him straight away when she got in and he'd immediately started issuing orders. First thing tomorrow she was to meet him in Meols and take over a stakeout while he got some sleep. Donna had grumbled loud and long that she had her own case to be getting on with, but Dexter had over-ridden all her protests. When she recalled her harsh words she knew she'd been unfair. This sharing of duties was routine and Dexter had been about to settle down for a cold uncomfortable vigil that would last the entire night. He'd pointed this out to her, suggesting that if she cared to exchange duties he'd be only too pleased to relieve her in the morning, but Donna had not taken him up on the offer. Her own case was going nowhere and Dexter knew that. Despite a few trivial inconsistencies, all the hard evidence concerning the death of Julian Carter still pointed to suicide. Tragic, but no more than that. Perhaps Kate would turn something up. Donna set her alarm clock for six o'clock, wished Peg a good night and took herself off to bed.

The air drifting through the open bedroom window was the hot rancid breath of an impending storm. Eyes fixed on the glowing light of the digital clock, Kate felt for her wrist and found a steady beat, watching and waiting for the minute to click over. As she'd suspected, her pulse was racing, heart thumping in her chest like a kettledrum. Seeing the house plunged into darkness had sent her reeling out of the chair, arms waving wildly in an utter panic. When the back-up power system switched itself on a few moments later, the relief had been so immense that she'd staggered and almost fallen. Knowing the deep primitive terror of sudden darkness to be an irrational reaction was one thing; dealing with it calmly and sensibly was quite different. The fail-safe power supply, superior to most hospital operating theatre systems, could deal with any interruption in power, maintaining her security screens at full power until the main system kicked back in. Calm down, she muttered to herself, but without any certainty of being able to act on her own advice. Eventually, at some point in the long night, her over-active mind put up its hands and cried uncle. Enough was enough and Kate sank into a dream-ravaged sleep.

Marcus stood silently in the darkness, as still as a crouching tiger, waiting for his senses to adjust to their surroundings. Computer screens surrounded him; red lights flashing intermittently as their respective hard drives acted out instructions. The programme he'd introduced into Kate's system was still working away. In a few more hours all data would have been permanently removed. Marcus moved stealthily through the room, carefully avoiding chairs and other obstacles. His night vision was exceptional and his other senses were on full alert. Shining a tiny penlight on the worktops, he picked up and discarded several sheets of paper. He was moving away when a laminated card took his attention. He flicked it over and stiffened as the logo was revealed. Marcus stood very still, concentrating fiercely. He had a sudden premonition that the identity card he was holding symbolised a threat to his security and slipped it into his pocket.

Reaching the door, he stepped through into a wide corridor and stood very still, listening for any sound which threatened to disrupt the absolute silence. At last he heard what he'd been waiting for. A soft exhalation of breath and the creak of some inanimate object. A sleeper turning over in bed. Moving like a wraith in a misty forest, he moved silently along the corridor and stood outside a partially open door where a faint glimmer of light penetrated the darkness. He heard a faint rustle from inside the room and smiled, white teeth flashing in the darkness. He eased through the doorway and, by the light of a bedside clock radio, saw a prone figure lying on a single bed in the centre of the room.

Marcus stood right next to the sleeping figure. Silent and immobile. Waiting. This was the best moment for him; that brief interlude when the sleeping victim gradually became aware of his presence. He'd experienced it many times; this remnant of an animal instinct for self-preservation, but never failed to be stirred by it. The sleeping figure would pass from a state of utter repose to one of abject terror, all without any action being required on his part.

Kate's eyelids fluttered, her chest rising and falling, then her eyes flew open and she looked unerringly at Marcus and screamed. Exactly as he'd known she would. He reached towards her and slapped her face hard, turning on the bedside light with his other hand. Dressed all in black, his tanned face impassive, he stared at her until he saw her turn away. There was no necessity for him to speak. She had never seen him before, but the air of menace emanating from every pore had conveyed to her more effectively than mere words that something unspeakably evil had entered her life.

Donna awoke, eyes stinging and head thumping, with a vague feeling of dread seizing her chest. She sat bolt upright, impervious to the chill in the room, eyes darting towards the partly open door. The house was silent and the air still. Donna sank back on her pillow, unable to explain the terror that had gripped her without warning. She'd had these feelings before and the prognosis was not good. Every single time she'd experienced this terror-struck wakening from a previously untroubled sleep, it had meant bad news for somebody. Very bad news. Donna lay very still, eyes wide open. She knew there'd be no chance for any more sleep this night.

Kate stiffened as Marcus reached towards her but could not move. Powerless, she lay still and watched his hand touch her naked shoulder. A faint sob, almost inaudible, escaped her cracked lips as she felt the warmth of his fingers caressing her body.

'You know who I am.' The voice was cultured, velvet smooth and seductive. In any other circumstances she'd have found it compelling.

'You're Marcus Green.' Her voice was flat and impersonal. She was hardly aware that she'd spoken but saw a gleam of pleasure in his eyes as she said his name. The cool professional aspect of her mind recognised that small weakness for what it was: a desperate need for recognition and approval.

'You've been interfering. I can't allow that.' It was the absence of menace that made his calm voice so threatening. Like a rabbit transfixed by car headlights, she'd frozen, unable to flee or consider any means of defending herself. Marcus reached out his other hand and stripped the sheets from the bed, leaving her naked and still she did not, could not, move. He removed his outer clothing, laying each item carefully on the back of a chair. Kate's eyes widened and he saw her fear and laughed.

'You're not my type,' he said. Marcus ripped a strip of cotton from the sheet, effortlessly, as if tearing tissue paper. He raised her head from the pillow and, fashioning the strip of cotton into a gag, slipped it into her mouth and tied it off.

'I don't need you to speak,' he explained, his voice as gentle as a parent reading a bedtime story to a child. 'When I've finished here there'll be time enough to scream.' He reached out and pushed her over, just flipped her face down without any warning and she felt the pressure of his hands on her neck. 'Relax,' he cautioned as she arched her back upwards and she settled down again instantly, hating her own compliance but seemingly powerless to prevent it. When the pain came, her eyes filled with tears. When Marcus touched her again, a sudden unbearable pressure, she heard a sharp crack from somewhere high in her back and now the pain was intolerable. It lasted only for an instant, to be replaced by a numbness that was, in its own way, as bad as the pain.

Marcus hauled her over again without any sign of emotion. Almost as if she were a sack of flour in a warehouse, she thought, irrationally. She lay on her back, gazing at the ceiling and tasted the sharp coppery taste of blood in her mouth where she bitten her tongue.

'Are you comfortable?'

Kate nodded. The incongruous nature of the question, considering the circumstances in which it had been posed, struck her as funny and she gave a harsh bark of laughter, reduced to a dull grunt by the gag between her teeth.

'I've moved a couple of small bones,' Marcus said, his voice calming and melodic, 'At the top of your spine.'

Kate nodded, scarcely taking in what he was saying. Her head ached and she felt sick.

'They're very important, these little bones. When they slip out of alignment, they damage the area around them. Its all nerve endings that area of the spinal column and very well protected. Once the nerves are damaged, they can never be repaired. Do you understand me?'

Kate looked blankly back at him.

'You're paralysed now. From the neck down,' Marcus said, with a hint of a smile as he saw the effect of his words. 'You're listening to me now, aren't you?' He reached out and yanked one end of the gag, allowing it to slip away.

Kate drew a deep breath, but didn't speak. The urge to scream was very great but somehow she kept quiet. When she saw the faint flicker of disappointment in his eyes she knew her instincts had been correct. This was a man who was turned on by the sound of his victim's screams and she congratulated herself on having predicted this aspect of his character. His words meant nothing to her. Paralysis, like rape and torture, was a nameless fear. She'd known from the first moment she'd seen him in her room that death awaited her. She resolved that anything else that happened to her would mean nothing. She faced him, striving to keep calm even as the blood ran down her chin, and felt a glimmer of triumph. He'd expected tears, screams, the full range of emotions, but she'd given him nothing.

Marcus turned away, moving out of her range of vision and she heard the soft creak of a door opening. Teeth grinding together, Kate attempted to move her legs, even one finger, to disprove the awful truth of what Marcus had told her, but her efforts were in vain. She froze as a door slammed in a distant part of the house and then a few moments later Marcus returned. He was carrying a thick hessian sack, heavy enough to cause a tiny tremor in his forearms as he reached across the bed and laid the clanking sack on the floor. He switched on the light at the side of the bed and Kate saw him clearly for the first time. His features were slightly misaligned, the skin on his cheek perhaps a little tighter than it should have been, as if he'd received a severe facial wound at some time in the past, but there was no denying he was still the most handsome man she'd ever seen. His expression was almost benign as he sat on the side of the bed, watching her face carefully, probing for any weakness. Kate resolved to say and do nothing to give him the satisfaction he sought. She expected to die in this room, had been convinced of this ever since she'd seen him standing by her bed, but she could at least die with her self-respect intact.

Marcus pushed her roughly to one side, manoeuvring her body roughly as he raised her buttocks and slipped a flat slender object between her and the mattress. Raising his other hand he showed her the blade and saw in her eyes a new fear. Moving his hand away for a moment, but keeping his eyes fixed on Kate, he smiled. When he raised his hand into view again, the razor was red with flecks of blood along its entire length. 'Now you believe me,' he said, 'I could carve you up like a joint of beef and you'd never even know it.'

Kate stared back at him, determined to blank from her mind everything he said or did to her. If she could die without giving him the satisfaction of seeing her terror, she'd have achieved a victory of sorts. It wasn't much, but it was all she had and she clenched her teeth with fresh determination.

Marcus smiled again, almost with approval and Kate knew he'd seen her purpose for what it was. A gesture. No more. He turned away again, out of her sight, as even the restricted movement in her neck was too painful to attempt any unnecessary movement. Her head was splitting, but she kept her eyes fixed on a spot on the ceiling. When Marcus spoke again, she closed her eyes, blotting him out.

'Can you smell that?' Kate gave an involuntary nod. She'd been conscious of the smell for several seconds at least.

'Roasting meat,' Marcus said calmly. 'You're helping me try out a recent purchase. I'm a great believer in road-testing new products. Like the griddle you're lying on. It's on the lowest setting; nothing dramatic, just a really slow cook-through. Very healthy, apparently, the way the grooves channel the molten fat away.' Kate began to cry, tears flowing freely, but she made no sound at all. Not even when Marcus showed her the searing flame of a butane gas blowlamp. He moved out of her sight once more as Kate sobbed quietly. She saw the ridge of muscle across his shoulders bunch as he made a sudden movement, followed by a crunching sound, as he brought his hand back into her field of vision and revealed the blackened and scorched stump of a toe he'd snipped from her foot. Kate had felt nothing which was far worse than any pain. The smell of burning flesh was stronger now and she sensed rather than felt the exact moment one of her internal organs ruptured and howled in anguish, all her previous intentions forgotten.

Marcus grinned at her. 'Ready to talk yet?' He reached into his pocket and produced the identity card he had taken from Kate's desk. 'Why don't we start with this? Anything you can tell me about this person?' He held the card up. Kate looked at the face of Donna's colleague, Andy, whom she knew by name but had never met, and began to laugh. The laughter was irrational but genuine. Marcus looked at her searchingly and replaced the card in his pocket.

He bent, momentarily out of Kate's line of vision, before holding up an electric drill and switching it on. The noise was appallingly loud when he held it to Kate's ear. 'Find this funny, do you? Not hurting yet? Why don't we concentrate on the parts you can feel?' Kate screamed and carried on screaming until her ravaged throat could produce nothing more than a raw croak. Marcus was impervious to her agony, smiling indulgently as he gently re-positioned her head, watching her face impassively as the drill crunched repeatedly through bone and sinew. His concentration was total. It had to be, as he knew his pleasure would be brief. After each withdrawal of the drill bit he asked the same question, but Kate continued to shake her head. When her struggles began to lessen Marcus gave a tiny hint of a sigh and placed the drill on the floor. He rose to his feet, his naked body glistening with sweat and took a small screwdriver from the bedside table. He showed it to Kate; an ordinary electrical screwdriver that she'd used to rewire a plug on the bedside lamp and not bothered to replace in her office toolbox. She looked at him with a sudden premonition that her agony would soon be over. Marcus bent and carefully placed the point of the screwdriver below the area of her vision. Most of her body was numb, completely without feeling, but her ravaged face was throbbing with a pain she could never have imagined. Marcus pressed down ever so slightly and Kate felt the tiny blade enter the skin of her neck. She gasped and he smiled down at her adding an almost infinitesimal inward pressure until his sensitive fingers confirmed that the tip of the screwdriver was touching the rubbery sheath that was Kate's carotid artery. A final touch caused a tiny rupture and systolic pressure forced the blood to spurt out in a fine mist. Marcus positioned himself directly in its path. Hot, coppery in taste, the lifeblood of a living breathing person striking his naked body was a pleasure to be savoured. Kate moaned softly, her eyes wide with shock, and Marcus shuffled closer as the spraying blood flow began to lessen. He took hold of Kate's hair, raising her head and grasping the shaft of the screwdriver firmly in his right hand. Looking into Kate's eyes Marcus ripped the tiny blade from side to side across the exposed taut skin, rupturing flesh and cartilage with brutal efficiency and prompting a deluge of blood from severed blood vessels. Kate tried to scream but her vocal chords were savaged and useless. Blood poured down her exposed windpipe, filling her lungs within seconds. Now there was panic etched across her ravaged features and Marcus took her hand in his own, holding her as gently as if she were a new-born baby while she drowned in her own blood. Tracheal spray exhaled as tiny flecks of blood and mucus added to the pools that were already starting to congeal on the floor.

When the moment came, Marcus held Kate's hand and planted a tender kiss on her forehead as he watched the spark in her eyes flicker for the last time, then fade and die. This was what spurred him on. No junky ever found such a rush from his daily fix as he did from holding the hand of a fellow human at the moment of their death. He sighed, genuinely regretful that she'd gone, but this was not the time to fully savour the experience. He still had to shower before dressing and packing his things away. The house would have to burn now, but even as a blackened smoking ruin he'd remember it with fondness. Not for what it was, mere bricks and mortar, but as a memorial to one woman's belief that her house would protect her. Marcus knew that could never be. His power was such that nothing could stand in his way. Now he'd removed one small obstacle it was time to move on. Many more would die before he accomplished what he'd set out to do.

CHAPTER 10

DONNA tiptoed her way to the kitchen, desperately trying not to wake Peg. Ensuring Peg got her full eight hours was way down the list; this was self-interest, pure and simple. It was bad enough climbing out of a warm bed at this unearthly hour without having to put away the huge meal Peg would insist on preparing.

Dexter had been pretty insistent last night. Getting up at six o'clock would allow her a whole hour to get washed, dressed and out of the door, ready to take over from him at seven. If only she'd had a decent night's sleep. The premonition of impending disaster that had woken her in the small hours looked pretty stupid this morning, but the damage had been done. Donna felt wretched and the clothes she'd just put on didn't help one bit. Major league snooping and all the nefarious activities that involved had meant only one thing. Get into the black gear. Donna knew black was supposed to be chic and sexy but that didn't seem to apply in her case. She looked terrible, like a skinny-legged street waif on smack. But it had to be done, so Donna had got out the ribbed leggings, tight polo-neck sweater and ski-hat that she kept buried at the back of the wardrobe. Slipping on a comfortable pair of black pumps, her attention was caught by a reflection in the glass door and she had to go over to the mirror to check that she didn't really look as bad as the quick glimpse suggested. The truth was even worse. Deathly pale with dangerously sharp cheekbones, Donna even managed to scare herself. The world's skinniest Ninja warrior. Pulling her cap down over her ears, she closed the front door silently behind herself, vowing to tell anyone who saw her that she was on the way to an audition for the Rocky Horror Show.

The car started first time but it was all downhill from then on. As Donna flicked the switch, the headlights flickered and died. Both of them.

'Oh shit,' Donna exclaimed, 'Not today of all days.' Having finally got round to replacing the dodgy taillight, this was the last straw. Torn between the risk of driving five miles in the dark with no headlights or leaving Dexter in the lurch was a no-brainer. Breaking the law was one thing; being late when Dexter had issued a three line whip was quite another. Donna pressed on, glancing in her rear view mirror every ten seconds for any signs of a police car.

Dexter was slumped on the back seat; his head only barely visible as Donna drew up behind his car. The streetlights were barely adequate and Dexter had parked up in the deepest shadow in the entire road. It was just about getting light and Donna shivered as she climbed out of her own car and stood on the pavement next to Dexter. He motioned towards the front passenger seat and Donna gratefully climbed in.

'God,' she complained, 'It's freezing in here.'

'What's with the headlights?' Dexter snapped, ignoring her complaints completely.

'Just went on the blink,' Donna explained.

'When?'

93

'Oh, just before I turned in,' Donna gabbled, not daring to confess she'd driven all the way here without lights, 'They were fine when I set off, but started flickering just now.'

Dexter grunted. 'Why don't you get yourself a decent motor? You can't expect to do this job with an old banger like that thing there.' He jerked his head in the direction of Donna's wretched car. Donna said nothing. What was there to say? She could plead poverty, had done so in the past when this same subject had cropped up, but that wouldn't wash with Dexter. He'd tell her what he'd told her last time: that she should manage her finances better before offering to lend her the money to buy a decent motor. That would have been a step too far. Donna couldn't imagine anything worse than being in debt to Dexter. Every time she splashed out on as much as a Mars bar, he'd take the opportunity to remind her of her profligate spending habits.

'Not much use for this job, is it? The bloody old wreck belongs in the scrap yard.' Dexter was still grumbling away, but Donna wasn't really listening. She'd just realised her car acting up meant that Dexter would be sending her back home any minute and the chance to grab an extra hours sleep was an enticing prospect.

'Give it another five minutes or so, be light enough to drive soon. I'll take your motor to the garage round the corner. I know them there and I'll leave the mechanic a note explaining the problem. A fuse packed in perhaps, or a twisted wire somewhere.' Dexter stretched out his arms, cupping his hand over his mouth to stifle a yawn,' I'll ring for a taxi to pick me up from the garage to get me home.'

'What about my car? When will I get it back?'

Dexter looked surprised. 'You can call round for me when you finish here. Give me a lift to the office. I'll need a few hours sleep, not much been happening around here for the past eight hours. You can borrow my motor.'

'Eh?' Donna was genuinely shocked; she'd never considered this possibility.

Dexter reached for the door handle, then caught sight of Donna's expression and stopped abruptly, 'Don't pull your bloody face. What can you do with no car? Give it three or four hours and if you get no joy, forget it and clear off. Be all right will you, on your own?'

'We're in Meols, not sodding Baghdad.' Donna's indignation was so obvious that Dexter chuckled. 'What's so important about this case that it needs twenty-four hour attention?' Donna continued truculently.

'Hardly twenty-four hours,' Dexter replied, 'One night plus two or three hours this morning, that's all. Don't start giving me grief, Donna. I've been here all night, remember? If you could be bothered to stay awake during meetings you'd perhaps remember me saying I had information from a good source that our pal Dennis is due to make a move. The exact words were sparrow fart on Wednesday. About now, in fact.'

'So, why have you been here all night?'

Dexter sighed. 'I've been at this game too long to take any chances. No bloody use rolling up at half-past five if he went out at quarter past.'

94

Donna nodded. Typical Dexter to take a belt and braces approach. Dennis Reece was an old friend of R and D security. This would be the third time he'd been the subject of an investigation. Each case had been referred by Regal Insurance, certain that Reece had submitted a fraudulent claim. The investigation of a dubious robbery at his home, involving a massive claim for missing property had fizzled out for lack of evidence. Dexter had remarked at the time that the thieves would have needed a removal lorry to take away their booty, yet there had been no sightings of anything larger than a family saloon in the area. Reece had moved on to motor claims, suffering the misfortune of having three high value cars stolen from outside his house in the past three months. Even on Merseyside that was stretching the boundaries of credulity. None of the vehicles had ever been traced and Dexter was firmly of the opinion that they were sitting in a lock-up garage somewhere, getting a fresh paint job and different plates, everything needed for a new identity. One of Dexter's legion of informants, a former associate of Reece, had confirmed the scam was about to move on to the next stage; shipping the freshly modified cars abroad complete with new identities where they would command a premium price. The theft of prestige cars for export was nothing new, but Dennis Reece wanted it all: stealing his own property and claiming the loss on his insurance.

'There's a hands-free mounting for your mobile under the dashboard,' Dexter said, opening the back door. 'All mod cons. Stick your 'phone in the cradle and I'll see you in a couple of hours or so. Give me your keys and I'll shift your motor before anybody thinks it's been dumped there.' He climbed out of the car and stood next to Donna, tapping on the window. Donna clicked the button and the glass slid smoothly down. She passed him her keys and he took them, glaring at the Homer Simpson key fob.

'Go on, then,' Dexter ordered. 'Put your 'phone where it's supposed to go.'

'I'll do it in a minute,' Donna snapped, 'It's in my pocket and I'll have to take my coat off first.'

'See you do,' Dexter grunted, turning away and climbing into Donna's car. A few moment's later Donna heard the characteristic clatter of the engine and Dexter pulled past her and drove slowly away.

Dexter had chosen a decent vantage point alongside a wheelie-bin with the front gate of Dennis Reece in full view. Donna would have expected nothing else. She could also just about see the wing-mirror of his car. Specks of dust floating in the glare of sunlight coming through the windscreen bobbed and fluttered like demented dancers at an Ibiza rave. Donna tried her best to keep a low profile, but was uncomfortably aware that being alone in the car she was more liable to attract the suspicion of a nosy neighbour. Dexter had taught her about observations. Two people in a car can be chatting away for an hour without attracting any particular attention. Like the two of us, he'd said at the time. People will think you're my daughter and I'm giving you the benefit of my fatherly advice. Don't kid yourself, Donna had replied, they'll think I'm your bit of stuff and you're a dirty old sod. Right now, Donna was sitting in the passenger seat, as if waiting for someone. One of the tricks of the Investigator's trade. For some reason, a lone passenger was regarded with less suspicion than a lone driver. If she had to follow the subject Donna could easily slide over the central console and be behind the wheel in moments.

Anyone leaving the house would have to pass through Donna's line of vision. She'd been sitting here for next to no time and already wanted a pee. The curse of the O'Prey genes. The other team members kept an empty plastic bottle in the car for situations such as this. Donna had not yet found an equivalent system applicable to a female that wasn't hazardous or mildly obscene. Hoping to distract herself, she reached down and picked up the brown paper bag she'd brought from home, withdrew a big chunk of chocolate cake and took an enormous bite. A door slammed and suddenly any bladder problems were forgotten as Dennis Reece came into sight. Donna glanced at the small photograph taped below the dashboard and confirmed his identity. Difficult to mistake him for anyone else. Mid-thirties, skinny build, with a lean vulpine face, protruding yellow teeth and greased-back hair. *Nice!* Reece moved away, out of her line of sight and Donna quickly checked that Dexter's keys were in the ignition. She waited for the sound of his car door opening and closing before carefully sliding herself over the gear-stick and starting the engine. Dexter's car purred into life like a contented moggie. The contrast with her own rattlebox couldn't have been more pronounced. To extend the feline metaphor, this was a pampered Siamese, while her own car was at best a dustbin scavenger, complete with fleas. Donna followed at a discreet distance, keeping the prescribed three cars between herself and the target. Reece turned right at the end of his road, heading for Hoylake and Donna nipped out in front of the next-but-one car, taking advantage of a slight gap. Reece's Volvo was twenty yards ahead, driving just under the limit. Donna hung back a little more to allow the driver she'd previously cut up to overtake. He glared as he went past, but she pretended not to notice. Market Street, even at this early hour, was busy, as usual with progress being of the stop and start variety. At the King's Gap roundabout Donna had been expecting the Volvo to go straight across. Instead, it turned left; heading for the random collection of prefabricated garages and glorified sheds that called itself an industrial estate. Which meant having to cross the railway line. *Shit*, Donna thought, slowing drastically. *All I need is for the barriers to be down and I'll be right behind him. A bit too bloody obvious.* Luck favoured the righteous. The barriers were raised and Donna followed the Volvo at a discreet distance across the railway crossing and into the heart of the industrial estate. Reece slowed and turned left by a 'phone box as Donna coasted almost to a stop fifty yards back. This place was a bit of a bastard for keeping track as the narrow roads all interconnected with one another. Donna rolled as far as the next corner and saw the Volvo carry straight on. From her local knowledge, she knew that this strip of road led only to the car park of the local rugby club and was otherwise a dead end. Donna parked Dexter's car on one of the side roads, locked it, carefully fitted the steering lock and walked into the cinder car park. The Volvo was parked behind the clubhouse. Empty.

Donna ran to the left where a narrow path led to a Bowling Green and the railway line. There was no one in sight. Starting to panic, she ran back in the other direction. The playing fields were deserted, but Donna caught sight of two distant figures on a grass path leading to a secondary car park. The rough path ended at the entrance to the next field where Donna came to a shuddering halt. There was nobody in sight. Not for the first time, she wished she'd borrowed a dog. Dog walkers went anywhere and were never challenged. As a snowy white cloud scudded rapidly right to left, momentarily obscuring the sun before passing on its way. Donna saw a movement at the far side of the field. Dennis Reece and another man were standing by a red panel van and as Donna watched, both doors opened and the two men disappeared from her view.

Donna set off at a gallop. By the time she reached Dexter's car and had clambered inside her heaving chest was brushing the steering wheel with each intake of breath. She twisted the ignition key and was relieved to hear the engine burst into life. Snatching another huge mouthful of cake, she tramped on the accelerator and arrowed through the narrow gap between two parked lorries in the direction of the car park recently vacated by Dennis Reece and his unknown companion.

'Shit!' Donna cursed as she caught a glimpse of the red panel van in the far distance. Her bloody phone was ringing.

In her pocket.

Donna twisted and turned while still travelling at top speed through the narrow roads of the industrial estate, but couldn't reach the 'phone. She should have done as Dexter had suggested – make that ordered – and stuck the bloody thing in the hands-free gadget when she'd had the chance. Donna slowed down, contorting her body in an ungainly and distinctly painful manner before finally managing to retrieve her mobile from the depths of her pocket. The law stated she should stop the car, switch off the ignition and actually remove herself from behind the wheel before using her mobile, but there was no chance of that. Compared to driving five miles in the pitch dark with no lights showing, using her mobile while still behind the wheel was a pretty trivial offence. Flicking the cover off the 'phone and simultaneously stamping on the accelerator, Donna clamped the earpiece tight to the side of her head while concentrating on renewing contact with the red van.

'Hello?'

'Donna?'

Dexter. Who else?

'Where are you?'

'Hoylake. Following Dennis Reece.'

'You sound as if you're underwater. Donna brushed crumbs from her jacket, frantically trying to swallow the huge chunk of chocolate sponge. God, he picked his moments. How did he know to ring the moment she'd crammed half a chocolate cake into her mouth? Very nearly half, anyway.

'Sorry,' she managed at last, 'I was just eating something.'

Dexter said nothing, his silence conveying annoyance more accurately than mere words. When he spoke again, he was all business.

'Right. Abort right now. Get back here and pick me up. Rapid.'

'I'm in pursuit. I can bloody well see him,' Donna snapped, swerving to avoid a cyclist. *Bloody hell, that was close.* 'Any minute now and I'll have him.'

'Forget him,' Dexter bellowed in her ear. 'Just get here right now. I've just had a call from the local law in Chester. Kate's place burnt to the ground last night. They've found a body.'

CHAPTER 11

THE uniformed policeman barring the way puffed out his cheeks, playing a sort of tune as he exhaled. Donna couldn't place the melody. Dexter walked straight up to him, face to face, his expression a sombre mask.

'The name's Dexter. Who's your Guvnor? Is he here?'

'DS Lawton. Back there, sir.' The officer straightened his back as he snapped out the reply. Donna knew Dexter had never worked in this Division, but even here the name alone was sufficient to gain respect. He may have been retired, but that old magic was still very much in evidence.

'OK to go in?' Dexter asked, raising the coloured tape and slipping under it without waiting for a reply. Donna smiled at the officer, marvelling once again at the effect Dexter's presence had on anyone in uniform, and made certain she followed close behind Dexter to forestall any objection. None was forthcoming.

The house was a burnt-out shell, gaping holes where there used to be windows and a black smoking beam projecting through the main entrance door. Dexter stood and looked at the scene of devastation, shaking his head. Donna caught up with him, standing a pace back, waiting for Dexter to speak.

'What a bloody mess. Looks like Kate's luck finally ran out.'

Donna flinched. She'd been hoping against hope that when the time finally arrived there'd be some evidence to sustain her belief that Kate could have somehow survived this disaster. That hope had now deserted her.

'Stay here,' Dexter ordered, 'May not be pretty.' He stalked off, leaving Donna standing alone. She felt the twin pangs of rejection and deprivation. Dexter was shutting her out and Kate had surely perished in the fire. Donna would not claim to have known Kate at all; she'd barely scratched the surface of the most secretive, paranoid and private person she'd ever met, but she still felt a deep sense of loss.

The smoke swirled away for a moment and Donna saw Dexter and another man standing outside the shell of the building. Dexter was pointing upwards, shaking his head. Donna had taken a dozen steps before she even realised she was defying Dexter's instruction, but she carried on and had reached the two men before either became aware of her presence.

'Bastard!' Dexter's voice was a raw scrape, pain and desperation forcing the words out between cracked lips. Donna followed the direction of his gaze and flinched. A body hung high up on the blackened wall, almost as if mocking the crucifixion scene in a biblical epic. A gasp escaped Donna's lips and Dexter whipped round, grabbing her arm and pushing her roughly away from the scene.

'I fucking told you,' Dexter snapped, his voice a savage rasp of anger.

'Sorry,' Donna gasped. His grip was vice-like.

Dexter released her arm and shook his head. 'Sorry, didn't mean to hurt you,' His voice was softer now, but the angry expression was still visible on his face.

'What happened? Is Kate…?'

Dexter nodded. 'Yes. To save you asking, the only thing that's certain at this stage is that it was no accident. Not that I ever thought it would be.'

The other man, dressed in a white zip-up jump suit, joined them, looking quizzically at Dexter.

'Donna O'Prey. Works with me,' Dexter said, 'Donna, This is DS Lawton. He's SOCO, so if he tells you to do anything, just bloody do it. It's his scene and nobody touches anything without his say-so. Got it?'

Donna nodded, noting that Dexter had described her as working with him, not for him which would have been far more accurate, but typical of Dexter to be so thoughtful. One of the reasons his old squad would have run through brick walls for him if he'd asked it of them. She was still in shock but determinedly tried to follow Dexter's lead and carry on as if finding the body of a woman she'd known and spoken to only a few hours previously was simply routine. Dexter had far more experience in acting in a detached manner than she had, but if she ever aspired to Dexter's professional standards it was something she'd have to learn. Starting right here, right now.

'What's that suit made from?' Donna asked DS Lawton 'Looks like paper.' *What a bloody stupid question.*

Ds Lawton gave her a look which suggested he thought it was a bloody stupid question too. Obviously deciding Donna was a retard; he switched his attention back to Dexter. 'I'll have to log you in if you want to go inside. Sorry.'

Dexter shook his head. 'No need. Just keep me up to speed, if you can. I was a friend you know.' He indicated the shell of the building.

DS Lawton nodded. 'An old mate of yours should be here any time. DS Abbott.'

Dexter looked startled. 'How's that, then? Bit off his patch this, isn't it?'

'Yeah, but he's on secondment for a month. Seeing a bit of real policing, I reckon. Not like that cushy billet he's used to.'

Dexter managed a faint grin. There was nothing cushy about Liverpool 8 and both men knew it. Even Donna knew that Toxteth was the toughest area of a tough city and Abbott's home base, Dexter's old stamping ground, was smack bang in the middle of the war zone. Dexter took Donna's arm, much more gently now, and walked her away through the main gate. He nodded to the uniformed officer and was back at the car before he released his grasp.

'What happened?' Donna had a thousand questions, but that would do for openers.

Dexter sighed. 'Someone got to her at last. She'd half expected it for years. One of the reasons she was such a mess.'

'No, I meant...'

Dexter's expression changed. 'Oh. You mean how?'

Donna nodded. She wanted to know, but didn't want to know. All at the same time.

'Tortured. Badly, I'd say from what Lawton and his lads have found so far. Made a right mess of her, even allowing for what the fire did afterwards, that much is clear. Then leaving her like that.' His voice tailed away. He took a deep breath. 'The bastard nailed her to the fucking wall. Left her hanging up there like that and then torched the place.'

'Any idea..?'

'Who did it? No. Not yet.'

'Could it have been Marcus?'

Dexter took a step back, his face twisting with anger. 'For fuck's sake, Donna. Don't start that shit again. Not today. Kate had a lot of enemies. Obvious in her line of work. Could have been one of a hundred.'

'The fire, though,' Donna persisted, 'It's his thing, isn't it?'

'Him and a good few others. It's not unknown to torch a crime scene, you know. Muddies the water no end, if you'll forgive the mixed metaphors. There's a lot of sick bastards out there and Kate's been involved in one way or another with most of them.'

'Do you know somebody called Sheehan?'

'Sheehan?' Dexter looked baffled.

'I don't mean that he would be involved in this. Kate said we should look into him, that's all.'

Dexter shook his head. 'Fat Stan Sheehan? Why?'

Donna looked puzzled. 'I don't know. Just something Kate said. We should talk to a man named Sheehan.'

Dexter grunted. Donna saw his expression and flinched, but suspected his frown masked a quiet pleasure. Dexter had never subscribed to the sit still, say nothing and never volunteer culture. He liked input. Even at the cost of Donna shooting her mouth off and spouting rubbish on a regular basis. Better one spark of original thought than nothing at all.

'Listen to me.' Dexter pushed his face down so he was at Donna's eye level. 'The Sheehan brothers are hard bastards. Well out of your league. Mine too. Mainstream drug barons. At least they used to be until they met up with someone even nastier. Someone who gave them a good spanking. Even if they were half-dead, I'd not be going anywhere near the Sheehan boys if I could help it. What does any of this have to do with the suicide of Julian Carter?'

Donna swallowed. 'I don't know,' she admitted, 'Kate just said we should….'

'Talk to the Sheehan brothers,' Dexter interjected. 'Yeah, so you said. What you didn't tell me was why. One thing's for sure. Kate won't be telling us, will she?'

Donna shook her head. 'No.'

'Right then. You get back. Go and get a decent breakfast inside you and I'll see you later.' He held up a hand to forestall her anticipated question. 'The minute I hear anything about what happened here, I'll tell you. I know you never felt less like eating, but it's what you need right now. Trust me.'

'What about you?'

'I'll manage. If Abbot's on the way I'll sort a lift one way or another. You get off.'

Donna nodded. 'Be nice to see Abbott,' she offered, trying to build bridges.

'Yeah. With any luck he'll be back up to DI any day now.'

Donna looked surprised. 'Thought he'd been put back to sergeant again. Didn't you say a new DI had transferred in?'

Dexter grinned wolfishly. 'Yeah. Some sheep-shagger from the Staffordshire Moorlands. What would he know about inner city policing? He lasted three months before he asked to be transferred back to Leek. Wherever that is.'

Donna nodded, understanding from Dexter's air of satisfaction that Abbott and the rest of Dexter's old squad would have made the new man's settling-in process as difficult as possible and had apparently got their own way by forcing their new DI out of the job. Abbott would have been the popular choice: an old-style copper in Dexter's image with a good track record and an enviable list of contacts, mostly of the type who frequented betting shops and drinking clubs. Rumour factories, but pure gold to a working copper keen on getting results.

Donna opened the car door. Dexter touched her shoulder. 'You feeling ok? Fit enough to drive?'

Donna nodded. 'Thanks for asking.'

'Best to be sure. That's my motor you're driving.' Dexter walked away, hands thrust deep in his jacket pockets. Donna allowed herself the luxury of a faint smile, the first since she'd received the news about the fire. She knew Dexter was trying to act as normally as possible and that it was all for her benefit, but Kate's death had been a shock she wouldn't get over in a hurry.

Marcus watched from the balcony as the two figures below him leapt and darted in turn. He'd never played the game of squash, but saw immediately that both players possessed considerable ability. One fair, one dark, but otherwise rather similar. Lean and agile, moving with the easy grace of natural athletes. A rally ended and the players turned to each other, laughing, the dark-haired man leaning on the side wall for support. Marcus concentrated on the other man whose photograph on the laminated card propped up on the ledge in front of him failed to do him justice. He was even more handsome in the flesh. A tap on the door immediately below Marcus indicated that the next pair were waiting to use the court and the players collected their bags from below the tin at the front of the court. A quick shared glance revealed a degree of intimacy that confirmed the early impression Marcus had already formed. He smiled. A gay man would be easy to entrap and once he had him in his power Marcus knew he would find the truth about the enquiries that were evidently being made about himself.

Donna studied her notes with mounting irritation. On the way back from Chester she'd decided against going home for breakfast. Food, especially a breakfast cooked by Peg, swimming in grease and of Desperate Dan proportions, held no appeal at all. Quite why she'd headed for the office and settled down at her desk she couldn't have explained. Peace and quiet, perhaps. Andy had left a note in her in-tray to say he'd be out for most of the day and she'd managed to avoid meeting Roper or his sister in the corridor. Her notes confirmed the progress she'd made so far.

Zero.

On an impulse, Donna powered up the computer she hardly ever used and checked for e-mails. In amongst the usual offers of pornographic material and easy loans, was a message from Kate. Donna swallowed. Peg would have called this a message from beyond the grave. The melodramatic thought made her pause for a moment as she double clicked on the message and saw a full page of text.

'Hi Donna. I dug this out not long after you left and reckoned you'd want to get straight onto it. No sense in waiting until I see you next.' Donna stopped reading, blinking away a tear. It seemed an age before she moved her gaze back to the screen.

'I'll be looking into any sudden deaths, like I said,' the message continued, 'but thought you'd like to see this. I can't imagine you having the resources to get a list of the jurors in the trial of Marcus Green, especially with a fussy bastard like Dexter making you go through official channels, but rest assured, Auntie Kate is on the case. List of jurors all present and correct − see attachment.' Donna blinked her eyes rapidly. She could envisage Kate tapping out this message last night, unaware of the horror that awaited her. She looked back at the screen and continued to read.

'Thinking ten steps ahead, literally, one thing occurs to me: if, and it's a big if, there's anything at all in this coincidence of two sudden deaths linked by the fact that each victim had a parent who was once on a jury; why aren't the parents the victims? Why pick on their kids? The suggestion I came up with would only make sense to a pure sociopath. Marcus Green, for example. If we look at it from his point of view, he was locked up at, what was it, thirteen, fourteen? In a way, his mother suffered the loss of her son. In his distorted mind, that could suggest wreaking vengeance on the jurors who wrongly convicted him through their children. I've not forgotten that Marcus had almost certainly been responsible for the death of his father and baby sister and would later kill his own mother, but his mind works in a different way to the rest of us. Anyway, I'm rambling on here, too knackered to think straight, but if he is targeting the children, think what he's achieving by choosing such methods. Certainly he'd want the parent to feel the loss of a child, but in the worst way imaginable. These people thought they knew their kids and a death like suicide, for example, would come as a shattering blow. They'd blame themselves. How could a normal well-adjusted kid kill himself? Could they have prevented it? Same goes for a drug overdose if the parents had no idea their son was a drug user. See what I mean? It's worse than losing a child through a motor accident, for instance. That extra burden of self-blame. I'll keep digging; see if I can find another link. Safe to say that if another of these jurors turns out to have lost a son or daughter in similar circumstances; then any thought of coincidence goes out of the window. As you probably know by now, coincidence is a concept with which I've never been entirely comfortable. Leave it with me. Too tired to carry on tonight, but first thing tomorrow, I'll be back at my desk slaving away for you. By the way, you left your identity card behind when you left. Obviously you haven't been flashing it around much as the photo doesn't really do you justice. Even on your best day you never looked this good.

Alas, nothing on Marcus Green at all. No records, nothing. Officially, he's dead, but that's about all the information I could find. Which is pretty significant for devious sods like you and I. Maybe he's been a bit too clever this time. Even looking in places I looked at last time you asked me to investigate him was no use. Any records that were there then have been wiped. Pretty good going for someone who's supposed to be dead, wouldn't you say? I can't imagine anyone else having any interest in removing all traces of Marcus.

One more thing, I mentioned a man named Sheehan. Dexter will know of him. He's a nasty piece of work. Used to run all the drugs in the Northwest until he suddenly retired and went back to Ireland. Men like Sheehan don't scare easily. I've hacked into a few dodgy sites and the word is out that a young Englishman took over Sheehan's empire. A complete unknown, but a hard lad, ruthless and cruel. The reference to cruelty caught my eye. Could it be Marcus? Who knows? Ask Dexter and see what he says. It's not a job for you, Donna. Not Sheehan. Way out of your league, but Dexter might fancy following it up. Like I said, mention it to him.

I'll get off now, screen getting blurred. Too long without sleep and I still haven't found the cheeky toe-rag who's trying to hack into my system. I'll have one more try and then call it a night. Ring me first if you're coming over.'

Donna sat back. No idle chatter, no best wishes or farewells, but every word spoke volumes. This was Kate's last message. Ever. Donna felt fresh tears on her cheek but didn't even try to brush them away. She clicked on the blue text indicating an attachment and a fresh page consisting of twelve names filled the screen. Twelve names. The jurors in the trial of Marcus Green.

Donna took a deep breath. This was gold. Even allowing for the tragic circumstances under which she was reading Kate's message, Donna felt a deep sense of vindication and gratitude for Kate's efforts on her behalf. She even half-smiled when Martha put her blue-rinsed head round the door, scowled and went away again, her expression threatening to strike Donna down on the spot. Donna thought through a list of possible transgressions, all without success, but breathing was enough of a crime when Roper's sister was in hypercritical mode.

She glanced around the confines of the tiny office. She'd seen a TV documentary a while ago about prison riots. The presenters talked a lot about prison over-crowding, describing the tiny cells as reminiscent of something out of the pages of Dickens. Donna had laughed out loud as her office was a good two feet smaller all round than the cells depicted in the programme and she had to share it with her equally messy and disorganised colleague, Andy.

Kate's reference to an identity card had baffled her, but Donna had a sudden idea. She pushed papers around on Andy's side of the desk and gave a squeak of triumph as a laminated card came into view. Flipping it over, her own face stared back at her. Donna immediately understood Kate's message. If her card was still here, that could only mean she'd been walking around with Andy's identity card in her pocket.

The slam of a door at the far end of the corridor made Donna jump. She stretched, pushing herself away from the desk and stood up. Dexter's face appeared in the doorway. He looked surprised to see her.

'What's this? Turned into a workaholic the minute my back's turned?'

Donna ignored the sarcasm and pointed to her computer screen. Dexter walked in, his bulk filling the tiny office, and peered at the words on the screen.

'What's this?'

'An e-mail. From Kate.'

Dexter frowned. 'When did you get this?'

'Just now. She sent it last night. You don't have to be online to receive e-mail, you know. A message stays in the system until you open it.'

'I know that,' Dexter snapped. Donna looked at him askance. She doubted it. Dexter was the ultimate Luddite.

'It's a list.'

'I can bloody well see that,' Dexter snapped, then took a step closer, squinting at the names on the screen. 'Is this what I think it is?'

'The jurors,' Donna said, 'There's more. A message from Kate.' She leant forward and clicked her mouse twice. The printer by Dexter's elbow clattered into life and they both watched in silence as a sheet of paper slowly appeared in the out-tray. Donna picked it up, shook it twice to dry the ink, and handed it to Dexter. He read it in silence, but if Donna had expected any sign of pleasure on his face she was disappointed.

'What's all this about?'

Donna blinked.

'I see you got Kate roped into your bloody crusade.' Dexter's face reddened. 'I told you to concentrate on the case you've been given. A suicide. Find some answers for the family. That's what they asked for, nothing more. Simple, I'd have thought. Even for you, but, oh no. You have to see the hand of some dead psycho in everything that comes your way. Bad enough to waste your own time, make that the firm's time, but you even involved Kate in your nonsense.'

'It's not nonsense. Kate agreed with me that there was something not right here. Two sudden deaths, both victims having a parent who'd served on the same jury.'

'It's coincidence. Nothing more. No evidence of foul play in either case.'

Donna stood up, her anger making her bold. 'You're a fine one to lecture me. You've always told me to look further than the obvious. Never ignore a coincidence. Have you forgotten that?'

Dexter's expression softened. 'No. But the way you're continually suggesting Marcus Green's involvement in some unspecified series of crimes is too big a jump. He's dead for a start.'

Donna was almost beside herself with rage now, stuttering in her haste to get the words out. 'He's not dead. I should bloody well know. He tried to kill me.'

Dexter sighed. 'Officially, Marcus Green is dead. Died in a fire at his house. Him and his mother. Identified by items such as a distinctive watch and other property. How do you expect anyone to take you seriously if you're flying in the face of facts?'

'That's not right. I saw him at the cabin. The cabin where he tried to kill me.'

'I know that. I believe you. But even so, except for me and you, it's not been given a lot of credence. Not exactly surprising. You were not the most reliable informant at the time. Babbling like a bloody idiot. A virtual basket case.'

Donna flinched. There was more than an element of truth in Dexter's harsh comments. Dexter wandered off into the corridor. Donna sat on the edge of a metal table and looked out of the window, a myriad thoughts battling for supremacy in her head. She thumped the table in frustration.

Dexter re-appeared in the doorway. 'You all right?'

Donna nodded. Dexter walked towards her. 'Don't suppose you want to tell me why you left your identity card behind? Burnt to a crisp now.'

Donna shook her head, rummaging in the pocket of her jeans and producing her identity card. 'No idea what that's about. I've got my card here.' Dexter glanced at it and shook his head but showed no inclination to pursue the matter further. Donna would have struggled to explain how she'd managed to be carrying Andy's card yesterday, plus she would hate to drop Andy in it by revealing he'd left the office without his identity card. She decided to change the subject.

'It wasn't just me who saw Marcus Green, you know. In the cabin. Celine Dobson and her mother were there. They saw him too.'

Dexter scowled. 'So you say. And where are they now? Skipped the country and went into hiding. Anyone's guess where they are now. Not that they ever said anything about what had happened in that log cabin, as I recall. Kept their traps shut and then vanished into fresh air.'

'They only disappeared because they knew Marcus could still be alive. Afraid he'd come after them again.'

'Maybe so. But it doesn't help, does it? As far as the official story goes, Marcus Green is dead. Case closed. End of story.'

Donna leapt to her feet. Eyes ablaze and finding new levels of courage from somewhere she prodded Dexter's chest violently. 'I bloody well know Marcus is alive. And he's involved in all this. Just as I know he's responsible for what happened to Kate. I brought her into this and now she's dead. My fault.'

'How sure are you?' Dexter was more animated now, fingers pinching the side of his leg as if to wake himself up. Up to now he'd been dismissive. Not any more though. Not in the face of Donna's untypical display of emotion.

'Sure as I can be. It all fits.'

Dexter shook his head. 'Not to me it doesn't.' he held up his hands as if to ward off another bout of chest prodding. 'Hold on. Convince me. Find me another link in that list, for a start.'

Donna took a step back, her previous temerity fading. 'You mean I'm still…?'

'On the job. Why not? It's still your case, remember. Hold onto that anger. Anger is good. Keeps you motivated. Just one thing though.' Dexter paused until Donna met his eyes. 'Run with it until you've got something for me. I'm all for gut feelings, as well you know, but there have to be limits. Twenty-four hours, that's all you've got. If you've got nowhere by this time tomorrow; forget it and get onto real cases. The ones that pay your wages.'

CHAPTER 12

MARCUS hoisted the body out of the boot of his car and onto his right shoulder. The boarded up flats of the condemned tower block were deserted with no other houses for several hundred yards in any direction. He climbed to the fifth floor, grimacing at the weight of his burden, but still moving freely and pushed aside a sheet of corrugated iron that he'd previously loosened. The bare concrete floor was dusty and a small cloud rose into the air when Marcus dropped the limp figure.

Marcus watched his captive intently while consciousness returned. Immediately he opened his eyes, Marcus leapt forward and struck him a savage blow across the face. 'Andy,' he said, his soft tone at variance with the violence of his actions, 'I've got a few questions for you.'

Andy opened his eyes and looked directly at him. He said nothing but Marcus saw the defiance etched on his features and rejoiced. He'd been concerned that this would be too easy and that the pretty boy on the floor would fold before he'd had time to enjoy the questioning process. Andy writhed, testing the strength of the thin nylon cords that bound his wrists and ankles, but to no avail. He lay back and looked at Marcus coolly. 'Go ahead. I don't mind a bit of rough stuff now and again.'

Marcus grinned. 'I'm more interested in what you have to tell me. Does the name Marcus Green mean anything to you?'

Andy tried to keep his expression neutral, but saw from the other man's smile that his attempt had been a failure. 'Nothing at all.'

'Oh, I think you know who I am. I need to know your connection with Kate Davies. Now, why don't you tell me why you've been taking such an interest in me and we can all go home.'

Andy looked at him impassively. His brain was racing with the implications for Donna if this man knew she'd been attempting to track him down. He knew instinctively that it was almost certainly too late for himself but resolved to shield Donna at all costs.

'Well? I'm waiting.'

Andy turned his head away. 'Fuck off.'

Marcus smiled, rising to his feet and removing his clothes, folding them carefully and placing them on a hook jutting out of the wall. He returned to Andy and stood watching the prone figure still struggling against his bonds. 'No sense in ruining good clothes,' Marcus said over his shoulder as he walked away, out of the room.

Moments later he was back, smiling broadly and carrying a red plastic washing-up bowl, brimming with water. 'Better and better,' he said, his tone almost conversational, 'Water still on in the kitchen. I can clean up after you've told me what I want to know.' Marcus placed the bowl on the floor and effortlessly lifted the struggling figure of Andy, grasping his hair and slowly lowering his face into the bowl. Andy struggled fiercely but was no match for Marcus who kept him under water despite struggles that became more and more frantic with every passing second. A minute passed and then Marcus heaved Andy's head out of the bowl. Andy spluttered, gasping for breath, but Marcus allowed him only an instant before thrusting his face back under the water. This time, Andy's struggles were desperate and for the first time Marcus showed the strain of holding him, but his grip was relentless and nothing Andy could do was to any avail. The second immersion was longer than the first, perhaps a minute and a half, and it was only when Andy's struggles began to abate that Marcus wrenched him out of the water again. Andy heaved for breath, his eyes wild. Marcus still held his hair tightly and brought his own face down towards that of his captive. 'Ready to talk now?'

Andy took another ragged breath and spat full in the face of Marcus. As a gesture of defiance, it was feeble enough and Marcus grinned, recognising the fact. He came closer still, squatting on his haunches with his face inches away from that of Andy. Suddenly, and with blinding speed, Marcus clamped his teeth on his captive's left ear and shook his head from side to side grinding his teeth together. Unable to defend himself, Andy bellowed in pain. Marcus spat the torn flesh out of his mouth, blood spatters mingling with the rivulets coursing down the side of Andy's face. 'Why don't I jog your memory a little more? Perhaps you'll remember things better when you're not quite such a pretty boy. Not even old lags just out of Walton will fancy you when I've finished here.' He reached behind himself and showed Andy the blade, exalting inside at the other man's expression. 'This razor has been a good friend to me. You'd be surprised how effective it can be at helping people regain their memory.' Without waiting for a response Marcus whipped the blade left to right and then back again, opening deep slashes across the face of his captive. Blood spurted out from the wounds, a deepening puddle on the floor soaking into the dust. Andy bellowed in agony, writhing from side to side in a vain attempt to escape his attacker.

'Squeal as much as you like,' Marcus hissed, 'No-one will hear you.' His wrist cocked and the blade flew down, removing the sole undamaged ear cleanly. Andy looked up at his assailant, teeth clenched, and swore to himself that he would say nothing to this man. Marcus caught a hint of this fresh defiance and the blade rose and fell another half dozen times until what remained of Andy's face was unrecognisable. Marcus knelt alongside the other man, the razor now held loosely in front of him. He slit the waistband of Andy's jeans and peeled the denim away. Even through endless surges of pain, Andy felt the chill on his exposed flesh and tensed.

'You were keen enough a while back to give me more than a hint as to what you'd got on offer inside your pants. Are you sure you've nothing you'd like to tell me before we go on? Last chance, pretty boy. Talk to me.' Marcus waited patiently for only a moment and then the razor flashed once more. Andy screamed, his voice cracking at the unimaginable pain.

'Not such a pretty boy now, are you? Not even a boy any longer. Don't imagine it will end now. Me and my little friend here,' Marcus showed him the

109

blade again. 'We've got more tricks to show you. Lots more blood left in you yet.'

Donna parked her car, now restored to health by Dexter's mechanic, on the deserted car park of the Seven Stars public house. The picturesque village of Thornton Hough was delightful on a sunny summer afternoon when the thwack of ball on willow enlivened the village green, but early on a damp miserable morning, its appeal was muted. Donna locked her car, slipped the keys into the pocket of her jeans, and set off at a fair pace, skipping over shallow pools of water and sopping grass verges.

The house was set well back from the road, almost as if it were attempting to hide from view altogether. Donna reached the sanctuary of a shallow porch and pressed the brass door push with a sopping finger. The front door creaked open almost instantly, revealing a middle-aged woman wrapped in a blue towelling robe and squinting out at the damp apparition on her doorstep.

'Mrs Jackson?' Donna enquired, seizing the initiative.

'Yes,' the woman confirmed, somewhat dubiously.

'My name's Donna O'Prey. I wonder if you could spare me a few moments.' Donna offered her card, but the woman waved it away.

'Can't find my glasses,' she said, 'Are you selling anything?'

'No, not at all. I work for R and D Security.'

'What's that, burglar alarms and such?' Mrs Jackson asked dubiously.

'No. Nothing like that. I'm an investigator.'

'You don't look like much of a private eye to me. Still, no sense in standing out in the rain. You'd better come in, but mind you wipe your feet and don't drip all over the hall.'

Donna wiped her feet and shook the worst of the rain off her coat as she entered the hall. The floor was magnificent, gleaming black and white diamond patterned tiles and Donna took the opportunity to wipe her feet once again on the mat positioned just inside the door. Mrs Jackson watched her approvingly and beckoned Donna to follow her.

'Just me, I'm afraid,' she called over her shoulder, 'My husband's away on business. That's what he tells me, anyway.' She gave a nervous giggle.

By the time they reached the kitchen Donna had completely re-evaluated her intended approach, deciding on direct action. This was a house straight out of the pages of the glossy magazines. The dinner set arranged on the pine dresser was par for the course. With the possible exception of blue and white Delft, nothing sets off a Welsh dresser like Crown Derby and its one hell of an investment.

Donna looked out of the window. From where she was sitting, a strip of lawn extended almost out of sight to a row of mature trees. She moved up a bit and saw that it wasn't as big as she'd first thought; not much more than a good-sized football pitch. The grass was a bit long. Good enough for a pub team, but not up to Anfield standards.

Donna took a deep breath and came straight to the point. 'Can I ask you something that may be upsetting?'

'What?'

'Do you have children?' Donna enquired, watching the woman's face crumple in front of her. Mrs Jackson gave a stifled cry, clutching the edge of the centre work unit for support.

'Samantha.' The voice was no more than a whisper.

Donna felt a chill across the back of her neck. She moved across the room and stood next to the woman, reaching out to her. 'Did something happen to Samantha?'

'She ran away.' The voice was flat, expressionless, but Donna immediately discerned that there was even worse to come.

'Shall we sit down?' Donna kept her voice low, battling to contain a feeling of anticipation. She hated herself for feeling a flutter of excitement but was certain that her suspicions were soon to be confirmed. Mrs Jackson sank into a wooden hard-backed chair, looking drawn and pale.

'She was a happy girl, never any trouble, you know?' Donna nodded, noting the past tense with a mixture of dread and expectation. 'Not that we didn't have the odd falling-out. Teenagers have to rebel, don't they?' Donna nodded; seating herself on the chair next to the woman who didn't appear to be even aware of her presence any more. 'We thought Samantha was staying with a friend from school. In a caravan. When the police came and told us, we said it couldn't be right. What they were saying, you know? Couldn't be our Samantha. She was miles away, staying with her friend.' She stopped speaking, her face a tortured mask.

Donna held her breath as the silence grew more intense. This was another of those judgement calls: to speak or not to speak. Wishing Dexter was with her, she decided to wait it out.

'Samantha had taken her best clothes. She looked so grown-up, but of course she was still only a child. What we can't understand, my husband and me, is why she lied to us. Said she was going to stay with a friend from school, but she wasn't. My husband rang the family. They knew nothing about it. Why would she do that?' She turned her anguished face to Donna.

'I don't know,' Donna confessed, 'Had she done anything like this before? Run away perhaps?'

'Certainly not. Samantha was a good girl. Always kept her room tidy, did her homework as good as gold. Never went on her computer until she'd finished her homework.'

'Was Samantha keen on the Internet?' Donna kept her voice impassive, but felt a tremor deep in her chest.

'Oh yes. Listening to music, chatting away, all the usual teenage things.'

'What exactly happened to Samantha?'

'An accident. Samantha was crossing a railway line and must have got her foot trapped somehow. An express...' Mrs Jackson's voice tailed away in a sob. Donna winced.

'The police said she didn't suffer, but how could she not have suffered? Seeing a train rushing towards her and not being able to get out of the way?'

Donna took a deep breath. 'I need to ask you something,' she said, 'In connection with a case I'm working on.' The woman looked at Donna impassively. 'Were you or your husband ever members of a jury?' She had the list from Kate, but needed the confirmation.

'Yes. I was, many years back now. What a question; that was so long ago. A terrible business, a schoolteacher's two little girls murdered by one of her pupils.'

Donna sighed. She had the confirmation she'd both anticipated and dreaded. Mrs Jackson rose slowly to her feet, swaying slightly. 'Would you like to see Samantha's room?'

Donna nodded. In reality, she wanted nothing more than to leave, putting this woman's grief behind her, but felt an obligation to stay. Her presence had re-opened raw wounds and it would be impossible to just walk away now.

Samantha's bedroom was a shrine. Immaculately tidy, not a trace of dust, no scattered clothes. Donna had no way of knowing whether the room's present condition was its original state or whether the mother's grief had caused her to tidy up and present the room in a more favourable light. Taking a second step into the room, Donna's glance took in the scattered bouquet on the floor by the bed. Under different circumstances she'd have been distressed to see it abandoned like this. The flowers were exceptional. Roses and carnations, red being the dominant colour offset by a froth of green fern, the whole creation would originally have been swathed in shiny cellophane and tied with ornate strips of pink ribbon.

'Dennis threw those there. Dennis, that's my husband, isn't dealing with things at all well, I'm afraid. He's been a different person since we found out about Samantha. We hadn't been getting on very well for a while, but Samantha was the apple of his eye. He blames me for her running away. These things here are from one of the neighbours,' Mrs Jackson said, kicking disconsolately at the wilting flowers on the floor. 'Fat lot of use I've got for flowers when I never got the chance to see my little girl for the last time. They wouldn't let me.' Donna nodded, speculating on the damage done to a human body after colliding with a speeding train and shuddered inwardly. Composing herself, she walked over to inspect the wardrobes. Something to do. Real wood, not chipboard. The brass door furniture and hinges alone must have cost a bomb. Talk about how the other half lives. Donna remembered this woman's anguish over the fate of her daughter and hurriedly put any envious thoughts aside.

'The police brought us her bag.' The woman's voice intruded on Donna's thoughts and she turned round with a guilty start. 'Samantha must have thrown it to one side when she realised she was trapped. That's how the police knew it was her. There were things inside that... ' She began sobbing, shoulders heaving gently.

'What sort of things?' Donna knew she was being a tad insensitive, but the question had to be asked.

'A pack of birth control bills. And some other tablets that the police took away with them. Said they were a controlled substance.'

'Drugs?' Donna's voice was sharper than she'd intended, but her surprise was genuine.

'Ecstasy, according to the police. Ridiculous. I can only imagine Samantha must have been holding them for some friend or other. My daughter would never be involved with drugs. No matter what Dennis says. He blames me for losing touch with my daughter, letting her get involved in drugs, having sex, running away because she was so unhappy at home. I kept telling him, it wasn't like that at all. I knew my daughter.' Her voice broke and she sobbed into a handkerchief.

'Have you any idea where she was going?'

'No. Samantha's friend from school said she was going to meet some boy or other, but that can't be right. Samantha didn't have a boyfriend. She was only sixteen and was too busy with her schoolwork to go round chasing after boys.'

Donna nodded, but was beginning to form a picture of the dead girl's home background. Pampered and cosseted by parents reluctant to accept their little girl was growing up and eager to spread her wings.

'Did Samantha's friend say any more about this boy?'

'No. That's because there was no boy in the first place. Melanie, that's Samantha's friend, told her mother that Samantha told her she'd met a boy and was mad about him. Asked Melanie to cover up for her so she could go away with him. The very idea.'

'Did Melanie know anything about this boy?'

'Not a thing. I think she made up the whole tale. She's a devious little madam, that one.'

Donna realised she was dealing with a closed mind, blanking out anything that would have reflected badly on her lost child. Nothing more would be gained by staying here. The friend, Melanie, was a far better bet.

The Range Rover glided up to the tollbooth and Marcus flung coins into the hopper. A clear run down from the Wirral had faltered at the M25; bringing heavy traffic and drizzling rain. The Dartford crossing had been particularly bad, but he saw the opportunity of a clear run down to Kent as the traffic congestion eased. His thoughts were racing. The little gay-boy had surprised him by biting through his own tongue and choking on his own blood before he'd given up his secrets. Marcus had been enjoying himself, perhaps a little too much and, with the benefit of hindsight, wondered whether he could have actively pressed the man to talk a little earlier in the proceedings. It was behind him now, but he felt a sense of regret that the man had cheated him right at the end, certain now that the man's actions that ended his life had been deliberate. He would need to investigate the firm of R and D Security at some future time. Loose ends were never to be tolerated and he still had no firm idea why he, a dead man, was being investigated. Both the man this morning and the woman, Kate Davies, had chosen death rather than enlighten him as to their interest in his affairs. But that could wait. He had his own agenda to pursue now.

The latest target would be the most difficult. He'd had little opportunity for research and would need to force himself into a familiar discipline over the next few days. Patience was essential. The target would need to be watched and appraised until he was ready. At that time, and not before, he'd know how to proceed.

CHAPTER 13

DEXTER sifted papers on his desk and with a sigh of exasperation recovered his mobile 'phone from beneath a mound of files. 'Hello?' he barked.

'It's Donna. I've just left a Mrs Jackson. She was one of the names on the list that…'

'I know what list you mean,' Dexter interrupted with more than a hint of annoyance, 'Just get on with it.'

'Mister and Mrs Jackson had a daughter. Samantha. She died three weeks ago. Run over by a train.' Donna was gabbling, desperate to pass on her news, but Dexter let have her say. 'A friend reckons she'd met a boy and ran away with him.'

'Did you confirm the jury business?'

'Yeah. The mother was the juror. She's well gutted by all this. Her daughter's dead and her husband blames her for it all. She's in a right state.'

'Right. Anything more?'

'Possible drugs involvement. Ecstasy found in the girl's bag, birth control pills as well. All too much for her mother. Seems she didn't know her daughter as well as she thought she did. That's the worst thing of all, it seems to me. Punishing herself.'

'Maybe that was the intention,' Dexter mused.

'Eh?'

'Just remembering that e-mail from Kate. How the intention may be to punish the parents in the worst way imaginable. More than just losing a child. God knows, that's bad enough, but realising it may have been their own fault? That would make it much worse. Where was the bag found?'

'Near the body.'

'Could have been planted, the pills and that. To wind up the parents, make them think their kid had drifted away from them. Even been driven away.'

'That's it,' Donna burst out.

'Maybe. Maybe not. But, it's possible. What else?'

'Thought I'd look up the girl's best friend. See if she knows anything about this mystery boyfriend.'

'Good. Keep me up to speed with anything you find out. I'll pull a few strings. See if I can work my way through that list of jurors.'

'You believe me, then?' Donna's voice was shrill with excitement.

'Told you I'd take it further if you found out any more. As you saw fit to remind me, I don't like coincidences. Two names on the same list mean its well worth a look. Three makes a big difference. Good work, Donna. Watch yourself and keep in touch.' Dexter pressed the off button, cutting Donna off in mid squeal, then rose to his feet and walked slowly down the corridor.

Roper sat at his immaculate desk, laboriously adding a column of figures on a pristine white sheet of paper. Dexter saw the opened office accounts ledger and frowned. Roper was capable of spending an entire day perusing the records of income and expenditure in an attempt to reduce operational expenses by a fraction of a percentage point and, not for the first time, Dexter questioned his own presence in a partnership between two such vastly different characters.

'Put that away,' Dexter grunted, 'We need to talk. That case Donna's working on?'

Roper looked surprised. 'Not the suicide enquiry? Surely she's finished that by now? Wasn't much of a job, I wouldn't have thought.'

Dexter grunted. 'Depends how well the job's done. There's been a development.' As Roper sat in open-mouthed astonishment, Dexter outlined Donna's progress to date.

'Surely, this is a police matter now?' Roper interjected as Dexter paused for a moment.

'Not sure,' Dexter said, frowning. 'Far as I'm concerned, yes it is, no question, but my former colleagues may not see it like that. Not at this stage. We have three sudden deaths so far. All of them easily explained. Suicide, drug overdose, railway accident. No evidence to justify any investigation.'

'What about your friend? Kate, wasn't it? Surely there's no question about foul play there?'

'No. But, Kate had many enemies and there's nothing to link her death with our case.'

'I see,' Roper said, his expression belying his words, 'I assume you'll be handling the matter yourself from now onwards.'

Dexter's surprise was genuine. 'Why? It's Donna's case. I'll give her some background help but she's done pretty well so far.'

'But, she's very inexperienced for what may develop into a major inquiry. Hot-headed and rather inclined to jump to conclusions. I really think....'

Dexter thumped the desk angrily, cutting off his partner's voice in mid-sentence. 'Now listen. We wouldn't have a case at all if Donna hadn't jumped to certain conclusions. Without her input, her bloody-minded obsessions, we'd be nowhere. She's the only reason we've found this possible, better make that probable, link between a list of jurors and the apparently unconnected deaths of three young people. Donna stays on the job. That clear?' He didn't wait for an answer, storming out of the office, brushing past the concerned figure of Martha as she hovered uncertainly outside the door.

Marcus leant back in his seat as the Range Rover came smoothly to a halt. He parked alongside the statue of William Harvey; a former Royal physician who, according to a metal plaque at the base, was credited with discovering the manner in which blood circulated around the body. Marcus climbed out of the car and walked a few stride across the grass verge. The weather had improved and he smiled as he looked across the leaden expanse of the English Channel towards the distant coastline of France. The Leas, high above the harbour of Folkestone, had been a popular spot in the Edwardian era and still retained much of its legendary style. Vast white houses faced out to sea while further along the promenade the turrets of the Grand and Metropole Hotels were just about visible. The next target was almost within reach and a sigh of anticipation escaped his lips. He returned to the car and drove a further quarter of a mile, pulling up on the forecourt of the Burlington Hotel. He'd made a reservation before leaving Merseyside and, looking up at the ornate façade, he was content.

Five minutes later, having registered and settled into his room, Marcus unpacked the leather valise that was his only item of luggage. The razor gleamed in the sunshine bursting through the open first-floor window as he removed it reverently from its case. It was time for this old friend to earn its keep once more. A few miles along the coast lay the port of Dover, headquarters of a vital aspect of his business empire. Hashish from the Rif Mountains flooded into Dover, hidden in camper vans, lorries, family saloons and sealed containers, all of it destined for customers of Marcus. A section of his organisation had recently shown a downturn in profits. The only explanation was that the man in charge had become greedy and skimmed off part of the take. He'd deny it, of course he would, but Marcus knew he'd find the truth. The razor would loosen his tongue. One way or another.

Marcus turned his back on the view. Errant employees could wait a little longer. There was work to be done here and the sooner he set about it the better. According to her former neighbours Alison Lea had left her home in Ruthin some weeks ago and was now shacked up with a man many years her senior. By all accounts, her parents had been far from pleased, but she'd turned eighteen the week she left and there was little they could say to prevent her giving up her college place and going to work as a maid in the same hotel where her boyfriend had been taken on as a chef. The man was ten years older than Alison, not in itself a barrier, but it had been his complexion, which had seemingly upset Alison's parents. Neighbours had insisted that racism had no bearing on the concerns of Alison's parents, but in staid respectable Ruthin, the colour of a man's skin was still a significant factor. Particularly when the man in question had encouraged their only daughter to throw away her education and future prospects.

A soft tap on the door alerted Marcus and he scooped the razor back inside his bag with practised ease.

'Come in,' he called.

The girl looked even younger than her years. The trim uniform fitted snugly, but it was the hair that took his attention. Long, dark and straight, it flowed around her shoulders like a silky curtain.

'Sorry to bother you, sir,' she said her voice a soft lilt, 'But your room 'phone must be off the hook. A message for you, left at reception.' She handed over a long white envelope.

Marcus smiled, glancing at the bedside table where the telephone had apparently been dislodged when he'd thrown his jacket on the bed. 'My fault,' he confessed, 'Clumsy of me. Sorry you've had to come up to bring this.'

'No problem, Sir. Part of the job.' The girl turned to leave and he treasured the sight of her calves and trim ankles.

'Hang on,' Marcus called, reaching into his trouser pocket and producing a ten-pound note. 'Please take this for your trouble. Sorry, what's your name?'

'Alison,' the girl replied, reaching out hesitantly for the proffered note. 'Thank you, Sir. Thank you very much.'

Marcus smiled back at her. He'd known her name already, but had enjoyed hearing her say it. Thus far, she had exceeded his expectations. Soon he would have the opportunity to hear her scream and watch her innocence and youthful promise fade away as the utter certainty of her death approached.

There were worse places than the tree-lined avenues of Heswall, and after the early drizzle the sun was out with a vengeance, but Donna was still not happy. She'd tracked down Samantha's friend, Melanie, supposedly revising in the garden, but there was no sign of a school textbook anywhere. Just a particularly annoying sixteen year old girl working on her tan. Donna refused to accept that she'd ever been as immature as Melanie, even at birth. There were only half a dozen years between them, but it may as well have been an entire lifetime. Worst was a rising intonation at the end of every sentence turning the most prosaic remark into an apparent question. Donna didn't watch 'Friends' and would slit her wrists rather than suffer 'Neighbours' or 'Home and Away,' but Melanie was clearly an addict.

'It was a real shock, yeah? I was, like, in shock, you know?'

Donna sighed. It wasn't getting any easier. 'Did you know where Samantha was going, the weekend she said she was staying with you?'

'Oh, no way. Samantha was real secretive. She never told me no details.'

'Nothing at all?'

Melanie shook her head so vigorously Donna feared she'd suffer brain damage. Not that there was much of a brain to damage. A grey squirrel ran along the high wall bordering the garden and Melanie cooed with delight, Donna's questions forgotten. Behind them the sandstone gable end of the house was marred by a hideous square of grey plastic containing an air vent. Donna sighed again. Now she was catching the distraction bug. She touched Melanie's arm and the girl jumped. 'So, you knew nothing about a new boyfriend?'

'Eh?'

'Samantha? A new boyfriend?' Donna's patience was almost exhausted by now and her voice contained more than a hint of irritation.

'Oh, yeah. I reckon that would be Miles?' Melanie's vapid expression gave Donna the impression she'd perhaps had a close encounter with some alien species.

'Miles?'

'Yeah. I think that was his name. I dunno nothing about the guy. Just that he was loaded and his name was Miles.'

'Anything else? How did Samantha meet him? Where did he live? How long had she known him? Was she going to meet him that weekend?' Donna fired off questions, watching in vain for any spark of intelligence in Melanie's expression.

'Dunno.'

Donna sighed. 'Nothing at all? You don't know anything about him, apart from his name?'

Melanie shook her head. 'He's got a sports car, yeah? Samantha told me that. He was well loaded, she reckoned. Jammy cow.'

Donna looked at the girl in disbelief. Her supposed best friend had died in tragic circumstances, but her dominant reaction appeared to be jealousy.

'Not so jammy, as things turned out,' Donna pointed out. Melanie turned her head slowly towards Donna and her baby-blue eyes filled with tears. 'Oh yeah,' she said, 'That was, like, so unfair. What happened to Samantha.'

'So, you know Samantha had a boyfriend, his name was Miles and he drove a sports car. Anything else at all?'

'No. Sorry. Just she met him in a chat room, yeah? Miles said not to tell anyone, but Samantha had to tell me, you know? She had to tell her Mum she was with me or she'd, like, never let her go off for the weekend.'

Donna started. 'A chat room? Had she ever been out with him before?'

Melanie shook her head. 'No. I know. It's not fair, is it? Like, never getting the chance to be with him.'

Donna looked at the girl in disbelief. Had she no conception of the dangers of arranging to meet a stranger she'd only met on the Internet? More to the point, had Samantha been equally unaware of the dangers of such an arrangement? Donna attempted to convey her shock at this dangerous practise, citing examples of adult paedophiles posing as teenage boys with the intention of meeting impressionable young girls, but lapsed into shocked silence when Melanie burst out laughing.

'That's all such, you know, bollocks, innit? The sort of thing your parents are always going on about. Samantha wasn't stupid, you know and Miles wasn't some old pervert making out he was a young lad or anything like that. He went clubbing, Samantha said, not what some old bloke would do, is it? And, he sent her a photo.' This last sentence was delivered with an air of emphasis, as if it were the final proof that Miles could only have been who he said he was.

'Did you see the photograph?'

'Yeah. Samantha printed it out off the screen so I could see what he looked like.'

Donna gave a start. 'Did you keep it? The 'photo?' The note of excitement in her voice was palpable.

'Nah! No chance. She kept it in her top pocket. Next to her heart.' The expression was uttered without a trace of irony.

'Can you describe him?'

'Dunno really. Dead fit. Dark hair, cut sort of short. Like tanned, really brown, a bit moody looking?'

'How old would you say?'

'Nineteen? Hard to say. Look, I didn't get much chance. Samantha just let me have a quick look at break and then she put it away again.'

Donna pondered a moment. Melanie wasn't the most reliable informant, but she was all that was available. The age of the mystery boyfriend was a

119

worry. Marcus Green would be in his late twenties by now which cast a certain amount of doubt on Donna's precious theory, but she'd at least gained the knowledge that Samantha had left home with the specific intention of meeting a boy or man that she'd met on the Internet. She even had a name, Miles, but the chances of that being the mystery boyfriend's real name were pretty slim. The last time Donna had seen Marcus Green, his nose had been badly broken, his face bruised and most critically of all, he'd been pinned to the wall of a wooden cabin by a knife which Donna had stuck through his cheek.

'What about his face? Any marks that you could see?'

'Not really. He was dead fit, you know? He looked a bit like that lad who used to be in East-Enders, only he'd got dark hair not blonde. The one what got run over.'

Donna shook her head in irritation. The lack of any obvious facial damage was a further blow. She decided she'd keep these awkward details to herself for now. No sense in Dexter pouring scorn on her ideas until she was ready to admit defeat.

'You got a boyfriend, then?'

Donna shook her head. The absence of anyone who could realistically be termed a boyfriend in her life was something else Donna needed to get her head around at some time in the future. When she could find the time. Her track record in that department was pretty ropey, actually, but personal relationships were a bit of a luxury just now.

The last man in her life, Donna mused, if you could call him a man, or if you could call this a life, had been Stuart. Terrible name, she knew, but trying to be fair, Donna hadn't held his name against him. She'd taken the line of least resistance while recovering from her near brush with death at the hands of Marcus Green and had become accustomed to staying in and watching the soaps with Peg every evening. Stuart was a young farmer. Donna knew that because she met him at the first, and last, Young Farmers' dance she'd attended after allowing her so-called friend, Andy, to persuade her that she should 'Get out more'. Hence the Young Farmers' dance.

What made it worse was that she'd actually found she was enjoying herself. Stuart was a bit of a surprise too. Handsome, slim-hipped and fit as a butcher's dog; what more could anyone want? Donna soon became aware that his family farmed half of Cheshire, but that was never a factor.

Honestly!

It had all started well enough when Donna had her wicked way with him, while managing to give him the impression that it was all his idea. Fortunately, Stuart was no Einstein, but Donna was on heat the minute he took his shirt off.

Stuart seemed almost too good to be true and of course, that was exactly how it turned out. He was keen, but not clingy. Good company, almost funny in his own way and Donna started to get a taste all over again for having someone else in her bed. Then, poor, soppy, thick as pig-shit Stuart dumped her. For some hairy-arsed farmer's daughter who worked at the Artificial

Insemination unit in Neston. He told Donna it was because of their common interests: her good farming stock background and all that crap, but she knew the real reason and accepted it well enough. How could she ever compete with someone who wanked off bulls for a living? With that sort of expertise behind her, the farmer's girl had both feet under the table.

With no prospect of boyfriend talk to occupy her mind, such as it was, Melanie appeared to have drifted off to sleep, mouth gaping open and arms akimbo. Donna walked away, certain she'd got all there was to offer from this particular source.

The strident clamour of the bell reached every area of the hotel. From a storeroom under the main stairs Marcus watched guests and staff troop through the lobby and spill out onto the pavement, green-uniformed figures striving to assert some form of control. He waited for a further minute, senses on full alert, until certain that the premises were empty apart from himself. An earlier anonymous call had already ensured that the area's only available specialists trained to deal with bomb threats were presently conducting a painstaking sweep of a building a mile away on the East Cliff overlooking Folkestone harbour. His second telephone call to the hotel had also been anonymous, but Marcus knew that no chances would be taken. The drill was always the same: evacuate the building and wait for the experts.

Marcus moved silently along the deserted corridor and pushed open the double swing doors at the end. The kitchen gleamed, the ambient luminescence of ceiling-mounted light strips reflecting pure white light from stainless steel hobs and rows of hanging pans and utensils. A simmering pan popped and bubbled as the surface area of the liquid contents seethed gently. Marcus walked confidently to the chopping block and rapidly scanned the area. Slipping on a pair of latex gloves, he picked up a slender filleting knife, enclosed it in a clear plastic bag and placed it carefully inside a leather pouch he drew from his inside breast pocket. Replacing the pouch into his pocket, he retraced his steps and slipped out of the hotel by way of a rear exit. By the time he joined the milling crowds on the main car park, the faint sound of an emergency siren was just about audible in the distance.

The cup rattled in its saucer as Dexter banged down the telephone receiver. Three names into the list and already he'd struck gold. Ben Adams had been keen on scuba diving from a young age; one of the reasons his father had taken early retirement and moved the family to a villa on the Roussillon coast of France near the picturesque town of Collioure. Two months ago, the lad had gone out on his own, strictly against the orders of his father, and got into difficulties. Ben had been fifteen years old. The verdict of accidental death by drowning was clear enough and Dexter wouldn't have given the matter a second glance except for the fact that Ben's father, Terence Adams, had been foreman of the jury that sent Marcus Green to prison.

Dexter stabbed out the number of Donna's mobile 'phone, clapped the receiver to his ear and the teacup rattled once more as a metallic voice informed him for the third time that the mobile he'd been calling was switched off. Frustration etched into every line of his craggy features, he angrily paced the boundaries of his office.

Donna almost ran up the drive, her coat flapping, watched by Mrs Jackson from the kitchen window with open-mouthed astonishment. As Donna reached the top step the door swung open and she practically fell inside.

'Why, whatever is the matter?' Mrs Jackson looked as if Donna's previous visit had taken its toll. Her hair was all over the place and her eyes were red and sore.

'Sorry to just barge in,' Donna gasped, 'I need to look at Samantha's room again. If you don't mind?'

'Of course I don't mind. But I fail to see what earthly use all this rushing around is. Its not as if there's anything to be gained from it. My daughter is gone. An accident. I just don't see how whatever case you're involved in can possibly benefit from poking around in Samantha's things.'

Donna took a deep breath. She'd only given a sketchy explanation for her previous visit, reasoning that until she had hard evidence of wrongdoing there would be nothing to gain from causing this grieving family any more cause for concern. Her quandary was eased by her hostess's sudden acquiescence to her request to view the room without any need for further explanation. Seemingly, she'd by now become accustomed to a state of bewildered confusion. Donna suspected this was a device to mask her true feelings. Self-deception in its purest form. Donna doubted that the woman would ever allow her inner self to accept a scenario where her daughter had routinely deceived her parents. Lying about her whereabouts, birth-control pills and recreational drugs found in her bag, and all of it unknown to the parents. Easier to block it all out. What it came down to was finding a way to cope with a devastating loss while avoiding personal blame. Donna thought back once again to Kate's e-mail in which she'd speculated on the possible reasons behind the targeting of the children of the jurors, rather than the jurors themselves. This woman's grief provided further support for Kate's theory that the grieving parent, by blaming themselves for lack of foreknowledge, would suffer for the rest of their lives from the tragic death of their child.

On arrival in Samantha's room Donna made directly for the computer. 'Is it all right to have a quick look at this?'

'Oh. I suppose so. You young people all seem to be such experts on those wretched things. I suppose you learnt it all at school?'

Donna grunted, reaching down to push the plug into its socket. Not in her case. Her final years at school must have been the very last to receive only traditional teaching. Nowadays, computers in schools were everywhere, thanks in no small way to the inspired marketing ploys of major supermarkets. Donna could type a letter, send and read an e-mail and just about manage a search on Google but the finer points of spreadsheets, desktop publishing or image manipulation were way beyond her capabilities.

Mrs Jackson backed out of the room and Donna heard her footsteps clattering down the stairs as the screen brightened and the Microsoft logo appeared. Donna battled with an unfamiliar set-up for ten minutes before eventually gaining admittance to Samantha's Internet history page. It was distinctly unsettling to see the date of her last entry, the day before her death. Donna scrolled down the entries, noting that there were very few items that could conceivably be construed as relating to schoolwork, but numerous entries for dating sites and pop music trivia. One site in particular took her attention, having been visited every day. Its sole purpose was to bring together singles of both sexes and seemed, to Donna at least, to be heavily biased towards overtly sexual innuendo. Perhaps she had become an old fart overnight. Clicking on Samantha's last visit to the site produced only a blank page. Frustrated, Donna clicked on the entry before last; an attachment entitled 'Miles pic,' and again found only a blank screen. Each entry with any connection to the mysterious Miles had been erased.

Donna leant back in the flimsy typist's chair with reckless abandon. All the other entries were still available, but of Samantha's new boyfriend not a trace remained.

CHAPTER 14

THE rise of Islam brought Arabic, the language of the Koran, to Morocco and saw the ancient language fade into disuse. However, in the mountain regions and especially in the High Atlas, where the Berber tribes were strongest, the old ways remained. Surviving purely by word of mouth, never having existed in written form, the Berber dialects remained in common currency. Marcus had seen the potential of a language which was known only to its closest intimates and had studied hard to attain fluency. All his most trusted employees were Berbers from the mountain regions of Morocco. A race of people committed to survival through reliance on their wits had proved an ideal work-force. Marcus gained respect through fear, well aware that these tough men of the mountains revered strength and resolution above all other leadership characteristics. The harsh climate of their isolated villages, baked by blazing heat in summer and frozen for months in the winter, together with a compulsion to retain their old traditions and beliefs, ensured their respect for a strong leader. The financial benefits for villagers living far below any Western indications of poverty levels were obvious, but a leader who both promised and delivered riches while actively encouraging avoidance of contact with established authority figures would earn their absolute loyalty.

Marcus watched the man approach and felt a brief frisson of regret. Abdullah had been a loyal and trusted lieutenant during the past year, but his cruel nature, previously a major asset, had now become a liability. Discipline had been Abdullah's forte, but recent excesses had attracted the attention of the police and this situation could not be allowed to continue. A group of Somali migrants, hidden in a specially modified container had been moved across an entire continent without mishap and safely delivered to their destination. When the final stage payment was not forthcoming, Abdullah had extracted drastic retribution. The leader of the Somali group had been brutally killed in front of his companions, thus ensuring that the overdue payment was immediately made. Marcus had no problem with the method of assuring payment, but the later discovery of the mutilated body had been a grave error. Abdullah's judgement, occasionally suspect, was now deemed to be fatally flawed.

'*Maneek antgeet?*' Marcus enquired, extending his hand in friendship.

'*La bes imandulah,*' Abdullah responded, taking the hand of Marcus in a double-handed grip, grasping wrists in the manner of the Bedouin. Both men spoke in the *Tashelhait* dialect used in the High Atlas region, although Marcus was equally fluent in the *Riffi* dialect commonly used by his employees from the Rif Mountain range.

In the far distance, where the sea mated with the land, a barely discernible light appeared. Dawn was approaching as Marcus beckoned his lieutenant to a gap between two lines of containers stacked three high on the Dover quayside. Both men were of similar stature, but the Berber's breadth of shoulder testified to massive strength and Marcus took care to alleviate any suspicions on the other man's part by volubly praising his efforts and promising the payment of a substantial cash bonus. In the faint light of an orange sodium light spilling out from the quay, he flipped open the lid of the valise he held in his left hand and showed the other man the substantial quantity of bundled notes it contained. Abdullah licked his fleshy lips and took the proffered case with an eagerness that momentarily overcame his natural caution. Marcus handed over the case with a smile; subtly re-positioning his body as he did so, satisfied that Abdullah's attention was elsewhere.

His recent experience with Kate Davies determined his next actions. Marcus reached out with his right hand, cradling his palm under the other man's chin and pressing the heel of his other hand into the soft flesh at the back of the neck. Jerking violently upwards with his right hand and pressing forwards and downwards with the other, he snapped Abdullah's neck like a twig between the third and fourth vertebrae. Bracing himself, Marcus took the full weight of Abdullah on his forearms and lowered him slowly to the ground. Abdullah lay on his back, eyes open and watching the face of Marcus in confusion. Marcus had been careful; the manoeuvre could easily have resulted in death, but he wanted Abdullah alive for a while longer. Below the break in his spine he was paralysed and would soon lose the ability to control his breathing, but he remained conscious and able to understand the meaning of the words Marcus was about to utter.

'You have been careless, my brother,' Marcus whispered. The prone figure blinked, wincing as Marcus produced his razor and showed it to him. 'The Somali was a mistake. He had to die, but leaving him to be found was an error.'

Abdullah was feeling no pain but his face creased in anticipation as Marcus drew the blade of the razor across the line of his vision. Marcus showed him the blade, crimson now with stray drops of blood glistening in the faint light of the overhead lights. The blade dipped again, repeatedly criss-crossing the torso of the motionless man. Marcus raised the blade again and paused from his labours for a moment. 'There is another matter we should discuss,' he said. 'What reason could there be for a decline in income? Your section is the only one to show a fall in profit.'

Abdullah struggled to speak, his face stricken. 'Don't bother,' Marcus told him, 'I don't want excuses. You were in charge; the responsibility is yours.' Abdullah closed his eyes. He knew pleading would be useless.

'You will feel pain now,' Marcus said, his voice flat and expressionless. He drew the blade of the razor across the face of Abdullah who hissed as the blood spurted. Abdullah remained silent, biting his lip at each slash of the blade, right up to the moment the razor passed across his eyes. The loss of sight confirmed he was about to die and a croak of agony bubbled out from his chest, immediately stifled when Marcus reversed his grip and cut deeply into the throat. A fresh torrent of blood poured from the open wound as Marcus rose to his feet, looking at the body of his former lieutenant without a trace of emotion.

The body lay against the side of a rusty container and Marcus dragged it further into the darkness, throwing the flapping corner of a tarpaulin cover

over the crumpled figure. Abdullah's replacement's first duty would be the safe disposal of his predecessor's body. It was essential that the death of Abdullah and the manner of his demise, be known to the rank and file members of his organisation in order to reinforce the penalties for failure, but the body must never be allowed to come to the attention of the authorities.

'Where the hell have you been?' Dexter's voice demanded. Donna sighed. She'd returned to her car, noticed her mobile was switched off and within seconds of switching it back on she'd got Dexter giving her grief.

'Sorry. Had to switch off while I was doing an interview.' The explanation sounded pretty feeble. Even to herself

'How many bloody times do I have to tell you to keep in touch? Especially when you're doing an interview. I'm talking about your safety, Donna.'

'Okay. Won't happen again. I said I was sorry.'

'You're always bloody sorry. Doesn't stop you leaving the bloody thing off, does it? Your mate Andy's no better. I've been trying to reach him all morning. Not turned in, no 'phone call, nothing. Must be bloody catching.'

Donna held the 'phone at arm's length and pulled a disrespectful face. 'Do you need to tell me anything, or did you just want to give me a bollocking?'

Dexter's voice softened slightly. 'I wanted to tell you about the names on Kate's list. I've used up a shit-load of favours with a few old mates and checked three so far. Two no results, happy families all round as far as I can tell, but Michael Steven Adams is a different story. Self-made man, done well for himself. Well enough to retire early and swan off to the South of France to live the good life. Near some place called Collioure. Famous for artists, apparently.'

'So what?'

'The part where it gets interesting is what happened when he got there. There's a son, Benjamin, known as Ben. Aged fifteen. Apple of his dad's eye from what I've been told.'

Donna's pulse quickened. 'Something's happened to Ben, hasn't it?'

'Got it in one. Drowning accident while out diving. Family are devastated. The father especially from what I could gather. Seems he was too busy playing golf to take the lad out diving as often as he wanted. You can guess the rest; the boy went out on his own, got into difficulties and drowned.'

'I knew it,' Donna burst out. 'What about you? Convinced yet?'

'Getting there,' Dexter admitted, 'Something else about this list.'

'Oh?'

'Yeah. I've been checking dates. Ben Adams died just under two months ago. If we count him as number one on the list, it looks like Julian Carter could well have been number two. Christopher Wright died a few days later, but we now know his real father was named Hudson. Anything strike you so far?'

'No,' Donna admitted.

Dexter chuckled. 'Too bloody obvious for words. Alphabetical order. First Adams then Carter. Wright would have thrown the whole idea out of whack if we hadn't found out the name of his real father. Hudson. He's on the list. Robert Hudson.'

'Right,' Donna chipped in, noting Dexter's joint claim to the discovery of the real name of Chris Wright's father, but letting it pass for now.

'All easily explained deaths with nothing to suggest they died from any outside influences. Then there's the girl, Samantha Jackson; you've got somewhere with that by now, I'm assuming?'

'Yeah.'

'Go on, then.'

'I've found a link on Samantha's computer. Some lad she'd been in contact with recently. Her best mate reckons Samantha set off to meet this boy, Miles somebody or other and met with an accident on the way.'

'And you think there's more to it than that?'

'Yes. When I said I found a link on her computer; what I meant was I didn't find anything about this mysterious new friend. Every reference to him had been wiped and overwritten. Everything else she'd been looking at lately is still there, but not what I wanted to find. Anything at all to do with this Miles character has disappeared. I don't think it was Samantha who wiped the documents either; there's loads of entries left on her hard drive that could be embarrassing if her parents saw them, but only this one particular area has been deleted.'

'Can you do that? Clear something off a computer without having direct access to it?'

'Well, you couldn't. Nor me come to that. But to anyone who knew what they were doing it wouldn't be difficult. The sort of thing that Kate used to do all the time. Basic hacking.'

Dexter was silent for a moment. 'I see,' he said eventually, 'Where are you now?'

'Thornton Hough. On the pub car park.'

'Seven Stars?'

'Yeah.'

'Good enough. That's on the way. Stay put and I'll meet you there in twenty minutes or so. We can go together.'

'Go where?'

Dexter sighed. 'Where do you think? If we accept the idea of alphabetical order, the next name on the list is a Megan Lea. Lives in Ruthin. Time we paid her a visit, don't you think?'

The hotel was packed and the well-dressed man seated alone in a window seat attracted no more than a casual glance. A glass of water at his arm, his concentration on the sheaf of papers before him on the round table appeared total, but his apparent ease was deceptive. Even at times of apparently minimal danger, Marcus took extreme precautions. Always seated with his back to a solid wall, facing the door and senses alert for any change in his surroundings, his defences remained at maximum vigilance. The change of personnel caused by the enforced removal of a key man from the payroll would have a limited effect on his business affairs, but the new regime would take time to settle in before he was satisfied that Abdullah's replacement could be allowed to work without close supervision. The financial rewards were huge, far beyond the imagination of the Berber tribesmen who made up the bulk of his workforce, but their loyalty was beyond dispute. Every man knew the price of treachery: certain death and in a manner designed to cause prolonged and unbearable agony to the wretched offender. Faced with such a prospect, even the most venal subordinate would scarcely contemplate crossing his savage employer. Marcus was presently torn between the demands of his core business; the illicit movement of people and commodities across national borders, and his personal crusade to wreak vengeance on those who had once been directly responsible for the deprivation of his liberty. The decision had not been easy, but having reached a conclusion he would now give it his undivided attention. The next stage of his plan was well advanced; the mode of death for both of his next victims already decided and he would allow himself sufficient time to complete this phase of his plan before devoting all his attention to the further development of his business empire. The expansion of the European Union, with its guaranteed movement of subjects between member states, together with the vast numbers of wealthy Russians and Chinese thrown up by their exposure to the concept of a free market economy, had greatly increased his trading range. In particular, expansion into the satellite states of the former Soviet Union, brought problems which required specific solutions. His existing work force was predominantly Moslem who wouldn't necessarily be welcomed in such areas, riven as they were with religious strife. The solution was a stroke of genius. The man he had chosen to recruit his new army of key workers was already hard at work.

Nobody knows how many gypsies there are in the world. A lot. By their very nature, they fall outside the scope of the procedures nation states use to control the lives of their citizens. Gypsies are everywhere yet nowhere. They neither possess nor require any of the documentation that most other residents of consumer driven countries take for granted. No birth, marriage or death certificates, no medical records, no Social Security numbers or educational qualifications. And yet they exist. When it becomes necessary, a family member, always male, will obtain a driving license, but in other respects a true Romany will blend seamlessly into the society around them without any sign of their passing. This reclusive behaviour is both intentional and necessary. The lessons of history have been well learnt, never more so than in the Europe of the nineteen-thirties. The Nazi's feared the dilution of bloodlines would weaken and endanger the Fatherland, but their concerns were groundless. Gypsies are an ancient race with their own obsessions who avoid contact with their host nation as far as possible through a determination to avoid contamination of their own unique way of life. Gypsies learn from birth that their existence is conditional on an avoidance of official attention. They move freely in their own shadowy world, unchecked and uncounted, keep themselves to themselves, and are fiercely loyal to their extended family. Lias was of that ilk. A true Romany who could trace his family history through a dozen generations or more. Which made him ideal for the purpose Marcus had in mind.

In any event, Marcus needed to assure that suitably trained personnel were in place in the key markets of Western Europe before the planned expansion took place. That would necessitate a return to the inner regions of the High Atlas where the last vestiges of his present image, that of a prosperous and successful businessman, would be stripped away.

At the approach of the young waitress Marcus thrust his concerns to the back of his mind and smiled broadly.

'Anything from the bar, Sir?'

'No thank you,' Marcus replied, white teeth flashing as he indicated the glass of mineral water by his side. He'd already noted her excessive use of make-up and sun-streaked hair.

'Will you be dining with us tonight? I could fetch you a menu, if you like.'

'That would be most kind. Tracey, isn't it?' The girl's face lit up with the realisation that he'd noticed her sufficiently to remember her name. 'That's right, Sir.'

'I rather think I will eat here tonight. Perhaps you could reserve me a decent table?'

'Certainly, Sir. I'll make sure you're in my section so I can be certain you'll be well looked after.'

Marcus nodded his thanks and the girl reluctantly departed. The stupid little bitch would pay for her simpering manner, but that pleasure would have to wait. Pleasure was important, but business was his main priority now. An image of the young waitress, naked and screaming, flashed through his mind and his smile broadened. Glancing back from the bar area, Tracey caught his eye, imagined the smile was meant for her, and smiled in return. Marcus felt a stab of excitement. Work had to come first but he made a vow to return here at the earliest opportunity. He'd hate to deprive this girl of the treat she was presently imagining. Thrusting her face into a bowl of boiling water would do an excellent job of removing the excess make-up. It may even be an improvement although he doubted she'd find much to smile about by the time he'd finished with her.

CHAPTER 15

DEXTER thrust a scrap of paper into Donna's lap. 'Come on, navigator. Earn your keep. Where the hell do we go from here?' Donna squinted at Dexter's scrawl and sighed. She'd never been to Ruthin in her life and Dexter was acting as if she ought to know the place like the back of her hand.

'I can ask at the paper shop,' Donna suggested. Dexter flicked the left indicator and pulled up on double yellow lines outside a newsagent. Donna scuttled inside and stood behind a group of three women waiting at the counter. All three, together with the middle-aged man behind the counter, regarded her with deep Celtic suspicion.

'Can you tell me where this is, please?' Donna stepped forward, deciding that if she was going to be stared at it would be best to get the ordeal over with. Four pairs of eyes swivelled to the proffered scrap of paper, but it was the newsagent who reacted first.

'Which way have you come?'

'That way,' Donna replied, gesturing in the direction of the road outside.

'You've passed it, then. Turn round here and go back as far as the pelican crossing. It's the next road on the right. Can't miss it.'

'Thank you,' Donna said, turning to leave.

'What you be wanting with Megan, then?'

Donna blinked. She was used to blunt northern ways; difficult to be otherwise living in the same house as Peg, but this was pure nosiness. Even when uttered in a singsong lilt.

'I'm a friend of the family,' Donna replied. This was stretching the point to say the least, but she felt she had to say something. Perhaps she should have claimed to be recruiting staff for the Ann Summers sex shop chain.

'You'll be knowing the daughter then, I suppose?' a tall woman in a grey duffle coat enquired.

'Oh, that one.' This came from a thin dowdy woman, no doubt a pillar of the local chapel. 'No better than she should be, if you ask me.'

'*Nobody did ask you,*' Donna thought, but delayed her departure for a moment. Nosy neighbours had their uses occasionally. 'Oh?'

The thin woman sniffed scornfully. 'Running off like that with a man twice her age. Disgusting. Her poor mother.' Outside, Dexter's horn sounded twice. Donna ignored him.

Donna wished she'd not claimed friendship with the daughter. She couldn't really ask too many questions, not now she was apparently accepted as a close family friend.

'Of course, I'm not surprised,' the duffle-coated woman assured them all, 'She always was a bit flighty.' Nods of agreement all round. 'Poor Megan. All that sacrifice for nothing. Telling everyone how her daughter was all set to go to Teacher Training College, then the girl runs off with a man like that.' Donna detected a faint note of triumph in the air and suspected that the general opinion locally was that Megan Lea was paying the price of what was perceived as excessive boasting over her daughter's achievements.

'What do you mean, a man like that?'

'Well, so much older than her. Not a local. Not very likely either.' This produced knowing smirks all round.

'How do you mean?'

The thin woman looked askance at Donna. 'Didn't you know? Alison's boyfriend? He's coloured. Black as your hat.'

Donna backed away and rejoined Dexter who was revving the engine impatiently. 'Well?' He demanded.

'Back there,' Donna said, pointing over her shoulder. 'Turn round at the petrol station and its back there, on the right past the pelican crossing.' Dexter snorted and pulled away from the kerb. As they turned into the road, Donna motioned to Dexter that he should pull up well short of the house they were seeking.

'What now? Dexter grumbled as he parked the car.

'What do we know about Megan Lea? Apart from her being a member of a jury years ago?'

Dexter shrugged. 'Bugger all.'

'Well, we do now. She's got a daughter, Alison, supposed to be going off to college to train as a teacher. Mother very proud of her. Except there's a snag. A black boyfriend. Twice the daughter's age and some sort of tribal chief, according to the neighbours. Alison ran away with him.'

'Did she now?' Dexter looked impressed. 'Good stuff, Donna. Forewarned is forearmed.' He started the engine again and drove slowly down the road checking the house numbers.

The house was identical to its neighbour on either side in a neat terrace with smartly painted windows and gleaming brass letterboxes on solid wooden front doors. Dexter's assault on the knocker would have woken the dead and Donna thought once again how her companion's former profession had formed his doorstep habits. Dexter seemed incapable of imagining a situation where a resident would willingly come to the door to answer a stranger's knock. It was always the full police-style battering on the door. Donna hoped it would be answered before Dexter resorted to plan B and kicked the door off its hinges.

'Hello?' The woman standing in the doorway looked and sounded harassed. Dexter introduced himself and Donna, asked if he could talk to her on a personal matter, but gave out no other information.

'Won't you come in?' The woman said, standing aside and waving a hand towards the hall behind her. Donna stepped inside, marvelling at Dexter's ability to gain the trust of complete strangers who rushed to welcome him into their houses. Perhaps it was his unspoken air of command, but whatever the reason, the result was always the same.

The front room was small but immaculately tidy. No sign of a television or any items of a personal nature. Donna surmised that it was reserved for visitors and that the family actually lived in the rooms at the back of the house.

Dexter confirmed that the woman was Megan Lea and that she'd been a member of the Marcus Green jury. 'Heavens! Fancy bringing that up after all this time. I'd almost forgotten about it.' Her troubled expression gave the lie to her words and this was confirmed when she spoke again. 'Of course, I'll never forget that Marcus boy laughing out loud when the details of how those two little girls had died were read out. Made my flesh crawl. What on earth do you want to know about that trial? It was all so long ago. You're an investigator, did you say? What about the young lady? Are you learning to be an investigator as well, my dear?'

Donna wanted to laugh at Dexter's expression. Unable to get a word in as the enquiries came thick and fast, he made a typical Dexter decision and ignored her questions completely.

'I actually wanted to ask you about your daughter?'

'Alison? Whatever for? What's she done now?'

Dexter waved a deprecatory hand. 'Nothing, as far as I am aware. I'm interested in where she is at the moment, that's all.'

'As if I know,' Mrs Lea snapped. 'And I'd like to know just who you think you are to burst in here asking questions about my daughter.' She stuck out her chin, daring Dexter to respond. Donna waited with bated breath for Dexter's response to the allegation that they'd burst into the house as her recollection was that they'd both entered by invitation. Dexter revealed a hitherto unknown degree of diplomacy, smoothing away the woman's concerns without revealing more than the absolute minimum level of information concerning the real reason for their presence in the house.

'That's all right, then. Would you like a cup of tea? A biscuit, perhaps? What about you, dear? I bet you'd like a nice cup of tea, wouldn't you?' Donna would have loved a cup of tea, but Dexter got there first.

'No thanks,' he replied firmly, 'We're both fine.'

'Well, if you're sure.'

'Quite sure. Now, your daughter. Alison, did you say?'

'Alison, that's right.' Mrs Lea's face clouded. 'Roger would tell you the same as me. Sorry, Roger is my husband.' Dexter nodded. He'd worked that out for himself.

'Did Alison leave home?' Donna broke her silence, earning herself a glare from Dexter. Donna never knew whether she should speak or not while Dexter was conducting an interview. Sometimes Dexter praised her input; on other occasions he was rather less pleased. Such as now.

'Sorry, I've forgotten your name,' Mrs Lea said, her face creasing in concern.

'Donna. Donna O'Prey.'

'Hello Donna. Call me Megan, won't you?' Donna glanced at Dexter but he was looking out of the window. Megan hadn't asked him to call her by her first name. Emboldened, Donna pressed on with the interview.

'You were saying about Alison leaving home?'

'Oh yes. A few weeks ago. She'd been acting up for months before she left. Broke my heart. Roger's heart too although he pretends he's washed his hands of her. You know what men are like?' She exchanged a conspiratorial smile with Donna, ignoring Dexter completely. 'Alison has always had an independent streak, but this was the last straw. All set for college, done well in her exams and everything. Always wanted to be a teacher. Talked of nothing else until she met up with that chef. Longhaired scruffy devil. How he manages in a decent kitchen I don't know. Wears a cap, I suppose.'

Donna blinked. She'd not been expecting this and by the look on Dexter's face she wasn't the only one. Donna's expectation had been the discovery of a recent friendship, almost certainly developing without the knowledge of the girl's family, as had been the case with Julian Carter and everyone else she'd subsequently investigated.

'Had she known the boy long?'

'Well, I'd not call him a boy; he's a grown man, probably ten years older than Alison, but yes, she'd been seeing him for three or four months, I suppose. Roger was convinced she was doing it to annoy us.' Megan looked directly at Donna; seemingly she'd forgotten Dexter was even in the room. 'You'll know all about teenage rebellion, I suppose. Roger said best to ignore it and she'll come to her senses. Far from cooling off, Alison took off with Tony, that's his name, without even consulting us. Left us a note saying she'd got a job in the same hotel as Tony and she'd ring when she had settled in.'

'Did she? Ring, I mean?'

'Every week for the first three weeks. Then we had a row. My fault. I couldn't bear to see her throwing her life away with a man like that. I mean to say, how if she had children? What chance would they stand?'

Donna had the sense to look baffled. Thanks to the local gossip she'd picked up earlier, Donna had a fair idea what Megan meant but had not been told anything directly as yet. Megan saw her confusion and laughed nervously. 'Oh, I didn't tell you the best bit about Tony. He's black.' She sat back in her chair, looking expectantly at Donna. An awkward silence ensued.

'Not that I'm racist,' Megan announced, 'but when it's your daughter involved, you just have to say something, don't you? Alison started a big row. Said I was a prejudiced old cow and that's when Roger took over. He told her good and proper. Get back here and go off to college like we both wanted for her and he'd forget about her bad behaviour and rudeness.'

'What did Alison say to that?' Donna asked. She had a good idea what she'd have said in the girl's place.

'Only told him to get stuffed, didn't she? Roger was furious. He told Alison straight that if she wanted to waste her life away that was up to her, but as far as he was concerned she wasn't welcome back here if she intended bringing that Tony with her. I agreed with him and I told Alison so. She put the 'phone down on us and we've not heard a peep out of her since.'

'Oh, I see. Do you have a photograph of Alison we could look at?'

'I can give you one. I don't want it. You'll understand why when you see it.' Megan stood up, straightened her skirt and left the room.

Donna looked across at Dexter. 'Good, so far,' he said, 'She doesn't seem very interested in why we're here, so try and keep it that way. See if you can get an address off her for the girl. Looks a bit different from the other cases and she'll be even more vulnerable living away from home.'

Megan clumped back into the room, having slipped on a pair of orthopaedic clogs during her absence. 'My feet are creasing me,' she announced, 'High arches, you know? I found you that 'photo.' She handed a small colour print across to Donna. Alison was a pretty girl with long dark hair framing her face, but it was the other figure that caught Donna's attention. Far from being, to quote her informant in the paper shop, as black as your hat, the man standing with an arm around Alison's waist was of mixed race. Café-au-lait would have been Donna's description, and he was almost indecently handsome.

'Tony?'

'Yes. See what I mean? Just imagine the problems if, God forbid, they had children.' Donna thought any children produced by the couple in the photograph would be gorgeous, but had enough sense to keep her opinions to herself. This was Ruthin, not the cosmopolitan streets of Liverpool 8.

'Would you have Alison's address handy? I may have to go and see her?'

'It's him isn't it? That Tony. What is it? Drugs, I suppose. They're all on drugs aren't they, those sort of people?'

'No, nothing like that,' Dexter interjected as Donna hesitated. 'Just routine. Don't suppose for a minute we'll ever follow it up. It's just to keep the paperwork tidy.'

'Oh, I see.' Megan left the room once more, returning almost instantly with a glossy leaflet. She handed it to Dexter and remained standing. 'That's the address of the hotel. Fancy place in Folkestone. If you do get to see Alison, ask her to ring me. She can reverse the charges if she's short of money.'

Dexter nodded. He glanced at the leaflet. 'There's a telephone number down here. Have you not thought about ringing your lass? See how she's getting on?'

'No, I've not. She knows our position well enough. She can ring me if she wants, but I'll not be chasing after her. Not while she's still with that Tony.'

Dexter glanced at Donna and she rose swiftly to her feet. Megan led the way to the front door, glancing at the sky as she opened it. 'We'll have rain later,' she pronounced, 'Mind you get yourselves back before it comes down.' She closed the door and Donna followed Dexter back to the car.

'The boyfriend was a surprise,' Dexter said as he fastened his seatbelt. 'I was expecting some sort of fuzzy-wuzzy with a bone through his nose.'

Donna flinched. Although he was far less extreme in his views than most other policemen of Donna's acquaintance, years of conditioning had produced a distinct absence of subtlety regarding the colour of a man's skin or his sexual inclinations. She gave a non-committal nod. 'What now?'

Dexter didn't answer until he'd eased the car out into the main road. 'I'll ring the hotel later. Check there've been no accidents we should know about, but that's about it for now. I'll have a word with Abbott. See if he's interested in making it official.'

Donna gave him a sharp look which he missed. 'Involve the police, you mean?'

'Maybe. If I can make out a decent case, why not? Face it, Donna; if there's any truth in this theory of yours, we're talking murder not just a random collection of tragic accidents and sudden deaths. That's police work. Not that I've any great hopes.'

'Why not?'

'Look, to you it's all as clear as crystal, but coppers don't think like that. To Abbott, it'll be nothing more than coincidence. Tragic for the families, but all easily explained. A suicide, a drowning accident, a drug overdose and a young girl getting hit by a train while trespassing on railway property. Nothing that stands out there. All too common, I'm afraid. Each case has been looked at already, investigated by the coroner and filed away. Nothing to justify the manpower of a major investigation.'

'But, what about the list of jurors and the connection with Marcus Green?'

Dexter smiled mirthlessly. 'A list of jurors obtained in some dubious manner by Kate. I don't know the details, but I'll lay odds she didn't get hold of that list by any legal means, so best not push that angle too hard. And as for Marcus Green, I can tell you now what Abbott will say. He's dead. Just another statistic.'

'That's bollocks,' Donna exploded.

Dexter grinned. 'That's right,' he agreed cheerfully, 'You know that and I know that, but where's the evidence? No evidence, no case. I've said it myself often enough over the past thirty years, I'll be stunned if Abbott sees it any other way.'

'It's not fair,' Donna grumbled.

'Look on the bright side for once. Assuming the law isn't interested in your fancy theories, it still leaves you with a case to get on with.'

Donna waited for a moment while his words sank in. 'You mean we're still going on with it? Whatever Abbott says?'

'If you're still interested.'

'You know I am.'

'Right then. I'll do the telephone stuff and arrange to put our case to Abbott. Why don't you have a poke around? See if you can find any trace of your mate Marcus. Try his mother's place and that island he used to hide out on." Dexter held up a finger and waited for Donna to look at him. 'Watch yourself. If there's one chance in a hundred that your idea about Marcus Green makes sense, he's bloody dangerous. I don't need to remind you of that, do I? Get hold of Andy and take him with you. He's not exactly an all-in wrestler, but he's better than nothing.'

The last time Donna had passed this spot, the charred timbers and fallen masonry had re-opened the lid on memories best left undisturbed. Now, as she coasted to a halt outside the mesh screen, she saw that the site had been cleared.

135

Not a single brick or broken slate remained. Not even a weed disturbed the perfect symmetry of what was clearly intended to become a building plot.

'Nothing here,' Donna mused aloud. The house where Marcus Green and his mother had supposedly died was no more than a patch of bare earth. She'd often speculated on the identity of the poor wretch whose size and approximate age had so closely resembled Marcus Green. Donna shivered, remembering the furious blaze in which the unfortunate body double had perished, along with the mother of Marcus and the old man and his son who'd been unlucky enough to have lived next door to a monster. Her irritation flared at the continuing failure of anyone in authority to accept the true facts: namely that Marcus had not been one of the victims at this site. She'd seen him after the event, almost died at his hands, yet only Dexter seemed prepared to give her story any credence. She'd often suspected that even Dexter had his doubts, but at least he was prepared to listen to her.

Not that Dexter wasn't still a pain in the arse. The manner in which he had laid down the law when Donna had made a perfectly innocent enquiry about Kate's funeral still rankled with her. "Forget about a funeral. There won't be one. Kate wouldn't want any weeping on her account. Funerals are for sanctimonious bastards. Just forget you even asked and get on with your job." End of discussion.

A woman tottered past; ridiculously high heels clip-clopping, and Donna woke from her dismal reverie. She grinned. Andy would have had some ribald comment to hand if he'd been here. Donna had rung him, sent text messages and eventually gone round to his flat last night, but there was no sign of him. The old bloke in the bottom flat told her he'd not seen Andy since yesterday morning when he'd gone off all of a rush. She'd not told Dexter; he'd have only made some remark about Andy's sexual inclinations, especially as the old boy had given a strong hint that there had been a man involved. If Andy had met someone special and wanted a day off work, good luck to him. Her only regret was that she was alone now. Andy was such great company. Irreverent to the point of flippancy, amusing and with looks to put any matinee idol to shame. His only flaw, as Donna saw it, was in the unfortunate nature of his sexuality. What use was a Greek God if he was also gay? Donna had long since settled for Andy being her best mate, but the prospect of what might have been still rankled within the devious depths of her mind. A long-forgotten fragment arose from the depths of her memory and Donna smiled. She'd been out for the evening with Andy, touring the Liverpool pubs, and had been accosted when she went for a pee by a girl about her own age, breasts bursting out of her satin top and a skirt just about covering her arse.

'That your feller?' The girl asked. Straight to the point.

No,' Donna had replied, 'Not a chance. Not much chance for you, either. Be a different story if you'd got a good-looking brother in tow.'

'Never?' The girl's face was a frozen mask of disbelief.

'Yeah. Queer as a nine-quid note,' Donna had confirmed.

The girl looked at Donna for a long moment. 'What a fucking waste of decent tackle,' had been her eventual response.

Donna tapped her fingers on the steering wheel. 'Earth to Donna,' she called out, 'Move it.' She'd noticed this recent tendency to talk to herself while alone in the car. Why not? At least she could listen to someone whose opinions made sense.

Donna wiped the smile off her face and sank back in her seat and then her face brightened. The island. That was it. Marcus Green had kept a number of young women captive on a remote island in the middle of a lake. Donna had spent a few hours there and the memories were still painful, but she had to be certain in her own mind that Marcus wasn't still around. 'Where else can I look?' she muttered, 'All I know is where he used to spend his time? So: we work with what we have. Dexter wants proof; let's see if I can't find him some.'

A strong breeze threw swirling clouds of dust into the face of Dexter as he climbed wearily from his car. Grimacing, he collected a buff folder from the boot, locked the car and strode towards the two-storey building over the road. Explicit graffiti and mesh-screened windows revealed the identity of his destination as clearly as the familiar blue sign. Dexter paused at the entrance, remembering the many triumphs, and inevitably the occasional abject failure, which had marked the years he'd spent in the back offices of this building. As a career police officer, Dexter's experience pre-dated the political correctness and emphasis on Community Policing which dominated the working lives of his erstwhile colleagues, but the basic nature of the job remained the same: the prevention of crime and the relentless pursuit of offenders. Certain superficial aspects may have changed since the Police Force became the more user-friendly Police Service, largely related to finite budgets and financial constraints, but Dexter knew better than most the quality of the men and women who policed this tough city and was encouraged by that knowledge.

Abbott was already waiting. Dexter's old sergeant's waistline may have expanded since they worked together, but the firm handshake and beaming smile were as familiar as ever. Within moments, shirt-sleeved bodies surrounded Dexter; each eager to shake his hand and exchange shared memories.

'Come on, Guv. Let these tossers get on with finding lost dogs and come with me,' Abbott called after a few minutes. To members of the old squad like Abbott, Dexter was still the Guvnor and always would be. Dexter shrugged his apologies and followed Abbott through the double doors and into the squad room at the rear. It wasn't the largest room in the building, but it had been the nerve centre for major investigations for as long as most officers could remember. Dexter's arrival brought a flurry of excitement from the surviving members of his old squad, but the new officers all knew him by reputation. Marriott, tolerated by Dexter for his ability rather than any redeeming aspect of his personality, released a loud fart as his contribution to the chorus of greetings and Dexter smiled broadly. Abbott took Dexter's arm and led him to the small annexe that was his office. He left the door open, having adopted the habits of his predecessor; Dexter had never closed his office door.

'Hawkes not about then?' Dexter enquired casually. Chief Superintendent Hawkes was the notional commander of the Major Inquiry Team and Abbott's ultimate superior, but Dexter's opinion of the senior officer mirrored that of Abbott. Hawkes and others like him were partly responsible for Dexter opting for early retirement. For any dedicated working copper, the politically correct pseudo-accountants who made policy decisions and thereby determined which cases were to be pursued and which abandoned when investigation failed to pass some artificially imposed test of economic viability, were the complete antithesis of the principles which had governed Dexter's career. He knew the faults were not all on one side; Dexter had a maverick bloody-minded nature which ensured the loyalty of his troops but was anathema to the control freaks who dominated the upper echelons of Divisional Headquarters.

'Not likely. Divisional golf tournament at Royal Liverpool. Glad-handing the top brass and getting some Hoylake sunshine.'

Dexter snorted. 'Best place for him. Any joy with that list of names I sent you?'

Abbott frowned. 'Fuck me; you don't want much, do you? Supposed to be retired and out to pasture at that cushy firm you somehow managed to con into employing you.' His smile took the sting out of his words and he was reaching into the cluttered drawers of his desk even as he spoke. Abbott produced an unmarked file, containing about a dozen sheets of paper and tossed it towards Dexter. 'There you go. I've run a trace on all the names on the list. Most of them have kids, all still alive and kicking as of this morning, apart from the ones I've ticked.'

Dexter studied the top sheet of paper, noting Abbott's neat tick against the names of Adams, Carter and Jackson, but also alongside that of Kenneth Gilbride. 'What happened here?'

Abbott reached across and turned over several sheets of paper. 'Here you go. Kenneth Gilbride. One child, Rebecca Juliet. Died in 1996. No suspicious circumstances. Aged nine.'

Dexter frowned. 'How come?'

Abbott grimaced. 'Asthma attack. Poor little bugger.'

'Doesn't fit anyway,' Dexter growled. 'Marcus bloody Green was banged up when she died. Couldn't have been him.'

Abbott looked thoughtful. 'There was something odd about that. I spoke to the collator, a real old boy. Been in the job for years. He remembered seeing the name on a recent crime report. Turned out it was a case of vandalism. Rebecca Gilbride's grave was one of a number vandalised and defaced. Vandalism, random stuff. Headstones shattered, diesel oil poured over the graves. Nothing will grow there. The parents were devastated. The father especially. Especially when his wife had a nasty fall on the way out of the cemetery. The man who found her reckoned she must have slipped on the wet grass, fallen against a gravestone and banged her head. She's been in a coma ever since.'

'When was this?'

'About ten days ago. No question it was an accident. I made a point of following it up. She'd gone to put flowers on the grave. Went twice a week, regular as clockwork. No one remembers seeing anyone else around at the time. Just one of those things.'

Dexter grunted. 'Any thoughts on this?' he waved a hand towards the list of names. Abbott looked almost embarrassed, glancing through the open doorway at the crowded room beyond.

'This is more than just a list of names,' Dexter said, pointedly when the other man's silence persisted. 'One of the other names on that list has lost a son, but nothing will show up on any official records. Hudson: had a kid with some other woman. Nobody else knew he was the father. Well, not exactly nobody. If I'm right, then at least one person made it his business to find out.'

Abbott coughed nervously. 'That's all this is though, isn't it? One big supposition. One of your famous hunches.'

Dexter flushed, clearly annoyed. 'There's enough here to make it a bit more than a bloody supposition. Coincidence? Come off it. You should know better.'

Abbott shifted nervously in his chair. 'Be reasonable. You know what it's like trying to keep the cases we've already got up to speed without touting for extra work.'

Dexter grunted again. 'Suit yourself. Looks like it's just me and Donna then.'

'Donna? She's in on this, is she?' Abbott's face cracked into a smile.

'Her case. Most of it is down to her. She reminds me of someone I used to know a few years back. Before he turned into a fat idle bastard who wouldn't know a crime if it turned up in his front room and pissed on the mat.'

Abbott tried without success to ignore the rebuke. 'Donna's a good girl, right enough,' he agreed. 'Why didn't you say it came from her instead of letting me think it was all the idea of some old bastard who's forgotten how things are back in the real world? I'd have taken a bit more notice.'

Dexter grinned. 'Your loss,' he said, cheerfully, gathering the sheets of paper together and bundling them into the buff file. 'Do me a favour and keep one eye on this list.' He reached into the file, took out the top sheet and handed it to Abbott. 'Anything happens to any of these people, anything at all; I need to know about it.'

Abbott thrust the sheet of paper back towards Dexter. 'Already in hand,' he said, 'Anything else we can do while you're here?' The question seemed innocuous, but Abbott's eyes were wary. He knew better than most that giving Dexter an inch made it an absolute certainty that he'd go on to take a mile.

Dexter paused. 'Maybe. What's the crack on the Sheehan Brothers?'

Abbott whistled. 'Fuck me, now you're back in the big time. Fat Stan Sheehan took early retirement. His brother too. We've got a new kid on the block.'

'So I heard. What can you tell me?'

'Not a lot. Never thought I'd be saying this, but I almost miss Fat Stan. Better the devil you know, I suppose. At least we always knew what to expect. Nowadays, it's a fucking lottery. Drug shipments come and go. We get the occasional low-level bust, but that's about it. If anyone out there knows who the gaffer is these days, they're not telling me or my lads. Best we can do is plod on and wait for a mistake. Might be a long wait.'

'You got anything on Sheehan? Address, for instance?'

'Suppose so.'

Dexter stood up. 'Come on then. Shift your fat arse.'

Abbott sighed resignedly. He walked in front of Dexter and studied the desks that filled the room. 'Jock,' he ordered, 'Nip up to the canteen and see if the fat cunt's still up there. Tell him I want a job doing right now. Come on lad, move it.'

'Jock' Ferguson, despite his surname was of West Indian extraction with a rich Scouse accent. Dexter knew that DC Ferguson had battled harder than most for acceptance on joining the squad, his complexion being a greater barrier than any other aspect of his job performance. Any police station has elements of racial bias, usually explained by the undeniable fact that arrests of black youths in certain areas were up to five times more frequent than their white counterparts. Any dispassionate study of these statistics would conclude that there was an element of self-justification in the figures, but a police station is not the most enlightened of places, despite strenuous efforts to change the attitudes of the working troops. Political correctness imposed from the top had been one of the problems with which Ferguson had to contend. Minorities, meaning Asian or black officers, were actively encouraged by recruitment and promotion boards and this led to resentment in certain quarters. Being a different colour was enough in itself to cause problems with some colleagues, worse even than being female. Only officers who were openly gay fared worse and standard opinion was that they only had themselves to blame: If they had to be gay, at least they should have the sense to keep quiet about it. Dexter rated Ferguson as a good copper. His arrest record was as good as anyone else in the squad and he'd proved himself as a good team man. At Abbot's request, Jock left the squad room at the double in search of the fat cunt, also referred to on rare occasions as DC Edge. The name had been the result of Marriott, of all people, coming to his defence when Edge was suffering a particularly virulent attack from fellow squad members due to his preference for the warmth of the squad room over the bitterly cold pavements outside. 'Leave the fat cunt alone', Marriott had said, 'He's better off typing my reports than wandering round out there being a fucking traffic hazard.' The recipient of numerous warnings about his size, Edge was a good typist, his stubby fingers flitting rapidly over the keys and he kept the files up to date like nobody else. For once, Dexter had agreed with Marriott. Whatever the cause of Edge's weight problem, and he surmised it was less to do with glands than with the number of kebabs and burgers the man devoured, he was more use in administrative duties than he'd ever be out on the streets. When a quick reliable transcript was required, Edge came into his own and it was for this very reason that his natural sloth was tolerated.

Donna shifted her position as the sun burst through a cloud and shone directly into her eyes. Squinting, she shuffled the plastic chair around until her face regained some shade. She'd ordered coffee and cake and was waiting impatiently while she flicked through a complimentary copy of a tabloid newspaper. A rapid perusal was sufficient to confirm her prejudices; this was a paper she'd never consider shelling out money for.

Donna slid round in her chair as the man behind was trying to read over her shoulder and half-turned to glare at him. His face was red and shiny. Not the ruddy complexion of a hill farmer, but looking almost like he'd been scalded. Hair sprouted from his nostrils and ears as if making up for deficiencies elsewhere. A hint of pink scalp showed through the sparsely arranged hair on his head while facial hair was non-existent. This was one man who'd never known five o'clock shadow. Donna had divided opinions about male facial hair. Designer stubble looked great on the right person, but kissing the same person at nine o'clock in the morning and five o'clock in the afternoon was a very different experience. Some women forked out a small fortune for a facial scrub that did exactly the same thing.

Whether the meal was a late breakfast or an early lunch, the man was eating a steak that was so rare Donna had to check it wasn't still moving. The growing pool of blood on his plate caused Donna to give serious consideration to becoming a vegetarian. Then she thought about breaking the news to Peg and decided against it.

'You finished with that paper yet, girl? Either read the bloody thing or pass it over here. If you're eyeing up the competition I've got bad news for you. You're gonna need one hell of a boob job before you stand a chance of getting on page three.'

Donna's anger flared momentarily, subsiding instantly as she saw the broad grin on the affable features of the man seated behind her. She grinned back and placed the paper into his outstretched hand. The waitress was weaving through the pavement tables, clutching a laden tray protectively to her midriff. Donna studied her order with approval. A tall coffee mug topped with an inch of froth, thickly sliced carrot cake and a plateful of toasted teacakes.

As Donna tucked in she reflected on her wasted journey to the isolated island where Marcus Green had imprisoned his captives. Even from the distant shore of the lake it was clear that the cabin had been totally destroyed by fire. The memory of her last sighting of Marcus Green, pinned to a wooden beam by a knife thrust through his cheek as she and the other women scrabbled away from the blazing cabin was as fresh in her mind as if it had happened yesterday. Her relief at having escaped had turned to nameless terror when a police search of the charred remains had failed to find any trace of the body of Marcus. That last glimpse of Marcus, with a defiant expression on his battered and broken features, had stayed with her ever since and his was the face she saw in her dreams almost every single night.

Donna pulled out her mobile and rang Dexter. She gave a brief account of her progress, or lack of it, so far.

'So, what next? Any suggestions?'

'What about that girl? The one who showed you the picture of his island.'

Donna's face brightened. 'Margaret,' she exclaimed. 'Of course.' Margaret was the daughter of a couple she'd interviewed during the course of her previous case. Marcus had lived in the house next door until the age of seven and Margaret appeared to have been his only friend. Although she showed none of the physical characteristics of Down's syndrome, Margaret was severely retarded and yet she had been directly responsible for providing Donna with the information she needed to find the hiding place of Marcus Green. Deep in the woods behind the house where Margaret lived was an old house, long since abandoned and known only to Marcus and his former playmate. Donna had seen the picture of an island painted on the wall and had instinctively known that this was where she would find Marcus.

Twenty minutes later, Donna pulled onto the gravel drive outside a large detached house on Caldy Hill. As she stood on the doorstep Donna felt a sudden premonition of dread. She tried to ignore her shaking hand as she pressed the large ceramic bell push. She waited in silence, but no one came. As Donna resigned herself to failure, the heavy door opened catching her by surprise. Donna recognised the man standing before her, but only just. It had been not much more than two years since she'd last seen Mister Snape yet he seemed to have aged ten years in the interim.

'Donna, isn't it?' Even the voice was different. Shaky and brittle rather than the crisp baritone she remembered. Donna nodded.

'Please come in.'

Donna had stepped inside before she realised she'd not given any reason for calling unannounced, but Mister Snape didn't seem interested, much less curious. He ushered Donna inside like a farmer shooing a favourite cow into the milking parlour. *There you go, Daisy. Come on, old girl.*

The last time Donna had been a guest in this house, she'd been led to the main sitting room which she remembered as a lovely airy room overlooking the garden. On this occasion, a small conservatory at the very rear of the house proved to be their destination. The woman seated on a cane chair was a shadow of the person Donna had seen on the occasion of her previous visit. Drawn and haggard, thin as a rail and with an unkempt thatch of white hair, the contrast with the elegant woman Donna remembered could not have been greater. The woman looked up but gave no indication that she'd even noticed the arrival of her visitor.

'We'll go through to the garden, should we?'

Donna nodded, feeling a return of the chill she'd felt on the doorstep. Mister Snape touched his wife gently on the arm as he passed but her gaze was firmly fixed on the far wall. The once-glorious garden was neglected and dowdy but Donna gave it scarcely a glance.

The old man shook his head sadly. 'Sorry about all this. Not at her best today, I'm afraid. It's been like this for the last three weeks or so. Some days are bad; some are worse. Neither of us have good days any more.'

'What happened?'

'Margaret.' As he spoke his daughter's name Donna flinched. 'She wandered off. A car hit her. By the time I noticed the gate was open it was too late. They never found the driver.'

'Oh God, I'm so sorry.'

'She'd never done it before. Not once. She never went out on her own. Never. She knew it was wrong. Knew cars were dangerous. We can't understand what possessed her to wander off.'

Dexter sighed as he rose slowly to his feet. The past hour had been instructive but he'd no wish to over-extend his stay. Abbott had gone as far as he'd dared in sharing information which Dexter knew to be strictly off limits and it was time to go before he used up the last traces of goodwill which twenty years of friendship had bought him. He had a thick folder on the Sheehan Brothers and a list of contacts in the Irish Republic.

'I'd best be off,' Dexter announced. 'Can't hold up the fight against crime any longer. You must have better things to do than chatting to old farts like me.'

Abbott grinned, his failure to protest Dexter's statement giving the remark credence. 'About time too.'

The two men walked together through the crowded room while Dexter fielded quips and mock insults with the skill of long practise. At the main entrance, Dexter turned and grasped Abbott by the hand. 'Thanks mate.' The words brought a flush to Abbott's cheeks and Dexter regretted he'd not demonstrated such largesse during the course of their working relationship. He'd taken Abbott and the rest of his old squad for granted, expecting perfection and a similar level of commitment to his own without giving much thought to their feelings, but Dexter knew it was far too late now to make amends. Abbott gave a smile of farewell as Dexter turned to walk back to his car. A red-faced uniformed officer, late for roll call, charged past on his way into the building and Dexter frowned as the man brushed against him, causing him to step aside. He walked away; innocent of the bollocking the unfortunate officer was to receive on arrival inside the main entrance.

'Were you born without a brain or are you just fucking stupid? Do you know who that was? That man you almost knocked over, you clumsy sod?' Abbott rarely raised his voice, but his words carried clear across the room. The officer shook his head.

'No Guv.'

'No, didn't think so. Well, remember his face, sunshine, because that was Dexter. The best bloody copper that ever set foot in this place. Bar none. Just try telling any of the MIT lads that you tried to knock Dexter over and see where it gets you. It'll fuck up any hopes you might have had of ever getting somewhere in this job. So next time you see him, take your hat off, grovel at his feet and apologise for being a dozy young bastard who's in too much of a hurry to know when he's just met a real pro. Now shift your arse out of my sight before I really lose my temper.'

Mister Snape had returned to comfort his wife, leaving Donna standing on the gravel drive in a world of her own, her gaze fixed on the distant line of trees behind the white picket fence. When she spoke her voice was as faint and tremulous as that of an old woman.

'I need to see the house in the woods.' Donna announced to a blackbird pulling a stubborn worm out of the lawn. She set off, walking with purpose, and reached the double-barred fence where she slid between the top and lower bars almost without breaking stride. The route through the woods was tortuous and over grown with brambles, but Donna followed the path unerringly until the canopy of leaves above her head reduced her field of vision to the immediate vicinity. Donna gave a gasp of astonishment when she burst into the clearing and saw the old house again. It was even more dilapidated than she'd remembered with broken tiles littering the undergrowth and the wooden handrail around the entrance was broken and overgrown with moss. On her previous visit to this spot, Margaret had told her that the house used to belong to the Green family. They'd never lived here; their house was much further along, at the other side of the woods, but the old house was part of the estate. Marcus used to play here when he was a young child. He'd later painted a picture of the island where he was living on one of the walls.

Donna set her foot on the lower step, watching it flex alarmingly as she pushed her way through the fronds of an overgrown creeper and entered the dark interior. Above her head was a dense canopy of trees with the odd glimpse of sky. The roof had long since collapsed and the spars of the upper storey stood out starkly like the ribs of some gigantic skeleton. Towards the back of the house, part of the roof had somehow survived and it was there that Donna headed, stepping carefully on the large wooden joists that bisected the floor beneath her feet. Two rooms at the rear were virtually untouched by the ravages of time. The larger still bore the painting Donna had seen previously, but the picture was almost unrecognisable having been daubed with paint until the scene it had depicted had ceased to be a viable image. Donna looked above her head and saw a row of tiny corpses, mice, squirrels and even a tiny kitten, all of them pinned to the main beam by rusty nails hammered through each eye.

'Marcus,' Donna said aloud, her voice a harsh rasp. She'd seen this gruesome sight before. Two years ago at the home of Marcus Green's mother. But many of the corpses of these poor little buggers were recent. Which confirmed Marcus had been here. On this very spot.

Donna started to walk away, placing her feet carefully on the main joists and suddenly pounced on a small object in the corner of the room. The stub of a cigarette. The gold band gave it away and any lingering doubts evaporated instantly. It was identical to the one she'd taken to the old man in Bold Street and clear proof that Marcus was still alive. Still killing.

Chalk up one more victim. Margaret. The poor girl from the big house back there. She would have never left the safety of her garden. Not unless she was with a friend. Someone she trusted. Someone like Marcus.

Donna knew with a grim certainty that Margaret's death was her fault. She'd been wracking her brains, trying to remember if she'd ever let it slip that she'd seen the picture Marcus painted for Margaret. Once Donna had seen the picture, she'd known where to find him, had passed the information to Kate and Kate told Dexter where to find Marcus. Just in time, as it turned out. An hour later and Marcus would have been long gone and Donna would have been at the bottom of the lake along with all the other women that had been lured to that island.

A single tear ran down Donna's cheek. All of this was her fault. If she'd never come here two years ago, Margaret would still be alive and her parents would still have something to live for. Even if she didn't actually say the words, Marcus would have known Donna had seen Margaret. Talked to her. Seen that picture on the wall. Margaret had been the only possible link to him. That's why he killed her. Same with Kate. If Donna had never contacted her, begged for her help, Kate would still be alive today. Both of them had died because of her fucking obsession with Marcus Green.

CHAPTER 15

MARCUS finished the last of the marmalade and debated whether to ask for more. From his position against the back wall of the dining room he could see the entrance lobby as far as the main staircase and had been watching the girl with guarded interest as she dealt with a series of arriving and departing guests. The hotel had proved the ideal base while he dealt with pressing matters in Dover; close enough for convenience yet sufficiently removed from the troops on the ground to preserve his sense of detachment. The scorn he felt for the minions under his command was immense, but a degree of personal contact was necessary to ensure the smooth running of his operations when he was no longer available to enforce loyalty and maintain discipline. Abdullah's replacement, a desert warrior from the shifting sands of the Western Sahara, had responded well to the increased responsibilities which accompanied his recent promotion. Jela was a man of few words but the burning eyes promised total obedience. Marcus ensured loyalty by a traditional stick and carrot system, but his methods went far beyond anything taught at Harvard Business School. The rewards for unblemished service were vast and the corresponding penalties for failure equally off the scale. Abdullah had paid with his life for a solitary lapse, his greed momentarily out-weighing his fear, but Marcus had ensured that his own response had been sufficient to ensure loyalty from Abdullah's successor. He'd received confirmation that the last surviving member of Abdullah's family, a cousin working as a translator in a shipping office in Rabat, had been doused with petrol and set alight in full view of horrified work colleagues. This relentless persecution of offenders and their extended family was the key to his labour relations policy. His Berber work force understood strong leadership. A man who worked for Marcus would become wealthy beyond his dreams and it was only right that the man who was the source of such riches should expect unstinting obedience in return.

The girl glanced across the room and saw Marcus watching her. She smiled, brushing away a stray hair which had escaped the confines of the peaked uniform cap she wore. He would never have taken the chance of such overt surveillance under normal circumstances, but the girl was spectacularly lovely and he would soon be obliged to leave England to recruit fresh recruits for the expansion of his business empire. The rewards of his chosen employment were immense. Even the business ventures he'd set up as a means of legitimising the proceeds of drug deals, video hire shops and amusement arcades throughout Britain were flourishing although the money safely stored in tax havens where discretion and secrecy were assured had long since failed to interest him. True rewards were to be found not in balance sheets, but in pitting his wits against others and winning the battles.

A figure moving through his field of vision brought Marcus to full alert until he was certain the fellow guest was no threat to his security. The elderly man nodded as he passed by and Marcus inclined his head in response. The double life that had become his daily routine never ceased to fascinate him. Marcus was able to pass freely through any environment; secure in the knowledge that none of the men and women who noted his presence had any inkling of the unique threat he represented. This was important to him. His personal security depended upon this ability to blend into his surroundings. His present situation was a case in point. None of his fellow guests or any member of the hotel staff had the faintest idea that a man who was directly responsible for numerous murders had walked the same stairwells, eaten at the same table and chatted amiably to each of them over the course of the last few days.

Marcus pushed back his chair and prepared to leave the dining room. His work here was almost over and it would soon be time to move on. He had arranged to meet a man down by the harbour who rented out lock-up garages. Marcus had made preliminary contact by telephone to explain that he needed a secure dry garage to store a classic car. He'd been re-assured on all counts and had agreed to meet the man and pay three months rental in advance. Marcus had given his name as Tony Beech and had arranged to send a friend down with the money, explaining that he worked as a hotel chef and would be unable to get away from work to deal with the matter in person.

Marcus glanced across at the lobby and saw the girl was now chatting to an elderly male guest. He'd settled on the means of her death but would delay the execution of his plan until he checked out of the hotel. His other key lieutenants had received their instructions through Jela, who remained the only person able to identify him. New routes and methods had been discussed, allowing a thirty per cent rise in volume of the importation of classified drugs. He'd also set up a scheme where those of his contracted customers who required British passports following their clandestine arrival in the UK were provided with the necessary documents in return for a year's unpaid employment in one of the agencies which specialised in the provision of labour. One final day should ensure the completion of his business duties and then he would be free to continue his personal quest for vengeance. The death of Alison Lea would be a pleasure worth savouring and arrangements for his next victim had already been made.

Unforeseen difficulties at a late stage of the planning process meant that he'd initially considered diverting his attention elsewhere, before making a firm decision to continue with his existing plans. His next target had moved abroad but the decision of Marcus to press on with his original schedule had been fully vindicated. Far from inadvertently escaping Marcus, the target was now fully in the line of fire. The realisation of his plans was at hand and all the fates were conspiring to assist him in his quest.

Marcus walked to his room in excellent humour, bypassing the lift as usual and taking the stairs two at a time. He would complete his business today, check out of the hotel and make the necessary arrangements concerning Alison Lea. As he reached the top of the stairs, he sensed the hint of a familiar fragrance in the air. He walked softly along the corridor and saw a couple entwined in a passionate embrace outside the lift doors. Alison and her chef boyfriend were immediately recognisable and Marcus slipped the key into the lock of his door without alerting them to his presence. Let them take their moment of stolen pleasure; by the end of the following day they'd both have suffered agonies beyond their comprehension.

Dexter frowned; his expression dampening all of Donna's few remaining scraps of enthusiasm. She'd been ordered back to the office for a review of the circumstances surrounding the death of Julian Carter where her claim to a spectacular breakthrough had been treated with what amounted to contempt. They were sitting in the garden, Dexter's chipped coffee mug steaming in his fist, but despite the sunshine Donna was surrounded by gloom. She was deaf to the soft blandishments of the leaves in the tree above her head as they rustled and sighed. In this location, directly overlooking the sea, squalls were common and this particular year had been harsher than most. Many of the trees in these exposed positions were almost skeletal by now but this particular specimen was more resilient, exhibiting a greater instinct for survival than most of its companions.

'I hear what you're saying, but what's the bottom line?' Dexter asked, slurping from his mug. 'You've got supposition and hearsay by the barrow-load, but what's the one thing you don't have?' He paused for a moment, took a further drink and then answered his own question. 'Evidence. Simple as that. I've gone out on a limb by asking Abbott if he's interested in taking it on as an official enquiry and he told me to sling my hook. I'd have been disappointed in him if he'd have done anything else. You know why he's not interested as well as I do. No bloody evidence. None at all.'

Donna said nothing. She could have gone over all the old ground again by pointing out the undeniable fact that a disproportionate number of young people, connected only by their parents having been members of a jury fifteen or so years ago, had somehow managed to die in tragic circumstances. Dexter knew all this. He'd not have allowed her to proceed with this one-trick-pony of an investigation and with only a single suspect in mind, unless he was satisfied that the facts amounted to far more than mere coincidence. Intensive efforts had failed to produce a single shred of hard evidence of a crime and without that evidence they had no case.

'I'll have a chat to Roper. Tell him I've suggested you take a couple of day's leave,' Dexter mused. 'No sense in running up any more debts on the client's account. Even former rock stars aren't made of money and I can't imagine Roper will be best pleased if you carry on without us billing the client.' He rummaged in his pocket and drew out a battered brown leather wallet. He examined the contents and flicked through the notes in the rear compartment. 'Here. Take three days off. There's two hundred quid there. That should last you until you get back to work.'

Donna looked at him blankly. Her case had apparently come to a dead end, in Dexter's eyes at least, and her frustration was now joined by confusion. 'What's that for?'

'Expenses. I can't justify putting this through the books, so bear in mind I'll only get repaid if you turn something up that we can bill to the client's account. I want an answer, one way or another, in three days.'

'What the fuck are you on about? What's this money for and what am I supposed to do with myself if I'm to take three days leave?'

Dexter stood up. He looked down at Donna and frowned. 'I'll scrub out that gob of yours with carbolic one of these days. For the benefit of what passes for your dim brain, I'll set it out as simply as I can. As far as Roper is concerned you're on leave. As far as I'm concerned, you're very much at work and while I'm paying your expenses I'll want results. Get down to Kent, find Alison Lea and make a decision as to the likelihood of her suffering some accident or other in the near future. If your ideas make any sense at all, she's next in line. Get down there and either find me some evidence or put it out of your head once and for all.' Dexter took a step back as Donna rose to her feet and threw her arms out towards him. 'Get off, you soft little mare. Try hugging me just once and I'll have that money back in my wallet and you on filing duties for the next month before you can blink.' He walked away and Donna was left to beam her appreciation at his broad back.

Peg looked askance at Donna and pursed her lips. 'Where did you say you were going? Folkestone? That's miles away. Don't know how long you'll be gone either? This is a right carry-on, Donna. How am I supposed to put meals on the table if I don't know when you'll be back?'

'I'll ring you,' Donna promised, 'Just as soon as I know anything.'

'I've a good mind to ring that boss of yours and give him a piece of my mind. Sending a chit of a girl off like this, it's a disgrace.'

'Don't you dare,' Donna cautioned in alarm, 'I want to go. It's all to do with the job I'm working on. And, I'm not a chit of a girl; I can look after myself.'

Peg looked dubious but lapsed into silence. Donna carried on with packing a small suitcase, wishing Peg would find something else to do. Every item she'd packed had to be scrutinised and queried, making the job three times as difficult.

'Is that an ambulance at the end of the road?' Donna asked, glancing through the window and barely managing to withhold a cry of triumph as Peg rushed over.

'Mister Day. He's been waiting to go in any time now. They'll be opening him up again, but it's a waste of time if you ask me. Poor old devil's been waiting for them to find a bed for him for weeks now. He's got a case packed and waiting by the front door and one of them dole cards for eyes, kidneys and the like. Ready for when he gets to hospital.'

'Oh, right. They're a good idea, those donor cards.'

'Bit of a to-do, I reckon,' Peg continued, 'As if they haven't got enough to do in hospitals without having to take everyone apart for spares just because they've got one of them cards in their pocket.'

Donna nodded distractedly, closed her suitcase and slid it off the bed while Peg's attention was elsewhere. 'Finished,' she announced.

Peg turned away from the window and scowled. 'You think on, ring me every day and mind you keep out of trouble. I've got enough to do without fretting myself silly while you're off gallivanting.'

CHAPTER 16

JAMIE looked out over a crescent of gritty sand broken by rocky outcrops. He'd arrived in Tarifa an hour ago and this first glimpse of the ocean was confirmation that it was vastly different from the Mediterranean. Propelled by a stiff breeze, the waves were bigger on the Atlantic seaboard and a small group of surfers rode the breakers like brightly coloured water sprites. Facing inland from the ochre shoreline, towering palms and a solitary leafy eucalyptus framed a mist-shrouded vista of distant hills. Jamie took a fresh grip on the heavy surfboard in its nylon carry-bag which was his only luggage. He'd been on the road for a fortnight, hitching throughout France and Spain and sleeping where he could, but this was journey's end at last. The wind freshened and a tumultuous mass of sun-bleached hair spilled exuberantly from beneath the confines of his baseball cap, dancing and swaying like a field of ripe corn.

Cornwall had been his home and he'd built up a formidable reputation amongst the surfing crowd, but this was the big league. As the best surfer on Newquay's Fistral Beach, Jamie had been a big fish in a small pond. Now he needed to prove to himself that the ability to ride the waves of his home beaches could transfer to the wild Atlantic breakers of Tarifa.

Marcus had walked down the same street three times before he was certain. He crossed the road and approached the man directly.

'What do you need, Brother?' The dealer was surprisingly well spoken, a nervous tic jumping at the corner of his right eye. 'Charlie perhaps? Anything you need, I got it.'

Marcus smiled. His instincts had not failed him. The man was playing a dangerous game. This was Jela's home territory but none of his legion of suppliers would have acted so brazenly. The man was almost begging to be arrested, but in present company that was the very least of his worries. Marcus named a quantity of cocaine that he knew the man would be unable to supply on the spot yet with sufficient profit as to be impossible to decline. When the man vowed to return in an hour with the requested merchandise, Marcus showed him the wad of cash he was holding as evidence of his seriousness and agreed to wait for his return.

The dealer was careful to conceal his destination but not careful enough. Marcus followed him to a block of three-storey flats overlooking the Channel. A rudimentary system of lookouts was in operation, but the watchers were lazy or stoned and he saw a figure in a first floor apartment wave down to the dealer. Marcus gained admittance to the rear car park without being questioned, climbed over the concrete barrier and leapt upwards to reach the railing around the balcony of the flat next door. The apartment was empty and he clambered silently onto the neighbouring balcony without being seen. Curtains fluttered over a partly open metal-framed window and the faint sounds of conversation filtered through to where Marcus was crouching. As the sounds of speech faded away, he slipped carefully through the narrow gap

150

in the curtains. The room was filthy, stained mattresses on the floor attesting to its use as a crack house. A faint hum of conversation emanated from the room beyond. Marcus risked a glance through the doorway and smiled. He slipped the knife he'd stolen from the hotel kitchen into his right hand and walked boldly into the room. Seated at a kitchen table were the dealer he'd followed and a large black man with severe facial scarring. The dealer reacted with predictable alarm, leaping to his feet and overturning his chair, but the calm response of the other man was confirmation that they were not the only residents of the flat. Moving swiftly, Marcus leapt to one side as the door to his left swung open to reveal a third man holding a dull automatic pistol.

Marcus swung his arm in a wide arc and the razor-sharp blade opened the man's cheek like a gaping sardine can. Bellowing in pain, he dropped the gun and pressed both hands to his face as the blood spurted. Marcus ignored him and turned back to the two men at the table. The dealer was already halfway to the door but Marcus reached him in a single stride and despatched the man instantly. Unable even to utter a sound as the knife severed his windpipe, the dealer dropped like a stone. The remaining man backed away, eyes fixed on the knife, its gleaming surface now dripping blood. Marcus motioned for him to resume his seat at the table and he sank slowly back into his chair. Both ignored the keening man lying on the floor, still trying vainly to stem the blood seeping between his fingers.

'Taking a chance, aren't you? Dealing around here without a permit? On my manor.' Marcus kept his voice low, forcing the other man to lean forward. The air of command emanating from Marcus left no room for doubt as to his right to demand an explanation.

'I'm connected,' the other man blustered, 'Abdullah came round here himself.'

Marcus nodded at this further confirmation that he'd been right to dispose of the treacherous Abdullah.

'Shame you picked the wrong team.' Marcus walked across the room and turned up the volume on the television. Reaching down to the stained carpet, he picked up the pistol and pointed it towards the scarred face of the man seated opposite him. The other man sat immobile, his face impassive as Marcus wrapped the gun in the thick folds of a maroon sweater that lay on the back of the sofa and pulled the trigger. The muffled explosion was barely audible over the soundtrack of the television game show, but the man's head snapped back and his body flew backwards off the chair. Marcus strode across the room and fired twice more. When he'd satisfied himself that all three men were dead, Marcus searched the flat and removed a large quantity of his own merchandise together with an assortment of weapons. Bundling everything into two canvas bags, he slipped out of the front door and walked casually down the stairs. When Marcus reached the Range Rover, he threw his burden onto the back seat and bent his head to look underneath the dashboard. Ripping a wire free, he touched it to the bare metal of the steering column and the engine burst into life. This car had almost served its purpose but he needed it for one final task. A job that would require the vehicle to give the appearance of having been hot-wired. He dropped the car keys into a drain and drove away from the area. Leaving the estate behind, he reflected on the effrontery of his former lieutenant in making under the counter drug deals almost within sight of the docks that were the epicentre of Marcus's empire. Abdullah had paid for his disloyalty but the lesson was not lost on Marcus and Jela would be watched carefully. As the one person who could implicate his employer, his role was crucial. The rewards for continuing loyalty were considerable, but he'd ensure that the penalties for failure were equally commensurate with the stakes involved.

Donna tried for the fourth time to re-fold the map only for her efforts to be rewarded by the sound of rending paper. "Bloody maps," she muttered, throwing the unwieldy bundle onto the passenger seat. Junction 13 was approaching and she could put this wretched journey behind her. A long drawn-out slog down the M6, including the seemingly obligatory delays either side of Birmingham, had sent her rushing for the sanctuary of the relatively trouble-free M40, but the worst was still come. Maidstone had signalled the start of a traffic nightmare and every foreign-registered lorry in the UK had seemingly elected to choose the day of her journey to head towards the Dover ferries.

Donna negotiated the roundabout at the far end of the exit road with extreme care. She was stressed out, bone tired and starving. Not a good combination. The Leas, her destination, was clearly signposted and within five minutes Donna saw the ornate façade of the Burlington Hotel appear in front of her. She'd talked Dexter into booking her in for one night at least and he'd reluctantly agreed that the best way of getting in touch with Alison Lea was to see her at her place of work. She still had most of Dexter's two hundred pounds available and toyed with the prospect of ordering a meal in the hotel restaurant. The lavish nature of the main lobby soon dissuaded her of this idea. Given a choice between blowing a sizeable chunk of her budget on fancy meals or a visit to KFC, Donna's thrifty nature came to the fore. She'd book herself in, dump her case in her room and head off to town in search of the cheapest means of satisfying her hunger.

Alison writhed and struggled, but the thin nylon cord that restrained her held firm. Her nakedness was no longer a concern; she'd long since blanked the indignities she'd suffered from her mind. Marcus had raped her twice but she suspected that even worse was to follow. His expression revealed nothing as he sat beside her on the narrow bed. Beneath the tight gag, Alison had bitten clean through the end of her tongue and the sharp metallic taste of blood in her mouth made her feel sick. With a rare insight into the mind of her attacker, Alison knew with absolute certainty that even the ultimate indignity of rape had been almost dispassionate. Forcing himself upon her had been more of a demonstration of his absolute control over her than any hint of sexual satisfaction. She was not to know that Marcus was frustrated by the need to ensure her absolute silence and that by gagging her he'd removed any element of his own pleasure from the act of rape. He'd long since refined his methods whereby rape would be only the start of the escalating assault on his victim that would result in their death. Only when the girl had nothing left to fight for would he allow her to die.

Marcus stood and walked slowly out of her field of vision. His naked body with its ridges of hard muscle standing out in stark relief had no discernible weakness. The perfect killing machine. When he returned, Alison flinched at the sight of the blade he held in his right hand. This was confirmation that the agonies she'd suffered so far were to be only the start of her ordeal. So far Marcus had said nothing and she started at the unexpected sound of his voice.

'Recognise this, do you?' He held the knife out, waving it in front of the soft beam of the bedside light. Alison turned her face away, refusing to acknowledge the question.

'Your boyfriend's knife. You should be proud of him. He really looks after his tools. Nice to see a man's pride in his work.' Alison squeezed her eyes shut, trying in vain to shut out the sound of his voice. A muted hum from the small bedside 'fridge was the only sound in the room. Marcus reached out his hand and casually touched the blade of the knife against the swell of her breast. Moving achingly slowly, he drew the blade from right to left leaving a thin red line in its wake. Alison felt no pain from the razor sharp knife, but a fat tear escaped the corner of her eye and rolled unchecked down her cheek. Marcus raised the blade a few inches higher to the junction of Alison's shoulder and neck and made a more deliberate pass from right to left. Alison's spine arched, raising her clear of the mattress as the flesh parted and blood gushed onto the white sheets. Behind the gag she moaned in anguish and begged in vain for mercy. Wielding the flashing blade with dispassionate skill, Marcus sliced the delicate flesh of his victim, his attention totally focussed on his grisly work. By the time he laid the knife carefully aside, the girl's upper torso was weeping blood from numerous cuts.

Marcus eased one of the cords that bound her wrists and with a swift and decisive movement flipped her face down on the bed. He re-tied the restraints, checking the security of each knot, and stood watching the slow rise and fall of the girl's shoulders. Marcus experienced a *frisson* of excitement, anticipating the manner in which his next actions would re-engage her sense of violation. A fresh condom in place and massively erect, he pinched the tender flesh of the girl's inner thighs and wrenched her legs wide apart. Alison could not have imagined any circumstances in which the pain she had previously endured would count for nothing, but the agony she now felt was beyond any comprehension. This invasion went far beyond mere pain and her spirit finally acknowledged defeat. Marcus felt her resistance fade away and experienced a surge of disappointment. The imposition of his will on an unwilling victim was always better when their resistance prolonged his pleasure. His predilection for violently sodomising his victims as a means of provoking some fresh token of resistance had served him well in the past but was by no means infallible. The circumstance of this girl's death was mitigation against any further delay and he put aside his expectations of enjoyment in the interests of finishing the job and moving on.

Donna had eased the pangs of hunger, rang both Peg and Dexter to report her safe arrival, and was now ready to start work. The hotel lobby was deserted and the urge to press the brass bell on the counter proved irresistible. A uniformed figure appeared briefly from behind a linen screen, gestured wildly and disappeared again. Donna looked at the bell longingly but resisted the urge to press it again.

'Sorry about that. Julie lost a lens and that carpet's all swirls and patterns. Like looking for a needle in a haystack.' A uniformed girl about Donna's age rose from the floor behind the screen and took up station behind the counter. She had a great mass of frizzy hair, a massive cold sore on her upper lip and a rich variety of metal studs, rings and other and ornaments dangling from various areas of her visible person. Donna felt an attack of premature middle-aged indignation coming on and fought valiantly to keep it at bay.

'I'm Donna O'Prey. In room 36? Would it be possible for me to talk to Alison Lea? I understand she works here.'

'Allie? She's off this afternoon. You might catch her later on though. Tony, that's her boyfriend, has to work evenings so they don't normally stop out long.'

'Oh, right. Do you happen to know if they're out at the moment?'

'No idea. I could ring her room, if you like?'

Donna nodded. Despite her unprepossessing appearance, the receptionist was being helpful. Having gained no reply from Alison's room, she next tried the boyfriend's extension and spoke briefly to whoever answered before replacing the receiver.

'Tony says Allie went back to her room to check she hadn't left her key in the door. She couldn't find it anywhere. Maybe she's still looking for it somewhere in the hotel. Tony said she'd left him a good hour ago and didn't come back. He's just going out to check if the garage has been out to look at his car yet. Someone smashed into it last night and he's been waiting all day for the garage to tow it away. He'll be down in a minute if you want to talk to him.'

Donna thanked her as the 'phone rang again. She stood in the entrance for a few minutes, but saw nobody even remotely similar to the man she'd seen in the photograph provided by Alison's mother. A sudden thought struck her and she returned once more to the desk.

'Is there another car park or just this one out front?'

'There's another one out the back. Just through that door over there. Tony usually leaves his car in the side street. Bet he wishes he'd left it on the car park last night, eh?'

Donna nodded and thanked her. As she walked through the side door she saw a man she thought she recognised as Tony sitting in the passenger seat of a Range Rover. The photograph was all she had to identify Alison's boyfriend but his appearance was so striking that Donna felt confident she would recognise him on sight. She'd only caught the barest glimpse of the driver yet something about him had also struck a chord. Donna watched the car drive smoothly away, feeling a vague sense of unease. Acting on impulse, she scurried round to the front of the hotel and jumped into her car. As she pulled away from the entrance she caught a glimpse of the Range Rover in the distance. She thought she'd lost the other car twice in the next five minutes but somehow managed to maintain contact. The road heading down towards Folkestone harbour was nowhere near as busy as the High Street and Donna had no problems keeping her quarry in sight. She concentrated on keeping a safe distance from her quarry and studiously obeying Dexter's oft-repeated surveillance and pursuit instructions. Other than a vague sense of unease, she still had no particular reason to suspect the other vehicle was suspicious in any way, but it was a good opportunity to hone her skills.

At the bottom of a steep hill, the Range Rover suddenly turned sharp left. Donna slowed down and when she saw the entrance to a narrow arched tunnel she decided to hang back for a while. Leaving her car on a small car park outside the Tourist Information office, Donna jogged back across the road and cautiously entered the brick-lined arch. Beyond the narrow entrance the road continued along the quayside of the small harbour. There were a few seafood stalls and a couple of pubs but no sign of the Range Rover. Donna was almost running now, deliberating whether she should go back to fetch her car in case the other vehicle had continued further along this road. It was what Dexter always referred to as a judgement call and she decided to stick with her instincts that the Range Rover was very close. Her guess was vindicated when she caught a glimpse of the car driver in the distance. He was opening the door of a blue Ford Sierra and Donna was once again struck by a strange sense of familiarity with the manner of the man's walk. The Ford started up and moved away. She was unable to see the driver's face but there was something about him that brought about a fresh sense of unease. Where was Tony? What had happened to the Range Rover? Donna stood still, dithering with indecision on the rough cobbles. If the other man had dropped Tony at a garage in connection with his damaged car, where the hell was it? She'd seen no evidence of a garage around here and the whole area had an air of desolation. A sudden instinct made her retrace her steps and she walked quickly past a boat storage yard towards a large metal door set into a brick wall. She could hear the faint sound of an engine from behind an up-and-over garage door. Donna banged on the metal door but no one answered. She looked around, but the area was deserted. Her sense of unease was now overwhelming and she ran back to the boatyard, picked up a short length of scaffold pole and hurried back to the garage. Half-hoping she was only about to commit an act of vandalism, Donna fitted the end of the scaffold pole around the door-handle and heaved. Her efforts were rewarded with a loud crack as the lock snapped. Dropping the scaffold pole behind her, Donna took hold of the handle and heaved upwards. A dense cloud of engine fumes billowed out. Donna saw the Range Rover, with its engine still running, and a motionless figure seated in the passenger seat. Eyes streaming, she wrenched the garage door fully open and squeezed her way inside. Feeling her way through the dense fumes, she somehow managed to open the passenger door. There was no key in the ignition, but Donna saw a length of bare wire protruding from the dashboard and when she yanked it away, the engine spluttered and died. Taking a firm grip under the man's arms, Donna found a strength she did not know she possessed and somehow managed to drag the unconscious body into the fresh air. There was still no one else around and Donna's panic mounted as she realised any resuscitation would be down to her. She'd done a first aid course, part of the routine at R and D Security, but could remember almost nothing about emergency procedures. There was no longer any doubt in her mind. The man she'd seen in the photograph, Alison Lea's boyfriend Tony, was lying next to her on the oil-stained cobbles. Donna knelt down and began to breathe air into his apparently lifeless body. Just as she was about to admit defeat, Tony drew in a great gulp of air. Donna watched his chest swell and subside and, when he took a second breath, she sat back, supporting her weight on her hands, utterly exhausted. Tony gave a wracking cough and opened his eyes. He looked at Donna blankly, eyes glazed over, and Donna was too tired to start explaining her presence to him. A man passed by the end of the road, glanced at the two figures lying on the road and walked on. The fumes had already dispersed and the air was clear and sweet. The only sounds were the screeching calls of seagulls in the harbour and, very faintly, a police siren far away in the distance.

CHAPTER 17

DEXTER replaced the receiver with a thoughtful expression on his face. His instincts had served him well over many years and he had no reason to doubt the concern that his abortive telephone call had occasioned. Trying to reach Donna, he'd telephoned the Burlington Hotel but had been unable to obtain any reply. After hanging on for three or four minutes while the 'phone rang out repeatedly, Dexter knew with absolute certainty that something was very wrong. Hotels are not in the habit of allowing calls to ring out unanswered. He dialled the number again and waited with mounting concern until a harassed voice eventually answered. 'I'm sorry. We're unable to deal with reservations at this time,' the young woman informed him, her voice almost breaking.

Dexter drew on all his thirty years in law enforcement and snapped out an order. A few moments later a man's voice came on the line. He sounded almost as shell-shocked as his receptionist had as Dexter confirmed he was speaking to the Hotel Manager.

'What's going on there?'

'I'm sorry, sir. I'm not at liberty to give out any information at this time,' the man replied and Dexter switched into overdrive. Speaking very clearly and giving the impression, without actually saying as such in words, that he was still a senior police officer, he made it plain to the manager that he had no option but to talk to him.

'There has been a sudden death in the hotel. The police are here at the moment, but I've been advised to say no more at this time.'

'Who died?' Dexter's voice cracked like a whip.

'A young woman.'

Dexter flinched. 'Donna O'Prey?' He could scarcely hold the receiver in place.

The manager sounded surprised. 'No. Although I do recognise that name. I remembered it as it was so unusual. Miss O'Prey is a guest in the hotel.'

'She's also one of my colleagues.'

'Oh, I see. The person who died was not a guest. She was a member of my own staff.'

Dexter now knew the identity of the dead woman with absolute certainty. 'Alison Lea,' he said.

'Yes.' The manager's voice betrayed his astonishment. 'That is correct. How did you know that?'

Dexter ignored the question and replied with one of his own. 'Was Alison's death an accident?'

'Not at all. The police are here now. A brutal murder.'

'What?' It was Dexter's turn to be astonished. This was a major deviation from previous cases. He thought for a moment before asking the manager if it would be possible for him to speak to the senior officer presently in attendance at the hotel. The manager did not demur, but left Dexter hanging on for at least five minutes.

'Hello? Who is this?' There was more than a hint of irritation in the voice. Dexter kept his tone deliberately low-key, explaining his own background and that he had information relevant to the murder enquiry. Dexter added that he would be arranging for DI Abbott from Northwest MIT to be in touch. The DI in Folkestone had the sense to keep quiet while Dexter laid out the bare bones of his own conclusions concerning the near certainty that this present murder was linked to a number of other sudden deaths elsewhere in the country.

'Are you able to give me any details that I can pass on to my contact in the MIT?' Dexter enquired.

'Like what?'

'Circumstances of the death would be a start.'

There was a lengthy pause before the DI replied. 'It's a bad one. That much I can tell you. Rape, anal rape, multiple cuts and abrasions and finally strangulation; he really put the poor little sod through the mill. Nasty business.'

'Sounds it,' Dexter agreed. 'Any suspects?' He wasn't really expecting an affirmative.

'Oh yeah. The boyfriend. Name of Beech. Tony Beech. Worked in the hotel kitchen. He's done a runner, but we've got half of Folkestone looking for him.'

'The boyfriend? You sure?'

'Seems pretty clear. He'd cut her with one of his own knives. We found the rest of the set in the kitchen. Plus, there's a button off a tunic we found behind the sofa. It's part of his chef's outfit. The dead girl still had hold of the button in her hand.'

Dexter took a few more details before hanging up. Frowning, he tried Donna's mobile without success. He reached Abbott straight away and explained about the new development. 'This time it's no accident. Clear case of murder. Remember I showed you the name of the dead girl's mother on that list of jurors and said a member of her family was at risk. I was dead right, wasn't I? Too many deaths now to be regarded as coincidence. Even for you. Do yourself a favour and get in touch with DI Gerrard in Folkestone. He's expecting you to call and I told him the murder of Alison Lea is linked to a series of deaths up North. You're in pole position on this one; make sure the Kent lads know it's your case.'

The seagulls wheeled overhead, calling in excitement at the first sight of the returning fishing fleet. Tony was asleep in the passenger seat of Donna's car while she paced the quayside and waited impatiently for the opportunity to get in touch with Dexter. Her mobile had run down and she'd had to resort to the in-car charger that was achingly slow. Under normal circumstances, she'd have tried to ring from a call box, but was too concerned about Tony's condition to leave him unattended or risk waking him by driving away. His absolute refusal to receive medical attention had been a concern, but looking at his sleeping form Donna felt more optimistic. The pallor that had transformed his features had left him and he now looked to have completely recovered from his recent ordeal.

Donna started as her mobile bleeped to signify it was now charging and, almost at once, the 'phone rang. Donna flung open the driver's side door and snatched the mobile, still attached by its charging cable to the cigarette lighter socket.

'Hello?'

'Donna? At last. Where the fuck have you been for the last hour and a half?'

Dexter' anger was obvious, but Donna grinned in relief. Recent events had overwhelmed her and she needed Dexter's advice urgently. 'Sorry. I'm with Tony. The chef. Alison's boyfriend?'

'I know who he is. Just tell me where you are at the moment.'

'By the harbour. Someone tried to kill Tony. I think it was Marcus. I got him out, but we need to get back and make sure Alison is still safe.'

Dexter's voice softened. 'Is he there with you now, you say?'

'Yes.'

'Put him on.'

Donna passed the mobile to Tony who was now wide awake and watching her intently. He took it and Donna heard for the first time his explanation of the situation which had almost resulted in his death. The man who'd attacked him had been a guest at the hotel for three days. A good tipper, according to the waitresses and very friendly and good-natured. Alison had become friendly with the man, causing friction between Tony and herself when he'd accused her of flirting with the guest. Alison had made a point of introducing Tony to the other man and his jealousy had eventually subsided. Tony explained how the guest had asked him to join him at the bar. He'd only had time for a single drink as he he'd arranged to meet a mechanic in the car park. The guest had walked out to the car park with him, but Tony remembered nothing more until he'd woken to find the concerned face of Donna staring down at him. Donna couldn't hear Dexter's side of the conversation, but it was clear enough to her that the guest, whom she was now certain, was Marcus, had drugged Tony's drink and kidnapped him. When he finished speaking, Tony listened in silence while Dexter spoke to him and Donna watched in astonishment as tears flowed from his eyes. He didn't speak again, but handed the 'phone to Donna and crumpled his face in his hands.

'What's happened?'

'Too late to save Alison,' Dexter explained, 'I've just spoken to Abbott. He's in touch with the Folkestone police. Alison's body was found two hours ago. She'd been murdered. Very brutally. The knife used by the killer had been left near the body. It was part of a set belonging to the boyfriend.'

'Tony didn't kill her,' Donna interjected, 'It was Marcus.'

'I know he didn't kill her. Do you think I'd be letting you have cosy chats with a murderer? The point is; the police are looking for him. They've also linked him to a triple murder in Dover. Drug related. The same knife was used on three more victims. They'd been shot as well, but the killer cut them first using a knife that left a very distinctive signature. SOCO spotted it straight away.'

'Why was Alison murdered? All the others were made to look like accidents.'

'I don't know. The only thing that occurs to me is that Alison's parents were dead set against the boyfriend and believing him to be the apparent murderer would cause them maximum heartache. The killer's suicide would have tied up all the loose ends. Until you happened along and rescued him, that is.'

'What do I do now?'

'Take him in. Let the police sort it out.'

'I can't do that,' Donna protested, 'Not if they think he's a murderer.'

'Just do it and get your arse back here,' Dexter ordered.

Donna looked at Tony. He was looking away from her, staring out of the car window and she doubted he was even conscious of her presence. She took a deep breath and spoke once more to Dexter. 'Can't do it. Sorry.'

'Listen to me...' Dexter began. Donna clicked her thumb over the 'phone button and switched him off. She sat for a moment, appalled at her own temerity, and turned the mobile on again but it remained silent. Tony was still looking out of the window. His whole body was shaking, his hands were trembling and he looked almost as bad now as he had when she'd pulled him out of the smoke-filled car.

'My boss thinks you should turn yourself in,' Donna said. Tony swivelled round and looked directly at her, but said nothing. 'I don't think it's a good idea,' Donna continued, aware that she was directly defying Dexter by this act of sedition. 'Not if they've got evidence linking you to a murder. More than one murder, by the sound of it. The police have found a knife that they say belongs to you. It was used to kill Alison and they seem to think the same knife was involved in the murders of three other victims. Drug related, or so it seems.'

Tony looked stricken. 'I didn't kill anyone. I noticed this morning that one of my knives was missing, but thought it would turn up sooner or later. Alison was my whole life. How could anyone even imagine I could kill her? And as far as killing three other people, that's even more ridiculous.'

'I know,' Donna said. 'But that's where we start to have a problem.' Tony looked at her, baffled. 'You see, I think I know who killed Alison. And those others as well. He's a man named Marcus Green and he's the real danger as far as you're concerned. At the moment he thinks you're dead. A suicide. Filled with such remorse at the murders you'd committed, you did away with yourself. Clever, really. The problem, as I see it, is what happens when you surrender to the police? Marcus Green will know you're not dead. You can identify him as the real killer. Where does that leave you?'

Tony shook his head. He looked bewildered.

'Up shit creek is where it leaves you. If you turn up, pleading innocence and able to tell the police what really happened, Marcus Green will come back. To finish the job. Being in police custody won't keep you safe for long. You turn yourself in now and you might as well put out a bloody great sign saying here I am, come and get me.'

'So, what do you suggest?' Tony looked stricken. In the past few hours, he'd narrowly escaped death, heard how his girlfriend had been raped and brutally murdered and now he was not only the chief suspect for multiple murders but in great personal danger.

Donna shrugged. 'I haven't a clue. I know what you shouldn't do, but that's about as far as I've got so far.' Tony looked at her as if she'd been speaking Martian for the last ten minutes. He shook his head and looked away, gazing across the harbour at the approaching fishing boats, an air of absolute desperation etched across his features.

'I know the man who did this,' Donna said and saw the expression on her companion's face change from dull resignation to one of keen interest. 'I've met him before. A couple of years ago. I'd just started work for the security firm and it was my first real case. A missing teenage girl.'

'You're telling me you're some sort of detective?'

Donna didn't like his disbelieving tone but couldn't really justify the word detective as a job description. 'Not really. If I'm honest, I just do Mickey Mouse stuff most of the time. That was what that case should have been. It started with a missing girl, Celine Dobson, and the parents wanting me to find her. It should have been routine, but turned out to be anything but.' Donna paused. The memories of that time were still painful.

'Go on.'

'It turned out there was a lot more involved than just a missing teenager. Like murder. Throw in rape, kidnapping, arson and everything else you can think of and that was my easy little case. My boss, that was him on the 'phone just now, kept me involved when everyone else wanted me to bow out gracefully and let someone who knew what they were doing take over. I got a bee in my bonnet about someone called Marcus Green and had a lot of help from a woman named Kate Davies. With Kate's expertise and my own stubbornness, I eventually made myself into a bit of a nuisance. So much so that Marcus Green kidnapped me as well.' Donna glanced at Tony and saw he was hanging on her every word. 'It ended up a right mess, but I managed to escape with Celine and her mother while Marcus was trapped in a burning log cabin. He should be dead. But, I know he isn't. He's behind the murder of Alison and I need to stop him before he goes on to kill anyone else. The trouble is, I seem to be the only one who knows that Marcus is still out there somewhere.' Donna stopped talking. The words just dried in her mouth like ashes and she shivered. Tony reached for her hand and gripped it tightly.

'What about that woman who helped you last time? Surely she believes you?'

'She's dead. Murdered. Only a few days ago.'

Tony sucked in a great gasp of air. 'Is there a connection?'

Donna shrugged. 'I think so. I hope not.'

Tony looked at her quizzically. 'Why?'

161

'Because I got her involved in looking for Marcus again. If he killed her, then it's my fault. Kate would still be alive if I'd kept my mouth shut.'

Dexter's face was a mask of impotent fury. The news from Abbott had been less than promising. Abbott had presented the facts linking the recent deaths to the men in suits who made policy decisions and been rebuffed. Insufficient evidence to justify re-opening old cases, particularly where all the circumstances had already been investigated and resolved, had been the gist of the decision handed down to Abbott and his squad. The murder of Alison Lea in Folkestone was already under investigation by local officers and Abbott had been told to leave it all to the locals, unless they made an official request for information. This now looked unlikely as the Folkestone police already had a prime suspect and were not looking to widen the scope of their enquiry. Dexter had experienced frustration with the decisions of senior officers many times in his long and distinguished police career, but the limitations of his current status, unable to fight his own corner or impose his own will on the decision, was much worse than anything he'd ever previously endured. His absolute certainty that Donna's original suspicions had been validated made the situation much worse. Dexter now had to tell Donna that all the work she'd put in so far had been deemed worthless. The prospect was not pleasant. He flicked through the pages of notes he'd intended for Abbott's use and scowled. Assuming the deaths were following a specific order, the next at-risk juror was Jamie Marshall and here Dexter thought there was good news to report at last. His enquiries had revealed that Marshall's only son, also named Jamie, was safely out of harm's way having recently left England to travel the surfing beaches of Europe. The next vulnerable juror would now be Anthea Peters. With three daughters and a son still at school, Dexter's resolve to protect them all would seriously stretch his resources.

Dexter dialled the number of Donna's mobile and grunted in satisfaction when the tone rang out.

'Hello?'

'Donna. I need you back here pronto. We've got four school kids to look after. Abbott put our case to the top floor, but they've let us all down. I want you to know I'm gutted about all this. You've done a bloody good job and I'm no happier about waiting for the next body to turn up before anyone takes us seriously than you are.' *He'd never even mentioned me hanging up on him last time we spoke*, Donna thought.

'What four kids?' Donna sounded perplexed.

'Anthea Peters. She's got four kids. All at school.'

'She's not the next name. Jamie Marshall is next. He's got a son aged seventeen or so.'

'Forget Marshall. The lad's gone swanning off on some nonsense or other. He's not even in England now so he should be safe enough for the time being. He's mad about surfing from all accounts. Family expected him to settle down and start looking for a proper job, but it wasn't to be. The lad told his folks to stuff their ideas of working for a living and buggered off. Apparently, he was useless at school and only interested in sport. Left home a week ago and should be well on his way to Tarifa by now, according to his father. Wherever Tarifa is.'

'That's not how Marcus works.' Donna snapped. She was furious. 'If Jamie Marshall is next on the list, then Jamie Marshall will be the next victim. I don't care if he's on a sheep station in the Australian outback; he'll be next.'

'Just get back here today and we'll talk about it then,' Dexter snapped. It was clear from his tone that he'd already made up his mind. 'Has that Tony bloke turned himself in yet?'

Donna looked at Tony seated alongside her on the park bench and sighed. 'It didn't happen. He's still here. With me.'

'What?' Dexter exploded, 'For God's sake, Donna. Half the Kent Constabulary will be looking for him by now. I even rang the DI in charge and told him you'd be bringing him in.'

For the second time in an hour, Donna hung up, switching off her mobile and dropping it on the back seat of the car. She'd no desire to hear Dexter's hectoring voice at the moment. He'd made decisions about the case with which she disagreed violently, but her chances of changing Dexter's mind over the course of a telephone conversation were nil.

'Where's Tarifa?' Donna asked, making up her mind.

'Tarifa?' Tony could possibly have looked more baffled although Donna doubted it.

'Yeah.'

Tony shrugged his shoulders. 'Somewhere in Spain, I think. Why?'

'I need to go there.' Donna reached into the glove box and rummaged around inside.

'What are you after?'

'A map,' Donna snapped, slamming the lid on the glove box in frustration. Tony reached into the inside pocket of his jacket and withdrew a battered wallet containing a small blue diary. He flipped it towards Donna who snatched at it gratefully. She flicked through the pages, disregarding the close-written pages of handwriting, until she found the map section at the rear. Tony scooted over until he could see the map as well and traced a finger down the southern coast of Spain. 'Here you go,' he exclaimed, 'Right next to Gibraltar on the Atlantic coast.'

Donna studied the tiny map with mounting excitement. She knew with an absolute certainty that she had to go to this place. A life depended on it. Tony shifted back into the passenger seat and Donna looked at him with some concern. He still looked terrible. She made a decision to explain the reasons behind her sudden appearance in his life, reasoning that she owed him that much at least. Tony listened intently as Donna gave a detailed précis of the events that had brought her to Folkestone, his eyes glistening with tears as she skipped rapidly over the final section, specifically the fate that had befallen Alison. Donna picked up the diary again and peered once again at the tiny map of Spain. She found Tarifa and placed the tip of her finger as a marker. 'It's a hell of a long way from here,' she mused.

Tony nodded. 'Do you have your passport with you?'

Donna nodded. 'Yeah. God knows why, except I thought it might come in handy if I needed to show identification. At the hotel, for instance.'

'Then, the logical thing would be to fly to Malaga, then hire a car for the last bit. 'Course that's no good to you now.'

Donna's head flicked in his direction. 'Why not?'

'I'm a wanted man, remember. The police will have already circulated my details to all airports. I'd planned to take a day trip to France, just to buy Alison a couple of presents, so I've got my passport with me, but it's no use. I can't travel under my own name. There'll be an alert out for me by now. We'll have to take a ferry and drive down.'

'We?' Donna stared at him in astonishment.

Tony nodded. 'I'm part of this now.'

Donna shook her head. 'Oh no. This is my job. Nothing to do with you. You've got enough troubles as it is.'

'I'm part of it,' Tony insisted, 'This man, Marcus. He's killed Alison. Would have killed me too if you hadn't happened along when you did. Anyway, what choice do I have? Like you said, I can't give myself up without risking him coming back to finish the job. Plus, I know what he looks like.'

Donna started. This aspect hadn't even occurred to her. Two years ago she'd seen Marcus Green at close quarters and her memory of that ordeal would never leave her. But Marcus would almost certainly have changed his appearance since she'd seen him last. Marcus had always planned to kill Tony and would have had no concerns about being subsequently identified which placed Tony in a unique position. He had seen Marcus in his new guise and it was this knowledge which prompted Donna to reflect on her initial outright refusal. Tony seized on her hesitation to press his case further. 'Two pairs of eyes must be better than one. Then again, I can share the driving and help out where necessary. You're the boss. Just tell me what to do and I'll do it.'

Donna looked at him quizzically. The prospect had its attractions. The driving alone was a daunting prospect; it looked a hell of a long way to Tarifa. She nodded thoughtfully. 'Just remind me,' she said. 'Why do I have to drive all the bloody way through France and Spain? What's wrong with flying straight to Spain?'

'Passport,' Tony answered with alacrity, 'I'll never get through passport control. The police will be watching all ports and airports. The ferry is the only way to get out of the country without anyone knowing I've left.'

'Sorry to be a smart-arse' Donna said, 'but, last time I heard, you still needed to show a passport to get on and off a ferry. They'll pick you up straight away.'

Tony smiled. 'Not if they don't see me.'

'Eh?'

'I'll hide on the back seat. Under a travel rug, say. We only need to get you past check-in and onto the ferry. They don't worry too much about people wanting to leave the country; those travelling the other way catch all the flak.'

Donna stared at him, astonished at the level of his audacity. 'That's your great plan, is it? How if it goes wrong? What about spot-checks? How about if I'm stopped and asked to empty my car?'

Tony grinned broadly. 'Oh, I never said it was a perfect plan,' he said, 'If you get stopped, we're both fucked.'

CHAPTER 18

MARCUS glanced out of the tiny window as he felt the wheels lift from the tarmac. The woman seated next to him was apparently engrossed in a newspaper but her knuckles were white. Marcus had never understood fear as a concept and fear of flying was even more difficult to comprehend. The safety of each passenger was out of their individual control and Marcus had no problem with that. Dust flecks, reflected in the brilliant light from the window, swirled slowly past his blank and empty eyes, mimicking the lethargic drift of his attention. He'd never experienced sorrow and a sense of joy was equally alien to his nature, but at this moment of languid contemplation he felt the stirrings of a feeling hitherto unknown. A profound and resonant satisfaction. His work was progressing well. Not that he'd ever doubted he'd be successful, but it was comforting to see the fruits of his labours. He had no need of any other human being to achieve his ends. He made use of other men in his daily work but they were merely tools. It had been a long time since he'd had to rely on anyone else. Not since prison, and even then he'd only required the basic necessities of existence. He'd never asked for anything. Now, he had both money and power. Money, far more than he could ever spend, piled up in far-flung bank vaults, was a mere by-product of the life he'd chosen. He could afford to wear the finest clothes and stay in the grandest hotels but luxury meant nothing to him. He was equally content to wear a simple *djellaba* and sleep on the bare earth in a filthy shantytown.

Power was much more important and his power knew no limitations. He could buy anything he wanted. Procure any service. Give any order to the right person and know it would be obeyed. None of his underlings ever questioned an order. Refusal of his wishes was unknown. It had not always been the case, but the ones who'd defied him had gone to a painful lingering death, leaving a legacy of unquestioning loyalty to their successors. This ability to have anything, do anything, would have been more than enough for most people, but Marcus had never been motivated simply by the urge to garner wealth or impose his will on others. Satisfaction came from seeing his plans come to fruition and the vindication of his decisions.

A headline at the top of an inner page of his neighbour's newspaper caught his eye and he quickly scanned the body of the text while pretending to adjust the strap of his seat belt. A Daily Mail reporter detailed the tragic death of Alison Lea whose body had been discovered in a room at the hotel where she worked. Her grieving parents were said to be 'devastated beyond belief' at the loss of their only child. Police were seeking Alison's boyfriend, Tony Beech, a chef at the hotel in connection with the crime and also with regard to the murders of three illegal immigrants in Dover. A senior policeman warned the public to be vigilant as the man was considered to be extremely dangerous. Marcus skimmed over an account of the parents' remorse at their failure to dissuade their daughter from leaving home with Beech. It was evident that they'd harboured suspicions of some unspecified nature concerning the boyfriend but the reporter did not elaborate on these misgivings. Even allowing for tabloid exploitation of a tragic event under the guise of a human-interest story, the reference to a grieving family was ample recompense for his efforts.

Marcus was travelling under the name of Derek Latham, an insurance broker from Wolverhampton, and had no reason to suspect he was arousing any more curiosity than any other of his fellow passengers. The passport and other documents in his flight bag were genuine and would pass any official scrutiny. As the angle of the aircraft's climb levelled out, Marcus looked down on the green and brown checkerboard-patterned fields that were so characteristic of rural England. He felt no sentimental attraction to the country of his birth, but his recent trip had given him many treasured memories to savour. It would be necessary for him to return eventually to complete his mission, but he'd already made a good start. Half way through his project and the next target was now identified and in place. He smiled at the irony of his next victim having left England but, far from delaying the moment of his death, this action had actually hastened the process by moving to an area which placed him directly in the path of his unknown pursuer.

The woman in the next seat stood to open the overhead locker and remove a black leather satchel. Marcus gave her a cursory glance as she resumed her seat and saw the embossed crest on the side of the bag. Not a tourist, then, but a business traveller thrown in with a planeload of holidaymakers due to the parsimony of her employers.

Marcus sensed the woman's gaze on him and turned to face her. The tight planes of skin covering his razor-sharp cheekbones shifted and in an instant the transformation was complete. His eyes crinkled and softened tiny creases either side of his mouth widened, and like a fissure of sunlight breaking through a cloud, his face came alive. Without being aware of her response, the woman smiled. Her delicate features delineated a shallow prettiness that would never stand the test of time, but right now she was doing just fine. Marcus appraised the pallor of her neck, shot through with a delicate tracing of faint blue veins and felt his interest quicken. This one could be worth a small delay.

By the time they landed at Malaga, Marcus had learnt that the woman was the PA of a prominent academic and would be travelling onward to Seville to join her boss, a criminologist invited as one of the guest lecturers, for a pan-European conference on drug trafficking. As one of Europe's leading dealers in narcotics, the delicious irony was not lost on Marcus. The woman, Tania, was going out a few days early at her own expense for a short holiday and had yet to finalise her plans. By now openly flirting, Tania had stressed the fluidity of her arrangements and Marcus was only too pleased to offer his assistance in obtaining accommodation. His suggestion that Tania could stay at his own villa for a few days prior to travelling onward to Seville was accepted with an eagerness that Tania would very shortly regret.

The churning wake of the ferry trailed behind the bow railings where Donna stood, watching the familiar white cliffs fade into the distance. Her heart was still pounding from the ordeal of passing through check-in, handing over her ticket and passport and trying desperately to ignore the bulky mound that covered the back seat. She'd bought two sleeping bags, a tent and an assortment of clothing from a charity shop; all chosen without consideration to suitability or fashion sense. Bulk was far more important as their primary function was to provide sufficient covering to hide the stowaway lying across the foot-well of the rear seats. Donna had checked and re-checked the effectiveness of the camouflage before she'd approached the check-in booths, but the wait for her ticket and passport details to be checked had been the longest three minutes of her life. When the man in the booth handed back her passport and a paper tag showing the lane in which she had to park, Donna had slipped the clutch and belted away from the check-in area like a Formula One driver. She followed a stream of traffic and located the correct lane without mishap. The ferry waited, gleaming in the sunshine, with earlier arrivals already beginning the loading process. Ten minutes spent drumming her fingers on the dashboard later she'd followed a fully laden Renault Kangoo up the ramp and into the bowels of the ferry. Donna heaved a great sigh of relief as she bumped over the metal ramp and was finally on board, but was only too well aware she still had to go through the whole procedure again when the ship reached the other side of the Channel. The folly of her actions, both in following the trail to Spain and specifically in harbouring a stowaway in her car, was only just sinking in. Dexter would have been apoplectic with rage if he'd known what she intended to do and Donna resolved to keep him in ignorance a little longer. She'd telephoned Peg before setting off for Dover, explaining that she was intending to take a short holiday. 'I've got my passport with me and France is just over the water from here, so it would be stupid to miss the opportunity.' Peg had cautioned her on the dangers of foreign food, but sounded happy enough. Donna left a cryptic message for Dexter, saying very little while at least giving the appearance of checking in, but remained full of doubts. Two hours later, with Tony hidden under a mound of camping equipment, her doubts had multiplied seven-fold.

Tony whispered a few words of encouragement when she pulled on the handbrake, but Donna had hissed at him to be quiet and keep under cover. Theoretically, it may have been possible to have spirited Tony out of his place of confinement for the duration of the crossing, but Donna had thrown a major wobbler when he'd made the suggestion. She wasn't prepared to risk hiding him again under the scrutiny of a few hundred fellow passengers and had expressed herself in the strongest terms. Tony had acquiesced, Donna having made him realise it would be her way or nothing.

The rented Porsche whisked them away from the airport and within an hour Marcus and Tania were taking in the sights of the shoreline from the terrace of an isolated villa high in the hills above Marbella. The house was one he had chosen for its remote position amongst the cork forests. Members of his organisation constantly scoured the area for likely properties such as this. Property purchase, always under an assumed name and brokered by a respectable lawyer, was an ideal means of legitimising the vast sums of cash which his business empire created. The sumptuously furnished villa was very much to Tania's taste, but the price she'd shortly pay for such luxurious surroundings would be steep.

Tania perched on the marble balustrade surrounding the pool, arching her back provocatively and giggling as Marcus approached. He smiled appreciatively at the scanty bikini accentuating her high breasts and tiny waist and stooped to press his lips on her shoulder as gently as the breeze from a summer zephyr. Leaning forward, he flicked his tongue into the shallow declivity of her navel as Tania shivered in anticipation. She never saw the fist that broke her nose or the second punch that split the tender flesh above her right eye. Marcus grasped her arms and dragged her away from the drop down to the terraces, her legs twitching in shock and her open mouth gasping in silent agony. Inside the bedroom, pinioning her arms above her head and wedging her thighs apart with his knee, Marcus raped her and then beat her until black marks covered most of her body. The translucent nature of her skin excited him; bruising was always spectacular on such a pale background. If sex was all he wanted, he could have had the woman by now and discarded her, but his desires were far deeper and darker than such a basic need. The manner in which the woman had offered herself to him, a stranger, had been the catalyst for the pain that was to be her reward. Marcus enjoyed wielding power over weaker individuals and a forced sexual act afforded him the greatest pleasure of all.

Tania sobbed, scarcely able to manage more than a whimper as Marcus buggered her with a savage violence that was so far beyond her comprehension that the last vestiges of her sanity departed. Tania would never arrive at the conference, much to the annoyance of her superiors, but her talents were not to be wasted.

Marcus summoned one of his local contacts. El Jaffeh, his skin creased like old leather, had been recruited from the nomadic tribes of the desert. His ancestors had valued the pale flesh of captives since the time when the great expanse of Barbary was known only to the nomadic tribes who alone could tame its savagery. Such men were loyal unto death and would die rather than betray a comrade.

El Jaffeh looked at the sprawled limbs of the woman and smiled. Below the hem of his *burnous*, his skeletal legs resembled twin sticks of liquorice, riven with rope-like sinews and sharply defined bones, but he could march for three days and nights without stopping through pitiless terrain that would defeat a highly trained athlete. It was for this capacity to survive in the face of overwhelming hardship that Marcus had recruited him and his followers. As a Bedouin, El Jaffeh was bound by a strict code. The death of a young boy while in his care was unfortunate, and the circumstances of the boy's death even more so. The boy had belonged to a tribal chief whose certain displeasure would have had only one outcome. El-Jaffeh had travelled for many days before he could feel safe and had been eager to put himself under the protection of such a powerful leader as Marcus. Men such as El-Jaffeh and the others he recruited in turn were of great value to their new leader. Impervious to suffering, steadfastly loyal and with a natural distrust of anyone in uniform, they formed the beating heart of a smuggling empire that would transcend anything that had gone before. To a desert Arab, the sea was alien, but the new recruits learned swiftly and were now as adept at making the short crossing between the two continents as the fishermen who had plied their trade in these waters for a lifetime. Provided with EU passports and valid documentation, the couriers had no fear of a random check, but in the event of being captured in the actual course of their illicit duties, it was then that the true value of the Bedouin became evident. These men would never inform on their employer or any of their companions. Marcus had spelt out his requirements and had seen the expression on the face of the men. Any suggestion of disloyalty was an affront to their pride and their response had surprised even Marcus. Invited to choose a man at random, he'd indicated one of the younger members of the small group. The man accepted his selection with stoic resignation. He had taken four hours to die at the hands of Marcus, watched by an encircling group of his companions. Fingernails had been pulled away, hot irons placed on his exposed flesh and only when his testicles were crushed between two boulders did he utter a faint cry of agony, instantly suppressed. Marcus would have spared the man for his courage, but his former companions insisted on torture being prolonged unto death. The point had been made and Marcus had gained a work force whose loyalty was beyond reproach.

Marcus gave his orders and left the villa. Tania opened her eyes as the car engine started and looked at the face of the man who knelt by her side. El Jaffeh opened his mouth revealing broken and stained teeth in a grotesque parody of a smile. His hand caressed the pale skin and long limbs of the woman. Truly, she was a gift from the Gods. His men would work with a will on their next journey across the straits with the memory of such pleasures as this to sustain them. When he removed his robe, revealing the great bunch of his genitalia, and reached out for her, Tania wailed in terror, her cries echoing unheard around the lonely canyons surrounding the villa.

'Shit!'

Dexter thumped the sturdy top of his battered desk and cursed Donna in her absence. The message she'd left with Martha had seemed innocent enough, but Dexter was adept at deciphering the hidden meanings behind such bald phrases and was troubled by the clear evidence of Donna's deceit. He liked to think he'd always encouraged freedom of choice and expression among his staff, but he drew the line at outright rebellion. Dexter stood and paced the gap between the desk and the single window which overlooked the garden and had a view clear across the Dee Estuary to the looming bulk of the Welsh hills, but his attention was far away.

The strident tones of a telephone interrupted his reverie. Dexter frowned and crossed back to his desk where he shuffled paper with mounting impatience until he unearthed the telephone.

'Dexter,' He barked.

'What's up with you, you miserable old bastard?'

Dexter ignored Abbott's question and responded with one of his own. 'What do you want? He demanded.

'Just passing on a message,' Abbott replied urbanely, 'Fat Stan wants to talk to you.'

Dexter whistled, surprise banishing his former irritation. 'Sheehan? How come?'

'Beats me,' Abbott said, 'All I know is he sent a message through a contact of mine in the drug squad. Asked for you by name. Heard you'd been asking around about him and wants to talk. He won't leave the Republic, but will meet you in Dublin if you're up to it.' Abbott gave a mocking laugh. 'He won't talk to me, or anyone else who's still connected to the job, but sad has-been ex-coppers are apparently a different story. Gave his personal guarantee of your safety. For what that's worth.'

'Quite a bit, from what I know of Sheehan,' Dexter insisted, 'He's old school. His word is his bond.'

'You're not intending to follow it up?' Abbott asked.

'Why not? Nothing else to do here. You got anywhere with that Alison Lea murder yet?'

'I've done like you said and kept the pressure on. The Kent mob are interested enough to ask me down for a briefing. Hawkes gave me the green light to travel down to Kent, but you know what he's like. If we're not offered a full share of the collar, I'm supposed to tell the Folkestone boys bollocks, forget any offer to pool resources and get my arse back up north again.'

Dexter grunted. 'I expected nothing else. I got a good feeling from talking to the DI in charge. Seemed a good bloke to me and when he gets the full SP from you about links to other suspicious deaths in our region, you'll be in business.'

'Maybe,' Abbott said, doubtfully, 'I checked with Folkestone CID before I rang you. Still no sign of dead girl's boyfriend, but he's definitely their prime suspect. They've got a shit-load of forensic linking him to three murders in Dover as well, so it'll be a full-scale manhunt by now. Fuck knows where he's got to.'

'Not a word of this to anyone, but he's with Donna.'

'Donna?'

'Yeah. The silly little twat should have turned him in, but she put the bloody 'phone down on me when I told her to let the local lads sort it all out. She's got some idea or other in her head and won't listen to reason.' Dexter heard chuckling at the other end of the line and snapped his annoyance at Abbott. 'What's so bloody funny?'

'Nothing. Just thinking about Donna, that's all. Ignoring direct orders, running amok with wild theories and sticking two fingers up to anyone who tries to tell her what to do. Sounds like you've trained her a bit too bloody well.'

'What's that supposed to mean?' Dexter's voice was an Arctic blast.

'Reminds me of a bloke I used to work for some time back. Stroppy old bastard never admitted anyone else knew anything better than he did. Always wanted to do things his own way. Most of the time he got it right and came out smelling of roses. Mind you, there was the odd exception. Sammy Talbot, for instance.'

Dexter said nothing. No working copper was infallible and everyone called it wrong sometimes. He'd made one big mistake in his career. Many years ago now, but the consequences of that single error had been immense. Sammy Talbot had been a petty scam merchant, nothing more. Never a hint of violence. When Sammy had resisted arrest for the only time in his career, taking a neighbour hostage and barricading himself behind the doors of his flat, Dexter had taken the decision to go in. Ordered to wait outside for Hostage Rescue to mobilise, he'd argued that waiting around while a crowd gathered was only making Talbot appear more important than he really was and unilaterally ignored a direct order. The few sticks of furniture piled behind the door had been no more than a minor irritant to Dexter's men, but the forced entry had tragic consequences. Sammy Talbot had cut the neighbour's throat at the first sound of footsteps on the stairs and it had needed a five-hour operation to save the woman's life. Only Dexter's excellent track record had saved his career at the inevitable Inquiry. There had still been enough real coppers then among the ranks of senior officers to ensure the waters were well and truly muddied, casting doubt on whether the decision to call in the Hostage Rescue squad had been a direct order or merely an option. Nowadays, men like Chief Superintendent Hawkes, obsessed with targets and financial constraints, ran the top floor and Dexter's record would have counted for nothing in the search for a scapegoat. Damage limitation was the name of the game and Dexter knew better than most that his breed of copper had effectively ceased to exist.

'You still there?' Abbott enquired.

'Yeah. Let's hope Donna's little bit of rebellion doesn't end up as another Sammy Talbot fiasco. Keep me informed, will you? Oh, and get back to your Mick contact. Tell him I'll be glad to buy Fat Stan a pint of the black stuff any time he wants to meet.'

'I don't think he'll be supping any Guinness. From what I heard, he's a shadow of his former self. Drinks his meals through a straw.'

Dexter grunted and replaced the receiver. He dialled Donna's number once again but there was no reply. Dexter thought for a moment, then sifted through the papers on his desk until he found his address book. Dialling a number he waited impatiently until it was answered, but with every question he asked his frown deepened. Slamming the telephone back in its cradle, he sat for a moment in thought then rose with a sudden blur of motion and rushed out of the door.

Roper was seated behind his vast empty desk, fiddling with an electric pencil sharpener that was attached to the rim of his desk. He looked up in surprise as Dexter burst in.

'Just look at this thing,' Roper complained. 'Can't get a decent point on a pencil no matter what I do.'

Dexter dragged a chair across the room, leaving deep grooves in the pile of the thick Axminster, and sat down. 'Never mind all that bollocks,' he snapped, 'Listen to me for a minute, will you?'

Roper dropped the handle of the pencil sharpener as if it were red hot. He glanced only briefly at the grooves in the carpet, then sat back and waited for his partner to speak. Dexter's very presence indicated a matter out of the ordinary. The two men were not friends and were never likely to be, but co-existed happily enough in their respective fields of endeavour. Dexter handled the bulk of the actual investigations and Roper concentrated on keeping the paperwork under control and saw that the accounts were up to date.

'Donna's sloped off somewhere,' Dexter began, his expression grave. 'Left a message saying she was taking a few extra days leave.'

Roper frowned. 'I've not had a chit from her. There's nothing on the chart. Most irregular, booking additional leave without authority. Bad enough that she took leave anyway at such short notice.'

Dexter thumped the pristine surface of the desk, his features contorted with rage. 'Never mind your bloody leave chart. I've just been on to Donna's Gran. She tells me Donna rang her and said she was going abroad for a few days with a friend she'd met in Kent.'

Roper's frown deepened. 'I'm sorry. I don't quite see....'

'Oh, for fuck's sake. Donna's got no mates in Kent that I've ever heard of. I'll lay odds she's buggered off with that Tony Beech bloke.'

'Oh,' Roper exclaimed, 'Isn't he the one...'

'That the Folkestone boys want to interview about three or four murders on their patch?' Dexter interjected. 'The very same. I told Donna to turn him in. Let the local coppers sort it all out.'

'But she didn't?'

'Did she bollocks. Put the 'phone down on me when I made it a direct order. She gave me some tale about how she'd saved his life and it was up to her to protect him as she saw fit. Now this.'

Roper held up his hands in supplication. Dexter's support for his troops was the stuff of legend, yet his criticism of Donna's actions appeared well founded. In Roper's experience, this recent defiance of Donna's was nothing out of the ordinary and he told Dexter so.

'I'm not bothered about Donna putting the 'phone down on me,' Dexter bellowed. 'If she had good reasons to make a snap judgement which was different from what I'd told her; fair enough. What I'm worried about is what the daft little sod has done now. If she's with Tony Beech and she's gone abroad like she told her Gran, then she's breaking every bloody law in the book.' Roper started as comprehension dawned on his features. 'Yeah,' Dexter continued. 'Harbouring a witness to a murder enquiry. Worse, a bloody murder suspect. And as for skipping the country with him...' His voice tailed away.

'I see.'

Dexter looked askance at his partner. 'I doubt it,' he said frostily. 'Donna going off all of a rush tells me one thing and one thing only. She's following a lead and going after the next kid on that precious list of hers. The one I told her was a waste of time as the potential victim had scarpered. Jamie Marshall. Gone to Spain as I recall.'

'And you think Miss O'Prey would be so foolish as to follow him?'

Dexter paused. Roper looked at him and could almost be certain that there was something very like pride amidst the concern etched across Dexter's features.

'Oh, she's well capable of doing just that. Stubborn little sod. Now we need to work out how to do something about it.' Dexter stood up and began to pace the area between the desk and the bay window. 'Assuming she's not been caught in a random swoop, I reckon Donna will be in France by now. I'll have a word with an old mate and get him to lift the registration numbers of cars using the ferries today. Ten to one, Donna's motor will turn up. If it does, there'll need to be a few changes round here.' Roper looked concerned. Change was never part of his agenda. 'You will have to hold the fort for now, until Andy turns up again' Dexter said, 'I'll chase up all my contacts, see if I can find any trace of her. In the meantime, I need to go over the water and see an Irishman. Man named Sheehan. Might be nothing, but if Kate Davies thought it was important enough to suggest I spoke to him, I reckon that's good enough reason.'

'Kate Davies? Wasn't she that woman in Chester whose body turned up in a fire at her house?'

Dexter nodded. 'Bit more to it than that, but yeah. That was Kate. I'll get myself off to Dublin while I'm waiting for anything to break about Donna. Expect me back when you see me.' He slammed the door behind him, leaving his bemused partner still trying to contemplate running the firm for an unspecified period without the comforting presence of Dexter.

CHAPTER 19

THE car was a red Porsche Boxster, specifically chosen to impress a teenage boy. Marcus pulled off the road and looked at the waves breaking on the shore. Surfers dotted the water, skimming across the tips of the waves and Marcus watched them for a while through the open window, feeling the breeze on his face and savouring the beginning of the next stage of his quest.

On leaving the arrivals hall at Malaga airport with his female companion, Marcus's attention had been momentarily diverted by the name on a card being held aloft by one of the travel reps. Memories invoked by the name had transported him back twenty-five years to his early school days.

Marcus had been bullied at school. After the sudden death of his father, his mother had indulged his every whim. School bored him, so he stopped going. It took a Court Order to persuade his mother that Marcus should resume his education. When he returned to school, outside lessons he never spoke to anyone, just sat in a corner reading. The teachers were too busy dealing with a class size in the high thirties to concern themselves with the quiet new boy. If he preferred to read instead of playing in the yard with the other children, that was fine by them.

Marcus possessed a level of intelligence far in advance of his fellow pupils, but knew instinctively that by revealing too much he would set himself apart. He reined himself in and became an average student. No better and no worse than the majority of his class. In reality, he was light years ahead of them, even surpassing his own teachers in some subjects. He was an assiduous reader, not children's' stories, indeed not fiction of any kind, but textbooks and articles on specific subjects.

All would have been bearable if only schoolwork had taken up the entire day. Lunchtimes were more problematic. For an hour and a half, the regimented supervision of a professional teacher was replaced by that of a poorly paid auxiliary helper and the results were inevitable. To his fellow students, everything about Marcus was different. Solitary by nature and from a background where money was always available. The bullying started when envy turned to hate. He'd become accustomed to handing over his pocket money when it was demanded of him, but when the money had gone, one of his class-mates went further. David Whittaker was the biggest boy in the class and accustomed to getting anything he wanted. Threats escalated into violence and, by the age of eight, Marcus was being beaten and tormented on a daily basis. He never fought back, never reported the assaults to anyone in authority and his tormentor, perceiving this as weakness, devised ever more fiendish means of torture.

At home, Marcus sat for hours on the branch of a cherry tree in the garden, gazing at a school photograph. He was immediately recognisable, centre row, on one end, his body half turned from the boy next to him, an expression of implacable serenity on his face. There was no attempt at a smile, only a defiant stare at the camera lens. Marcus would gaze at the group photograph, his finger tracing the outline of each child in turn until he reached the tall figure of David Whittaker when Marcus would start to smile. There was not a trace of warmth in the smile.

The David Whittaker for whom the travel rep was waiting would probably enjoy his holiday, but Marcus doubted the man's namesake would be visiting the sun-kissed beaches of the Costa del Sol. His former nemesis had been blinded and facially scarred beyond recognition since the age of eight. Other children at the Bonfire Night display had escaped with slight burns when the box containing the fireworks had somehow exploded sending searing jets of flame towards the watching spectators. In the midst of the panic and the milling crowds of children and parents, David Whittaker had apparently tripped and fallen directly into the red-hot embers at the base of the towering bonfire. Marcus had watched the arrival of the ambulance with a calm detachment and could see even now the anguish on the face of his teacher when she gave the class the sad news that David would be unable to return to school. Marcus had suggested taking a collection from among David's classmates to buy flowers for the boy's mother and had been hugged by his teacher for his thoughtfulness. The gesture cost him nothing; the removal of his tormentor had only cost the price of a box of matches and a homemade fuse connected to the box in which the fireworks were stored. David Whittaker would have taken his pocket money anyway. A floral tribute was a small enough sacrifice in the circumstances.

The woman on the plane had delayed his arrival in Tarifa by twenty-four hours, but had been worth it. El-Jaffeh would share the woman with the men of his tribe in the traditional manner, taking her in turn until even their legendary appetites for the pleasures of the flesh were sated. The remains would be disposed of over the stern of a fishing boat in the deep and treacherous waters between Spain and the North African coast.

Putting such pleasant reveries aside, Marcus glanced back at the beach where the surfers were deserting the ocean and making their way to the shore. Starting the car, he glanced in his mirrors and pulled smoothly away.

Donna pulled up at a road junction and waited for the steady stream of traffic to ease. She'd been sharing the driving with Tony: three hours on, three hours off, and Tony was presently asleep in the passenger seat. She'd just about finished her shift and was exhausted. All that driving on the wrong side of the road was wearing her out. The first motorway toll barrier had caused her some concern as the booth was situated on the opposite side of the car. She'd managed to wake up Tony and order him to hand over one of the Euro notes they'd changed on the ferry and accept the change. After that, the journey had quickly settled down into a routine, although Donna realised with a guilty start that she'd not been woken by Tony when he'd been driving, meaning that, faced with the inevitable toll booths, he'd somehow managed to crane an arm past her to make the payments without waking her. She glanced across at him and smiled indulgently. The pain lines in his face had softened, smoothing his features. He's a good-looking sod, Donna thought, perhaps a little rough around the edges, but with cheekbones like that it was hard to quibble. She reached towards him; touching the dark stubble of his cheek with a tenderness she'd have thought impossible a few hours ago. He stirred restlessly and Donna quickly converted the caress into a light slap on his cheek. 'Come on Sleeping Beauty,' she said lightly, 'Your turn again.'

Their entry into France had been a doddle. Passport Control consisted of a solitary official sitting in a booth waving a languid hand at her brandished passport. In a state of euphoria, Donna had travelled half a mile before remembering Tony was still squashed down behind her seat. Not to mention that she should have been driving on the right hand side of the road. She'd screeched to a halt after a narrow escape involving an on-rushing lorry and climbed out to open the back door and release her passenger. Tony claimed to be as stiff as a board, but otherwise none the worse for his confinement. He'd studied the pathetic map and worked out their best route for which Donna was grateful. Map reading was just one of the numerous skills she lacked and left to her own devices would have ended up in Bulgaria or somewhere equally unlikely. According to the last checkpoint on the rough and ready directions that Tony had scrawled on the back of an envelope for her benefit, they were almost through France and would be in Spain within the next hour or so.

Tony had woken, stretched his arms above his head and managed a brief smile, but he wasn't fooling anyone. Even Donna could see the hurt in his eyes and the worry lines around his mouth were back with a vengeance. Donna slipped from behind the wheel and they passed each other in crossing over to their new positions without speaking. Tony was a good driver with a light touch on the controls and Donna closed her eyes. Thoughts of Dexter and the annoyance he would be feeling intruded for a moment or two, but faded away as she drifted off to sleep.

The Porsche gleamed in the sunlight as Marcus strode across the dusty tarmac and opened the door. He climbed inside and hammered the steering wheel with his clenched fist. His enquiries had revealed that his intended quarry had left Tarifa on the previous day and taken the ferry for Morocco. Essaouira, an ancient port on the Atlantic coast favoured by surfers for its strong winds and huge waves, would take him far from his intended route, but he would allow himself one further day's delay before devoting his attention to his business interests. Marcus rarely experienced regret, but he was aware that if he'd not broken his journey to seek pleasure in the pale flesh of the woman he'd met on the 'plane, Jamie Marshall would have still been in Tarifa and easily available to him. Now he would be obliged to seek out the target once again, but the irksome delay had its compensations: he had many contacts in Morocco and the sudden death or disappearance of a single back-packer would be far more unlikely to invoke the interests of the authorities. He'd leave today and collect a fresh car from one of his contacts on arrival in Tangiers. A major shipment was due and it would be easier and safer to ship it out in sealed refrigerated lorries rather than entrust such a valuable cargo to the risky trips across the water in a fleet of small boats. Money placed in the right hands would ensure the correct seals and documentation for just about anything and, not for the first time, Marcus gave serious consideration to expanding his interests into the arms trade. He knew the men who controlled the movement of weapons throughout Europe and was certain that he could take over their lucrative business. All it would take was a few high profile executions and the arms dealers would soon retreat to their boltholes in the Swiss Alps. They'd made enough money to contemplate retirement and amputating the limbs of a favourite grandchild or two would surely hasten the process.

Fat Stan was fat no more and Dexter scarcely recognised the man who pulled up a chair and sat opposite him in the darkened corner of the bar. The bar staff found sudden pressing business elsewhere at the arrival of Dexter's companion and any remaining drinkers supped up and left the two of them in peace. Even in retirement, Stan Sheehan had an aura of menace about him. Dexter was no drinker, not any more, and he made no attempt to enquire whether Sheehan would take refreshment. This was business. Not a social call.

'Retired, I hear,' Sheehan said, his voice a conspiratorial murmur, 'Me too. Although a smart feller like yourself would know that.' Dexter nodded but said nothing. This was Sheehan's turf and it was he who'd asked for the meeting.

'I'll not waste your time in idle chatter about the old days,' Sheehan continued. 'You've been asking about me.' It wasn't a question and Dexter nodded, his face giving nothing away. 'The thing is, now I'm retired I get itchy when coppers, even ex-coppers like you, start to show an interest. So, I make it my business to find out what they want to know. Seems it's got something to do with the reasons I decided I'd had enough of the nine to five life and settled for sitting in the sun and watching the world go by.' He paused and fixed Dexter with a glare. Dexter looked back at him impassively. 'Now, I've got no reason to fret myself if you want to waste your time and energy in worrying about a retired businessman, but when I heard who was doing the asking, I got a little curious. We never actually came into contact, did we?'

Dexter shook his head. 'Not as such,' he said.

'No. But I know you. Same as you know me. We were on opposite sides long enough and I learnt a lesson from that German general. The one Montgomery did for with his desert rats.'

'Rommel. Know your enemy'.

'Exactly. And what I heard was enough to make me glad you kept your nose out of my business. Now we've both retired, and after all this time, here you are asking about me.'

'Not so much you as the person behind you giving it all up.'

Fat Stan smiled. 'I was right,' he said, 'I told Dermot we'd be hearing more about that little toe-rag one of these days.'

'How is Dermot?' Dexter enquired innocently, 'I heard he'd had a bit of an accident.'

Sheehan's face darkened and Dexter glimpsed the savage power that had built and held onto a vast drugs empire through sheer force of personality.

'Dermot's not good. Not good at all. He took it hard. Losing his legs was bad, but he's lost a lot more than that. Always was a ladies man was Dermot. Not any more. He's nothing to offer in that department, if you get my meaning. That's why I'm here talking to you. I'm not up to the old ways no more. I thought I still had it in me, but I don't. Not to do what needs doing. It's a young man's game now.'

'Why ask to see me?'

'Because you're still out there, putting yourself about. You were good. Even I could see that. You're still at it; still got the drive to get out there and do what needs doing. Seems to me, we could help each other out a little.'

Dexter frowned. 'I don't do deals. Never have, never will.'

Sheehan smiled. 'Hard bastard still, aren't you? I wouldn't be here if you were still doing the same job. You're not the only one who draws the line at fraternisation. How about if we both wanted the same thing, though? Wouldn't that be interesting?'

Dexter didn't speak but his mind was churning. Everything he'd ever heard about Fat Stan Sheehan had indicated that the man was almost pathologically secretive, yet here he was getting all chummy.

'You're interested in my replacement, aren't you? Come on, Dexter, you wouldn't be here if you weren't looking to get something out of it.'

Dexter thought about it for a moment. He wasn't entirely sure why he'd agreed to the meeting. Apart from Kate's final suggestion that he took a look at the Sheehan brothers. Honouring her wishes was good enough reason, he supposed. 'Is there some point to this conversation or are you just pissing me about, Sheehan?'

'Oh, there's a point all right. I need you to flush out the kid that did for me and Dermot. Not for me. I took a good hammering, but I've had them before. A dozen lads with baseball bats can do a fair bit of damage, but I survived. But Dermot was a step too far. What that bastard did to him was fucking barbaric. He's my kid brother and I've always looked out for him, you know?'

Dexter nodded. Dermot Sheehan was a vicious thug, plain and simple. His elder brother had a veneer of civilisation and most of the family brain cells, but Dermot was a nasty piece of work with no redeeming features. Whoever reduced him to an impotent cripple had done society at large a major favour, but that was a point of view best not aired in present company.

'He came from out of nowhere,' Fat Stan said, a vacant look in his eye, 'One minute we'd got the whole fucking shebang wrapped up; next thing this bit of a kid comes along with a gang of fucking Arabs in tow and starts making moves aimed at taking over. A shipment going missing here, a courier arrested there, fuck-ups all round. When it graduated from knee-cappings and a good kicking, when my best lads started turning up with the backs of their heads blown off, that's when I said he'd gone far enough. Me and Dermot, we went over to Tangier to get it sorted.' He paused; staring into space while Dexter waited him out. 'He asked for a meet. Talk terms, he said. Cheeky little bastard. Dermot was all for putting a bullet in his head, but I wanted to talk to him. See what we were up against.'

He paused again, looking at Dexter as if pondering the wisdom of speaking freely. 'He wasn't what I'd expected. All dressed up in them robes they all wear, but he was no Arab. Came from that arsehole of a place you call home.'

Dexter started. He'd not expected the revelation. 'Liverpool?'

Fat Stan shook his head. 'Where you live now. Across the water. He said he'd waited for me to come over in person so there'd be no misunderstanding.'

'What did he say to you?'

'Told me he was taking over and offered me a retirement present.'

'What was that?'

Fat Stan grinned wolfishly. 'My life and health.' He gave a great bark of mirthless laughter. 'I told the cheeky bastard to fuck off. Dermot was off looking for a fucking gun when a mob of Arabs turned up with bloody great knives and baseball bats. Gave me and a couple of my best lads a good going over. Dermot comes bursting in waving a shotgun like something out of a Jimmy Cagney film. Fires both barrels straight at one of the Arabs and blew a fucking great hole in the bastard. He dropped like a stone and that kid took a swing at Dermot with his bat and laid him out. They picked up the dead Arab and took Dermot with them. Next time I saw him, his legs were gone and I could scarcely recognise him.' He shuddered and Dexter watched a tear spring to the corner of an eye. 'That was enough for me. The minute we were fit to travel I had us both shipped out to Sligo. The kid could have the business. He's fucking welcome to it.'

Dexter said nothing, his mind churning at the possibility that Kate and Donna had been right all along and that the person tying all the links together could be Marcus Green. Which meant that while Donna was acting on her own account, she was in deadly danger.

'Any use to you?' Sheehan enquired.

Dexter nodded. 'What do you need from me?'

'Find the little fucker. I've got good enough reason to want to see him hung out to dry, wouldn't you say? I'll give you all I've got. When you find him, talk to me again. You'll not get anywhere with trying to lock him up. Your old mates aren't up to dealing with the likes of him. Just let me have one last crack at him. I'll hold my hands up after it's over. Do you a bit of good, retired or not, to be the one that brought in Stan Sheehan. I don't give a toss about anything any more. Not with Dermot like he is.' He looked at Dexter quizzically. 'What's the problem?'

Dexter shook his head. 'Nothing. Just thinking about how one of my staff is heading out to look for him on her own.'

Fat Stan gave another bark of laughter. 'God help the silly bitch,' he said, 'She's as good as dead if she goes within a mile of that bastard who did for me and Dermot.'

CHAPTER 20

TONY braked suddenly and Donna's lolling head nearly came off her shoulders. She bounced back against the restraining seat belt and glared. Tony grimaced. 'That woke you up, didn't it?' He jerked a finger towards the windscreen through which Donna saw the grinning face of a young boy on a moped who'd stalled his machine right in front of the car bonnet.

'Came out from nowhere, little bugger,' Tony grumbled, 'How I managed to miss him I still don't know.'

'Where are we?' Donna watched the moped rider scream away and dart into a narrow alleyway without looking to the left or the right. No hand signals. No helmet. No fear.

'Nearly at Algeciras. Tarifa is just up the road and all the road signs are in Arabic as well as in Spanish here. You can see Gibraltar if you look to your left.' Donna looked through the window at the hulking lump of rock and marvelled at how big it was. A thought struck her. 'How long have I been asleep this time?'

Tony shrugged. 'About seven hours or so.'

Donna frowned. 'Why didn't you wake me when it was my turn to drive?' Tony shrugged, ignoring her peevish expression and Donna subsided into her seat once more. By her reckoning, she'd driven no more than a quarter of the way through France and Spain, but Tony looked knackered and this wasn't the time to start hitting him with recriminations and accusations of chauvinism. Also, she had to admit the fact that she felt refreshed and alert for the first time in days. Which may have had some bearing on her ready acceptance of the unequal share of labour.

'Do you want to drive the last bit?'

Donna nodded and they went through the rigmarole of swapping seats once again. As she pulled away from the kerb, Donna was aware of the fierce heat for the first time. 'Hot here,' she said. *Full marks for observation, Donna.*

'Costa del Sol. Supposed to be hot.'

The road climbed steeply from the town and Donna saw Gibraltar fade away behind them. The coast road wound its way through the scruffy outskirts of Algeciras and suddenly the car was barrelling along an open stretch of road along cliff tops with the blue sea far below. 'Is that....'

'Africa? Yeah. Only about a dozen miles from here to Morocco. Perfect smuggling territory.'

'Wow! I never realised it was so close. I wouldn't mind going across for the day when we've found Jamie Marshall and made certain he's safe. Is there a ferry? There must be.'

'Back there, where we've just come from. There've been signs to the ferry for the last fifty miles or so.'

Donna smiled and then checked herself. This wasn't a holiday. She was here to do a job and any thoughts of gallivanting, as Peg would say, could wait until they'd found Jamie and got him to a place of safety.

Dozens of gigantic wind turbines dominated the hills, their huge blades turning steadily in the stiff breeze. Donna looked at them in amazement. 'Is it always this windy here?'

'First time for me too, but it's where the Atlantic meets the Mediterranean which means a thumping great weather system whistling through a narrow strip of water at the mouth of the Med. Bound to be windy. That's why a surfer like Jamie Marshall would come all this way.'

Donna nodded. 'I don't even know whether he's a surfer or a windsurfer.' Dexter hadn't given her any details, although her anger at being told to ignore the next potential victim may have been a factor in her failure to obtain much information. 'Is it windsurfing or sailboarding? What's the correct term these days? I see them whizzing up and down the Marine Lake often enough, but never know what they call themselves.'

Tony gave a troubled sigh. He looked as if he didn't give a toss one way or the other and Donna suspected that her constant prattling was getting on his nerves. No wonder he'd been happy for her to sleep most of the journey. The entrance to Tarifa was high on a hill with the town stretched out below and a vast stretch of beach beyond the harbour. A huge road sign informed visitors that they were entering Tarifa, Costa del Windsurfing and Donna pointed at the sign in delight. 'That settles it,' she cried, turning towards Tony but his eyes were closed and she held her enthusiasm in check. He must be exhausted. They'd covered fifteen hundred or so miles since arriving in Calais, with only snatched breaks for drinks and toilet facilities and Tony had done the bulk of the driving.

The vast expanse of beach, complete with the crests of breaking waves, was testament to the reputation of this small fishing port as a Mecca for the surfing community. The numbers of young people in shorts and bright tee shirts thronging the narrow streets was confirmation that if you wanted to be at the cutting edge of surf fashion, this was the place to display it to best advantage. Tony stirred as Donna swerved to avoid a pair of jaywalking teenage girls, their heads thrown back in excessive laughter, and tooted her horn in annoyance.

'Are we there?'

'Yep. This is Tarifa. Journey's end.'

'Let's hope you're right. What next, boss? May I suggest a beer before we do anything else?'

Donna nodded. Her own throat was parched and the water in the plastic bottle from which she'd been sipping as she drove was now at blood heat. Parking the car in a tiny patch of shade near the port, Donna and Tony took the narrow lane on the right and were rewarded by the sight of not only a café, but also a bar as they rounded the corner. The café offered yoghurt drinks and salads, but Tony was far more interested in the sign outside the 'Beach-house' bar. 'Guinness!' he exclaimed, 'That'll do me.'

Donna sighed. 'Go on then. Poison yourself while I take the healthy option. See you in fifteen minutes.' She entered the café while Tony strode through the doors of the neighbouring bar with the air of a man who was bent on doing some serious damage to the beer stocks. The café was not exactly packed. Two women with kids in pushchairs munching sandwiches and talking ten to the dozen. Not German, but similar. Dutch perhaps? They looked up as Donna entered and then resumed their intense conversation; their dozing infants sprawled in their respective buggies. The entire wall to the left was covered in bookshelves containing second-hand paperbacks, mostly English titles, but a fair few being German or French.

'Can I help you?' The voice was that of a young English girl and Donna turned from her perusal of the shelves to see a teenager in a red apron standing behind her. Donna smiled to herself at the manner in which the question of her nationality was so immediately apparent. 'Could I have an orange juice please and a tuna salad?'

The girl nodded. 'Coming right up.' She went behind the counter and through a bead curtain. Donna heard a muted conversation and then the girl was back. Donna took a seat next to the window and sighed. It was cool and comfortable here: a far cry from the cramped conditions in which she'd spent the past couple of days. On impulse, Donna rose from her seat and returned to the counter. This was a surfer's town and the waitress was the right age group to know the leading surfers. 'I don't suppose you know an English boy named Jamie Marshall? He's not been here very long.'

'Sorry. I don't know many people here. I've not been here very long myself.'

'Oh. Not to worry,' Donna replied.

'I can ask Sean,' the waitress said, her face brightening, 'He's been here for years.' She darted away, through the curtain and re-appeared a few moments later with a blonde Adonis, complete with sun-streaked long hair and a full set of body jewellery.

'Who are you looking for?' *Australian. What else could he be?*

'Jamie Marshall.'

'Jamie? Sure I know Jamie. English boy from Cornwall?'

'Yeah.'

'You're the second person in the last couple of days to be asking for Jamie.'

'Oh?' Donna said, her senses on full alert at the possibility that she may already be too late. Who else but Marcus would be looking for Jamie?

'I can only tell you what I told the other bloke,' Sean continued, 'Jamie was only here a few days. Most of the kids here come for the wind. For windsurfing, you know. But the waves are great too and the surfers know that. Real surfers I mean. Board surfing like back home in Manley. Jamie's a nice kid and a real shit-hot surfer. Can do everything. Hang-ten, riding the tube, all the fancy moves, you know?'

Donna nodded vaguely. What she knew about surfing could be written on a postage stamp. 'Has he moved on to a better beach or something?'

Sean grinned. 'You could say that. Jamie took the ferry a couple of days ago. Heading for the Purple Isles.' He shook his head at the folly of youth. 'Same waves as right here. Cheaper dope though.'

'The Purple Isles? Where's that?'

Sean's expression revealed his incredulity at Donna's ignorance. 'You never heard of Essaouira?'

Donna shook her head. 'No. Where is it?'

Sean laughed and waved a hand at the entrance door. 'Over the water. In Morocco.' Donna felt suddenly light-headed. Jamie Marshall had moved on and it appeared certain that Marcus was hot on his trail. Donna had never met Jamie, but she'd never felt more certain that he was important to her. She was all that stood between Marcus and his next victim and it was down to her to save him.

Sean was watching her closely, a crease of concern bisecting his brow. 'You ok?' Donna nodded.

'Hey, just hop on a ferry and you'll catch up with your mate, no worries. Essaouira is easy to find. When you get to Morocco, just follow the West Coast down until you get there. Windy as hell and waves to die for.'

Donna knew the words were innocent enough, but she felt herself swaying and held onto the rim of the counter. As Tony appeared in the doorway, she slid slowly to the floor, her complexion as pale as the ancient putty peeling away from the frame of the glass chilling cabinet on the counter.

Marcus walked through the blinding light of the central courtyard and entered the dark shadows at the rear of the *caravanserai*. The travellers' hostel had been a place of sanctuary for hundreds of years and its patrons were of essentially the same nature as the day it first opened for business. Men who traversed the pitiless wastes of the Sahara were in need of food, water and shelter for themselves and their animals and the man who stood to greet Marcus bore all the hallmarks of a seasoned desert traveller. His blue robes emphasised his stature and he held himself erect as he greeted Marcus.

'Marcus, my friend. *La bes darik?*'

'*La bes,*' Marcus responded, studying the face of the other man. The eyes were deep-set, surrounded by fine lines where the man had squinted against the sun's brilliance, and his hands and face were burnished to the colour of polished mahogany. The pair clasped hands and Marcus noted the complete absence of any subservience with guarded approval. The man owed his prosperity to Marcus and had proved his total loyalty on many occasions, but would never acknowledge the existence of a master and servant relationship between them. These men of the desert were a proud race imbued with a rare dignity and an aura of self-sufficiency that was not replicated elsewhere in the world. Suleiman would carry out any task that did not directly conflict with the traditions of his tribe, but Marcus was obliged to follow a fixed ritual when dealing with men such as the Bedouin. A direct order would be regarded as an insult and Marcus prepared himself for a lengthy interchange of pleasantries before the main reason for their meeting could be broached. He had a predator's patience and would follow the approved rules of engagement even though the ritual was tiresome. Imprisonment in his early teens had been the ideal training. Long hours of solitary confinement, interspersed with a battery of psychological tests, had ensured he could switch from a state of torpidity to full alert in seconds. The testing had been intended to determine whether Marcus was likely to be a continuing danger to society, but he'd been ready for his inquisitors and their subtle questions. It would have been expected that a boy of thirteen who'd been placed in a secure unit following the apparent callous murder of two young children would have scored highly in any test of sociopathic tendencies, but Marcus ensured that his test results demonstrated a high degree of normality. Having researched the subject thoroughly in advance, he had no difficulty in feigning conventional morality and convincing a succession of psychiatrists that the offence had been at variance with his true nature. It had been a long battle, but one he'd been determined to win. Since his release, he'd taken immense care to ensure his liberty would never again be placed in jeopardy. Almost all his business affairs were carried out by subordinates, few of whom knew his true identity, and Marcus was content to remain a shadowy figure in the background as far as his work-force were concerned. His propensity for sudden unannounced checks and the savage way in which he punished misdemeanours or failures had fostered the legend of the leader throughout his realm. Such tactics ensured blind obedience from his troops without risking his personal involvement in the illegal trades on which his lucrative business empire was based. Occasionally, it was necessary to deal with a matter in person, albeit under a name which was not his own. The passport and documents currently in his possession identified him as a French oil company executive on vacation. He'd spent a great deal of money to ensure that his fingerprints or DNA profile were no longer on file in any known database and all of the identities under which he travelled related to men of unimpeachable character. The man he had travelled so far to meet was important to him. Knowledge and influence were valuable commodities and commanded a high price, but these men of the desert expected more than money; they demanded to do business face to face.

Suleiman was the leader of a caravan that followed the shifting trails across the great desert, leading hundreds of men and beasts safely through a journey of a hundred days or more. Even in the 21st Century, the camel was unmatched for this specific task. Police surveillance was unknown in these remote areas which made the caravan trails an ideal method of transporting illicit products across vast tracts of land. The Bedouin were also a valuable source of information and it was this aspect that made Suleiman such an asset. He acted as an agent for those men and women from the interior of the African continent who had both the desire and the means to escape their present circumstances and make a new life in Europe, but lacked the necessary documentation to be accepted by their intended host country.

An hour later, Marcus rose to his feet and exchanged bows with the robed figure. Suleiman's vast knowledge was not confined to the desert and he was in frequent contact with the hill tribes of the High Atlas. The supply of fresh drug couriers was always a problem and Suleiman had recruited a group of young boys during the period Marcus had been away. Teenage boys reared in a tribal culture were fearless making them ideal for use as drug mules and had the added advantage of being utterly reliable in the event of capture. To betray a comrade, even in the face of imminent death, would be unthinkable and Marcus knew he could rely on this unshakeable loyalty to a fellow tribesman, an elder or an employer without question. His only concern was that exposure to the vast sums of money involved in his business would be a corrupting influence, but this was a known factor and he would be vigilant.

Suleiman clapped his hands and a tall slim youth strode through the arched doorway where he had evidently been waiting patiently, just out of earshot, while the two men talked. As the youth drew level and bowed deeply and respectfully, Suleiman reached out and stroked the boy's arm. He'd recognised at once the value of such a boy to Marcus, but regretted that such a prize asset would no longer be sharing his sleeping mat in the cold nights under the desert stars.

'This is Khaled,' Suleiman said, his voice rough and halting as the moment arrived when he would have to be parted from such a boy.

'*Maneek antgeet?*' Marcus said, his eyes glinting with approval. The youth had a clear air of intelligence in his open expression.

'*La bes imandulah,*' Khaled responded, bowing deeply from the waist. 'Would you prefer we spoke in your own language?'

'You speak English?'

'Of course. I speak five European languages, as well as Arabic and all the Berber dialects.'

Suleiman laughed aloud, a fierce bark of joy. 'What did I tell you, *Effendi?* This one is a pearl beyond price.' Marcus nodded, aware that he should be attempting to disparage the boy's value in some way in order to reduce the outrageous commission that Suleiman would demand and yet he knew that Suleiman was right. The boy was indeed a pearl beyond price.

As the daylight fled swiftly from the sky, Marcus bade farewell to Suleiman, now richer than even he had imagined, and walked with Khaled to where he'd parked the Toyota Land Cruiser in the shade of a towering date palm.

The features swam across her line of sight like a fairground distorting mirror. Donna blinked and the concerned face looking down at her was revealed as that of Tony. Behind him, Sean looked equally relieved as Donna propped herself on an elbow and tried to rise.

'Oh no you don't,' Tony cautioned. 'You stay right where you are for a minute.'

'What happened? Did I faint?'

Sean gave a faint smile. 'You went spark out, girl. Just missed the edge of that table or I reckon you'd have a bump the size of an egg on your head by now.'

'I think we ought to get a doctor out,' Tony said and Donna felt a twinge of alarm. The last thing she wanted was a doctor prodding her about when she needed to be up and about. Jamie Marshall was in danger and every minute she spent on this café floor was a minute wasted.

'I'm fine,' she insisted, struggling to her feet and successfully evading Tony's protective arm. 'Too much sun and not enough fluids, that's all.' The explanation was pretty feeble, but if she was to mention that she'd blacked out in the past and suffered from panic attacks, Tony would have immediately summoned the men in white coats. As it was, he looked doubtfully at her, but made no further mention of fetching a doctor. Sean had made a cup of strong tea, sickeningly sweet and piping hot, but she managed to gulp it down and make a start on the tuna sandwich which he offered next.

'We need to catch a ferry to Morocco,' Donna gabbled through a mouthful of tuna, 'If you fetch the car round we can get off to Algeciras straight away.'

Sean put his head back through the bead curtain. 'What's wrong with right here? It's a few euros more, but the trip only takes just over half an hour. You'll get a ticket at the port and this time of year there'll be no problem in getting on the next ferry.'

'When's the next one due to leave?' Tony asked. He seemed to have accepted Donna's change of plan without asking questions for which she was grateful.

Sean thought for a moment. 'Half four is the next, then seven-fifteen.'

Donna glanced at her watch. 'Five past three,' she muttered, 'Plenty of time.'

Sean shook his head and pointed to the red plastic clock above the counter. ''Afraid not,' he said, 'You need to get your watch fixed.' Donna's gaze swivelled to the clock which ticked around to seven minutes past four as she watched. 'Bugger! I'm still on English time. What is it here, an hour later?'

'Yeah.'

Donna bolted the last of her sandwich, threw a handful of euros on the table and took a tight grip on Tony's arm. 'Come on,' she said, 'If we run, we can just make it.'

Sean sprinted to intercept them at the doorway and pressed the coins into Donna's hand. 'Medical emergencies are on the house,' he said, 'Hope you find your friend.'

Tem minutes later, after a breakneck dash across the quayside to the booking office, Tony was inching the car up the ramp of a creamy white catamaran and taking the last space on the car deck. He parked the car and as they reached the passenger area on the upper deck the floor shook to the vibration of powerful engines. The ship moved slowly away from the dock and eased through the narrow harbour entrance while Donna sank gratefully into the end of one of the rows of aeroplane type seats. She looked out of the window and was amazed at the speed they were travelling now the ship had cleared the harbour. Blue-green water foamed in their wake and even the gulls were left trailing far behind. There were television screens everywhere in the vast cabin, all showing safety instructions to be followed in the event of an emergency. The cartoon figures of passengers sliding down plastic chutes into life rafts were hardly likely to reassure a nervous passenger and Donna looked away. While she fiddled with the adjustment of her wristwatch she brought Tony up to date with what she'd discovered. It was no surprise that Tony had heard of the Purple Isles. The revelation that Donna appeared less knowledgeable than almost everyone else she'd ever met was nothing new. The embarrassment of a recent game of Trivial Pursuit with her best mate Andy and a couple of his friends when she'd failed to answer even a single question correctly was still fresh in her memory.

'Jimi Hendrix went there in the sixties,' Tony informed her, 'All the hippie crew ended up in the Purple Isles at some time or other. Free love, loads of dope, the usual sixties stuff. It was one of the places to see and be seen in. Marrakech too. Then times changed, fashions changed and they all moved on to Goa, Nepal or Thailand, wherever the next trendy place on the globe happened to be.'

Donna looked at the nearest TV screen that was now showing a silent Charlie Chaplin film. A group of young kids, all wearing bright robes and eating crisps, sat in front of the screen, eyes glued to the action without any change of expression on their faces. The passengers were dark skinned Arabs in the main with the odd European tourist mixed in. A long line of people snaked around the edge of the seats to where a fat man in a fancy uniform was seated in a booth. Tony nudged Donna's arm and grimaced. 'Passport check,' he murmured, 'Need to get it stamped on board. Saves time at the other end, I suppose.' Donna froze. In the rush to get abroad, Tony's situation had been completely forgotten.

'*Que sera sera,*' Tony said, pulling his passport out of the pocket of his jeans, 'Let's just go for it, should we? I don't see we have a great deal of choice.'

Donna shrugged and stood behind him, her passport ready for inspection.

'Did you fix your watch then?' Tony enquired.

'Yeah Eventually. It's a right pig to alter.'

Tony turned round and smiled wickedly. 'Shame,' he said, 'Morocco is the same as England. Greenwich Mean Time. You'll have to put it back an hour again, won't you?'

'I don't bloody well believe it,' Donna grumbled, sounding like a particularly peeved Victor Meldrew, snatching at the strap of her watch to go through the whole laborious process once again. By the time she'd re-set the watch to its original time, the line had moved on and Tony was handing over his passport. The fat policeman barely glanced at it before stamping a blank page and handing it back. Donna's heart had been in her mouth for an instant and she suspected that setting her the task of altering her watch had been a clever strategy on Tony's part intended to prevent her fretting over what would happen when they reached the head of the queue. Her own passport stamped and returned, Donna slipped it into her pocket and sat down next to Tony.

'Looks like we're out of Interpol's jurisdiction,' he muttered and she gave a nervous giggle. They sat in silence, watching the sea foaming beneath the hull of the ship. Within twenty minutes the coast of Morocco filled the forward windows.

'Tangiers,' Tony announced, trying for an exotic pronunciation and failing dismally. Donna grinned, pleased that he was attempting to introduce some levity. The tragic murder of his girlfriend, closely followed by his own narrow brush with death, had been enough to devastate anyone and Donna had made no real effort to intrude on his grief. It wasn't something that he was ever likely to laugh off, but the last hour or so had seen a partial lightening of his dark mood.

Donna let her thoughts drift and it was Dexter's face that swam into her mind. Given his background, it was no surprise that Dexter's expectations had diminished over the years. She was aware that he'd long since stopped wishing for something good to happen. It either would or it wouldn't and there was nothing he could do to change that. In a rare moment of candour, he'd once told Donna that hopes and expectations were alien to his nature. Hope only ever brought disappointment and he had enough disappointment in his life already without seeking more. 'Why bother hoping that tomorrow will be better than today,' Dexter had said, 'I'll settle for today being no worse than yesterday.' Donna had made some crack or other about a mid-life crisis and Dexter had nodded gravely. 'Your time will come,' he'd said. Donna thought about that conversation. Her own expectations had taken a dive just lately. Was she really destined to end up as a miserable old scrote like Dexter? Even worse, had that moment already arrived? At her age? Peg would have an answer ready if Donna ever voiced any of these dismal thoughts in her presence. 'Life isn't fair,' Peg would tell her, 'You should have learnt that by now. Just buck up and get on with it.' Donna pursed her lips. The advice was good enough; now all she had to do was follow it. Easier said than done.

Arrival on African soil was a major culture shock as far as Donna was concerned. If pressed, she'd have said that her only previous experience of the Third World had been Birkenhead on a Saturday night, but this was the real thing. Teeming crowds thronged the port, mostly men, all in robes and flowing gowns of many different colours, apart from a few harassed officials in bottle green uniform. Tony pulled up behind the car in front as crowds of men, all clamouring at once and waving their arms wildly, besieged them. Tony spoke to the most voluble of the company, a tall man with a great jutting nose and a cast in one eye. Donna watched in amazement as Tony took the car documents from the glove box, together with both their passports and handed everything to the man who instantly vanished.

'What was that, Arabic?' Donna asked in amazement.

'French. Most people speak French or Spanish here. Just as well.'

Donna shrugged. It made no difference to her. She wasn't even fluent in English, never mind French. 'Where's he gone with our papers?'

'Booking us in. He does this for a job and will get us to the front of the queue. It's not like anything we're used to here. Loads of regulations about how long we can stay and that includes the car. There was a leaflet on the boat, didn't you read it?'

Donna shook her head, ducking as a robed figure appeared next to her in her open window. He handed her the papers and a scruffy green form. Donna took the papers and examined the green form closely, trying vainly to look like it meant anything to her. The man stayed at the window, grinning with blackened teeth.

'I think he wants a tip,' Tony pointed out and Donna reached forward to look for change. As a non-smoker, the ashtray was a valuable place to store coins and she plucked out a handful of euros. 'I've only got this,' she whispered to Tony, 'What sort of money do they have here?'

'Dirhams, but he'll be happy enough with euros,' Tony replied and Donna counted out five euros into the man's outstretched palm. The green form was covered in scribbled pencil, her own name had been spelt incorrectly and most of the details of the vehicle were, to her eyes, illegible. 'Five euros to get my name wrong. That's three and a half quid,' she grumbled. The surrounding crowd had dispersed, but Tony was unable to drive away as the car in front was still blocking the route. A uniformed officer approached them and demanded the green slip of paper and both passports. He took the documents and entered a low office immediately to the left of where Donna was sitting. She could see other officers inside. All appeared to be smoking and talking constantly. The wait this time was longer; at least ten minutes, and then the official was back to hand over the precious documents.

'*Allez*,' he said, waving them off and Tony pulled away, only to halt again fifty yards further along. The crowds were as dense as ever, pressing all around the car and filling Donna's field of vision.

'What now?' Donna demanded, noting with some alarm that Tony was preparing to get out and leave her with all these men surrounding the car.

'Money. We need local currency. How many euros have we got left?'

Donna shrugged. 'Not many. I changed most of my own money on the boat. I've still got my expenses though. Two hundred pounds in English money if that's any help.'

Tony gave a wry smile. 'It'll have to do for now. I've got about fifty quid or so and I don't want to use a credit card if I can avoid it. Too easy to trace and I'm supposed to be a desperate fugitive, remember?' He opened the car door.

'Oh no you don't,' Donna said, clambering out of the passenger door, 'I'm coming with you.'

Tony shrugged, bent to remove the car keys from the ignition and locked all the doors, double-checking each, including the boot. He pointed towards a sign that said 'Bureau de Change' on the wall of a dilapidated shack. 'Not exactly palatial,' Tony said. Donna nodded. This whole place was a dump if what she'd seen so far was an example. They entered the tiny box and Tony showed his passport once again and negotiated a rate of exchange for their pounds sterling. The wad of crumpled currency, many of the notes torn and dirty, they received was dauntingly thick. Tony had mentioned that the exchange rate was in the region of 150 or 160 for a pound and the 100 Dirhams notes just kept on coming. Tony put it all in an envelope and jammed the bundle into an inside pocket. Donna had no objections; the bulk of the money may have come from her, but she was not rushing to cart a great wad like that around with her. Not carrying a handbag may have been a nuisance sometimes, but if she'd possessed a bag, filling it to the brim with cash and tucking it under her arm was not much of a prospect. She might as well have hung a sign around her neck saying, 'Here I am - rich foreign tourist available for robbery at your convenience. Help yourselves.'

Back in the car, they set off for the exit to the port, but were stopped twice more by uniformed officials wandering into the road with hands raised demanding papers and passports.

'For fuck's sake,' Donna grumbled under her breath, 'Who in their right mind would be trying to sneak into this God-forsaken bloody country illegally?' Tony cracked a faint smile while patiently answering the questions of their latest inquisitor. Mercedes taxis, old diesel models at least twenty years old, were everywhere, interspersed with what Tony had said were called *petit taxis*, a random collection of small cars all painted in vivid turquoise with a yellow flash down each side. No wing mirrors and dented on every body panel. Peugeot, Fiat, Renault, just about every make and model of cheap run-around was represented. Donna pointed to a particularly battered Peugeot 205. 'That looks as if it's been rolled over a cliff,' she said.

'Maybe it has. The *petit taxis* do all the local runs and the big lads look after the long journeys out of town. By the looks of the traffic on the other side of the gates, your motor will end up looking like that Peugeot before long.' Donna followed the direction of his gaze to where cars were whizzing around at breakneck speed and shuddered.

'You drive,' she said and hunkered down in her seat.

The road surface was dreadful with potholes everywhere and the traffic relentless, but after the first mile or two things began to improve. The congestion of Tangiers lay behind them and the road to the south was far less frenetic.

'How far is it to wherever we're going?' Donna had picked up a complimentary map in the Bureau de Change but had not yet mastered the task of opening the wretched thing to a section of the country that was even remotely close to where they were at the moment. 'I don't think Tangiers is even on the map and as for the Purple whatever they're called, I can't find them either.'

Tony pulled into a filling station and parked in a patch of shade. He took the recalcitrant map from Donna and within seconds had folded it open to show the Atlantic coastline from Tangiers as far down as Essaouira. 'The Purple Isles are here,' he said, jabbing an area of the map with his finger. 'Just off the coast from Essaouira. It's a fair run. No chance we'll get there before dark.' Donna pondered the prospect of arriving in a strange town in darkness and weighed up the prospect of spending another night sleeping in the car. It wasn't a pleasant thought. She felt like she'd been on the road for weeks and would have gladly parted with every one of that huge wad of notes in return for a hot shower and a comfortable bed.

'We could drive until it starts to get dark and then look for a hotel?' Tony said, not looking at her, and Donna grinned with relief.

'Sounds great,' she replied. She understood his awkwardness. They'd spent a great deal of time together by now and she still felt grief coming off him in waves. To have even broached the subject of booking a hotel room with a member of the opposite sex must have appeared disloyal to someone like Tony, still wracked with pain over the death of his girlfriend. Donna would deal with that problem, if it were to be a problem, when the time came. She had no intention of seducing Tony, although a wretched and unworthy part of her psyche drew a modicum of satisfaction from the faint chance that someone as attractive as Tony may have considered it a possibility.

The countryside, bordered on the right by the relentless waves and pounding surf, was a complete change to the frantic bustle of Tangiers. Even the roads had improved slightly although Tony swerved occasionally to avoid a pothole or piece of debris on the surface. There were cows and sheep in the fields, crops too and when Donna saw her first camel she exclaimed aloud. The tracks bordering the coast road were filled with men and women riding on the backs of donkeys, their legs sticking straight out at the side of the donkey's belly. There were horses and carts, mopeds and pedestrians and they were obviously passing through at the time when all the workers were returning to their homes. People waved and smiled and Donna was forced to rethink her previous impressions of the country in which she now found herself.

As dusk approached, Tony stretched out the kinks in his back and reminded Donna that they should start to look for a hotel. 'Where are we, exactly?' Donna enquired, having been half-dozing in the passenger seat for an hour at least.

'Exactly? I'm not sure, but we've passed Casablanca. I think the next town of any size will be El Jadidas. It's been sign-posted for a good few miles now so it should be important enough to have a couple of hotels. It's about half way to Essaouira, maybe a little bit more.'

As they approached, El Jadidas revealed itself as a substantial town with an historic walled quarter around the ancient port and the mediaeval medina was teeming with pedestrians. Donna had the task of finding a hotel and was pleased to be spoilt for choice. Her concerns over car parking led her to focus on the Hotel Royal whose faded grandeur extended to ornate iron balconies overlooking the main street and ample space to park immediately outside the front entrance. Tony parked up and they walked together into a cool dark entrance lobby richly decorated with glazed tiles where raised benches surrounded fountains and exotic ferns. The man seated in a carved wooden cubby-hole gave them a huge smile of welcome and an assurance that their quest for a room was at an end. He led the way up a broad staircase, the ornate handrail swaying to the touch, and threw open the door of room 8 on the first floor. Donna walked in and stopped in amazement. The room was vast. Two double beds flanked a separate single bed and a cane table and four chairs were placed in front of the lace curtains leading to the small balcony. When the curtains were parted, Donna glanced down and saw the comforting sight of her precious car immediately below. Any embarrassment over the necessity to request a second room for Tony was immediately vanquished. In a room such as this it would be possible to co-habit for an evening in conditions of the utmost propriety. She looked across at Tony and surmised he was equally relieved.

As they descended the stairs once more, the frescoed ceilings high above their heads reminded Donna of the interior of a church and, as if in response to this thought, a loud wailing cry assaulted her ears from a position immediately behind her. Through an open latticed window she glimpsed the great dome of a mosque and the call of the faithful to worship rang out from speakers positioned high on the walls.

In the entrance hall, the green slip of paper from their arrival in Tangiers had to be produced once again and their details laboriously transposed into an ancient ledger. The manager, magnificently attired in flowing blue robes, was no scholar; every item had to be carefully scrutinised before it could be entered into the book. When the passports were produced, he took an age over each section; even the many blank pages had to be examined in minute detail. He took Donna's passport photograph, not one she was particularly proud of she had to admit, to compare with the flesh and blood original standing before him. The man raised one languid brow with a practised skill Roger Moore would have envied and looked at Donna, those clear blue eyes making her feel like a slave-block specimen being evaluated as potential breeding stock, until, finally satisfied, he copied her name and place of birth into the ledger.

After their documents were returned, Donna realised to her astonishment that she was suddenly ravenous. Not so surprising as they had not eaten for many hours. She dragged Tony into the town centre and, after a quick wander around the historic *Cité Portugaise* and the bustling walled *medina*, they settled on *Restaurant Charazade*. It looked clean and inviting; cool too which was a major consideration. The sun completed its daily passage across the sky and dipped from view, leaving behind its legacy of flame and bringing a touch of splendour to the evening sky, but the heat in the air showed no signs of lessening.

Seated in a rush-backed chair, Donna studied the menu with mounting horror. Written in Arabic with French 'sub-titles,' she hadn't a clue what to choose.

'I can't cope with this,' Donna hissed, wondering why she felt compelled to whisper as the nearest fellow diner was four tables away. Tony looked at her in surprise.

'I don't understand a bloody word,' Donna whispered, 'You're supposed to be a chef. You must know what all this stuff means. Help me out.'

Tony shuffled his chair a little closer and held his own menu up for her perusal. 'Well, the first section is a list of *entrées*. That means starters. Then there are the main courses.'

Donna slapped his arm. 'I know that, smart-arse. Just tell me what they are and whether I'll like them.'

Tony grinned. He'd settled down a lot since they'd arrived in El Jadidas, was less stressful and somehow less sad. Donna hoped he was beginning to come to terms with his loss, but was well aware that a tragedy such as the sudden death of a loved one was not something that he could learn to cope with in a hurry.

'Do you like Chinese food? Sweet and sour, perhaps?'

'Yeah.'

'Right. Then we should have a *tagine*. It's a Moroccan speciality.'

'Have you cooked it yourself, or is it one of those foreign dishes that only the locals know about?'

'I've cooked *tagines* many times. Nothing to worry about. No eye of newt or wing of bat involved. May I suggest Madam may enjoy the *Tagine Barkouk* with mutton and prunes?'

Donna pulled her face and looked doubtful. 'What's in it?'

'Well, let me see. Mutton and prunes for a start.' Donna pursed her lips and he grinned at her across the table. 'That's the sweet and sour blend. Add garlic, cinnamon, a dash of saffron, perhaps a little coriander, sugar, olive oil and garnish with sesame seeds and roasted almonds. That's how I'd cook it.'

Donna sat back in her chair. 'Sounds lovely. Do we get chips?'

Tony shook his head. 'Couscous would be better.' He looked at her and anticipated her question. 'That's fancy semolina to you. Forget school dinner semolina, this is very different.'

'Bring it on,' Donna ordered and Tony motioned to the waiter to take their order. They had a vast salad to start and when the main course arrived, hot and steaming in its earthenware dish, devoured it like starving refugees. Eventually, Donna wiped her chin and sat back in her chair. 'That was a bit of all right,' she declared. 'I could get used to grub like that. I really enjoyed it.'

'So I see,' Tony said, pointing at the debris from the meal that littered the floor beneath Donna's chair. He looked rested for the first time in days and the dark shadows beneath his eyes were not as prominent.

'What's our next step?' Donna asked and Tony looked grave. They both knew Donna hadn't been wondering how they should spend the rest of the evening.

'Get to Essaouira, find Jamie and hope we're not too late, I suppose.'

'And then what?'

Tony shrugged. 'Beats me. One step at a time, eh? Try and persuade Jamie to return home and get your pal Dexter to take it from there.'

Donna frowned. Dexter kept intruding on her thoughts. Defying him had been scary enough, but anything less than a triumphant return home with Jamie Marshall in tow, safe and sound, was unthinkable. Dexter had told her many times that dealing with runaways was the worst aspect of his new job. While he'd been a copper he'd taken his fair share of kids back to the homes they'd escaped from and had seen at first hand the reception committee that awaited the runaways. His job had ended at the doorstep, but he'd refined his methods since leaving the police service. R and D Security took on the jobs the police didn't, or couldn't, deal with and tracing runaways formed a big part of their caseload. Dexter would find the kids and report back, but would never seek to persuade the young fugitives to return home unless it was what they really wanted. He'd seen too many cases where the kids had left home to escape abuse or ill treatment to drag even one more child back to the place they'd found intolerable enough to run away from in the first place. Donna had no idea why Jamie had left home, but the circumstances were far different in this case. She had no thoughts one way or the other, apart from a conviction that Jamie was in danger and she alone was in a position to protect him. In these circumstances, telling Dexter to get stuffed should be the least of her concerns. Defiance of Dexter that brought a positive result was one thing; slinking back with her tail between her legs having failed in her self-appointed mission was another question entirely. Not a prospect that appealed to her at all. And, what about Tony? How would he come to terms with his inevitable arrest on a charge of murder if they had failed to prove the link to Marcus Green? Donna wondered whether she should ring Dexter, but shuddered at the response she'd get if she tried to justify what she was doing. Best to leave Dexter out of the picture a little longer and see what tomorrow brought.

The width of a continent may have divided them, but Donna was very much on Dexter's mind. He'd spent a stressful hour with Abbott, shamelessly using their long working relationship as a lever to ensure the other man's co-operation. Folkestone CID were reluctant to consider any other suspect than Tony Beech for the murder of Alison Lea and the apparent link to another three murders in Dover made the subject even more difficult to broach. Abbott, with Dexter at his back, had suggested an alternative scenario: one in which Tony Beech had narrowly escaped being a victim himself and had been set up for the murders. It wasn't a suggestion that went down too well, but Dexter hoped it had been sufficient to broaden the search sufficiently for other possibilities to come to the fore.

The discovery of Andy's mutilated body, emasculated and repeatedly slashed with what appeared to have been a straight-edged razor, had been enough of a shock for one day. The local police had contacted Dexter in the small hours of the morning, but their enquiries were going nowhere. 'Picked up the wrong one this time,' Dexter had thought when the policeman gave him a list of the injuries Andy had suffered. Part of the risk of a gay life-style. Dexter's sense of shock had been immediate but was already beginning to dissipate. Andy would be mourned in time, but life was for the living and Dexter knew he had to put the tragedy of Andy's death behind him for now. The sudden death of one colleague was bad enough; a second death could not be countenanced. Which meant Donna had to get in touch.

Now.

Dexter fumed, watching the telephone on his desk and willing it to ring. His anger at Donna's mutiny had long since been replaced by concern for her welfare. If her theory was to amount to anything, she'd be placing herself directly in the path of a sociopath with a ruthless disregard for human life. Dexter was under no illusions as to Donna's chances of survival if her path should once again cross that of Marcus Green. Dexter would like nothing more than for Donna's famous theory to be discredited and for her to crawl back home defeated and disillusioned. There'd be no need to say I told you so or revel in her failure. Donna's safety was his only concern. He'd pushed her, bullied her, even ridiculed her; all with the intention of forcing her to stand on her own two feet and put aside the chronic inadequacy that had dominated her recent years. Now, with Donna making a stand and defying a direct order, Dexter wondered if his efforts had been counter productive. Showing independence and having the courage of her convictions were one thing; rushing headlong into a meeting with a vicious killer was quite different. The telephone didn't ring. The other staff had long since departed and Dexter was alone.

'Ring me, you stupid little sod,' he muttered aloud, 'At least let me know you're still in one piece.'

CHAPTER 21

THE breaking surf roared like a tropical storm as it crashed against the rocks and poured white foam onto the yellow sand. The tiny figures far out on the green ocean were low in the water. Both lying lazily on their boards with heads turned to watch the on-coming waves. As if on some unspoken signal, they turned to face the shore, paddling furiously as the huge wave swelled beneath them. One slipped behind and almost missed the opportunity, but the other stood immediately upright, swaying against the pull of the water beneath his feet. The sound of laughter reached the watcher on the distant shore as the riders in their brightly coloured wet suits swerved and dipped with the curling wave as it crested, following the line of breaking water. The taller of the two darted under the overhanging lip of the water that towered over him as it reached its height, his board acutely angled for maximum speed. He vanished from sight as the massive wave crashed down, breaking from right to left. With a gasp of astonishment the watcher on the shore saw the yellow wet-suited figure re-appear from the far end of the wave, his speed keeping him a fraction ahead of the destructive power of the breaker as it crashed and foamed behind his board. A triumphant cry reached the shore and the watcher realised he had witnessed a considerable feat of skill and courage. The yellow suit flashed in the sunlight, skimming across the water and traversing the diminishing power of the wave as it roared towards the shore. The other board shot aloft, the rider crashing into the trough of green water, while the first rider rode his wave right to the edge of the shore. Leaping to the sand at the very last second and waving an arm above his head in triumph, he turned to watch his companion struggle ashore.

They slapped hands together, laughing loudly. The slighter surfer wearing a scarlet wetsuit removed a tight rubber cap and a cascade of black curls sprang free. She took the hand of the other surfer and pulled him towards a row of beach huts at the far end of the beach. The watcher stood and removed his shoes, stepping out from the shadow of the overhanging roof and walking briskly towards the approaching couple.

'Hello,' the girl called, 'You came?'

'I'm glad I did. He's everything you said and more.'

The girl laughed at the expression on her surfer companion's face. '*Mon petit*, I have deceived you. Speaking to others behind your back. Can you ever forgive me?'

The stranger spoke to the girl softly and she stood on tip-toes to bestow a kiss on his cheek before taking her board and walking slowly across the sand towards a battered Renault van parked on the narrow strip of concrete that served as an access road.

'You know Yvette?'

The other man nodded. 'I came here today because she told me about you. She likes you a lot and has great respect for your talent. I saw you ride that tube. It was awesome. Please excuse me for involving Yvette, but it was my idea. When she told me you were good, I had to see for myself. Even in

197

Hawaii, I have never seen anything like that.' He paused and smiled. 'Sorry. I've not even introduced myself. My name is Marcus.'

'Pleased to meet you,' the youth replied shyly, 'I am Jamie.' Marcus took a step forward, extending his arm and shaking the youth's hand. Jamie smiled, his eyes downcast. When he raised his head to look directly at Marcus, there was a hint of interest in his previously diffident manner. 'You have been to Hawaii? To surf?'

Marcus grinned. 'Why else?'

'I'd love to go. The best waves of all.'

'The best,' Marcus agreed. 'You should go there. You owe it to yourself. Imagine riding the tube in a forty-foot wave.'

'Have you done it?'

Marcus looked at him in chagrin. 'I've been there for two years. Surfing every day. Up until I misjudged a break and wiped out. Big-time. Fell awkwardly and dislodged something in my spine. I'm slowly getting there; that was three months ago, but no surfing for at least another month. Maybe more.'

The expression on Jamie' face revealed the sympathy of one surfer for another. Denied the waves for four months was a pain almost beyond comprehension.

'Still,' Marcus said lightly, 'Never mind about an old crock like me. What about you? Are you into competition or is this just a hobby?'

'If this is a hobby,' Jamie said with a broad smile, 'I'm a sad bastard. I surf every day. Have done since I was a kid. But, I don't know whether I'm ready for competitions. I've no backing; just pick up a few quid here and there to see me through. Enough to buy food and pay my share for lodgings. It's cheap to stay here, but not exactly the lap of luxury.'

Marcus grimaced in response and they shared a conspiratorial grin. 'Tell you what. If you really fancy trying the big waves, you can come with me when I go back to the Islands. I won't be fit enough to enter the all-island competition, which is bad news for me as I've won it twice before, but you could. I'll sponsor you, pay the airfare and see you right for food and lodgings. We'll split the prize money, one third to me, two thirds to you. What do you think?'

Jamie pushed his hair away from his eyes. 'What do I think? Jesus, what a question. You're on is what I think. Are you sure about this? It's taking a lot on trust. I mean, we don't even know each other.'

Marcus smiled. 'What's to know? I've been around long enough to spot a natural and you're the real deal. That's enough for me. As for risking money to sponsor you, that's a no-brainer. I'll get all my stake money back and show a decent profit too. I've seen all the other guys, the Yanks, the Aussies, seen them and competed against them. I know what they can do. They're good, bloody good, but so are you. They're due a shake-up and who better than an unknown kid from little old England. Tell you what, don't make your mind up right now; I wouldn't expect that. Talk it over with your folks. Ask their advice.'

Jamie grimaced. 'No need for that. My folks want me to settle down, get a job. Just surf at weekends, you know? I'm not ready for that stuff. No, I've taken all the time I need.' He held out his hand and Marcus grasped it firmly.

'I've got some business to do later. Why don't we meet here tomorrow? About this time suit you? I'll watch you surf and I'll try and get you a decent place to stay as well. I'm meeting a friend later who owns property in Essaouira. He's bound to know somewhere decent you can stay. See you tomorrow, yeah?'

'Yeah. Sure.'

Marcus reached into his pocket and produced two cigarettes. 'Try this,' he said, handing them to Jamie, 'Very special. A bit different from what you've been used to. This is high-grade dope from the Rif. The stuff the growers keep back for themselves. Try it and you'll see why they are so reluctant to part with the best of the crop.'

Jamie grinned broadly, accepting a light from Marcus and drawing the smoke deeply into his lungs. 'Fuck me,' he exclaimed, 'This is dynamite.'

Marcus laughed, slapping him on the back. 'What did I tell you? Do surf dudes rock or what? Tell you what, why don't you come into town with me now? I'll drop you off at Jack's Kiosk. Yvette will be on her way to work at the restaurant so I'll need to hang around for an hour or so.'

Jamie grinned. 'That'll be great. Yvette kept that quiet. About you, I mean. I've only been here for a few days, but always assumed she was pretty heavily involved with someone back in France. Have you known her long?'

Marcus shook his head. 'No. Not long. She's a good kid, but I'll be moving on soon. Yvette knows the score.'

They walked to the beach shack where Marcus waited in the shade as Jamie changed out of his wetsuit and donned shirts and shorts. The wetsuit was hung out to dry and Marcus tossed a set of keys to Jamie as they walked behind the hut. "Drive, if you want.'

Jamie grinned at the sight of the Land Cruiser and slid behind the wheel. Marcus sat in the passenger seat and drew deeply on a cigarette. 'Take it away, Jamie,' he shouted, 'Take the short cut across the sand. Open it up. That's what it's for.'

Jamie turned the key and spun the wheel furiously as he tramped on the accelerator. The engine roared and the spinning wheels fought for grip. Jamie bellowed with laughter as the massive tyres flung clouds of sand in the air and the car tore away across the soft sand, bucking over hummocks and splashing through shallow pools, heading for the hazy collection of buildings in the far distance.

Donna had been left sitting in the car while Tony went to pay for petrol and she was not at all happy. The weather was glorious; she'd slept well in one of the vast double beds and feasted like a pig on sticky cakes and honey at a café near the hotel. But, everything had been downhill since then. Tony was morose and distant, too preoccupied for idle chatter. On leaving the hotel, he'd walked straight to the driver's side of the car without consulting Donna as to whether she would like to drive. It was her bloody car, but that seemed to count for nothing. Actually, Donna had not the faintest intention of driving, but it would have been nice to have been consulted. Now, two men had appeared from nowhere and were eyeing her in a very familiar fashion. Back home she'd have stuck her head out of the window and told them to piss off, but in a strange country where everyone wore robes and jabbered away in an unfamiliar language she kept her head down and willed Tony to hurry back.

The car door opened and Donna nearly jumped out of her skin. Tony sat down, looking at her oddly.

'What's up?'

Donna inclined her head towards the two men. 'Nothing. I thought it was one of them getting in the car.'

'Oh,' Tony said, shaking his head.

'What?'

'Nothing. Just thinking you must be a bit jumpy, that's all. I hate to disillusion you, Donna, but I can't imagine that either of that pair will be very interested in you.' Tony looked pointedly at the two men who were walking towards the kiosk, arm in arm.

'Oh, I see what you mean.' Donna managed a shame-faced grin of sorts. Tony turned the key and pulled away from the forecourt. The sun was beating down and the dusty road, familiar potholes and all, looked distinctly uninviting.

Tony pulled up sharply and turned to face Donna. 'I should have asked you. Do you want to drive?'

Donna shook her head. 'No. I'm fine. You carry on. You're doing great. Any idea how long we'll be?'

'Before we get to Essaouira? Not really. Depends on the road. It's not exactly the M25, but at least there's no traffic to speak of. Four or five hours I should say but don't hold me to that.' He drove off, passing a cart laden with plastic pipes which were swaying precariously and threatening to spill onto the road at any moment. The man sitting at the front of the cart was smoking a pipe with obvious contentment, flicking a stick idly across the back of the stout mule that was pulling him and the cart along, seemingly indifferent to the mayhem which his unsafe cargo was causing to other road users.

Progress was soon delayed by a police checkpoint at the edge of town. These had been a feature of their journey, but on each occasion until now the foreign plates on Donna's car had been sufficient reason to be waved through without delay. This time, the two policemen were seemingly intent on stopping everyone. The baking heat came off the road surface in waves as they waited for the cars in front to be checked. One of the uniformed officers wandered along the line of cars, unsmiling and serious. As he came alongside Donna, he checked his stride and rapped on the roof with his signet ring. Donna smiled ingratiatingly up at him, falling back on her traditional reaction to officialdom: look stupid and harmless and hope they go away. Tony leaned over and spoke to the policeman in a rapid volley of French. Donna had no idea what he had said, but his expression was fierce. The other man looked at

Donna and frowned, then shouted urgently to his colleague who left his position alongside the lead car and waved an imperious hand. Tony pulled out and drove past the entire line of cars, waving to the second policeman as they passed. Donna noted the occupants of the cars looking curiously at her as they drove by.

'What was all that about?' demanded Donna.

'Did you really want to spend half an hour waiting for Plod and his mate to check our papers?'

Donna shook her head.

'Thought not. I told the copper you'd eaten a dodgy *tagine* last night and had a bad case of the shits. That's the gist of what the copper shouted out to his mate. Seemed to do the trick, didn't it?'

Donna cringed and then exploded in laughter. Her embarrassment was nothing compared to Tony's returning good humour and the next few miles passed in companionable silence interspersed with one or the other of them breaking out in a fit of the giggles.

Yvette stretched out on the bed, arching her back like a cat. Marcus watched her with hooded eyes. He'd collected her from the restaurant after she'd finished her shift and they'd gone straight to bed. Yvette marvelled at how a modest young woman like herself had turned into such a wanton within the space of two days. She'd met Marcus by chance when he'd intervened to save her from the persistent attentions of a tall Arab youth who'd followed her home from the restaurant. The stranger had materialised at the sound of her scream and had put her assailant to flight. The manner in which he'd punched her attacker in the face, once, twice, so fast she couldn't see his hands move, had excited her in a way she couldn't explain. The sound of fists striking flesh and the blood that splashed onto her own face had been an insight into a violent world she'd never previously known. She'd clung to her rescuer in relief at her narrow escape and found her body responding to the feel of his muscular arms around her. He'd spent the night in her bed, her vows to her fiancé, the safe respectable young lawyer whom she'd left behind in La Rochelle long since forgotten. This was to have been their last fling; a last chance to do the things each enjoyed the most before marriage and careers intervened. It had been Guy's idea, this final separation before they were joined as one forever. For him, one last trip to his precious mountains with his climbing friends; while her love affair with the wild breakers would take her far from the flat sandy beaches of her homeland to the tumultuous West coast of Morocco where the full force of the Atlantic trade winds, *Les Alizeé*, whipped the breaking waves to an almost unimaginable power.

Yvette had never thought of herself as a sensual woman; her carnal experience, such as it was, had been fleeting and unsatisfactory, but that first night with Marcus had changed her forever. He had unleashed a tigress, willing and even eager to explore the boundaries of her sexuality. Now, two days and nights, later, Yvette could scarcely recall the face and body of Guy whose solid respectability she'd previously thought to represent her future life.

The idea of settling down with Guy was actually repugnant to her. He'd have used that expression: settling down. Just what wild lifestyle Guy imagined himself to have given up for a life of cosy domesticity in rural France she'd no idea. Now, all that was in the past. Marcus had aroused sensations in her that she'd never even imagined existed. She knew it wouldn't last; the affair was too intense, too overwhelming to be anything more than a fleeting episode, but she was determined to make the most of their time together while she could. Every moment spent in her narrow bed with this man who had come into her life by chance was to be cherished. Secure in her relationship with Guy, never dreaming that there was an alternative out there to the carefully planned life which had been mapped out for her, Yvette had ensured that the people she'd met since leaving France had been only casual acquaintances. Even the young English boy, Jamie, had been nothing more than a friend. So good looking, so brilliant on the waves, but still only a boy with no real experience of life and no conception of how to discover the real Yvette which she'd kept hidden for so long. Even from herself. Marcus had been interested in Jamie from the first time she'd mentioned him. Especially when he learned the English boy could ride a wave like no one she'd ever met.

'Will you and Jamie be leaving now?' She tried to make the question seem innocuous, but her sense of despair at the brief nature of this affair was almost overwhelming. Surely, he'd stay a few more days. Just a few. Even one more night would be a bonus.

Marcus reached out for her and Yvette saw the extent of his arousal with a sense of wonderment and anticipation. He'd made love to her once already; reducing her limbs to jelly and her nerve endings were still on fire. Yvette opened her arms and shifted to one side to welcome his body next to her own. Marcus loomed over her and slapped her, very hard and very deliberately, across her upturned face. She cried out in pain and Marcus struck her again, two open-handed slaps that sent her reeling backwards until she crashed against the wall which bordered the far side of her bed.

'What is it to you?' Marcus snarled, his features contorted in a sudden inexplicable rage, 'You got what you wanted, didn't you?' He seized her wrist and twisted it savagely, making her cry out.

'Shut it,' Marcus snapped. He took a corner of the sheet that her struggles had dislodged and tore a long strip away with no sign of effort. The muscles in his shoulders bunched and writhed like mating snakes as he took her head between his hands and squeezed. Yvette gasped. The pain was appalling, yet she saw the expression on his face and the calm manner in which he was gauging the extent of her suffering was somehow far worse than the pain itself. The betrayal and the unexpected nature of that betrayal in particular, were far worse than any physical pain. Releasing her head, Marcus wedged her mouth open, still bleeding from the slaps which had split her lips, and tied off the strip of sheet as a rudimentary gag.

'You've had your fun,' Marcus said, the menace in his voice even more evident for the matter of fact tone in which he spoke, 'Now it's my turn. One thing I can promise you; you won't enjoy it.'

Yvette heard a door open and slam closed and her heart leapt. Someone was coming. Marcus rose from the bed like a phantom, his naked body uncurling as he strode to the door and flung it open. Yvette's eyes widened in shock as she saw the face of the Arab youth whose attack on her had prompted her rescue by Marcus.

'Khaled,' Marcus said and they grasped each other's wrists in the Arabic fashion. Yvette noted the fact that Marcus was naked appeared to have no relevance to either man, marvelling at her own sense of distraction which allowed such a thought to intrude on her present predicament.

Khaled looked down at her and she flinched. The bruising on his delicate features, brought about by the fists of Marcus had already started to fade. His eyes were dark expressionless pools and his smile contained no hint of warmth. If she'd anticipated any pity or assistance from his arrival, she now knew the hope was false. Marcus made a gesture and the other man smiled in anticipation, removing his clothes until he stood at the bedside naked. His body was magnificent, not as muscular as Marcus whose every sinew stood out vividly, but he was truly a beautiful specimen, tall and slender with the coltish limbs of the adolescent.

Khaled sank down on the bed. Yvette realised that she'd wet herself in terror and felt shame, but Khaled ignored her completely. She realised with a sudden flash of insight that she was a trophy, bestowed by a leader to a subordinate. Nothing more. Khaled gripped her thighs, his long fingers strong and unyielding, forcing them apart. He gave an almost inaudible gasp as he entered her, thrusting himself roughly into her body with a callous indifference for her as anything but a means of attaining his own satisfaction. Yvette moaned behind the gag and turned her head to one side as a bead of sweat from Khaled's brow dripped onto her own face. With a final savage thrust, Khaled reached his orgasm and immediately rolled off her. He rolled to one side, leaving her with legs wide apart and studied her for a moment before rising to his feet. Yvette realised that Marcus had been watching and felt fresh shame at her own stupidity in allowing herself to be taken in by this man. Marcus stood over her and she knew he was about to hurt her again. He took her wrists between his hands, twisting them cruelly and looked at Khaled who stood expressionlessly by the bed, awaiting orders. Marcus had used this method of gratifying the need for savagery amongst his underlings on many occasions. The offer of a woman in these circumstances was the ultimate expression of male bonding. The girl meant nothing to him. His only concern was that a clumsy action could result in her death, depriving him of an anticipated pleasure that he wished to reserve for himself alone. On a previous occasion, a hitherto reliable and trusted lieutenant had reacted violently when the woman he'd just sodomised had raked his eyes with her nails and, in his rage he had strangled the woman. The other men, patiently awaiting their turn at the woman, had delivered their rash colleague, naked and pleading for mercy, to Marcus. The man had recently married the sister of Jaffra, another member of the group, and it was Jaffra who took on the responsibility for punishment. As each strip of flesh was torn from his body by the skinning knives wielded by the women of the household the screams rang around the surrounding hills, but no-one sought to intervene. The man had brought shame on the group by his rash act and his punishment must be seen to be suitably appropriate. When Jaffra brought his own sister from her hut and slowly strangled her while her dying husband watched, Marcus knew he had found a reliable replacement for the condemned man. Now, Khaled showed promise of becoming even more of an asset than Jaffra.

'Don't be so gentle this time,' Marcus said, wrenching on Yvette's wrists and turning her body to face the wall. She felt the weight of Khaled on her hip and bit into the strip of cotton at an unimaginable pain as Khaled impaled himself between her buttocks. The pain came in waves, receding slightly for a moment before returning even more strongly. Yvette was in agony by the time the two men exchanged places, but the renewed savagery of Marcus made everything that had gone before seem trivial in comparison.

When Yvette regained consciousness, Marcus was dressed. Khaled lay alongside her; the blood stained sheets a reminder of the pain she was feeling throughout her body.

'Do not kill her,' Marcus commanded, 'Anything else, but leave that for me.' Khaled nodded. 'I'll be away for an hour. When I return you can take the car and wait for me at the village. Prepare the couriers. I shall need them very soon.' As Marcus rapped out his orders, Yvette watched the expression on the face of Khaled. It reflected total obedience and she could not imagine any circumstances in which this man would defy his commander. She had been toying with the idea of appealing to Khaled to allow her to escape in some way, certain in her own mind that Marcus intended to kill her on his return, but Khaled's silent respectfulness meant that this last hope of mercy was stillborn. Khaled would die rather than defy Marcus; his whole demeanour revealed this fact to her and her last remaining hope was banished.

CHAPTER 22

THE *Iles Purpuraires,* or Purple Isles, lying just off shore from the ancient port of Essaouira, were named after the dye workshops built by Juba of Mauritania and used to colour togas in that shade of Imperial purple favoured by successive Roman Emperors. Tiny shellfish, indigenous to the region, were crushed to produce the dye, although the precise secret of the recipe was a jealously guarded secret. Juba's son, Ptolemy, was reputed to have been killed on the orders of the Emperor Caligula for having the temerity to wear a toga of the exact shade as that reserved for the Emperor. The islands are now a bird sanctuary, having been uninhabited for many years. The largest of the islands, Mogador, contains a ruined prison built to contain political prisoners and had been a place of pilgrimage for the sizeably hippie community which had settled in Essaouira in the sixties.

Donna looked out at the islands and the great swelling crescent of sand which was the main beach on the mainland and could understand why Jamie would have sought out such a peaceful place. The sun beat down on the white sand where dozens of scampering figures pursued a football on a vast pitch with no obvious boundaries and Donna turned excitedly towards Tony.

'Worth the trip,' she exclaimed, 'Now all we need to do is...' Her voice tailed away as the enormity of the task that still confronted them sank in. The water was filled with sails and surfers, too many to count, while to the far left and right were yet more beaches, each with their own collection of surfers dotting the breaking waves. Tony turned the wheel and headed for the promenade that ran for miles along the shore.

The town centre was compact, consisting of a high walled *medina* with wide battlements and a harbour in which numerous brightly-painted boats floated at anchor. Tony drew up in a tiny patch of shade and was immediately besieged by two small boys offering their services as guardians while he and Donna explored the town. Tony handed them each a note and they squatted either side of the car, glaring fiercely at anyone rash enough to approach within touching distance of the vehicle. While Donna sought refuge from the sun, sipping mint tea in the shade of a kiosk near the harbour, Tony accosted anyone of vaguely European appearance attempting to discover whether the boy they had come to find was actually living in the town. A small wiry girl waved her arms excitedly when Tony spoke to her and Donna saw from his expression that the news was promising.

'Well?' Donna demanded while Tony was still twenty metres away, but he waited until he had joined her on a stone bench before he spoke.

'The good news is that Jamie is here. Caused quite a stir apparently. Anyone who's a half-decent surfer soon comes to the notice of the regulars and, by all accounts, our boy is rather more than half-decent. The dog's bollocks, to quote my friend over there.' Tony nodded to the girl who waved back, simultaneously favouring Donna with a venomous glare. Donna could understand it, and under different circumstances, may have reacted in exactly the same way. Tony was the best looking bloke she'd seen in many a while, but neither Donna, nor more realistically Tony himself, could forget the fact that his girlfriend had been brutally murdered only a few days ago. Tony was just not on the market at the moment and Donna at least was well aware of the fact. His new friend, still glaring at Donna from across the square, was wasting her time batting her eyes at this particular hunk.

'Where is he then?'

Tony shrugged. 'Out surfing I suppose. Apparently, they stay out on the water for most of the day and only come into town to scrounge a beer or a bite to eat. He'll be camping out somewhere, like most of the recent visitors who haven't had time to get themselves fixed up with a room.' Donna frowned sulkily and Tony saw her expression and grinned.

'What? Donna demanded angrily.

'Oh, there's more. A possible contact. Some French girl who does a bit of waitressing work at *Ladyoune*. That's a fish restaurant in the main square somewhere. Find the French girl and we'll find Jamie. They're just mates, so I'm told. She's a surfer too, but not in Jamie's class.'

'Your skinny little friend told you all that? Don't mess about, do you?'

Tony smirked. 'Can I help it if I'm irresistible?'

Donna frowned. One little slapper coming on strong shouldn't have annoyed her, but it had. She had no claim on Tony; not that he'd shown the faintest interest in her, but the girl's obvious animosity to herself had irritated her no end.

'What's the plan then?' Donna asked, falling back on an old friend. Subservience.

'Try and find the restaurant for starters. Then ask around for a waitress who happens to be French and see where we go from there.'

Donna nodded. Sounded easy enough.

Marcus pushed the battered Mercedes to its limits along the winding curves of the coast road. The car, a former taxi, had been well maintained and his contact had assured him of its complete reliability, but there were many miles of hard driving ahead and he needed to be convinced that the car was fully up to the job. Its chief virtue was anonymity; blending in with the hundreds of similar vehicles that were a common sight on the roads. Khaled had taken the Toyota into the mountains, but there was much work to do before the two were re-united. The girl had been spectacular, fighting him every step of the way and he'd postponed the moment of her death interminably out of the sheer pleasure of watching her struggle. When the moment came, he held her face in his bloody hands, watching with a lover's smile the light in her eyes gradually fade away. He'd cleaned up and then slept for five hours next to the girl's body, finally sated and exhausted by his efforts.

He'd have liked to have developed his burgeoning friendship with the young boy, Jamie, but the demands of business required his attention and he could no longer justify any further delay on his own private project. The boy would die tomorrow, leaving him free to concentrate on matters that were becoming more urgent by the hour. Several couriers had been arrested in a well-planned police operation on the European mainland. Marcus knew he was immune from any direct involvement; all his couriers knew only the name of their immediate superior, but the suspicion persisted that someone higher up in the organisation had talked to the authorities. A senior courier, one trusted with knowledge of future shipments had been caught in an apparently random police raid several weeks previously, since when the man had disappeared. Faced with the certainty of a life sentence in a Serbian prison, even the most loyal employee would consider the alternatives on offer. As a Moslem and a drug runner, the prospects of prison life in Serbia held little appeal. Marcus had already decided to entrust to Khaled the task of locating this man and disposing of him in a manner intended to demonstrate the folly of treachery. He had great plans for the Berber youth and Khaled's command of languages and general intelligence marked him out for this particular job. Having witnessed Khaled's treatment of the French girl at first hand, Marcus was convinced that he had the aptitude and the ruthlessness the task required.

'What are you trying to tell me? She's skipped off and bloody well vanished?' Dexter's irritation revealed the depths of his concern.

Abbott nodded. 'Looks that way, Guvnor. I pulled a few strings, even took the liberty of mentioning your name when I needed it, and guess what? She booked herself on a ferry three days ago. Dover to Calais. Car and driver only. No passenger, so that Tony Beech character is still missing.'

Dexter shook his head. 'Oh no, he's with Donna. Without wishing to drop the silly little sod in it even further, if she's scarpered, then Beech will be right with her. He's a waif and stray in Donna's eyes and she'll be carting him round with her until she can figure out how to get herself out of the mess she's got into.'

Abbott grunted. He'd no wish to hear about further offences where members of his ex-Guvnor's staff were concerned. 'Not a peep from her since she landed in France until yesterday.'

Dexter stopped pacing the room and glared at the other man. 'What?' he demanded.

'She booked another ferry. To Morocco this time.'

'Jesus! Where the fuck is she now?'

Abbott shrugged. 'I'm a copper, not a bloody miracle worker. We're talking North bloody Africa here. Even your name carries no weight over there. Best I can do, I'm afraid. She buggered off to Tangiers and since then nothing. God knows where she is now.'

'I suppose you checked for Beech as well?'

Abbott's crestfallen expression was sufficient answer. Dexter indicated the telephone on his desk and watched while Abbott consulted a scrap of paper and dialled a number.

'Hello, Terry. DI Abbott from the 'Pool back again. Yeah, sorry mate. Just one more, then you'll never hear from me again. Remember that passport check? That's it, Donna O'Prey. Do me a big favour and see if you've got a record of a Tony, suppose that'll be Anthony, Beech. Try the same sailing as

O'Prey.' Abbott drummed his fingers on the desk as he waited for a reply. 'Hello? Yeah, still here. Right. Thanks again, mate. I owe you.' He replaced the receiver slowly on its cradle. 'Looks like we can call off the hunt for Tony Beech. Fuck knows how he got there, but he was on the same ferry to Morocco as your little mate Donna. That was as far as I can go. My jurisdiction doesn't go as far as Spain, as well you know, but no matter how many favours we call in, once they've left Europe, it's a black hole. Don't ask me where you go from here. Bloody Africa 'aint part of my beat. Not yours either.'

Dexter nodded. 'Too bloody right. Thanks. You've done enough favours off the books to last anyone a lifetime. You can forget about it from now on.' He paused, fixing Abbott with a steely eye. 'That includes anything you may have learnt about Donna's escapades. She's my staff. I'll deal with her when the time comes. You don't need to get involved. Best to leave Tony Beech on the missing files. Vanished without trace sounds about right to me.'

'Tony Beech? Never heard of him, Guvnor,' Abbott said, picking up his coat and walking out of the door.

CHAPTER 23

DONNA stretched out the kinks from her neck; certain that the bed on which she'd tossed and turned all night had been part of the furniture in a mediaeval torture chamber. Tony had booked the room next door and she'd heard him fidgeting throughout most of the long hours of darkness, although this morning he appeared considerably more rested than herself. Breakfast was a revelation after the dismal hotel experience; coffee, freshly squeezed orange juice, croissants, butter and a selection of jam, honey and marmalade that wouldn't have been out of place in a Parisian pavement café. Donna buttered, spread and munched with abandon, feeling the life slowly seeping back into her cramped muscles. They'd found the restaurant where the French girl who'd befriended Jamie worked last night, but that was where the good news ended. Yvette hadn't turned in for work last night. That was nothing unusual according to the restaurant manager. 'These girls. They work a few days; they move on,' he'd grumbled in passable English which even Donna had understood. 'It is normal.' A fellow waitress, a cheerful girl with enormous breasts, told Tony that Yvette was very far from unreliable, despite the opinion of her boss. The waitress thought Yvette may have gone with Jamie to a beach a few miles out of town which was where all the top surfers gathered and where Jamie would surely be camping. It had been far too late to travel out there last night, but Donna was still regretting being the one who'd chosen the hostel in which she'd spent the longest and most uncomfortable night of her life.

Tony drank the dregs of his coffee and regarded Donna with obvious concern. 'You ok?'

'Fine,' Donna lied. 'Never better.'

Five minutes later they had checked out and regained Donna's car from the jealous clutches of the same boys who'd appointed themselves its personal guardians on the previous afternoon. Donna had forgotten all about them until they rose, yawning and stretching, from the strips of cardboard which had acted as a mattress. Tony gave them his profuse thanks, together with a handful of coins and they darted off well satisfied with the proceeds of their employment.

'They did a good job,' Tony said as he sat himself behind the wheel. By now, he had apparently decided it was no longer necessary to ask Donna if she wanted to drive. Donna nodded. She was wondering how a sheet of cardboard laid out on a pavement could look so inviting when compared to the room in which she'd spent the night.

The beach was still packed with boys playing football. There seemed to be a game taking place at any time and Donna had marvelled at the numbers involved late last night when Tony and herself had wandered along the promenade seeking a cool drink. The entire beach, miles of it, was floodlit, the lights turning the gleaming sand to gold and literally hundreds of boys and young men were involved in one or other of the numerous matches that were taking place simultaneously.

Leaving the town behind them, Tony glanced at the sheet of paper on which he'd scrawled rough directions supplied by the chatty waitress. The road meandered away from the shore, only to rejoin the coastal strip a mile or so further along where the sand dunes formed a barrier of some sorts from the relentless wind. When they joined the main road towards Agadir, Donna was ready to suggest they had somehow taken a wrong turning but kept silent. The wisdom of that decision was born out a few minutes later when a tin sign pointed them in the direction of Diabat.

'This was the village the hippies settled in, back in the sixties,' Tony said, showing off. Donna had spotted him reading a guidebook to the area in the hotel last night, but somehow she managed to avoid yawning. She'd read the same page of the guidebook after Tony had left to find a working shower. A vain quest as it turned out. The hippies had long since departed and the old Berber village had reverted to normality. Which was to say, as far as Donna was concerned, that it was a dump. This was how people must have lived before electricity and running water were even considered desirable for civilised living. The road was narrow but still passable with care. There was a run-down campsite at the edge of the village and Donna could see at a glance that it was deserted.

'No sign of him here,' Tony pointed out. Donna sighed heavily. She could see that herself.

'No-one camping here just now,' Tony continued. Donna wanted to scream. If he was going to go on all bloody day making statements that were already obvious to anyone, she'd go mad. She decided her lack of sleep was the reason behind her irritability and could delay throttling Tony for another five minutes. The road petered out beyond the village and they had to make a three point turn in a stream and laboriously retrace their steps. Everyone they'd spoken to last night had insisted the area around Sidi Kaouki was the best place for surfing in all Morocco.

The road to Sidi Kaouki was a few miles further on and Donna took a deep breath as they rounded the headland and saw a vast empty beach with a plume of spray at the shoreline indicating that some serious waves were arriving. A few sails dotted the blue ocean, but there were no surfers to be seen despite waves which to Donna's eyes were the size of a double-decker 'bus.

Tony parked up at the rather grand *Auberge de la Plage* and wandered off to seek further directions. He was back before Donna had time to get out and walk a full circuit of the car and indicated a dirt road running towards a line of sand dunes. 'That way for surfers,' he grunted, banging the car into gear with a loud crunch. Donna glared but he seemed oblivious to her angry expression. 'Cap Sim is just up here somewhere,' Tony muttered. 'The gardener at that *Auberge* place reckons anyone who is a half-decent surfer goes to Cap Sim.'

The waves were even wilder as they cleared the dunes and met the full force of the wind. Rows of huts were perched above the high water mark on the beach, virtually derelict shacks but with a roof and walls of sorts.

Tony parked up and they clambered gratefully out of the car which was uncomfortably hot, even with all the windows wound down. As Donna waded through the soft clinging sand she heard the sound of running water behind one of the huts. She was a pace or two ahead of Tony and stopped in her tracks when she realised there was a young man standing directly in front of her. He was holding a plastic water container with a sprinkler nozzle at the base above his head and luxuriating under the resultant shower. Donna realised two things immediately: The object of her interest was almost impossibly good looking and he was entirely naked.

Tony appeared in her line of vision smirking at the expression on Donna's face. While Donna tried to shuffle silently away, the showering figure half turned and presented a full frontal view which was even more disconcerting.

'Hi.' He'd spoken to Donna, but she was uncertain how to reply.

'Hi,' she said at last, managing to stir her feet into some form of retreat and avoiding looking at Tony. They waited for a moment without speaking until they were joined by the blonde-haired figure now wearing a pair of ragged shorts. Donna began to stammer a form of apology, but her words dried up as what had begun as a faint possibility coalesced into certainty.

'You're Jamie Marshall.' Donna's statement hung in the air for a long moment until the boy smiled at her. Imagine a teenage boy with a mane of blonde hair, a body like a Michelangelo statue and the face of a movie star and you'd still only be halfway there, Donna thought.

The vision blinked, almost prompting Donna to wonder whether he could read minds as well. 'I am,' he said.

'We've come a long way to find you,' Tony said.

Jamie looked at him for the first time. 'Well, here I am.'

'Can we talk to you?' Donna said; feeling uncertain now the moment she'd waited for so long had finally arrived. How did one go about warning someone that a man they'd never met was on his way to kill them? *Tricky.*

'Sure,' Jamie replied, 'Only, I need to dress. I'm expecting a friend any minute and if I'm not ready, I'm a dead man, believe me.'

Donna glanced at Tony and saw him flinch. The expression was unfortunate, but at least they had arrived in time.

'Who's the friend? Yvette?'

Jamie looked at Donna in surprise. 'You know Yvette?'

'Not exactly, but we did some asking around. That's how we managed to find you out here in the middle of nowhere. Yvette's friend told us you'd both be here.'

Jamie frowned. 'Well, Yvette should have been here by now. It's not like her to miss the morning waves. A mate from the campsite told me she'd not turned up for work either. He said she'd found a guy, but I said no way. Yvette's already got a guy back in France and she's always going on about him. Going back home and getting married. The full hit. Probably have a house full of kids in a few years and be too fat to climb on her board.' He spoke of Yvette with such wistful longing that Donna saw at once how smitten he was.

211

Tony had wandered off to look through the partly open door of the shack and joined them with a pained expression on his face. 'Not much of a place.'

'Nah,' Jamie agreed, 'But good enough to store the boards and dry the wet-suit off.'

'It's not very secure,' Donna ventured, looking dubiously at the gaping holes in the walls of the shack. 'Aren't you worried about your stuff going missing?'

Jamie looked at her in astonishment. 'No-one here would take another guy's board. We're all surfers,' he insisted as if that was all that needed to be said. Donna shrugged. She wanted to sit down and get out of the sun for a spell while she tried to convince Jamie that he was in danger, but was uncertain how to go about it. Anyone who entrusted his possessions to a rickety old shed on the beach would be too trusting and naive to readily accept her warning about him being in danger. Whatever she said would have to be pretty damn compelling if she hoped to persuade Jamie to leave his precious waves behind and return to England with Tony and herself. She decided she couldn't wait any longer and took a deep breath.

'Tony and I have come over from England to find you,' she began, talking too fast, but determined to keep on going until he started to take notice, 'Tony's girlfriend was killed because of something that happened a long time ago.'

'He tried to kill me too,' Tony interjected, 'If Donna hadn't been around, he'd have succeeded.' Donna glared at him. She was certain she would manage better without Tony interrupting her every few minutes. The glare had its effect and Tony stopped talking, looking suitably contrite.

'Your dad was on a jury once. That's what all this is about. The children of those jurors have been having accidents. Fatal accidents. You are next on the list.' She stopped to marshal her thoughts and Jamie burst out laughing.

'This is a wind-up, right?' He was shaking his head, blonde hair flopping and looking at Donna and Tony as if they'd dropped from some alien spaceship.

'No wind-up. It's real and you need to start bloody listening,' Donna snapped, her voice sounding dangerously shrill. She was on the edge and she knew it. Having travelled so far, it had never occurred to her that having found Jamie she would be unable to convince him of the danger which threatened him. Part of her mind could appreciate the position from his point of view. Here was this basically nice kid, minding his own business and living his dream surfing the waves which were his sole interest in life, when along comes this mad creature from Liverpool telling him he will die if he doesn't take off with her and the other bloke she's brought with her and return to England. All because his dad was once on a jury, probably before he was even born. From that angle, Donna could see she'd have her work cut out to convince him.

Jamie stopped laughing and looked carefully at Donna. 'You're serious aren't you?' She nodded.

'Fuck!' Jamie walked a few steps to the side of the hut and scanned the beach carefully, but there was no one in sight. 'Where the hell is Yvette?' His expression had more than a hint of the peevish teenager in it and Donna reminded herself that he was only a young boy and would almost certainly turn rebellious if she tried to insist that he returned to England under their protection.

Tony beckoned to Donna while Jamie's attention was focussed on the barren stretch of sand. 'How shall we go about this?' He asked. Donna had already noted the way in which Tony had been deferring to her since meeting Jamie and was grateful for this. This was her show and nothing would weaken her case more than a gender war over who was in charge.

'No idea. He's not exactly falling over himself with gratitude, is he? Can't say as I blame him. Two nutters turning up out of the blue telling him he's the target of a serial killer? Takes a bit of believing.'

Tony smiled. 'Why don't I leave you here with Jamie? Let you work on him one to one?'

'Where will you be while I'm working miracles of persuasion?'

Tony pointed past her shoulder. 'Out there. I'll ask if I can borrow his board. It'll keep him here long enough for you to talk some sense into him and also take his mind off surfing for a spell. He keeps looking at the waves, haven't you noticed? We need to remove that distraction.'

Donna nodded thoughtfully. There was merit in the suggestion, but a snag still suggested itself. 'I suppose you can surf?'

Tony shrugged his shoulders, trying to look modest. 'A bit, yeah. I wouldn't class myself as expert, but I can stand up at least. Mind you, I've never even seen waves as big as this before.'

Jamie returned and opened the door of the shack wide. He took out his board and examined it carefully. Tony looked over his shoulder. 'Nice board,' he said, 'Don't suppose you'd let me use it for half an hour?'

'Not a chance,' Jamie said, 'I'm not waiting for Yvette any longer. Donna laid a hand on his arm, gripping him with a fierce urgency and digging in her nails. Jamie turned to her in confusion. 'Christ, you're not going to give up, are you?'

Donna shook her head. 'Not until I know you're safe,' she said, 'Ben Adams, Julian Harrison, Christopher Wright, Samantha Jackson and Alison Lea weren't so fortunate.'

Jamie looked at her, his eyes widening. 'Don't tell me. They're all dead, aren't they?'

Donna nodded. 'All of them. Alison was Tony's fiancée. Tony was almost killed himself. You see now why we came all this way to find you? Just trust me for now. I know the man responsible for all these murders and you will be his next victim unless we can get you somewhere safe. Right now.'

Jamie took his board and passed it over to Tony. 'Keep away from the rocks,' he said, 'You'll need a wetsuit as well. The water's bloody freezing. Mine should just about fit you. There's a strong off-shore current if you go any further south than the edge of the dunes, but just about anywhere else will be fine.' He waved a hand in the direction from which they had just travelled. Tony grinned and took the yellow wetsuit off a metal hook fixed to a stout beam. Donna moved away to give him some privacy and watched a small group of birds darting and swooping just above the waves. Jamie joined her and noted her interest.

'Eleonora's falcons,' he said. 'From the bird sanctuary on the Purple Isles. It's a wonderful place. I borrowed a rig when I first got here and sailed around both the islands. The water is like crystal and the sense of history reaches out and grabs you.'

Donna looked at him in surprise. What had happened to the petulant teenage brat who she'd been talking to a few moments ago? Tony interrupted her reverie; his body shoehorned into Jamie's brilliant yellow wetsuit.

'What do you think? Mister cool, eh?'

'More like Mister Blobby,' Donna quipped and Jamie laughed. Tony looked good, actually, not a hint of spare tyre in that most unforgiving of all garments. Tony waved a hand and walked purposefully towards the water, the surfboard resting on his right shoulder. Jamie watched anxiously as Tony waded a few steps into the pounding surf before launching himself onto the board and paddling out to sea.

'Looks like he knows what he's doing.'

'Yeah. He'll be fine. Now can we talk?' Donna tried to keep the air of desperation out of her voice but failed dismally. Jamie nodded and they sat close together in the doorway of the hut, a dark patch of shade providing welcome relief.

'Go ahead,' Jamie said, 'I'm listening.'

Donna took a moment to collect her thoughts before she launched into a concise report on all she'd discovered about the sudden deaths of a certain group of teenagers, linked by the presence of a parent in a jury many years ago. The accused had been found guilty by that group of twelve men and women and had bided his time until now when he'd begun a savage revenge, choosing to kill children rather than the actual jurors in order to maximise the pain inflicted on his chosen victims.

'Did he do it?' The interruption stopped Donna in her tracks and she hesitated, confused and uncertain how to respond.

'The boy who was on trial? Did he do what he was on trial for?'

'Oh, I see. Well, actually, he didn't. It was the father of the two little girls who was responsible. Not that he intended to kill them; his idea was to kill his wife. The father's dead now. I saw him die.' Jamie watched her face carefully as she spoke, his attention rapt.

'So, the boy who was sent down has a case. In a way. If he didn't do it?'

'Yes, but even if he didn't do what he was sent down for, he's an evil sod who's killed many times before and since. He even killed both his parents and probably his baby sister as well.'

'Christ!'

'Yeah. Marcus is a bad man and you'll be better off staying well away from him.'

Jamie started, his eyes wide open. 'Marcus?'

Donna nodded. 'Yeah. Marcus Green.'

'But, I've already met him.'

'What?'

'He was here yesterday. Right where you are now. He's arranged to meet me here to talk about going with him to Hawaii. He's a surfer, knows all the top guys.'

Donna grimaced. 'Marcus may be many things, but I'll lay odds he's no surfer. What time is he supposed to be meeting you?'

'Not for a while,' Jamie responded with a shrug of his shoulders, 'He said he'd come after I finished surfing. Two or three hours at least.' As if he'd just remembered lending out his board to Tony, he glanced out to sea where Tony was perched on the crest of a wave. As Donna turned her head to look out to sea, Tony fell with a huge splash, the board spearing away from him. He was the only surfer, the yellow suit standing out brightly against the brilliant blue sea while a speedboat far out on the ocean carved through the waves leaving a white plume in its wake. Tony remounted and paddled determinedly back to where the burgeoning rows of breakers gathered their forces for their final surge to the beach.

'I think we should leave right now,' Donna said, 'Didn't you say you were expecting your friend to be here this morning?'

'Yvette? Yes. She's never let me down before. First in the water and last out as a rule.'

'Let me make a wild guess here. Marcus knew Yvette, didn't she?'

'She introduced us. I think she'd met him a few days ago.'

Donna pursed her lips. 'Sorry, Jamie, but if Yvette has come into contact with Marcus, the signs are not good.'

'Why would anyone hurt Yvette?' Jamie scoffed, 'She's just a real nice girl who loves to surf.'

'Believe me, if Marcus has…' Donna's voice tailed away as she saw Jamie was no longer listening to her. His attention was fixed on the solitary figure half a mile away on the ocean. The vivid yellow wetsuit was clearly visible, paddling furiously as the swell surged beneath him, only to sink back into the trough as he failed to catch the wave. Donna gasped as the sound of the fiercely revving engine of the white speedboat reached her ears. The boat was running at high speed, just outside the cresting waves and heading directly for the figure in the water.

'Jesus!' Jamie cried, leaping to his feet and running frantically down the beach, waving his arms in a desperate attempt to attract Tony's attention. The surfer raised a hand in greeting, then Donna saw his head whip round as he became aware of the speedboat for the first time. He raised himself from the board, trying to dive beneath the waves, but he was too late. Donna screamed as the razor-sharp prow of the boat hit the defenceless figure, shattering the surfboard and powering on without checking its speed. Donna's last memory, before she sank to the sand sobbing uncontrollably, was the sight of blood splashing the bows of the speedboat as it cut through Tony's body like a chainsaw.

CHAPTER 24

AT the moment before impact, Marcus had seen the face of the defenceless surfer and realised it wasn't Jamie. A surge of adrenaline heightened his senses and rage contorted his features. The face had been familiar although he'd not expected to see it again. Not since he'd locked the door of the fume-filled garage in Folkestone leaving Tony Beech inside. He eased back on the throttle, reaching into a locker and withdrawing a pair of binoculars. Marcus scanned the beach and focused on the two figures standing close together outside a beach hut below the dunes. As the pair separated, Marcus saw the delicate features of Jamie fill the lenses. The boy's face was contorted in shock and grief and he lingered for a long moment before switching his attention to the other figure. Marcus drew back his lips in a snarl.

Donna O'Prey!

The recollection of the last time he'd seen her would never leave him. Donna had glanced back as she made her escape from the burning cabin. He'd been pinned through his cheek by the blade of a knife and unable to free himself. He'd seen horror on her face, but also a fierce satisfaction at his impending death. As she'd left the cabin, it had been that final glance which had galvanised his repeated attempts to free himself. Ignoring the pain, he'd dragged his face from side to side, the knife blade ravaging his features as he sawed into his own flesh, widening the wound sufficiently to ease the hilt of the knife through his cheek. The pain as he deliberately dislocated his jaw to ease the passage of the dagger's handle had been beyond comprehension, heightened by the searing agony of flames licking his exposed skin, but he was free at last.

Hideously disfigured for months, it had taken all the skill of the old Berber man and his herb potions to return his features to normality. He'd endured the pain of the process necessary to reconstruct his features without a murmur. Even when bones had to be broken and re-set, it had been nothing to him. After the agony of his escape from the burning cabin, he knew he could withstand any pain without flinching. Even the old man had been impressed by his stoicism. Killing him had been difficult. Not for any feelings of sympathy or regret; the old man had seen his new face and had to die. Both men knew that. When Marcus strangled him, the old man had not struggled; his eyes contained not a hint of reproach and Marcus had been reminded of the manner in which these men from the high mountains valued their history and traditions above all things. Not for nothing were they known in their own language as *Imazighen*, meaning noble. Marcus had buried the body with a sense of unease at the expression on the old man's face at the moment of his death. It had stayed with him for months and surfaced once again as he saw the tearstained face of Donna O'Prey. He had no idea how or why she had tracked him down, but his senses were aflame at the knowledge of her presence. He'd taken his customary precautions, methods that had served him well for many years against a succession of dangerous foes, but seeing Donna O'Prey meant only one thing; somehow she'd bypassed all his defences and

216

succeeded in tracing him and following him here. She would die for her foolish bravado, but first he would have to discover the extent of her knowledge. Was she alone, or were others also on his trail? Thoughts of killing Donna and the boy alongside her, whose escape would prove to be merely temporary, sustained him as he pushed the boat to its limits in returning to where he'd left his car with a sense of excitement he'd not felt for some considerable time. He'd scanned the shoreline and seen a small car parked in the dunes. There was only one exit from the beach, the small saloon being incapable of taking the direct route across the shore and he would be ready by the time they'd recovered from the death of their companion and were ready to leave. He wasn't concerned about them making a report to the authorities and he already knew that the vagaries of the local system would prevent any calls being made on a mobile telephone. In such an isolated spot, reception would be non-existent and any attempt to ring for help would only serve to further delay their departure.

Five minutes later, out of sight of watchers from the shore in the shadow of a sheer cliff, Marcus unscrewed the drainage plug in the foot-well of the boat and seawater poured in. The route he'd travelled on his outward journey would have taken too long for it to be even contemplated. Desperate measures were required if he were to make up the time necessary to carry out his plan. He gathered together his binoculars and all his other belongings, weighed them down with a metal wrench, and threw them far away into the ocean before diving into the cool clear water. Swimming with powerful strokes, he reached the base of the cliff and immediately began to climb. The rock was slippery and handholds were few as he proceeded relentlessly upwards. Time was against him now, but the certainty grew in his mind that when Donna and the boy left the track leading from the beach, he would be ready for them. The overhang was difficult and treacherous and here he paused for a moment, studying the cliff face intently, seeking out the best route. The darkness of the sea below revealed nothing. The boat had sunk without trace and lay in deep water beneath the permanent shadow of the cliff, some three hundred feet below. The bunched muscles of his arms burnt with fatigue having supported his entire weight while he scanned the rock face, but the prospect of a fall and certain death never entered his mind. He blocked out everything but the series of tiny indentations that marked his chosen route to the summit.

When Marcus swung his legs over the lip of crumbling rock and pulled himself bodily clear of the cliff, he stood and immediately ran towards the place where he'd left his car. He would need to rest later, but there was no time now for any delay. The car started instantly and within moments he was driving the heavy Mercedes along the dirt road as quickly as the conditions would allow.

Dexter sighed, rubbing the back of his hand through the greying stubble covering his cheeks, unable to remember when he'd last shaved. He'd not left his office for thirty-six hours and now the light outside the window was fading once more. He glared at the telephone, willing it to ring. Reluctant to involve

Abbott any more than necessary, Dexter had called in favours from various alternative sources, bullying where necessary and even begging shamelessly where no other alternative suggested itself. After a lifetime as a working copper, many people in various walks of life had reason to be grateful to Dexter. It was time to call in a favour or two. An hour ago, he'd had to remind a certain journalist that the man owed much of his present eminence to Dexter's ability to keep a secret. Fifteen years ago, the journalist, then a lowly reporter for the Liverpool Echo, had got out of his depth while attempting an undercover investigation of the criminal backgrounds of some night-club doormen working the city's clubs and bars. Following a major investigation into protection racketeering in which the journalist had been caught in the net, Dexter had buried the details of the man's involvement. Certain people had been seeking a scapegoat for the loss of revenue that followed a series of high-profile arrests and the journalist would have been in serious danger if his involvement ever became known. Dexter had called in the favour and the man, now a leading light in a major news agency, had promised to give it his best shot. The telephone rang only once before Dexter snatched it from its cradle.

'Hello?'

'Dexter? It's Terry Quinn.'

'What have you got for me?'

'I've been onto our contacts in Morocco. You wouldn't believe the begging I've had to….'

'Get on with it,' Dexter growled, interrupting the man rudely. This was not the time for small talk.

'Right. I've just been told about a murder in a place called Essaouira. I think that's how it's pronounced. It's a port on the West Coast. Local police reports say a young girl has turned up dead in a place frequented by backpackers and the like.'

'Do you have a name?' Dexter's voice was a rasp, masking his anxiety.

'No name, but it all appears pretty nasty. The only details I've got so far are pretty sketchy, but it appears the girl was sexually assaulted and possibly tortured before death. No name as I said, but the body was discovered by a waitress from a local restaurant looking for her friend. If it turns out that the girl she found was her missing friend, then the victim was a French student. That's all I have. Anything else, I'll get back to you.'

'I'll not forget this, Terry,' Dexter growled and replaced the receiver without any further pleasantries. He sat for a minute or two, thinking deeply. His intuition, which had served him well in the past, told him that the dead girl was connected to his search for Donna and also that Donna was safe for now. He could not have explained the sense of relief that washed over him or why his tiredness had evaporated with the telephone call, but he was suddenly invigorated. A stab of guilt hit home at the thought that he had so lightly disregarded the brutal murder of a young girl, but he had to focus on Donna.

The sound of metal-tipped shoes in the corridor signalled the imminent arrival of Roper whose concerned features reflected his own disquiet. Dexter's opinion of his partner had undergone a severe transformation over the past thirty-six hours. Roper was no action figure, but he'd worked as hard as Dexter himself in an attempt to trace their missing colleague.

'Got a lead,' Dexter announced, 'Dead girl turned up in some port on the Moroccan coast.'

'Not Miss O'Prey?' Roper asked, his face ashen.

Dexter shook his head. 'No. I've no more details, but it looks like the victim may have been a French student. The way she died, sexual assault, torture, it all tells me that Marcus Green is involved.'

'So, Miss O'Prey was right all along?'

Dexter looked up sharply. 'I never doubted it. I've been playing devil's advocate long enough. Time to admit Donna was right in all respects. If she's in Morocco and dead bodies are turning up, the best thing I can do is get out there and see if I can be any help.'

Roper looked baffled. 'We haven't heard from Miss O'Prey. Where will you start looking?'

'Follow the bodies. That's all I can do. You stay here. Pass any messages on to me. Any contact with Donna, tell her to contact the local police and stay safe until I can get to her. Anything else that comes along, I'll need to know about it straight away. Can you talk to Abbott? It's about time we started putting our side of the story out.'

'What do you want me to say?'

Dexter handed him a file. 'It's all there. Basically, what's in the file is Donna's theory, fleshed out by everything I've been dealing with. Tell Abbott to treat it as gospel. It's about time the firm started to give our staff some real support. Everything I've seen lately leads me to the conclusion that Donna had it right all the way down the line. Make sure Abbott knows I'm staking everything I know on that file. He'll take you seriously if you tell him that. I'll get a flight out and see if I can be any use to Donna. It's the least I can do. I let her think I was angry with her for taking off like she did. That's not the case and she needs to be told that if and when she gets in touch. Make certain you tell her that she's only done what any good investigator would do: kept the case alive as best she could.'

Roper's expression was stricken. 'You're just going to head off to Morocco, without any idea of where to look?'

Dexter shrugged. 'What else can I do? If Donna turns up there she'll be in real danger. I need to be in a position to help. That means being on the spot.' He fixed Roper with a chilling stare. 'It may all be for nothing. For all we know, I may already be too late.'

Donna was driving, thrashing the little car through the ruts and hillocks that made up the road surface, a great cloud of dust marking her passage. Alongside her, Jamie held tight to the seat belt mounting, his face the colour of putty. He'd hardly spoken since the speedboat hit Tony, shocked into silence by the sudden realisation that he had been the intended victim. Donna had wasted precious minutes in a vain effort to find a signal on her mobile 'phone before bundling Jamie into the car and heading away from the area as fast as possible. She still didn't have a plan worthy of the name, but doing nothing wasn't an option.

Donna braked hard to avoid overshooting the turn onto the slip road, itself only a rough dirt track that led back towards the main road. She checked both ways and saw that the road was empty. Jamie stared blankly ahead and said nothing. His silence was beginning to concern her, but this was no time to start a reasoned discussion of what had just happened or what their next step should be. Donna would get them as far as a police station, or to someone in authority, and try and get in touch with Dexter. She'd reached her limit, over-reached it actually, and it was time to let the experts take over. Dexter would sort it all out. Comforted by that thought, she let in the clutch and drove away.

Donna was running over recent events in her head, driving on autopilot, when she rounded the next corner and saw the accident. An old Mercedes taxi had skewed across the track and come to rest with one wheel balanced over a drainage ditch. The driver lay slumped over the steering wheel, apparently unconscious. Donna reacted instantly, screeching to a halt and leaping from her car to offer assistance. She heard the passenger door slam as she ran across the road and was momentarily gratified that Jamie had managed to get his head together sufficiently to come and help.

The driver of the taxi was younger than she'd expected, under thirty, and the side of his face was covered in blood. Donna eased his head back to check the extent of his injuries, part of her mind taking note of the manner in which her reactions to another's misfortune had over-ridden her own problems, when the taxi driver reached out his arm and struck her a clubbing blow on the side of the head, knocking her off her feet. Donna sank down heavily on the grass verge, her head spinning. She saw Jamie skid to a halt a few yards away from the car, a mixture of anger and confusion on his face. The taxi driver leapt from the car and seized Jamie's shirt. With his free hand, the driver flicked the boot open and bundled Jamie inside. It all happened so swiftly that Jamie barely had time to struggle before he landed on his back in the boot. He managed to half-rise, but a vicious punch sent him crashing back to the floor of the boot as the lid slammed in his face.

The attacker stood over Donna, feet astride. 'Get up,' he ordered. He had drastically changed his appearance, was slimmer in the face with his hair darker and his body was bulkier than she'd remembered. Even his complexion was several shades darker than the last time she'd seen him, but one thing hadn't changed. The voice was exactly the same with that air of cruel disinterest that caused fresh terrors to rise up in her chest.

'Marcus!' she exclaimed, her voice a shrill treble. Marcus grinned, reaching down and lifting her to her feet with casual ease.

'Donna O'Prey. Did you miss me so much you couldn't stay away?' He didn't wait for an answer, but swung her inside the taxi and clapped a foul-smelling rag over her nose and mouth. Donna gasped in terror, struggling wildly as the impregnated cloth made her senses swim. Within seconds, she sank back on the back seat as Marcus threw an old blanket on top of her, hiding her from view. He climbed behind the wheel of the taxi and manoeuvred carefully away from his precarious position overhanging the ditch. Donna's car stood empty and forlorn, both doors hanging wide open like giant ears. Marcus looked in the rear-view mirror and carefully wiped away all traces of the blood that had covered his face. The open wound on his forearm which he'd gouged to provide realism, still leaked blood softly and he bound it tightly with a handkerchief before swerving past Donna's car and driving swiftly away in the opposite direction.

When Donna stirred into consciousness, the car was no longer moving. She had no idea how long she'd been out, but her hands were tied behind her back and a gag prevented speech. Apart from herself the car was empty. Donna's first concern was for Jamie. She tried to prop herself up, a task made more difficult by the confined space in which she lay, but a sudden fierce headache battered her skull and she dropped down again with a moan of agony. A shadow darkened the space above her and the car springs settled as a figure climbed into the front seat.

'Awake are we? Good. I think its about time for a few questions and answers.' Marcus looked over the bench seat at where Donna lay. He was smiling, but his eyes were dark pools without a trace of humanity.

'Where's Jamie?'

'Over there. Safe and sound.' Marcus pointed through the window and Donna forced herself to ignore the throbbing pain for long enough to look through the back window. Jamie was tied to a tree, arms behind his back. His face was marked, but Donna's spirits lifted at the realisation that Jamie was still alive. The memory of Tony's body as the speedboat hit him drifted into her mind and she groaned aloud and sank back on the back seat of the taxi.

'I'll not tell you anything,' Donna insisted, defiantly.

Marcus leaned closer, his eyes blazing. 'Yes, you will,' he insisted. Donna closed her eyes, shutting out the sight of him. He terrified her and she could imagine no way in which she could successfully defeat this man. She knew only too well that he would be ruthless without a trace of compassion..

'Why have you followed me here? Who told you where to find me?' The voice was soft and insistent but there was steel behind the gentle words.

'I didn't follow you,' Donna replied, her surprise invoking an answer when she had resolved to keep silent. 'I was looking for Jamie.'

If Marcus was surprised, he gave no sign. 'Why?'

'To stop you. I know about the others you killed. The police know all about you now.'

Marcus shook his head. 'I really don't think so.' He paused; looking reflectively down at Donna who realised with a chilling flash of insight that he was deciding whether to kill her now.

'I didn't follow you,' Donna gabbled, words tumbling from her lips, 'I was just trying to find Jamie.' Marcus held up a hand and she stopped talking, looking into his eyes and finding not a shred of comfort. Donna thought about Peg, then about Andy and Dexter. How would they ever know what had happened to her if she died in this patch of scrubland in a burning land so far

away from home? Marcus climbed out of the car and Donna flinched, certain
he would open the rear door and drag her out to be killed, but he walked away
out of her sight. She rose to a sitting position, cramped limbs protesting at the
movement. At least the pain in her head had lessened. Marcus was releasing
Jamie from the tree. Even now, she could scarcely recognise Marcus; the
changes in his appearance were so pronounced. Jamie staggered as Marcus led
him towards the car and Donna saw how was pale and drawn he was. She
looked past him and saw a vast plateau with only a few trees to break up the
desolation. She felt isolated in such an alien landscape where all the
advantages lay with Marcus.

Since regaining consciousness Donna had tried in vain to find any reason
for hope, but she could think of nothing. Even Dexter, whom she'd relied upon
so much, had no idea where she was and would be powerless to help. In his
anger at her disobedience of his instructions, he may even have given up on
her completely. The prospect was appalling, but Donna stopped torturing
herself the moment the prospect of Dexter deserting her flashed through her
mind. Dexter would never abandon her; she was part of his team and she knew
he would never rest until he found her. She couldn't imagine any
circumstances in which Dexter would be able to track her to this place, but the
thought of him looking for her brought some comfort and a fresh resolution.
She wouldn't allow Marcus to retain the upper hand; she would keep looking
for any sign of weakness and be ready to strike if she ever got an opportunity.
Where there was life there was hope, as the old saying had it. The
responsibility for her life and that of Jamie also lay in her hands. She would
keep on fighting to stay alive, in the same way that Dexter would be battling
all odds to find her.

The door opened and Jamie fell on top of Donna. Marcus slammed the
door and climbed into the front seat. Donna had a wild moment in which she
envisaged attacking him from the rear and somehow overpowering him, but
even that slender hope was extinguished when the passenger door opened and
a stranger climbed into the front seat. The man turned to look over at Jamie
and herself. He was skeletally thin, wearing a brown robe which only
accentuated his slenderness. Beneath the brow of his head-dress, black eyes
stared at her over a great beak of a nose. Marcus started the car and drove for
several miles in silence before regaining the road. His companion never took
his eyes off the face of Donna. She forced herself to meet his gaze even though
the man's impassive stare made her want to shudder.

Marcus drove for two hours. The sun was very hot and the air in the back
of the car was stifling. Jamie lay where Marcus had pushed him, his weight
crushing Donna's legs, but she didn't try to speak to him. She stared boldly
back at the watching Arab, determined to show that she would not be cowed
by her situation. When the car stopped, Donna heard voices and felt a tiny
surge of hope. Voices meant people and the prospect of finding someone who
would help them.

Marcus climbed out of the car and as the door opened the smell came in.
It was the stench of raw sewage, of unwashed bodies and rotting remains.

Donna felt herself gag and took her eyes from the face of the man in the front seat for a moment as she thought she was going to be sick. The car door swung open and hard bony fingers seized Donna by the shoulders, dragging her from the car. Donna sprawled in the dust, flat on her back, blinded by the sun directly overhead. She heard a moan from Jamie as he was also dragged from the car and a moment later he dropped down beside her. Donna forced herself up on one elbow and saw a view she could never have envisaged in her worst nightmares. Covering the hillside above her was a squatter camp, hundreds of makeshift houses made of flattened oil drums, cardboard and plastic; anything that had been to hand at the time. The huts overlapped and piled on top of each other in complete chaos. The smell was awful and the faces she could see peering from inside their ramshackle homes were filthy and almost without humanity. The man from the car rapped out an order and Donna felt herself lifted bodily from the earth. She struggled to free herself, striking out wildly until the man spoke again. The hands released her and Donna stood alone and unaided. Jamie was standing next to her and one look at him told Donna that she had to take control. Jamie's expression was a blank canvas and he'd seemingly retreated inside himself where he could blot out these horrors.

Donna felt movement below her and glanced down. The red earth beneath her feet was riddled with holes and from one of these pits appeared the face and forelegs of a huge brown rat. It scuttled out and ran over Donna's feet. She screamed and the rat stopped and looked up at her with it's whiskers twitching. Donna saw dozens of the loathsome creatures darting in and out of their burrows in the soft crumbly earth. The crowd around her burst out laughing. They disregarded the rats completely, but seemingly found her reaction hugely amusing. Donna looked at their faces and saw with horror that many of them were children, some no older than five or six. All were filthy dirty, their ragged clothes barely serving to cover their bony bodies and an air of hostility pervaded the foetid air. Marcus had disappeared. A car engine roared into life behind them and Donna whirled round to see the Mercedes taxi driving away with Marcus in the driving seat.

Many hands reached out for her, pinching and twisting the flesh on her arms and legs until a voice of command rang out and the probing fingers disappeared instantly. The man who had been with Marcus in the car strode through the surrounding bodies until he stood in front of Donna and Jamie. He spoke to them, seemingly asking a question, but Donna did not understand the words. The man turned away in irritation and fetched a plastic bottle from the nearest hut which he handed to Donna. She took it and drank greedily. The water was warm and brackish, but her thirst overcame everything else. She passed the bottle to Jamie who looked at it blankly. Donna put the bottle to his lips and he sucked on it until the bottle was empty.

The tall man in the brown robe rapped out an order and many hands pushed Donna and Jamie up the hill, winding their way through the narrow gaps between the shacks, stumbling over the rough uneven ground. Under the shadow of the overlapping plastic sheeting the heat was stifling and the smell hung in the air as a thick miasma of many-layered aromas in which the stench of sewage was dominant. Black flies swarmed around their heads and tiny creatures scuttled and darted at every step. At a further command, the little caravan of people halted and Donna was pushed into the dark interior of a building made of rusty corrugated iron sheets with old carpets and plastic covering the walls. The dirt floor was alive with writhing insects and the near darkness accentuated the smell. Donna belatedly realised the damp patch of earth in which she was lying had a strong scent of ammonia and shifted herself away from the corner of the hut where the urine stench was strongest. Jamie lay face down on the floor; exactly where he'd fallen. Donna reached out for him and drew him next to her. He was shivering despite the fierce heat and Donna realised he was still deeply in shock. They were alone now and she felt her resources dwindling with every moment she remained in this awful place. A grudging appreciation of the warped genius that was Marcus Green came into her mind. Who would ever think to look for herself and Jamie in a squatters' camp? The inhabitants were, through the very nature of their existence, accustomed to life on the outer edge of society and would never consider going to the authorities to report the presence of two European captives in their midst. Even Dexter with all his experience would surely never have contemplated the prospect of them being hidden away in this camp. Donna knew with all her being that this was at best a transitory arrangement. Marcus had left them here while he carried out whatever business was important to him without the encumbrance of their presence and Donna was convinced he would return. Marcus would not have abandoned them here unless he was going to come back. That would have been at variance with everything Donna had learnt of his character. The streak of cruelty was too strong for him to drive away without a backward glance. Like a cat toying with a mouse, savouring his ability to choose the precise moment he would kill them, Marcus had a far worse fate than this in mind for his captives. Donna contemplated the thought for a moment and shuddered. She remembered the face of Marcus, focussing on it. This was how she would survive. She was still alive and no matter what horrors awaited her, she would hang on to life for as long as it was possible. Dexter would expect nothing less from her. The thought that Dexter would be devoting all his energies to finding her sustained her for a long moment as she hugged the shivering body of Jamie closer and concentrated her inner mind on the face of Marcus Green.

Since his arrival in Morocco, Dexter had experienced frustrations that had driven him to the edge of despair. Speaking no Arabic and with only halting Spanish and French with which to make himself understood, he had found dealing with the local officials intolerably difficult. The manner in which the mere mention of his name would open doors and instigate actions meant nothing here. As a former policeman from a land so far away, Dexter's influence was minimal, but by sheer force of personality he had made one man at least take note of what he wanted to say. The police chief in Essaouira was a cultured man with a fair command of English and the wisdom to appreciate the value of the middle-aged man sitting opposite him. It had taken a long time for Dexter to reach this office and he resolved to impress the police chief with every force at his disposal. It had been heavy going so far, but he now appeared to have found a man willing to listen. The death of a tourist was already sufficiently important to warrant personal intervention by the man in charge and Dexter delivered his carefully worded briefing with all the emphasis he could muster. He'd already arranged to view the body of the French girl; a courtesy which he knew would never have been offered to a foreign police officer back home in England. No matter how great the visitor's reputation. The police chief had left the room ten minutes ago after Dexter had implored him to issue a bulletin instigating a search for Donna, Tony Beech and Jamie Marshall. Dexter provided as much detail as he could, together with the registration number of Donna's car which the policeman had already confirmed had entered Morocco through the port of Tangiers three days ago. Donna and Tony were known to have stayed at the Hotel Royal in El Jadidas and also stayed in Essaouira last night, but their present whereabouts were unknown.

Dexter turned as the portly officer re-entered the room. The man's face bore a troubled expression and Dexter half-rose from his chair before subsiding again and waiting with stoical resignation for what he feared may be bad news.

'My officers have discovered the car in which your friends were travelling.' Dexter leaned forward, but did not attempt to interrupt. 'It was empty and they found no sign of the passengers. I have also received a report of a drowning off a beach in the same area. A surfer, perhaps, but it is difficult at this stage to be certain.'

'Do you have a description of the victim?'

The policeman pursed his lips. 'Not at this stage. All I know at this time is that the victim was a young male of mixed race. The circumstances of his death make identification difficult.' Dexter questioned him with his eyes. 'A person from a local camping ground found a body washed up on the shore. Not a complete body. Just the lower portion.'

Dexter swallowed. The body may have been that of Tony Beech, but the fact that Donna's car had been found empty was even more disquieting. 'Hang on in there, Donna,' Dexter muttered under his breath. If she was in the company of Marcus Green, Dexter knew how fleeting were her hopes of survival, but he drew comfort from being so close on her trail. Even Marcus Green was not infallible. Perhaps he would make a mistake and if he did, Dexter would be ready.

CHAPTER 25

DONNA sensed the man's presence before she saw him. She'd drifted off to sleep at last, still cradling Jamie tightly in an attempt to provide the reassurance which would allow him to recover from the state of shock into which his mind had retreated. The heat was relentless and the sensation of the creatures that ran over her exposed bare legs made her flesh creep, but exhaustion had eventually overwhelmed her. Some deep instinct of impending danger yanked her from sleep and heightened her senses. Alongside her, alerted by her tension, Jamie stirred. The shape of a man appeared and Donna recognised the robed man who'd kept watch on Jamie and herself while Marcus drove them here. He'd disturbed the flap covering the entrance while gaining admittance and Donna could see his thin face clearly. The surface of his skin was marred by pockmarks and his eyes were those of a jackal preying on the weak and vulnerable. He reached out his hand and Donna shuddered at the contact, but momentarily lacked the strength to resist. The probing fingers sought out her breasts and the sensation as his rough skin grazed her nipples was the spur her body needed to shake off her lethargy. Donna lashed out wildly, catching him a glancing blow to the temple and had drawn back her fist to strike again when she saw the knife he held in his free hand. The limpid heat of the shack was oppressive and the smell of the intruder's breath made Donna gag. He brandished the knife an inch away from her face and dragged her to a corner of the hut. Jamie sank back to the floor when she released her grip on him, seemingly impervious to her plight. The man indicated that Donna should lie on her back and she did so, her eyes fixed on the threat of the blade. She had always had a fear of knives; a phobia that had been with her since childhood. There was no doubt in her mind that he would cut her if she made any show of resistance.

A faint scrabbling sound at the entrance caused the Arab to draw back but Donna saw it was only a pair of rats. She had seen many rats and heard the sound of dozens more, since she had been imprisoned in the hut, but the way in which this pair looked at her without fear made her shiver with loathing. The Arab still held the knife in his left hand; his other hand probing her breasts and thighs with rough bony fingers. Donna clenched her teeth, determined to stay alive whatever the Arab intended for her, but when he drew back slightly and removed his robe she gasped in a fresh paroxysm of fear. His naked body was so thin that she could have counted each of his ribs, but his erect penis was massively disproportionate to his emaciated body. Donna shrank back, a stone pressing sharply into the small of her back, as he loomed over her. The man was giggling softly to himself and drooling from his open mouth. Only the ever-present threat of the knife kept Donna's sense of loathing under control; the blade provided a focus for her fear and took away some of the horror that surely awaited her. She felt her shorts and underwear tear as he roughly tore them away. Donna clamped her thighs together and he reached forward and pressed the point of the knife into the soft flesh behind her ear. Donna felt the blood spurt out and gasped with fresh alarm. She tried to resist as he pinched the insides of her thighs, but froze again when he pointed the knife blade at her right eye. The first touch of his hard penis against the junction of her thighs took Donna to a place she'd never previously known and despite her fear of the knife she made a decision. She would rather die, here and now, than allow this beast to violate her. She reached under her back and, pulling out the shard of stone that had been cutting into her, smashed it into the face of the man lying on top of her with all her strength. He gave a shrill scream and leapt away. Donna drew her legs up and huddled defensively in the corner of the shed, waiting for him. Her eyes had gradually become accustomed to the meagre light and she saw the rage consume his face as he wiped away the blood from his cheek. The wound was nasty, but it was not disabling. Donna looked around for a weapon, but there was nothing. Even the stone with which she'd struck the man was well out of her reach. She gasped as he gripped the knife in front of him and moved forward. His eyes showed only a murderous rage; all sexual desire had fled at her violent response to his advances. Donna knew he would kill her and resolved to fight him with her nails, her teeth, all she had. As he drew back the knife for the killing thrust, Jamie unwound like a coiled spring from the floor of the hut, propelling himself full length and smashing his forehead into the face of Donna's assailant. The man dropped like a stone, the knife dropping from his fingers and Donna fled to comfort Jamie as he lay on the floor, hissing through his teeth and shivering uncontrollably.

The prone man stirred and Donna reached for the knife, determined to stab him if he showed any other sign of movement. Jamie was still shivering, but his eyes focussed for the first time as he reached out for Donna's hand and gripped it fiercely. She turned her attention to him, embracing him in return and felt his parted lips seeking out her own. Donna kissed him and felt the heat of his lower body. Jamie spoke her name, so softly that she could barely hear, and she moaned as his lips found her bare breasts. She'd never anticipated this, but clung desperately to Jamie, relishing the contact.

Donna adjusted her position slightly and gasped as Jamie entered her. Rained soft kisses on his neck, she felt a soft tenderness that transcended the sexual act. Jamie arched his back at the moment of his climax and Donna saw tears spring from his eyes. Donna was almost overwhelmed with affection for this boy she barely knew who'd loved her with a tenderness she'd never previously known. The moment may have passed, but it had been so right and she felt wonder at the power of the human spirit to find ways of surviving and bringing new hope even at a time of maximum danger.

Donna remembered the man lying between herself and the entrance and saw his eyes had opened but he seemed oblivious to what had happened. She looked across at Jamie and saw him start, his body tensing, at the sound of scrabbling footsteps beyond the boundaries of the hut and a moment later the strip of carpet that covered the doorway was flung back.

Donna knew, even before she saw his face, that Marcus had returned.

An hour later, Donna stood next to Jamie and watched the fury of Marcus continue without showing any sign of abating. There was a perverse fascination in being present while such anger raged about their ears, the more so as Donna's would-be rapist was the subject of the verbal assault. The words were in an unfamiliar dialect, presumably Berber, but their meaning could not have been clearer. The Arab charged with guarding the prisoners had betrayed his master's trust and Marcus was detailing the consequences of such a failure. The man stood alone, facing Marcus, his head bowed while all around the narrow gap between the alleyways faces were watching and listening with evident enjoyment. Donna realised that this lecture was part of the punishment ritual: the many shortcomings of the man awaiting punishment being revealed to his peers. When Marcus indicated the slight frame of Donna with a sidelong glance, a hiss of derision rang out from the ranks of the spectators. There would be no help for her from anyone here, Donna knew, but the attempted rape of another man's property aroused evident displeasure. Even in the centre of this reeking township whose wretched inhabitants were scarcely able to prolong a life of abject misery, the accepted rules were clearly marked out. Marcus walked forward and slapped the face of the man standing in front of him. The blow was nothing more than a token, but the crowd stirred and edged forward.

Marcus held a knife aloft and Donna recognised it as being the Arab's own property. The man stared back at his accuser, the bruises from Jamie's head-butt standing out clearly along with a deep cut across his cheek that Donna had inflicted. He showed no fear, having seemingly resigned himself to his fate in the Arab manner, and Donna tensed herself to withstand seeing the man killed in front of her.

Marcus spoke softly to the encircling crowd and four men leapt forward to seize the accused man and hold him securely. Marcus took the knife and walked forward. Staring directly into the face of the prisoner, Marcus reached down with his free hand and tore away the strip of cloth around his waist that had been the man's only garment. The great bunch of his genitals swung free and the spectators drew a collective breath and drew fractionally closer. Still staring into the man's eyes, Marcus seized the man's scrotum and a fresh buzz of excitement rippled around the arena.

Marcus looked downwards and studied the man's exposed groin. He took the knife and made two small cuts in the scrotum he held in his other hand. The Arab gasped and beads of sweat appeared on his brow, but the hands that held him captive prevented any movement. Marcus resumed his study of the other man's face, openly savouring the terror that manifested itself in the prisoner's chattering teeth and ashen complexion. Marcus smiled and whispered a few words that only the other man could hear. As his victim began to weep, Marcus reached down once more, then withdrew his hand and held it aloft. In the palm of his hand were two bloody testicles. The crowd went berserk, cheering and stamping their feet. The men holding the recently emasculated figure had not yet released their grip and Donna felt sick to her stomach as she realised the punishment was not yet over. An old man stepped forward, bearing aloft a rusty sword with a massive handle. He handed it to Marcus and bowed deeply as his offering was accepted. The old man, clearly a leader of some standing, grasped the hand of the condemned man and pulled it towards him. Marcus swung the blade in a great arc and Donna swayed as the hand fell into the dust and blood spurted freely. The man screamed once, shaking as he took a filthy rag offered by one of his erstwhile restrainers and attempted to stem the flow of blood by wrapping the cloth tightly around the stump of his wrist. No one attempted to assist him as he shambled away out of sight and the crowd melted away, bowing respectfully to Marcus as they left. When they were the only figures remaining in the tiny area, Marcus checked the knots on the bindings that pinioned the hands of Donna and Jamie and nudged them downwards through the stinking huts towards the road. The entire area seemed deserted, but Donna felt a hundred eyes secretly watching her as she shuffled along behind Jamie and prepared to leave this awful place at last.

Marcus fastened them to the side pillars of the taxi and re-checked the knots which were cruelly tight. He pointed towards the door panels and Donna nodded dully as she saw the door handles and winding arms had been removed. The engine roared lustily and they drove off in a cloud of dust. Their route took them higher, through rough country where stunted trees were the only signs of life and where it became evident they were the only travellers. Donna saw a dozen or so goats grazing high in the branches of a tree and gasped in wonder despite her feelings of impending doom. She recalled Tony, fresh from his study of the guide to Morocco he'd picked up in their hotel, telling her of a region where goats fed in the branches of the argon tree and had to bite her lip to prevent herself sobbing. The tragic circumstances of Tony's death had passed in a virtual blur and she'd not yet had time to mourn his passing. As if divining her thoughts, Jamie squeezed her hand and she rested her head against his shoulder for a moment in gratitude. Neither had mentioned what had happened between them. There had scarcely been an opportunity as subsequent events had been so overwhelming, but as the day lengthened Donna answered Jamie's grip with a soft caress of his palm while the heavy car pitched and dipped on the uneven road surface.

Four hours later, they were in the mountains, having crossed the desolate plains. The heat was stupefying and each turn of the road took them higher and higher. Donna's sense of isolation grew more intense with each mile they travelled. In such a remote area, the opportunities for escape grew ever fainter and even if Dexter had somehow managed to track them as far as the coast they were a world away from there now.

The mountains still towered above them, great jagged peaks tipped with pockets of snow. As they continued to climb, the clear air grew gradually cooler until Donna found herself shivering. The car was labouring up a steep incline and Marcus was obliged to devote his full attention to the road surface which was heavily rutted and strewn with boulders. Donna started as the car rounded the next corner and she saw a Toyota Land-Cruiser parked next to a rock-fall which had evidently defeated even its formidable abilities.

Marcus drew up alongside the other vehicle and clambered out, arching his back and grimacing. He walked back and flung open the door of the rear compartment. Freed from their bindings, Donna and Jamie staggered from the car and stood close together, sharing the pain as blood rushed through veins that had been compressed and constricted for too long.

Marcus tied them together with a length of cord and hobbled their ankles so that they could walk in short steps but would be unable to run. 'Now we walk,' he said.

Donna's calves were screaming after an hour and her feet ached unbearably. She'd always considered herself to have a good level of fitness and Jamie was a young athlete who swam and surfed every day, but he suffered equally from the killing pace that Marcus maintained. Their captor showed no signs of tiredness; his even stride ate up the miles regardless of the nature of the terrain and he stopped only when Jamie or Donna had fallen and were unable to rise without help. When the sun departed, they walked by moonlight. The cold chilled their bones and the sharp rocks administered cuts and bruises at every stumble yet still they walked on. Onward and upward. Marcus never spoke and Donna had no means of knowing how long this agony would be maintained.

The highest peak in North Africa, Djebel Toubkal, rises to over thirteen thousand feet and is at the centre of a wild tract of land where roads and even tracks are scarce. Three clan families had traditionally controlled the high passes. For many years the so-called 'Lords of the Atlas,' held sway in a region where officialdom was unknown, operating under a set of rules unique to themselves. Even now, residents of the more remote areas do not consider themselves bound by the same laws as their fellow countrymen far below on the Great Plains. The Atlas Berbers never adopted the Arabic language, even though this was compulsory for all citizens of Morocco for hundreds of years, maintaining their indigenous *Tashelhaït* dialect in the face of extreme provocation from the State. The same applied to the imposition of the Islamic faith with Berber tribes preferring to retain their traditional beliefs. These people of the remote mountain areas kept their distance from the materialism to which other regions aspired, cherishing their ancient ways and systems of government. Here in the rarefied air of the high plateau, small villages existed far from any road, unmarked on any map, in the same way as they had always existed. Trekking groups did not come here and the villagers rarely left the immediate environs of their settlement. For many months of the year the heavy snows of winter prevented any access at all and at other times, the only known tracks were difficult to find and even more difficult to traverse. It was on such a road that Marcus led his protesting companions. As Jamie fell for the third time in less than a mile while straddling a steep ridge, risking the certain death of a fall of hundreds of feet down a scree-strewn slope, Donna begged Marcus to let them rest. Marcus looked at her with disdain. He appeared unmoved by the ordeal of clambering over rocks and scaling steep slopes for the past six hours.

'Kill us now,' Donna pleaded, 'You're going to do it eventually, aren't you? Why are you letting us suffer like this?'

'You will die when it suits me for you to die. Believe me, if you think this walk in the hills is suffering, you will soon find you are mistaken.' He held up a hand as Donna took a breath and prepared to speak. 'Waste your breath in idle talk once more and I will deal with your little friend in the same way as I did that man back at the camp.' He held Donna's gaze, his lascivious expression flickering across towards Jamie, suggesting that he knew all about their brief sexual encounter. Donna said nothing, but turned to help Jamie. His feet were bleeding and the light sandals he wore gave no side support which was hampering his ability to climb. unlike Donna's trusty Reeboks which were holding up well. Jamie grinned, trying to lift her spirits, but Donna knew he'd heard the threat of Marcus and that their captor would not hesitate to carry it out.

They walked for another hour through a pitiless terrain of broken rock and loose pebbles. Hardly anything grew here; occasional outcrops of bare earth allowed a few lichens or straggly grasses to live a precarious existence, but otherwise it was exactly as Donna had always imagined the surface of the Moon to be. The first hint of dawn was streaking the horizon when they breasted a rise and saw a ruined castle with enormous stone walls on the summit of the next hill. Marcus stopped and Donna stumbled into the back of him. She was exhausted, barely able to do more than shuffle along and Jamie's feet were cut to ribbons.

'There is the *Kasbah*,' Marcus said, his voice breaking the absolute silence of the mountains. 'The village is a mile beyond that next ridge, but we will not be going there yet. I have friends waiting for me here.' He pointed to the forbidding rocky fortress and Donna shivered. Jamie rubbed the exposed flesh of her forearm, but it had not been the chilly air that had caused her to tremble. She looked at the great stone walls as they gradually became visible in the dawn light and had a vivid premonition of death. Her Grandmother, Peg had always claimed the gift of second sight and insisted that Donna had inherited this power, but she'd never given the subject much attention.

Until now.

Marcus led them at a killing pace through the piles of towering stones that flanked the ancient fortress and through a pair of tall gates. Donna smelled wood smoke and heard the distant chatter of voices speaking a language that was unfamiliar to her. She gripped Jamie's hand tightly and kissed his cheek. He held her gaze and winked solemnly, making light of their situation and his ravaged feet, as they followed Marcus into the interior of the fortress.

CHAPTER 26

A TALL column of yellow flames rose from the embers of a fire in the centre of a circle of robed figures who rose and bowed deeply as Marcus and his captives approached. Donna started in surprise as she saw that they were a group of adolescent boys, most of them no taller than herself. The solitary exception was a tall slim youth, perhaps the same age as Jamie, whose flowing robes marked him as a person of substance amidst his ragged band of compatriots.

'Khaled.' Marcus greeted the tall youth by name and he left his companions to confer with Marcus in low tones. Donna could not understand their speech though the conversation appeared to be amicable. Marcus kissed the youth's cheek and walked away to speak with the band of young men.

'Let us go, you bastard.' Donna's voice cracked as she shouted across the open space; 'You can stay here with this bunch of kids and your queer little friend, but let us go.' Marcus turned and she saw the extent of his fury. He walked across the dusty earth and stood directly in front of where she stood, still hobbled and bleeding freely from where the savage climb had ripped the flesh of her calves. As swiftly as a striking cobra, the hand of Marcus flew at Donna's face leaving a red welt and the clear imprint of a hand on her cheek. He reversed his grip and slapped her savagely on the opposing cheek. Tears sprang to Donna's eyes, but she forced herself to remain upright and stare directly into his eyes.

'Keep your mouth shut,' Marcus ordered and walked away, dismissing her as if she were of no importance whatsoever.

The tall youth named Khaled strode across to Jamie and Donna and spoke clearly in English with scarcely a trace of accent.

'You have offended our master. That was not wise.'

'You speak English?'

Khaled looked disdainfully at Donna. 'Woman, I speak five languages. Did you imagine that we were all barbarians here?'

Jamie gave a shuddering sigh of despair. He seemed to have diminished during the long climb to the summit of the mountain and Donna looked at him with concern. 'We'll get through this,' she whispered with a confidence that belied her own feelings, convinced that if either were to openly admit defeat, they would be lost.

A soft breeze wafted the scent of fragrant blossom from the valley floor far below, mingling with the blue haze of wood-smoke from the open fire inside the ochre walls, all overlaying that primal scorched earth smell that characterised this mountainous region. The gentle undulations of the distant hills melted away to a blue ethereal haze at the distant horizon. A vast expanse of khaki, riven through with an occasional slender ribbon of green where a trickle of water debouched from the hillside and meandered sinuously downwards, the serried rows of parched and hostile peaks marched ever onwards towards infinity. Jagged mountains shaped by the contingencies of wind and blazing sun surrounded the ridge on which the walled square was situated and immediately outside the walls, a series of rocky outcrops mounted guard like the bony spine of some great prehistoric creature. In other circumstances Donna knew she would have been captivated by her surroundings with its revelation of a unique beauty more spectacular than any human creation. A Golden Eagle soared overhead, its huge wings spread to catch the rising air, keen eyes scanning the slopes of the mountains for movement. Secure within the red walls, the courtyard was a work of art in the truest sense of the phrase. One that had survived countless ages with its grandeur undiminished and would continue to proclaim its graceful majesty to all those fortunate enough to stand on this spot and marvel. With a heavy heart, Donna dragged her attention back to the perilous situation in which she found herself and still saw no prospect of survival. She looked across at Khaled. Despite his arrogant attitude, when he'd spoken there had been a tiny spark of humanity in those intelligent eyes.

'What is this place?' Donna asked. The question was not based on any quest for information. Her only intention was to start some form of dialogue between them and hope to find a rapport with at least one of her captors.

Khaled looked around the courtyard. 'A *Kasbah.* A secure place to which the villagers would retreat if they were threatened by enemies. The tanneries and potters workshops are here and there is a deep well with good water." Donna looked past him and saw a conical oven against the far wall extending to a tall chimney. In the foreground were a group of six large circular vats lined with bricks and sunk into the ground, each with a broad lip around the circumference wide enough for a man to walk upon and evidently of great antiquity.

'You should understand that this land has provided for its people for thousands of years,' Khaled continued, 'Self-sufficiency in its purest form. The people who live here are able to feed and clothe themselves without the necessity of leaving their village. In this place, your Western obsession with choice and easy availability of resources is unknown. This compound is where the villager's process and dye hides to make clothes. The process is the same as it has been for many years. What more do you want from me? A guided tour?'

Donna shook her head. 'No. I'm interested. That's all.' It felt weird under these circumstances to be having what amounted to almost a normal conversation.

Khaled looked at her carefully as if suspecting that Donna was attempting to divert him in some way. 'Have you ever seen the tanneries at Fez or Marrakech? The leather workshops?'

'No.'

'The dying vats there are over a thousand years old. These here are not so old, only a few hundred years perhaps. The hides are brought here direct from the animal. Camel, bullock, goat; the process is the same.' He stopped and looked across the square towards Marcus.

'Go on,' Donna said urgently. Anything that promoted an impression of normality was welcome.

'The skins are pickled and cured by immersion in each of these vats in turn. The flesh has to be removed and the hide made ready for dying.'

'Are they all different? The vats?'

'Yes. Some contain a strong acid and salt to strip the remaining hair and animal fat away from the skin after the boys have scraped away the majority of the flesh. The partly cured skins are pickled in another vat containing lime. The guava of pigeons is best for the liming process.'

Donna giggled. 'Pigeon shit.' She was on the edge of hysteria, trying desperately to maintain an appearance of sanity and desperate to keep the terror she was feeling from communicating itself to Jamie. Khaled looked at her and stopped talking. He shook his head and walked away

Donna looked at the faces of the teenage boys. One met her gaze and held it, his deep-set reptilian eyes staring defiantly at the alien culture she represented. Donna understood for the first time that this was because Jamie and herself meant nothing to him. They were irrelevant. Marcus controlled the destiny of his followers and they would do exactly what he told them to do. He had only to give the order and these silent unsmiling youths would kill them instantly. Without a moment's hesitation.

Donna flinched as Marcus parted the circle of youths who drew back respectfully. He stood directly in front of her, saying nothing but words were not necessary. Donna's shallow well of courage had evaporated when she saw the expression on his face. There was not a trace of pity there, not a hint of mercy or compassion and Donna knew with absolute certainty that she would soon die here in this God-forsaken place.

Self-pity threatened to overwhelm her at the thought that she would die without any of the people who cared about her having any knowledge of the means of her death. She glanced at Jamie and saw the expression of defeat firmly etched on his features. The realisation that Jamie had already resigned himself to his fate was no comfort and a tiny spark of anger at her own spineless behaviour flared into life. Donna raised her head and faced Marcus, forcing herself to hold his gaze. Marcus reached out and touched her hair, brushing it away from her eyes. The gesture was almost tender, but his eyes were bleak and his expression cold and forbidding. Donna snapped her head back, his touch further fanning the flames of her defiance. She willed herself to show no fear. It was a pretty feeble gesture, but it was all she had to offer. She wished she'd had the chance to say goodbye to Peg and wondered for an inconsequential moment whether the circumstances of her death would ever be known or whether she'd join the ranks of those people who'd just vanished without trace. Never to be seen or heard of again. The prospect was somehow even more chilling than if the facts of her death had actually been made known to those select few who loved her. The realisation of what her death or disappearance would do to Peg sparked a surge of anger in Donna. She stood tall and faced Marcus head on, resolving to show no fear regardless of whatever cruel fate awaited her. Marcus looked at her, a tiny smile playing at the corner of his mouth. Donna saw he'd recognised her pathetic effort for what it was: a futile act of defiance born of desperation. Her heart sank, but somehow she found the strength to keep her expression impassive. Something of this battle of wills had conveyed itself to Jamie who also raised his head and made a mute gesture of resolve in support of Donna's actions.

Marcus turned away and gave a soft word of command to Khaled who spoke rapidly to the group of boys. They snapped to attention at his words and seized Donna and Jamie, lifting them bodily and preventing any possibility of resistance. Donna cried out as hard fingers pinched the tender skin of her inner thighs, but there was no sexual intention, merely the callous indifference of her captors. Marcus walked over and gave a nod of approval. He motioned towards the wall and the youths shuffled across the packed earth bearing their unwieldy burdens towards a row of dangling chains that hung from the red inner wall.

The heavy iron shackles were set into the wall next to a narrow stone bench. Donna suspected this had been a primitive stage upon which a row of captives could have been displayed. Donna flinched as her ankles were securely clamped. The rattle of the chain was disproportionately loud, disturbing a tiny red-tailed lizard from its hiding place amidst the rusty links. Jamie tried to resist the shackles, striking out at the arms that held him and opening a gash above the eye of one of the younger boys who cried out in pain. Another youth drew a curved dagger, but was immediately rebuked by Khaled. The arms reached out once more and Jamie was helpless to resist. The shackles were made fast and checked, then the circle of boys withdrew. Jamie and Donna struggled helplessly against the unyielding metal chains that held them securely fastened to the stone bench. Marcus walked closer and checked the shackles himself, tugging each in turn until he was satisfied. He glanced across at the young boy who was snivelling in pain, the wound above his eyebrow welling out crimson drops of blood, and snapped out an order. The boy was instantly silent, biting his lip to ensure he remained mute.

'You must learn that causing injury to my people will not be tolerated,' Marcus said, his eyes fixed on the defiant face of Jamie who stared back at him without fear. Marcus rapped out another guttural command and four boys stepped forward, pinioning Jamie' arms to his sides and forcing him to his knees. Another boy brought forward a slender object, an unglazed shard of pottery with a shallow depression in the centre, which Donna assumed to be some sort of rudimentary spoon. Marcus knelt on one knee and dipped the implement into the nearest of the stone vats, withdrawing a spoonful of viscous liquid and carrying it carefully across to where Jamie was kneeling.

Impassively, Marcus dripped a single spot of the liquid onto the forearm of Jamie and allowed the remaining contents of the makeshift spoon to drip down onto the parched earth. Every pair of eyes watched intently and a collective sigh rang out as the face of Jamie contorted in sudden agony. Donna watched in horror as a section of skin peeled away from his pinioned arm, widening in a red circle as the acid stripped away flesh. Marcus snapped out an order and the boys released Jamie who remained on his knees, acute pain robbing him of movement. As Jamie began to scream, the boys walked away, not even looking at the captives. The hooded figures walked away in single file, like penitents in an Easter procession, and Marcus followed them through the gates of the enclosure.

Donna shook her head, trying to flick the sweat from her eyes. Not much more than two hours since sunrise and the heat was already merciless making the stone bench at her back too hot to bear. Jamie stopped screaming as she touched his upper arm with the tips of her fingers, but his face was still contorted in agony.

Donna tried to whisper a few words of encouragement, but they died in her throat as she saw the shadow of an approaching figure. She looked up, expecting to see Marcus, but it was the tall figure of Khaled who approached and stood before them in silence. He turned away, scrabbling on the ground, ripped a few leaves from a plant growing in the sandy earth and pounded them with a round stone. Spitting on the bruised leaves, he took Jamie's arm and slapped the crude poultice onto the red wound. Jamie closed his eyes and Donna saw the pain lines diminish on his face. 'You were foolish to provoke him,' Khaled said. He switched his gaze from Jamie and looked directly at Donna. 'I respect your courage,' He said, 'It is rare for a woman to suffer in this manner without weeping. Marcus is our leader and I must obey him, although I fear he will kill you now. I will not interfere because this is a personal matter, between the two of you, but I will try to persuade him that he should be merciful in your case. A quick death without pain. It will be worse for you if he sees you are afraid. Be strong for death without fear is an honourable death.'

'He will not listen to you. Marcus does not understand mercy.'

Khaled nodded. 'That may be true. There was a way of putting enemies to death that was used here in the old days. I fear Marcus has brought you here intending to kill you in this fashion.'

'How will he do it?'

Khaled shook his head. 'It is best that I say no more,' he said gravely. He finished tying off the poultice and touched his fingers gently over the wound. 'That will draw out the acid,' he said, 'The boys who work here; they have accidents.' He drew back the sleeves of his robes and revealed a circular white scar, an ancient burn long since healed. 'I worked in this place as a young boy. The old ones, they taught us what to do when there were accidents. How to grow the plants that will heal a wound and always to make certain that the plants are watered every day.'

'Please help us,' Donna implored.

'You should not have come here,' Khaled said, 'You were foolish to involve yourself with this man.' He rose to his feet, preparing to walk away.

'Please,' Donna cried out, her voice a sob of anguish, 'You're not like the other boys. You speak our language. You know there is another world out there, a world where human life means something.'

Khaled hesitated; half turned to look at her up-turned face, and retraced his steps. 'Why should I care whether you live or die?' he asked, 'This is our land. You do not belong here. You know nothing of our ways. Yes, I have travelled far from my village. My father wanted me to live in the modern world. As a young boy, I was considered to be clever and I was sent away to learn from the Europeans. I studied in Spain and have visited France, England and Italy. I learned to speak the languages of Europe and understand their cultures. However, I am a Berber and when I heard that my father had died I came home to my own people. I have studied the ways of the Western world. Seen for myself the promiscuity of your women and the greed for money and possessions that dominates your lives. My place is here now. With my own people.'

Donna held up the chains attached to her shackles. 'These belong to the old days, Khaled. Not the world you now know exists outside these mountains. You have left here once. Do it again. Set us free and leave with us. Your village and other villages like it will die if men like Marcus are allowed to lure away their young men with promises of easy money. He is evil and what he promises is wealth based on drugs and human misery. Slavery and an early death are all that await the young men who follow him.'

Khaled stared at her. He shook his head. 'You know nothing,' he said, scornfully, 'The business in which Marcus is engaged is familiar to us. My people were trading in narcotics and slaves while your countrymen were still living in caves in the earth. This is a harsh land and men must take any means available to them to survive. These mountains and the great deserts to the south are the only world most of my people have ever known. The mountains and deserts have been our home for thousands of years. What do you know of my world? When I was five years of age I travelled with my brothers for forty days into the desert. We ate the roots of plants, trapped lizards and snakes and took only one drink of water a day. The word Sahara means land which is fit only for crossing. Did you know that?'

Donna shook her head.

'My people have been travelling through the great desert for thousands of years as merchants and traders. You talk to me of slaves. Yet thousands of men and women from the continent of Africa crossed the desert bound for the cotton plantations of America. More than one and a half million slaves while millions more died from disease or the effects of the journey. Yet now you speak to me of enslavement. Your own people, ship-owners from all the great countries of Europe, were the paymasters of the slave trade. As for drugs, where is the market for this business? Your own country and the other decadent nations of Europe whose young people have lost all respect for their elders and think only of their own selfish desires. Who controls the market? Who funds the growers and pays the shippers? Your own people.' Khaled turned away once more, setting his face against Donna's tortured expression.

Donna cast her eyes wildly around and saw the marks on the stone left by legions of former captives whose scrabbling fingers and broken nails had torn vainly at the unforgiving rock surface beneath the chains which held them. She knew then that Khaled was right and that the only reason Jamie and herself were here was to die in agony, as so many had in this place, while Marcus watched their useless struggles. 'Please,' Donna implored, 'You know he will kill us.'

Khaled turned back again. He retraced his steps and looked down at Donna. 'That has nothing to do with me. I cannot help you,' he said.

'Why are you here?' The voice of Marcus was as soft as a sigh, but his expression revealed the depth of his anger. Donna had not heard him approach and her heart began to race. Khaled said nothing, turning to face the rage of Marcus without a change of expression and Donna marvelled at his courage. Marcus glanced down at Jamie and saw the dressing covering his wound. He hissed through his teeth and was reaching down to rip the poultice away when Khaled moved forward and stood in his way. Marcus stepped back and his face contorted in a paroxysm of anger that chilled Donna's blood. His eyes were black pits in which a flame of anger burned like a forest fire. The slender figure blocking his way stood tall and still, seemingly unafraid. Marcus barked out an order, but Khaled did not move. Marcus reached under his robe and withdrew a knife, the sun glinting on the curved blade. Donna gasped and Marcus looked at her, almost as if he'd forgotten she or Jamie was there. Jamie hissed at a sudden stab of pain and Marcus turned his stony gaze upon him.

'Many years ago, slaves were sold here. A Boy Market.' Marcus was still looking directly at Jamie. 'A pretty boy like you would fetch a high price. I once knew a man from a village near here who had been sold in this actual market.' Donna looked away and saw a fleeting expression very close to pain pass across the features of the tall youth, Khaled. She almost missed it as within a second his face had reverted to passive indifference, but she knew she'd seen something.

Marcus looked away, dismissing Jamie and Donna, and gazed at the figure still separating him from the two captives. He reached out and touched the point of the blade to the corner of Khaled's eye, but the expression on the face of the younger man never wavered. Khaled stared at Marcus, eye to eye, in a contest that brought fresh dread to Donna. If the intention had been to protect further injury to Jamie, this was now something else. Something personal.

'Move away, Khaled,' Marcus demanded. Khaled looked at him, standing as still as a statue.

'Move away,' Marcus said once more. He drew the blade of the knife across the forehead of Khaled and a thin trickle of blood followed the knife's progress. Khaled remained impassive and Donna flinched as this battle of wills could surely only produce one victor. She had no idea why the tall youth had suddenly adopted this defiant pose, but knew that Marcus would kill him for his insolence.

'That man who told you about being having been once sold in the Boy Market. He would have a very old man.' Khaled's voice was soft, his expression blank, but his eyes flashed with restrained passion.

Marcus said nothing, but Donna saw a faint crease appear on his brow.

'I once knew a man like that,' Khaled continued, 'The only one old enough to remember those days.' Donna saw a faint trickle of blood appear below Khaled's eye, but if he felt the blade pierce his skin he gave no outward sign. The flow of blood increased and Donna realised that Khaled was deliberately moving onto the point of the blade, purposefully wounding himself as if in defiance of the threat that Marcus represented. Khaled's gaze never wavered from the face of Marcus as he slowly raised his left hand and pushed the blade of the knife away from his eye. Marcus allowed his hand to be deflected, standing equally still. He spoke a few words in what Donna presumed to be the Berber language and Khaled laughed aloud. He raised his head slightly and gave a shrill call which raised the fine hairs at the back of Donna's neck. It was a primitive sound, a high keening ululation from deep in the throat echoing long-forgotten memories of a time when men and women lived in caves, hunting wild beasts to survive. Marcus raised his knife once more, but a flick of Khaled's eyes diverted his attention. Donna followed his gaze and saw the boys returning through the stone doorway, fanning out in a circle and closing in. Marcus spoke again, his voice a harsh bark of command, but the boys acted as if they had heard nothing.

Khaled looked across at Donna and Jamie. 'This man,' He indicated Marcus with a faint inclination of his shoulder, 'He asks why we do not obey the orders of our elders. As Berber people, we are taught from birth to obey our elders. Respect and obedience are the cornerstones of our belief. In my own village, there was one man above all who commanded respect. The headman of the village. Old age had given him great wisdom.' He was looking directly at Donna and from somewhere deep inside herself she found the strength to speak to him.

'What happened to the old man?' Donna asked.

Khaled looked away from Donna and stared directly into the face of Marcus. 'I do not know. I was away from my village, living the life of a Western student. When I heard of his disappearance I came home. The people told me he had left the village with a stranger. A European. This man had been scarred and disfigured. He wished to change his appearance and knew our people have the skills to do such things. The visitor asked the village for help and we gave it to him. He paid much money, but money is not important to our people. It is part of our culture to offer help to a stranger. No matter how great the need. The old ones have powers far more valuable than money. The old man never came back to the village.'

Marcus stirred, a tic of anxiety flickering in his throat.

'Do you think the European killed him?' Donna asked.

'Yes,' Khaled replied. 'They left the village together and never returned. The headman of a Berber village would never have abandoned his people, his family. Even the youngest, the most ungrateful and unworthy of his thirteen children, knew the European visitor had taken from him all his skill and wisdom and then killed him.' Khaled turned to Marcus, his face pressing close and his voice soft as a sigh. 'My mother was the fourth wife of the headman of our village. She was fifteen and he was over seventy when her only child was born and became the youngest son of the leader of our village.'

Marcus faced him without flinching, but the intensity of Khaled's words cut through the dense heat like a sharp knife. 'I had been sent away to study. To learn the ways of the world far beyond the boundaries of our village. The youngest son. The one chosen by my father. Before I left, he told me all the history of my family. I remember it all. Amongst Berbers, nothing is ever written down. Our history, even our language, survives by word of mouth. From a very young age we develop our memory. I remember every word my father told me. One thing in particular I remember clearly. My father had been sold at this market when he was a very young boy.' Khaled's voice had gradually risen in volume and intensity until his final sentence was a harsh cry, full into the face of Marcus.

Marcus knew the ways of these mountain men and the price they placed on consanguinity, especially between a son and his father. He stood very still, as if seeking to defy the younger man by sheer force of personality, then turned away.

As Marcus moved, the circle of boys shifted slowly closer until Donna and Jamie could see only the backs of their robes. The head of the tall Khaled could be seen, but Marcus was out of their sight. A sudden commotion saw two youths stagger back from the circle, blood flowing from knife wounds, but they regrouped in silence, ignoring their wounds and closing the circle once again. Donna saw the flash of reflected sunlight from the blade of a knife as it dropped to the earth and was immediately stamped underfoot by a dozen pairs of sandals. The circle of boys shuffled a few feet to one side and Donna gave an involuntary cry as she saw them approach the edge of the bleaching vat. She turned her face away at the sound of a splash, screwing her eyes tightly together, but made herself open them once more. The boys had spread out around the exterior of the vat, their teenage faces still inscrutable. Donna could not see Marcus at first and then his face and upper torso erupted from the surface of the vat like a shark hooked by a gaff. The skin had peeled away from his body and his mouth was open but no words could be heard. He went under again and one of the encircling boys gave a shrill cry of excitement. Khaled glanced across at the boy who'd cried out and he lowered his face in supplication. When the head of Marcus surfaced again, it was no longer recognisable. Much of the skin and flesh had been stripped away leaving behind little more than a bony skeleton, but still he writhed and twisted in torment, forcing Donna to look away once more. The surface of the vat boiled and foamed and then was still. Donna looked at the face of Khaled but saw not a flicker of expression. Almost as if responding to some unspoken command, the youths turned towards Khaled, their new master, arms held aloft in a gesture of subordination and respect. He regarded them gravely, then singled out one of the younger boys and spoke to him for a few moments before looking back at the others and giving a nod of dismissal. The boys drifted away, each bowing respectfully to Khaled as they left, and within minutes all but Khaled and the young boy had left.

Khaled knelt beside Donna and released the heavy shackles from her ankles, then repeated the action to free Jamie. He turned to address them both, his implacable expression revealing no hint of his inner feelings.

'You were never here. You saw nothing. You will leave now and never return.' He threw a set of keys into the dust. 'There is a Toyota Land Cruiser back where the road ends. Take it and forget you ever saw me or this village.'

Donna nodded. She was aware of the meaning behind the statement. This was far more than mere self-preservation on Khaled's behalf. The Berber tribes who lived in these high mountains had their own methods of summary justice and the world outside had no right to interfere. Donna looked at Jamie who nodded acceptance of this pact of silence. Khaled called to the young boy who approached them but did not speak. He was sturdily built with muscular legs and was busily fastening three leather water containers across his chest. 'This boy will guide you. Do not attempt to speak to him. He does not understand your language. Follow him, but the boy will not wait for you.' Khaled looked down at Jamie's feet and frowned He slipped off his own sandals and slid them towards Jamie. They were thick-soled with broad leather straps across the instep and around the ankle. Jamie smiled, appreciating the kindness, and knelt to fasten the sandals to his feet.

Khaled looked at Donna. 'You are the stronger,' he said. 'If this one,' he indicated Jamie who was still fastening the leather straps around his ankles, 'If he cannot continue the journey, you should leave him and save yourself.'

Donna felt a surge of anger. 'We'll make it,' she declared defiantly, 'Both of us.'

Khaled shrugged as if the matter was unimportant to him. He clasped each of them by the hand and walked away on bare feet, the torn hem of his robe trailing a faint trickle of blood which was instantly swallowed by the parched earth, and the last traces of what had happened in this place disappeared for ever.

Printed in the United Kingdom by
Lightning Source UK Ltd., Milton Keynes
139769UK00001BC/8/A

9 781846 850653